have been ... as ... to the
... Relief Committee to apply ...
... have ... port as may be ...
for and the ... of our committee also
... the ... of our committee ...
... to ... Wall/Carrick Committee
... to ... Carrick Committee and
... Shackleton ... to Cork or
... Shackleton for ... where ...
... to Cork where ...
... to ... if to Cork ...
... to ... these for ... 14 here ...
... Mr Johnson 86 Patrick Street ... as ...
... Mr ... this application is ... at ...
... of Captain Sheridan
... I am ...
Henry Sheamy

A powerful and gripping piece of writing from a born storyteller, a tale shaped with the lyricism of a song writing giant.'

Joseph O'Connor

'The narrative is just like his singing voice, full of powerful strength and compassion; a born storyteller in words as well as in music.'

Michael Harding

'Declan O'Rourke's first novel, which is grounded in a deep knowledge of place and history, propels us into the world of "the broker and the broken". Through the eyes of Cornelius Creed, a reporter for the *Cork Examiner*, member of the Macroom Relief Committee, Repeal warden and pawnbroker, we see the tragedy unfold from a variety of perspectives. Through the suffering of Pádraig Ua Buacálla, we observe the cruelty and capriciousness of the various relief systems and we understand why so many people starved. Lucid, lovingly written and lyrical, *The Pawnbroker's Reward* faithfully captures the horrors of the early months of the Great Hunger.'

Professor Christine Kinealy

The PAWN BROKER'S REWARD

The PAWN BROKER'S REWARD

DECLAN O'ROURKE

GILL BOOKS

Gill Books

Hume Avenue

Park West

Dublin 12

www.gillbooks.ie

Gill Books is an imprint of M.H. Gill and Co.

© Declan O'Rourke 2021

978 07171 8632 7

Edited by Conor Kostick

Design and print origination by O'K Graphic Design, Dublin

Copyedited by Djinn von Noorden, Seán Ua Súilleabháin

Proofread by Ruairí Ó Brógáin

Printed by Clays Ltd, Suffolk.

This book is typeset in 11/17 pt Minion.

This book is dedicated to those reporters, correspondents, writers, artists and speakers who bravely record and reveal the truth. And to those historians, archivists, researchers and sharers of lore who gift to us the past, so that we may learn from its mistakes and better respond to its echoes in our own times.

Author's Note on Language

The original Irish text that inspired this story — contemporary to the Muskerry Gaeltacht of the 1840s — used characters and symbols no longer in general use today. Out of respect for those whose lives this book concerns, I have endeavoured to stay as faithful as possible to their Irish, when Irish is used, and to how they referred to themselves.

Though primarily presented in English, the linguistic landscape in which we are placed was a dichotomy of Irish and English. A person's name may therefore be spelled more than one way, subject to the perspective being that of a native Irish or an English speaker.

'Take off your shoes and walk on your country.'

– A thought shared from Gunditjmara woman AMY SAUNDERS.

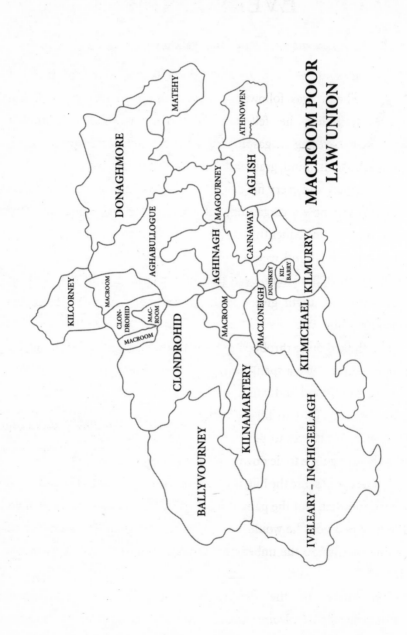

MACROOM POOR
LAW UNION

MATEHY

ATHNOWEN

DONAGHMORE

AGLISH

MAGOURNEY

AGHABULLOGUE

AGHINAGH

CANNAWAY

KILCORNEY

MACROOM

KIL-
BARRY

DUNISKEY

KILMURRY

CLON-
DROHID

MAC-
ROOM

MACLONEIGH

MACROOM

CLONDROHID

MACROOM

KILMICHAEL

KILNAMARTERY

BALLYVOURNEY

IVELEARY – INCHIGEELAGH

1

Every Sinew

A wheeze was followed by a gasping suck for air. With legs trembling he felt himself lurch forward, and stumble. Recovering ... gasping again ... in pitch-black emptiness, an arm reached out, blind, grabbing at the air but found nothing.

Every sinew and every fibre of his body burned from the ground up. Each step was now a gargantuan effort. The cold and damp air of the night, blowing infrequently, was the only balm to the fire in his skin. Exhausted – his mind teetering on the edge of consciousness – heart bursting under the strain, each part of him had pushed the limits of endurance and might give way at any moment. A raging fever was consuming him.

The choked pulse throbbed in his ears, the wheezing of his lungs, his tongue, panting like a spent horse, the intermittent coughs and groans from within. Blood and vomit stained the taste of his cut mouth. One at a time, the effort to lift each foot up and over the grass tussocks. The strain of his eyes to perceive the ground in absolute darkness. An overwhelming urge to lie down. His body begged for rest.

But he could sense the hill. It was just before him somewhere. He tried to focus on that. Not the pain. But how? To climb it seemed impossible. If he stopped now, he would never get there. Oblivious as a fallen roof leaning on him, to the unbearable burden, a dead weight pressed into his back.

Somewhere, in the depths of a dream, a voice chanted: 'Gurranenagappul ... Doire Liath ...' The mirthful laughter of a little girl.

'Síle!' he called out.

He saw the open pit below him and felt himself crash into it, pulled into the earth, then battered beneath the sprawling mass of black muck that pummelled and smothered him from above. But he was still walking. Unrecognisable voices swirled in his brain as his lungs heaved, ripping at his throat. And he was soaked. From sweat or rain, he could not remember.

Where are we? Who is crying? Is that me? Waves of sorrow and anguish were tearing him apart from the inside, rolling in a tidal surge of emotional flood. Outside, his limbs felt stiff … his neck was frozen and jammed. He moaned and struggled to free himself of the arms hung around it, dangling over his shoulders. *Whose? Hers?*

'Cáit! Poor Cáit.'

How far had they walked like this? Where were they coming from? *Six miles. That terrible place. Bodies. Twisted piles of knotted limbs. The children. Horror and sorrow.*

He stopped, dry retching, awake, choking on spit as thick as molasses, the heaviness of nausea deep down but everywhere, drooling, shuddering violence to clear his mouth of the dangling phlegm that refused to leave. And shivering … he fought desperately to steady his balance against the merciless pull of gravity, but ignorant will was stronger.

Muscle spasms. Tingling. Hair. Heat. Seized, unable to bend lower, or lift the burden higher, he stood stuck to the spot.

Fall here … or walk now. A voice within spoke.

And suddenly he felt it. The ground began to rise. One foot, drunk with emptiness. Struggling for breath he sucked and wheezed and moved forward again, steadying, breathing hard. Everything he had ever known … everything they had ever been … all experience: joy; pain; anger; even love were collapsing in on themselves. He just had to get to the top … one step at a time … without falling.

Up there, at the top of the hill … the cabin, the only place – once – they had felt hope, all four of them together. He just had to get her there.

Then it would stop.

1846

IÚIL

JULY

Bail ó Dhia ar an Obair

'*Bail ó Dhia ar an obair,*' a voice said. God bless the work. Pádraig, who was kneeling down pulling weeds out from between the stalks of the drills, barely heard the greeting above the turbulent breeze blowing overhead. He threw a handful of the virulent roots to one side and turned, squinting into the glare, to see a figure, which resolved itself to be Micilín Dubh strolling down the hill towards him.

'Micilín?'

''Tis looking healthy, neighbour,' the visitor said and came to a standstill beside him.

'With God's help it'll be a fine crop underneath it,' Pádraig answered.

Micilín was an easy-going kind of a character and Pádraig liked him well enough, but he stayed guarded and kept picking at the ground while they talked.

A full year and a half now they'd been here in Doire Liath, but it was still Pádraig's preference that he and Cáit took their time getting to know those around them.

Once they'd got a good crop landed, everyone would be on an equal footing. He'd be more comfortable then. Be it a failing or a folly, something within him said this was the way.

Micilín Dubh – Black Michael – was a nickname on his neighbour. Pádraig didn't know where it came from and didn't ask. His curiosity was only a mild one. Mícheál Ua Laeire was the man's real name.

To Pádraig, Micilín was a half-hen-pecked poor divil, who, when not on the receiving end from his wife, was trying to keep his many children under control. It was rare enough to see him on his own as he was now, but somehow Ua Laeire found time for himself away from the wild atmosphere in his own little bothán.

'Sure, a nose around the corner, and a bit of the talk with someone he sees as equal is probably enough to break the monotony for him,' Cáit had once reasoned in their neighbour's defence. 'He's nowhere far to go besides.'

Still busy at his task and sensing the inquisitive eye over his shoulder, Pádraig had a clear picture of the frown Micilín would be wearing. He could almost hear him wondering about the benefit of removing the weeds.

Pádraig knew that as far as Micilín was concerned you raked up the muck, threw in your slots, covered them over, and left them be until it was time to pull them out again.

But everyone had their quirks, Pádraig reasoned. He was well aware he had plenty of his own.

''Tis good to see the children out in the fresh air,' Micilín said as Síle shrieked, laughing in the background. 'Ye are well settled in now, anyway?'

'Ah. We're getting there. A day at a time.' Pádraig kept on with the weeding.

'God is good.'

A silence followed and Pádraig considered the probing nature of the talk.

The friendliness was genuine, but the timing of Micilín's visit was not purely by chance. With only weeks to go before the early crop would be ready to dig, there was nothing occupying the minds of the people more. But they tip-toed around the subject gently. No one was confident enough to bet their lot that the strange occurrence of the blight the year before had been a one-off and, like everyone else, Pádraig felt it would not be wise to tempt fate by talking openly about it.

'Well … If there's ever anything you need, we're only up the hill …'

'Thank you, Micilín. *Go mbeirimíd beo slán ar an am so arís.*'

Despite his reservation, Pádraig knew Micilín and Caitilín could not have raised their family in Doire Liath living on the poorest class of land in the outer reaches of the barony without their own share of misfortune, and whatever differences he felt existed between himself and Muintir Laeire, he knew they had more in common than he cared to admit.

They were the *daoine bochta* – 'poor people' – who worked the land, but would never own the land, the product of hundreds of years of subjugation and oppression, under laws that had removed every human decency, and each natural right of the human being, until, one piece at a time, they had pushed almost an entire race of people to the point of utter destitution and would keep them there to work the land for all it was worth. Pádraig, whenever he thought of it, supposed that it would not take much more of a push before the people themselves, and the system they upheld, would disintegrate like a house of straw and blow away on the drifting wind. But for now, Pádraig could do nothing other than to carry on making the most of it for his family each day that the sun brought up the light.

*

'What did Micilín have to say?' Cáit handed him a plate of boiled cabbage, then sat herself on the creel of turf in the corner while Pádraig took the stool.

He gave a soft grunt in reply, telling her they hadn't talked of much. Pádraig was too hungry to speak and rained into the steaming pile with a spoon, almost burning his tongue as he rolled the contents around his mouth to disperse the heat, the steam still escaping from the previous bite as he pushed the next mouthful in.

His wife suckled Diarmuidín at her breast while he ate.

'Did you say anything to him?' she asked.

'I didn't.' Pádraig chewed on and tried to catch his breath, as his loamy hands raced his mouth to see which could process the more, faster. But all too soon the heap was almost vanished and he had to stop himself, to allow some for her, and for little Síle, who was looking on hungrily.

The last remnants of their stock of potatoes were but a memory at this point and they were now running the gauntlet of *Iúil an Chabáiste*. 'Cabbage July' was the bridge between the last of the hungry months and the digging of the new crop.

While searching with his fingers for any last morsels hiding along the sides of his teeth, Pádraig found the time to answer Cáit.

'Children are children.'

'But they're wild, Pádraig. It's not right they let them run around trampling other people's gardens, breaking the stalks and doing them harm.'

'Ah, 'twas only one or two. There's no bad in them. I don't want to be getting at odds with my neighbours.'

'I suppose you're right,' Cáit gave in reluctantly. 'I think if someone else's children were treading on theirs, they'd have something to say about it though. Herself would anyway.'

'She is a bit of an aul' goat, right enough.'

They both laughed a bit, but aware that Síle was listening, Pádraig quietened, and sniffed, not wanting to encourage badness in his daughter.

'I suppose it can't be easy on her, having them all running around her all the time. Sure, how could you control them?'

Pádraig didn't answer, but flicked his head to acknowledge the observation, feeling he had no real opinion.

'Is anyone saying anything yet?'

'About the crop? Not yet.'

'What about the *Críodáins*?'

'Seems to be looking good all about the place.'

3

Coming of the Harvest

Cornelius Creed had high hopes that the past year, in which he had given out more tickets and advances in money than was normal, was about to turn back for the better.

July was the most straitened month traditionally, when the poor were stretched to their nth on the last of the old season's crop. But on the bounty that came with 'the earlies' – once digging had revealed a healthy and plentiful crop – they would, as the cycle went, sell off a portion to pay their debts and begin to redeem their pledges.

On paper at least, the season transitioning from '44 to '45 had turned out to be a bad year to take up the trade of the pawnbroker. But if Creed's calculations were correct, the bad year that had conspired to bring 'broke' and 'broker' together 30 per cent more frequently than was usual would – when all was back to normal, he predicted – result in 30 per cent more redemptions, and an exponential return. So long as *they* recovered and *he* didn't lose his coat, he thought, clasping his hands together.

But Creed had to admit that the season to come would be a tougher one than usual for the poor. The hidden variable was that with less seed gone into the ground that spring, less would naturally come out in the months ahead. Even if the crop was healthy, there would be more scarcity than usual. And it would most likely, he reckoned, take a season or two to stabilise.

'But still …' he told Paulellen, 'this is the lowest point. If all goes well, the up-swing of the pendulum will give effect any time now.'

It was with this buoyant hope in his step that Cornelius Creed picked up the morning papers and, returning to the shop, he spun them on the glass counter to peruse the ink in search of intelligence on affairs on the land.

Being situated on the south-west tip of the country, Cork tended to follow a week or two behind the rest of the country in reaction to the seasons. Therefore, it was usual for Creed and the inhabitants of Macroom to read east for what was to come.

The last of the sowing had seen seed go into the ground in April for the late crop. That would not be ready for harvest until October. But the fruits of those slots bedded in since February, after the frost, would be coming up soon. Early July was the time one would begin to hear rumours – good, bad, or in between – and it was in search of these that Creed was anxiously on the lookout for any information on the subject, especially following the appearance of the strange blight the previous year.

Was it a one-off?

It was unlikely that the strange new disease would appear again. Failures rarely occurred twice in succession, but the fates of millions hung in the balance. Of this, Creed was all too aware. For his livelihood depended on the ebb and flow of theirs.

Scouring the pages, he raced and glanced over articles he would come back to after he'd found what he was looking for: it appeared that the United States and Britain had finally come to peaceful agreement on the 'Oregon question' and that the territory had finally been settled. William Smith O'Brien had addressed the Repeal Association at Conciliation Hall, in Dublin, upon the occasion of his having been released from a short incarceration. A letter from 'The Liberator' stationed in London was also detailed. Sir Robert Peel's resignation was rumoured to have been 'refused' by the Queen.

Creed's eyes could scarcely avoid the many trifling advertisements that lay in the way of his search, such as 'The Curing Qualities of Cubed Water, Spring Water; Holloway's miracle Ointments'. He was met with a multitude of unworthy distractions before he at last found his way to an article that bore the heading 'Relief of the People':

> It is highly gratifying to find that the Relief Committees throughout the country are still continuing their truly benevolent labours to sustain the poor during the critical period that intervenes before the coming of the Harvest.
>
> From the very favourable state of the weather, it is probable that the Harvest business will commence earlier than usual, thus hastening relief from this source. The accounts of the new Potato Crop, which have reached us this morning are, with a few exceptions, of the most gratifying character.

With his chin thrust into the air, Creed let out a long sigh of relief and closed his eyes at the enjoyment of what he – and no doubt everyone else in the country – was desperately hoping to hear.

He spoke his thoughts aloud. 'Salvation is nigh upon us.'

*

A mere two days later, Creed experienced a resurgent sense of dread as an ominous air began anew to penetrate the tone of descriptions and reports.

In the *Cork Examiner* dated Friday 3 July, under 'The Markets', Creed read:

> The weather continues unsettled, and smart showers fall occasionally.
>
> The Spring crops have benefitted materially by the moisture, and are looking luxuriant. The late potato crop must also be much improved for the same reason.
>
> There is no doubt that it had suffered materially by the previous long-continued drought, and it is difficult to form an opinion as to what the final result may be, seeing that we have complaints of the disease from all parts of Europe.

Though the crop was yet to be examined as far west as Cork and Creed had heard no one definitely declare it to be a failure, by the tenth of July the situation was looking positively worrying:

> With respect to the Potato Crop, the reports we receive are so conflicting that
> we refrain from making further remark upon the subject at this moment.

'Oh, dear heavens.'

Creed sighed and closed the paper as a new, forlorn customer entered the shop: a young woman with a child by her side. The woman, he noted, was almost naked, but for a greenish black cloth, hanging from her shoulders.

'Good morning, ma'am. How can I help you?' he asked, eyeing the incoming cargo over the rim of his glasses as she approached. *Another blanket for my collection*, he thought with an inward groan.

4

Under the Magnifying Glass

By 15 July, Creed's worst fears were all but confirmed and *The Freeman's Journal* fed the words to his lips: 'There can no longer be any doubt upon the subject. The plague is upon us; and it behoves all who are interested to adopt those remedies and precautions which experience may suggest.'

'Merciful God!'

He pushed the paper across the table away from him and stared at it in disbelief. As a man of logic, Creed felt uncharacteristically taken by surprise, even physically unsteady at the prospect of the emerging reality. However profound the consequences were likely to be – ignorant of how much he or anyone had sermonised against the unprecedented nature of this eventuality – however much he knew the poor to have sent their prayers aloft for its opposite outcome, fate had not listened. It was almost impossible that they would escape catastrophe now.

From June to July one year before, the disease had spread from Belgium, to Holland, France, Germany and the Isle of Wight, reaching Ireland only by late September. But maybe this time it had not needed to leap across the continent. Perhaps it was already in the soil, lying in wait.

Lost in thought, absent from himself, Creed looked out the window, where his focus blurred through the general depth of sunken spirits and disastered bodies that peppered the square. They seemed to squirm and move about like insects under a magnifying glass in the midday sun.

Each among them, he reasoned, had just survived one of the hardest winters of their strained existence and, still on their knees, they had not even begun the effort yet to arise and regain their feet. Just as he who watched them now had felt that a reprieve was at hand, so too, surely, must have they. They too, before his gaze, had doubtless been tantalised by that which was almost within reach and by the hand that might have pulled them out of the mud, but that now was gone.

Assuredly, they too must have been tethered to hope. Is it not so, that every living thing clings to the hope, and struggles forth, on the presumption that its lot will improve? For what else can be the incentive to continue when you are scraping the bottom?

But few, perhaps none of them, were alive to this reality just yet. In one sense they were more aware of the danger than anyone. But as the bulk of the poor did not have 'the letters' – nor, in many cases, the English language – actual news from the east would penetrate the sphere of their class – the lowest social stratum – last of all, as a matter of course.

Some of them might never recover their footing as a result, though some, certainly, in accordance with the laws of probability, would. But Creed was certain now: if all that was ordained was to come to pass, then for a great many of them, their fate was sealed.

They would leave the world in the cruellest way, starved, succumbing to sickness, slowly watching their loved ones fall around them, one minute, one hour, one day at a time, some of them seeing their own demise through the eyes of a spouse or a child. Or worse still: alone, among none but the strangers and fellow inmates of the workhouse, too exhausted, or preoccupied with their own impending death, to worry for the next, dying alongside them.

Creed foresaw – with a chill – that for many of them, his premises would be the last stop on the way to that place. If not there, he would see them at the Poor Law Guardians' meetings, as they pleaded for admission to the workhouse. Whatever way he turned, whether in his role as a member of the local Relief Committee; as their pawnbroker; or corresponding on the business of the Poor Law Guardians in his vocation as a reporter for the *Cork Examiner*, Creed knew he was likely to cross paths with almost every pauper in the barony at some stage or another. Bound to witness their descent in its manifold stages, he reeled at the thought.

But what a wretched world – he stared on at the paupers on the square, some of them familiar to him, such as the old man with rachitis of the spine. *What a wretched excuse for a life. What a time to live.*

Perhaps it's better that the poor creatures don't know what's coming, he thought.

Even if they were among the portion who might survive and somehow escape the sweeping torrent that would tumble, swallow, drown and crush whosoever was found to be in its path … even for those, life would never be the same.

Were it possibly so that they somehow managed to stabilise their descent, and – when it was all over – get back to relative normality, they would inevitably find themselves just as miserable, just as impoverished, their existence just as treacherous and with as little chance for improvement as ever there had been under the 'Union' – the 'Empire' – and all that it entailed.

Perhaps they are as well off. He wished them the comfort of their unknowing for as long as it would spare them.

Though the news had wound its way as far west as Macroom and to Creed on the river of ink and words, a harbinger of what was to come, the digging itself was as yet uncommenced. The outer reaches of the barony, he knew – the peopled hills; the barren countryside of the district, and its sixteen parishes – would find out in their own time, with or without the outside prediction, and when it caught hold, news of the disaster would travel amongst them like fire on the wind.

If only by the grace of their ignorance, for just the moment, they were spared the inevitable sense of impending horror.

SCORE STICK

As Pádraig stepped across the fields with the spade on his shoulder, a strong summer wind was playing swirls through the tall grasses all around. He was a man who knew well the feeling of the grass between his toes, but there was something ancient and spiritual in the sensation when the good weather was on. Leaning forward, he began to ascend the hill with the jagged-toothed ridge at the top that was Doire Liath. Hidden from his view, just over its brow, was the stone cabin where Cáit and their two little ones waited. They would be expecting him there any time soon and after a good day turning soil for the Críodáins he was looking forward to seeing their mucky little faces.

It had been almost eighteen months since they'd landed here and the cabin they got from Taidhgí Críodáin was finally beginning to feel like home.

It was a hard-won prize, that feeling, but Pádraig knew they were lucky enough to have a home, with the times the way they were. A one-roomed, bare, stone cabin on boggy, untilled land in the wilds of the far-off hills. Another family falling down the ways might consider it a tough place to land, and one that would be hard to rise out of. But he knew where they had come from. Even lower. Much lower … From nowhere.

Ever since their marriage, in '38, life had been one slip down the ladder after another, so that when viewed from the outside, the path of his and Cáit's existence might have appeared to be a treacherous descent down a sloped hill, and one that offered very little to grab onto.

Cáit's people, Muintir Oiscín, were from nearer town. After their wedding in Macroom, he and Cáit had hoped they might get something down there and settle themselves. The thinking was that with more people around, there'd be more industry and more opportunity. But Pádraig's only skill was as a farm labourer and the one place that skill was not utilised, he soon discovered, was in the town.

When, not long after, Cáit had discovered she was to be a mother, he knew they had to strike out on their own. They couldn't stay on and be a burden on the kindness of her people and them with a child coming into the world.

They moved further west from Macroom and a little north. Three or four miles, out to where Pádraig's own people took a turn putting them up until they could get a situation of their own. From there, he looked for work and helped his brothers, to cover the trouble.

Mary was born in Inchinlinane and for a spell, Pádraig's brothers, Aindrias and Mícheál, kept him going with bits and pieces of work.

Things were good enough. But Mary was a sickly child and did not survive the year.

By the time Síle was born, they had finally got a place in Carrigaphooka, near to the Muintir Buacalla homeplace. But when the rates went up and every bit of land was being scrutinised for how much it was worth, many smallholders found themselves in danger of being swept off in a wave of evictions.

Anyone with holdings big enough to be worth over four pounds had to pay their own rates. That took the burden away from the actual landowner and put it on the occupier. But if the holdings were worth less than four pounds, the landlord still had to suffer it. It was then in the landlord's interest to have tenants with bigger parcels of land and the small man suffered under the clearances.

Not long after Diarmuidín came along, Pádraig and Cáit fell on the wrong side of this and they too lost their grip on the land.

With two young children now, they could not rightly put the burden on anyone else. Every family was close enough to the bone without another nest of mouths to feed, and no one in either family had the room. Aindrias and one of the uncles had good-sized chunks of land to their names, but each was struggling to hold on to what he had, and slowly losing the tug of war as rates went up and the return diminished. The bad year of '32 had taken a lot, Pádraig heard often, and uncomfortable noises were made about properties in chancery and such. At the home place in Carrigaphooka, the last possible refuge, Pádraig's father was still alive, being cared for by his sister, but the old bothán there was just big enough for them.

The only thing to do was to go further north and further west, away from the town. The land was rougher, but they had more of a chance of getting something of their own out there.

Pádraig had often heard his father, Pádraig Óg, say that at one time you could trample over the backs of Muintir Buaćalla all the way from the Sullane to the peak of Mullach an Ois without having to step down, they were so thick on the ground.

Pádraig knew there were droves of cousins and clan up out that way and they took to the roads carrying everything they had.

Winter was coming. It was the wrong time to go anywhere, but they had to move, and they almost paid dearly for it. No one was ready to take them in, though they tried many.

Pádraig offered his hands and tried the good name of his father. But they were not the only family being pushed out to the fringes and there were more open hands than there were strangers who could afford to accept them. No one seemed to have work to spare or was willing to take a chance.

But at the edge of their peril, after days sleeping out in the weather, and when Pádraig felt as though they were walking off over the cold, uncaring cliff of the world, it had been the kindness of a stranger that saved them.

Diarmuid Ua Laoghaire, a farmer above in Liscarrigane, found them in the snow: a young family, with a baby that he must have seen could only be months in the world … freezing and hungry all, by the side of the road. For reasons known only to Ua Laoghaire himself – perhaps it was the baby; other genuine cases were surely passed over – he had pity enough to take them in, exhausted, and devoid of much more hope.

Muintir Buaċalla took respite in the relative comfort of the stable adjoining the Muintir Laoghaire house until the turn of the year came and went. It was during that time that Cáit had decided on the baby's name, forever to stand as a reminder of Ua Laoghaire's gift to them. There they stayed for a few weeks more, until, early in '45, as the weather had thawed, Pádraig began to try the farmers of the area. At length, with the vouch of old Diarmuid, to whom he would forever be indebted, Pádraig fell in with Taidhgí Críodáin and his brother Con, who between them had the lease on three hundred acres of Massy H. Massy's land over on Doire Liath. The brothers had only recently acquired a great swathe of that land when the Scrivens had quit the lease and now needed all the help they could muster to tame it and turn its wild reaches into something that would yield a return on the huge rent.

Half an acre of manured land for Pádraig to plant his own potato garden and a cabin that would keep his family all together under the one roof in return for so many days of his labour throughout the year was – at that stage – practically a paradise and a golden branch to grasp onto and drag himself up, drenched, out of the river that had long been pushing them out to sea.

There was a period of respite for a while after they moved in, until the partial failure at the end of '45, which had put everybody's backs to the wall again certainly, but the visitation of the new disease was a freak enough occurrence that it was likely to be a one-off. Luckily for Pádraig, it didn't change anything for him in terms of his arrangement with the Críodáins. They needed to make up for the loss as much as he did, along with every other labourer they had working for them.

Though they hadn't managed to bring in the good harvest they were so looking forward to that first year, Pádraig had consoled himself that it would just be a leaner winter, with less seed to bed into the drills in '46 as a consequence. But with the grace of God, this year's harvest would balance the books for all their woes, or at least push them back in the right direction.

In July of 1846 Pádraig was in well now with the Críodáins and the crop was looking healthy. These were good days. Away off somewhere over behind the world there was talk that the blight might be again … that it had already shown up among the earlies at the roadside sessions in Macroom. But Pádraig wasn't dwelling on that when he threw his spade behind the cabin and stooped in under the doorway with a can of milk for his smiling little girl and a kiss for his wife.

'Daddy!' Síle, in her ragged little dress, made to pounce on him, before noticing the milk, which made her eyes bulge. She was allowed one big 'gullup', and the rest had to be kept to go with the dinner.

'Ah …' She hissed a sigh of satisfaction, then rubbed her tummy and licked her lips, clearly relishing every last taste of it.

'That'll make ye good and strong!' Pádraig told her, keeping one arm around Cáit as she handed him the baby.

'Say it, Daddy! Say it!'

'Oh!' he mock protested.

'Please Daddy! Do it!' Síle hopped on the spot and wrung her hands with excitement.

'Now Síle, pet, let your daddy get a bite of his dinner first.'

But Pádraig knew there was no stopping the game now. She was too happy for him to spoil her fun. It was his own doing anyway.

'Now, how does it go again?' He stuck out his neck and scratched at his stubbly jaw.

'Lackana … Hackna,' Síle said earnestly, then laughed, to her parents' amusement. 'You, Daddy! You!'

'Right so! All right! But you'll have to help me.'

She giggled again as he began …

'Gurranenagappul. Doire Liath. Currabeg. Corra Liath. Dangansillagh.

Carraganima. Lissacresig. Coolavokig. Barrantanaknock. Bawnatanaknock. Inchinlinane.Liscarrigane.Carrigaphooka.Lacknahaghny.Farranavarrigane. Ballinagree.'

'Ah, ha, ha! Again, Daddy! Again!'

Little Síle was beside herself as he grabbed her two hands and started again, reeling off the names of local townlands he'd had cause to visit over the years. He recited them in the ways they were often paired off, throwing in an additional tongue-bending one here and there, just for her fun.

'Gurranenagappul. Doire Liath. Currabeg. Corra Liath. Dangansillagh. Carraganima. Lissacresig. Coolavokig. Barrantanaknock. Bawnatanaknock ...'

Abandoning her giggle momentarily, Síle concentrated hard. Her eyes were aglow with determination as she tried to mouth along and piggyback his words as he said them. Her lips moved but she struggled to catch up. ' ... chinl ... ane. Lis ... gane.'

'Carrigaphooka,' he continued, courting her along, 'Lacknahaghny.'

She cackled and jumped with glee at the sound of her favourite one causing little Diarmuid to laugh his infectious baby laugh too.

'Farranavarrigane. Ballinagree.'

' ... nagree!' She managed to catch up with Pádraig at the last minute, if only a half a breath behind.

'All right. That's enough, Síle.' Cáit banged the spoon on the rim of the pot and turned to Pádraig with the bowl of cabbage, the smell of which instantly commanded his senses.

Placing the bowl under Pádraig's nose she took over the baby.

'My turn,' Cáit told Síle.

'Which one is your favourite then?' she asked their yellow-haired little girl.

'Lac ...'

'Hmmm. Let me guess.' Cáit pressed a finger to her lips. 'Is it ... Lackanahackana?' She trundled out the name as fast as she could to Síle's delight, who shrieked again in high-pitched ecstasy.

'Lacknacana! Lanckinahankna. Lank … anikankana!' Síle clapped and attempted to reel it off repeatedly, making herself bubble over again. 'Again, Mammy! Again!'

'Right … say it after me. Ready?' With an amused glance at Pádraig, Cáit began to bounce Diarmuidín on her knee and clap his hands along with the rhythm. 'Gurranenagappul. Doire Liath. Currabeg. Corra Liath. Dangansillagh. Carriga …'

'… nimma,' Pádraig helped her.

'Carriganimma! Lissacresig. Coolavokig.'

Cáit continued to list them, slowly so Síle could join in, then sped up again for amusement. Pádraig felt himself smiling, seeing it was even more fun for Síle when she tripped over herself.

At last, after the playing fun had calmed down, Pádraig said, 'Taidhgí Críodáin will be coming up to make an account.'

'Oh, right so,' Cáit answered with her back to Pádraig, letting Diarmuidín down to the floor. Pádraig glanced up at the stick perched over a nail above the door, then went back to his tea.

It was always an occasion for pride, and order, when the farmer came around, and the regularity of his visits put them at ease. But Cáit began to fuss regardless.

Síle ran in from outside a short while later. 'The man is coming,' she shouted.

Cáit brushed and dusted her shawl down once more, as Pádraig rose up, put his cap on, and stooped out under the doorway to welcome their guest.

The dark-haired man came right to the threshold, removed his cap, and gave the customary words, '*Bail ó Dhia oraibh.*'

'*Gurb amhlaidh duit,*' Pádraig replied.

'*A Thaidhgí.*' Cáit nodded a bow.

'*A Cháit.*'

The cabin was too small to receive another person when all would have to stoop, but Muintir Buacalla treated their guest as if he were inside regardless. Reaching his arm back inside, Pádraig took down the *bata* from above the door and stepped out to kneel on the ground beside Taidhgí, who had an identical stick in his hand.

The scoring stick was a piece of wood halved across its length. The labourer kept one end and his employer the other. Whenever the labourer had stacked up a few days' work and they needed to make an account of it, they would lay the two halves side by side on the ground, and cut a notch, or score, across both for each day of work clocked up. That way, whenever they were brought together again, each notch had a corresponding mark on the other stick. When the two pieces were apart, neither man could change the account and no man could cheat the other. Pádraig liked the system for its simplicity.

'*A cúig as a chéile?*' Taidhgí held the knife at the ready.

'*A cúig as a chéile.*' Pádraig rested one arm on a bent knee and held the other end of the two sticks as Taidhgí began to neatly saw the first of five notches across the pair.

'*Aon cheann amháin.*' Taidhgí rested the blade's edge across both sticks, then made a cut with two deliberate motions for each. Once across and once back, to make sure the cuts were even and clear. '*Dhá cheann.*' He repeated the action for each, until all five notches were made. '*Sásta?*'

Pádraig examined the cuts out of politeness but trusted the man implicitly. '*Sásta.*'

As the two men rose to their feet, Pádraig passed his own stick back inside to Cáit, then stood alongside the visitor. He felt proud and was acutely sensitive to how Taidhgí was taking in the rich, thick foliage idling under its own weight over the sides of the drills.

'What's above the ground is below the ground,' Taidhgí said at last, offering an earnest judgement.

Pádraig knew well it was a compliment, in the half-said old way – *you're making a good go of the land* – and, nodding, acknowledged it as gracefully as he could in the same spirit of cautious hope.

'Monday?' Looking straight ahead, Taidhgí Críodáin squinted the question at the line between the grass and the clouds in the far-off distance. He nodded his thanks to the same horizon when Pádraig agreed, then departed without another word.

'Come on, Síle.' Pádraig stooped in under the doorway again, happy he'd have Saturday to tend his own garden and Sunday to rest.

Inside, the *bata scóir* was back over its nail. The notches had not yet climbed to one quarter of its length, but the new stick had only been cut when they'd crossed the line between June and July. It would last until October when the late crop was dug.

THE UN-SOIRÉE

It came as an almost welcome distraction to Cornelius Creed when, on the twenty-second of July, it was purported in a newspaper article that he had attended a *soirée* in Macroom, for the quarterly gathering of the town's Teetotallers and Repealers.

Someone had gone to a great deal of trouble – out of malice or amusement – to paint quite an authentic scene in which two hundred people had met at the People's Hall, including some prominent members of the Roman Catholic clergy and several well-known local gentlemen, with Creed among them.

It was Matthias Ryan, the apothecary only a few doors along on the square, who brought the article to Creed's attention.

Stepping in out of the weather, Ryan entered with a copy of the *Examiner* under his arm and set off the bell above the door, causing Creed to look out from his office in the back. Rising out of the chair, Creed knew instinctively that Matthias Ryan was unlikely to be requiring the services of a pawnbroker but could not imagine what would bring him to visit the shop.

'Have you seen this?'

'Dr Ryan. I had only a glance – what did I miss?' Creed's interest was piqued further when the doctor raised his brows in a way that said he was going to enjoy Creed's reaction, but for all the wrong reasons.

'So you don't remember where you were on Saturday night then?' Ryan asked.

'Me? Saturday?' Creed said, meeting him at the counter where the paper was dropped flat onto the board between them. Ryan flicked over to the relevant page, dabbed his finger three times at what was apparently the offending article and turned away, as though to allow Creed time to absorb the essence in private thought.

'You are not mentioned until quite near the end,' Ryan pointed out. He began to walk through the shop with hands behind his back to examine the contents.

'Help yourself to a look around.' Hazarding a guess that Ryan had never even seen the inside a pawnbroking establishment before, Creed was nervous of what his guest might make of the range of items on display. All in a single moment he saw the contents of the shop through the visitor's eyes. From the most worthless of rags to the comparative opulence of fine jewellery – another kind of worthlessness to Creed's own way of thinking – from battered old furniture to elegant antiques; the strange and the exotic from far-off lands; toys; clocks; more ragged clothes; and a whole accumulation of items that Ryan would surely deem to be utterly bereft of value, as Creed knew them to be – with the exception of their value to the original owner, whose attachment to them was all that mattered to a pawnbroker and his business.

'Some people find *this* interesting.' Finding it hard to concentrate with a relative equal perusing the premises, Creed directed Ryan to the wall behind his head, pasted upon which was a large abstract of the fifty-seven laws of pawnbroking in Ireland, numbered in large print for ease of reference – there to the mutual benefit of the broker and the broken.

'Interesting, indeed,' Ryan proclaimed, suitably occupied.

With the wanderer's attention now trained upon something less embarrassing than the detritus of his poorest customers, Creed was free to stoop over the article and there gave it his undivided attention, until at last, aware again of the backdrop of numerous ticking clocks, he made a 'pffft' sound and raised his head to show his level of disbelief to the fellow Repealer. 'Where to even begin?' Creed blinked rapidly and shook his head, stuck for words.

'Your first thoughts?' Ryan asked.

'Well. It's perplexing … I mean, there was no meeting of any kind. Repeal or otherwise. Was there? At least not that I recall.'

'Correct. None such. I checked with Father Lee in case I'd somehow missed it myself. But he declared himself ignorant of the same.'

'Well, that's definitive. So the whole thing is some kind of mockery. But the purpose? I'm at a loss. I mean, there are obvious attempts at ridicule. Teetotallers "raising a toast" and such.'

'Agreed. And where is it? "The tea-equipage having been removed,"' Ryan added. 'But beyond those poor attempts at humour, I sense the author would like the whole thing to be passed off as an authentic event.'

'But what is there to be achieved by it?' Creed scratched his forehead.

'Did you notice the mixed-up names?' Ryan said.

'Names? No.'

'In the list there. There is no H. Linehan that I know of. A Henry Minihan, there is.'

'Oh, I see. H.' Creed shook his head.

'There are others. C. Loftus and so on. But here's the more interesting thing. Do you remember the Temperance meeting back in February, Mr Creed? When Father Mathew attended?'

'Of course. I wasn't in attendance myself. But …'

'No matter. The point is there was a temperance meeting back in February, chaired by Father Lee as it happens. I'm quite sure it was written up in the *Examiner*, and that the word *soirée* was used prominently somewhere.'

'Ah …' Creed sensed he was beginning to see where Ryan was leading him.

'Basically, although there are some differences,' Ryan went on, 'I believe this whole thing is likely just a re-hashing of that article. By someone with too much time on their hands.'

'Or an agenda, Dr Ryan!'

'True. They've obviously inserted some details of their own along the way.'

'Well, they've added me in for a start.'

'They have indeed. Can you offer any supposition as to why?'

But with this realisation, Creed, distracted, felt suddenly victimised. 'Not one as yet, Dr Ryan.'

'I can't see why anyone would go to so much trouble either.' Ryan sounded puzzled. 'Who would stand to benefit?'

'Well, given that it's someone who is anti-Repeal, anti-temperance and anti-Catholic, I can think of numerous people.'

'Yes?'

'I'll refrain from pointing the finger too hastily, but this much I will say … This is character assassination. And I tell you another thing – I will be getting to the bottom of who is responsible.'

'Indeed, Mr Creed.' Ryan seemed to hesitate. 'You have a relationship with Maguire, don't you? The Maguire who owns the *Examiner*, I mean?'

'Well … I wouldn't presume to call it that exactly, Dr Ryan. I do send in a reasonable amount of local correspondence.' Creed was taken aback. Though flattered, he felt somewhat uncomfortable with the question. He was not in the habit of flaunting his position as a correspondent publicly, but he knew that the general readership of Macroom was aware of his writing, and Ryan too, with certainty.

'I just thought that with your connection in there – perhaps someone in the *Examiner* could shed some light …'

'Of course. Good idea.' Creed regretted saying as much immediately. 'I was in the office only the other day.'

'Oh?'

'I was …' Aimlessly flicking through the pages of the paper, Creed fumbled over his words, trying to navigate the conversation. 'I won't be travelling back in again any time soon. But I'll get a letter off right away.'

'That'll do very well, Mr Creed.'

Having now seen Dr Ryan's motives for bringing the article to him specifically, Creed fought to hide his disappointment. But honour and responsibility overruled his *amour propre* and in the interests of a joint effort to expose the fraud he elected to ignore his wounded pride.

'It is downright outrageous, isn't it? The bust of O'Connell no less!' It was opportune to change the subject and he knew Ryan would be incensed at the sacrilegious mocking of his idol.

'Outrageous is too soft a word. Heinous!'

Creed was still trying to understand why the perpetrator had chosen to bring him into the satire. *This is far too specific to be accidental*, he thought.

'Right so. Well, if you hear anything.'

'Yes, of course, Dr Ryan. Thank you for bringing it to my attention.'

'Of course, Mr Creed. Good day to ye.'

Disturbed, Creed lingered behind the counter absorbing what had just taken place. To his mind, even more than being a prominent member of the temperance movement, Ryan was a stalwart of the Repeal Association. Though an unexcitable man for one of such a passionate standing, the doctor's level of dedication to O'Connell and the Association was second in Macroom only to that of Daniel Lucy. Ryan worshipped the ground the Liberator walked upon and was tireless in organising locally on the movement's behalf. But being a sometime collector of the national tribute himself, as well as acting as one of the Wardens of the Peace whenever meetings were to be held in the interests of the association by its Macrompian membership, Creed's own position among its ranks was not an unrespectable one. That they all shared in their devotion to the Liberator and his national cause was certain. But as proud as Creed was of his hard-won rank amongst them, it was one very much in the shadow of Ryan and Lucy.

What would the great O'Connell himself think of such a prank? Creed wondered. *The greatest statesman Ireland has ever known. He whose bosom, once upon a time, the innumerable political detractors and archers of the empire could not have hoped to pierce with their raining arrows; a man who for almost forty years has single-handedly spearheaded the national struggle to abolish the oppressive Act of Union between this land and that of the invader, thus to end his countrymen's woes.*

In his heart of hearts, Creed had to admit that O'Connell's movement might well have passed the high sun of its potency – now limping, biding its time, with the great ailing leader at its helm. O'Connell who no longer had the luxury of time and who was still licking the yet potentially mortal wounds sustained when the military might of the empire had called his bluff at Clontarf in '43. But Creed and his friends were patrons of the National Repeal Association – it was still active and still counted the vast majority of Catholic Ireland amongst its membership – *ever more the reason*, Creed thought, *to expose whichever small-minded unworthy was responsible not only for the insult to himself and his contemporaries, but for the glancing slight upon the glistening brow of their dear beloved Liberator, rumours of whose failing health were inspiring the protective ire of his allies the country over, as much as it was drawing his bloodthirsty assassins from the shadows, their blades sharpened and trained upon the heart of Ireland's own green Caesar.*

'Mr French!' Creed called out to the back, as the bell rang above the door after Ryan.

'Sir?'

'I need you to man the counter for a spell. Can you spare whatever you're doing?'

'I can, Mr Creed.'

'Good. There's a matter requiring my attention. I must get a letter in the post before the twelve fifteen.'

'Of course, sir.'

*

By Friday morning the *soirée* was the talk of Macroom. Nine proprietors in the town square alone had been mentioned in the article, along with numerous others on Main Street, Castle Street and beyond. When Creed returned to the shop with the latest issue of the *Examiner*, anxious to search its columns for a response to his letter, he found himself overwhelmed by an unusual gathering of 'customers' whom he judged to be only invested in the controversy and who were bent on witnessing his reaction to its next instalment.

'Bah!' Failing in his attempts to find the article amidst the sudden barrage of callers, he threw up his hands and abandoned the counter, taking to the back office. 'See if you can sort the wheat from the chaff, Mr French.'

But no sooner had he extracted himself than he changed his mind and returned to impolitely decline the last of them, then engaged the closed sign, drew the blinds, and locked the door. It was all too sudden, and displeasing.

'Scandalmongers and excursionists. There was ne'er a customer among them,' Creed told the worried-looking clerk. 'You may return to your duties in the store for the time being, Mr French.'

Back at the desk, Creed resumed the search. The article, when he found it, was quite short:

> From letters before us, we learn that we have been deceived by some very waggish individual, who sent what purported to be a sketch of a soirée held in Macroom, on the 19th – which soirée was never held. The sketch was accompanied by a note, which bore the signature of a gentleman who frequently communicates with this paper and was supposed to be in his handwriting.

'The whoreson dog!' Creed shouted. But there was more:

> After a good deal of search, we found the manuscript, which we have forwarded to Macroom. The writer will no doubt be discovered, and treated as he deserves. We cannot make room for Mr CREED'S letter this post.

'Aah!' Despite the rage that threatened to overtake him, spotting the word Macroom again in the next article, Creed could not help but follow with his eyes:

TO THE EDITOR OF THE CORK EXAMINER

Macroom, 23 July 1846.

SIR – My attention has been drawn to an announcement, in your journal of yesterday, of a 'Temperance and Repeal' soirée, reported to have taken place in the People's Hall of this town, on the evening of Sunday last: –

Amongst those assembled for the occasion, my unpretending name occupies a space; but unluckily for the accuracy of your waggish local contributor, I chanced that same evening to be in Cove.

I am Sir, your obedient servant,

VALENTINE McSWINEY, M.D.

'"Your waggish local contributor?"' Creed re-read the insult aloud to himself. 'How dare he!'

If, hitherto, he had been in any two minds as to whether or not the fiasco might damage his reputation, it was there before him now in black and white.

The letter's author was another doctor, also only doors away, but in the opposite direction. Unlike Dr Ryan, however, Valentine McSwiney – seemingly one issue of the newspaper behind the rest of Macroom – had very obviously pulled the proverbial trigger without utilising common sense first and without consulting with his neighbour first, at the expense of their both being a potential laughing stock, which, Creed contemplated, was exactly what the architect of the plot would have wanted.

But a compulsion for vengeance on the originator of the mockery was now blurred by his anger at the haste of McSwiney. Creed's newer, overriding instinct was to quench the flames of the fire sprung up on a second front.

And what was more, if Val McSwiney believed Creed was the author of the satire, how many other people did too? *If only the* Examiner *had published my latest communication instead of McSwiney's, it would have set matters to right,* he thought. *Now, whoever penned this farce and forged my name …*

Creed's blood curdled at the idea of someone laughing, wringing their hands at the news of the unfolding embarrassment. And he felt almost certain he had the identity of that someone.

'You may have your pound of flesh now, Massy Warren,' he whispered to himself. 'But may you choke on the fat.'

Though Creed was well aware that, until – before God – he was sure beyond doubt that Massy *was* the perpetrator, he could not utter that theory to a soul publicly, his reasoning mind along with his intuition kept leading him to visualise that stoat-faced individual whom he saw as the living embodiment of the ascendancy in Macroom, and who had lately seemed to enjoy abusing Creed as much as he enjoyed abusing his position as a Justice of the Peace and as a member of any committee in Macroom that might elevate his position in local society.

Whether right or not in his intuition, Creed had to out-think the invisible assailant.

To the sound of his own breathing, within the blackness behind his closed eyes, Creed sought to still his thoughts.

It was only 9.30 a.m. and the mail car would not arrive from Cork until noon, presuming no delays. The forged letter that the *Examiner* had publicly announced was on its way back to Macroom would surely be on that car. For now, that was his greatest chance of finding some proof as to the author. But that meant either having to wait or biding his time elsewhere.

Val McSwiney should have had better sense, Creed thought, disappointed in his neighbour's opinion of him. *To think I might have such fanciful notions of myself that I would concoct events that had not even occurred? That I would name people so close to myself, as to expose my vanity so easily. What must you think of my intelligence?* He imagined confronting the doctor.

If he had only asked around, McSwiney would have known Creed had denied writing the piece days before he sent in his own attack.

But who knew? Perhaps McSwiney wasn't aware of Creed's repudiation of the feature. Perhaps he *was* in Cove all week and had replied to the article from there.

Creed had no doubt that he could prove his innocence. His reputation would survive the satire. Surely most of those mentioned would have seen the paper by now and would have read the *Examiner*'s stance on the whole affair regardless of the misplaced letter that had followed it, and therefore the ruse was up. He was essentially vindicated. But there was still an urge to limit the damage. Or where next might this fiasco cause him trouble?

Preparing to leave the shop, Creed ignored the sound of someone banging on the door outside.

The knock came again.

'Mr French. Would you please tell whoever – in fact, don't worry, I'll see to it myself.'

But putting on his coat he heard a key turning in the door. 'Oh, it's you, dear.'

Creed greeted Paulellen, who'd gone out for the morning visiting her sister, and who had said she wouldn't be back until that afternoon.

'Why is the door locked, Cornelius?'

'Oh. You're back so early? I was just about to go out.'

'I can see that. But where are you going?'

'What do you mean, dear?'

'I heard about the letter, Cornelius. Who does Val McSwiney think he is?'

'Well, that's where I'm going. I must put things straight with him.' Paulellen looked aghast. 'To keep the peace,' he added quickly.

'Cornelius! If anything, he should be coming to you with an apology.'

'Now, dear, I think if …'

'I'm sorry, Cornelius. I don't like to interfere. But I'll be upset with you if you go lowering yourself to that man. He insulted you.'

'I know. But …' As he tried to shuffle his coat on, Paulellen, who was taking her own off, began taking his off too, and he found himself frozen between the confusion of the two actions.

'Your name has been cleared for all to see and that also shows Val McSwiney acted without thinking. He can come to you now.'

Creed took a deep breath in preparation for concession. And realising it might reflect well upon him if word got around that McSwiney had come to apologise instead of the other way around, he grew suddenly bolder.

'Maybe you're right,' he told her.

'Are you so surprised?' she said, brushing down his waistcoat.

'Always the fairer sex to see a way through the mire, Mr French. Ha?' Creed, noticing the clerk, who up until then had been doing a good job of making himself invisible, his escape route temporarily obstructed, invited him into the conversation.

The man responded nervously. 'Eh, yes, sir.'

'I'll wager Thomas treats all opinions with full respect and deference, Cornelius. He needs no reminding. Do you, Thomas?'

'No, ma'am.' He smiled.

Creed hung up his coat again and gave a wry grin to the clerk who was disappearing behind the counter.

'You have no reason to be hiding away in here, Cornelius. It looks like you've something to be ashamed of, with the blinds down. You've a business to run, dear. There are people in need of your services at this difficult time.'

Before Creed had expressed agreement with this, there came another knock to the door.

'Oh! Maybe that's him now!' Paulellen's eyes grew suddenly wide at the prospect of confrontation and she retreated behind the counter but stayed within earshot.

The thought of confrontation was suddenly not so attractive to Creed either, who steadied himself behind the door before unlocking it and turning the handle. 'Ah, Samuel Welply.'

'Hello, Con.'

'I was just about to open up again. 'Twas all a bit … busy for a while. I trust you've seen the …'

'I have. I was at James and Mary's just after Paull was there.' Sam acknowledged Paulellen across the room.

'Hello, Sam.' Creed's wife returned the greeting with affection.

'What do you make of it, Sam? Would you credit Val McSwiney's swipe at me?' Creed enquired of his friend, hoping for moral support.

'Mmm.' Sam responded with a reserved sound that seemed to say everything and nothing. 'Have either of you come to any conclusion yet as to the originator?'

'Well ...'

Sensing her husband's reticence, Paulellen interrupted: 'I just caught him in time and stopped him going off with the olive branch.'

'Oh?' Sam laughed. 'A bit of diplomacy might not be a bad thing.'

'Really? I think he should come to Con. I mean, writing that in the paper before coming to speak with his neighbour. That's really a poor show, isn't it?' Paulellen shook her head.

'Yes. I suppose it could be viewed that way.' A word at a time, Sam's measured tone was already having a calming effect. 'Now, I know when we talked yesterday, Con, you said you felt someone might be trying to sully your name. And you'd be forgiven that suspicion.'

'I'm sure of it, Sam.'

'Oh? I thought you said you weren't sure,' Sam said.

'Well, I have no proof. But a certain Justice of the Peace ...'

'Now, this is a delicate situation – for both of you – for all concerned. And it could be easy for things to get blown out of proportion. That's why I came over. Maybe together we can view it from a different perspective.'

'I'm listening.' Creed was happy to entertain Sam's opinion, but not convinced it would change his own.

'You're a dear man, Samuel. We do appreciate your kindness greatly.'

'It's no trouble, Paull. Glad to help any way I can. Now, Con, have you considered – and hear out, have you considered that perhaps this is not aimed at you directly at all?'

'I have not. But go on.'

'Well, supposing someone wanted to rag the temperance movement, locally.'

'But I have no direct association …'

'Exactly my point. However …'

'Sorry, do go on.'

'If someone wished to send up the Temperance Association as a group … Let me put it another way. You must have noticed there were a lot of names mentioned – but yours only once – in the first article?'

'I did. But I don't follow.' Sam, Creed noted, was always dressed impeccably, in tailoring that even suited his rather round figure. Light blue seemed to be his hue of choice for materials.

'Well, if someone wanted to make sure the article actually got into the paper, whose name would most likely be passed without question as the bona fide correspondent?'

'Aaah. I see where you're going.'

'In other words, they'd try to pass it off as coming from a regular contributor – someone the *Examiner* trusts – so that it wouldn't be questioned. Who better than Cornelius Creed?'

Creed found himself nodding, now convinced of a new possibility.

Paulellen sought clarity. 'So, on the pretence of being Cornelius, even though Con has no direct ties with the Temperance Association …'

'Of course, the *Examiner* would not be aware of that,' Creed added, 'but they *do* know I'm a warden with the Repeal Association.'

'And on that basis,' Paulellen continued, 'the author would have had a much better chance of the article being taken as authoritative. I see. I see.'

'Very interesting, Sam.' Creed was impressed.

'In a way, somebody is, in fact, paying you a backwards compliment, Mr Creed.'

'Well now, I wouldn't put my hat on that, Mr Welply. I think at very best I'm a convenient scapegoat. Whoever the prankster is, it's clear they have no respect for me. But I see your point. I'm just not sure that's how it will come across to everyone else.'

'I can't guarantee my theory absolutely, I feel obliged to say,' Sam smiled.

'But it's enough to throw some water on the fire for now,' Paulellen reassured him.

'It is also possible you are right, my friend.' Creed felt pleased with the prospect of another opportunity to save face. 'But I'll tell you this,' he hastened to add. 'It's a sorry individual occupies themselves with such a scurrilous contrivance – at a time when the public mind should be singularly concentrated upon the impending crisis and the state of the country in general!'

'That is fact, my friend. I won't argue with you there. In any case, the main thing is to maintain your composure. This will fade away before too long.'

'Good advice,' Paull offered.

'We are indeed grateful,' Creed added. 'Thank you, Samuel. We appreciate the thought and you taking the time. I'm sure you've better things to be getting on with …'

'So what about Val McSwiney?' Paulellen interrupted.

'Leave him to me. This shouldn't be allowed to get out of hand. In fact, the sooner a line is drawn under it the better.' Moving towards the door, Samuel Welply gestured reassuringly.

'Ah, you're too good,' said Paulellen. 'No wonder my sister married you.' Creed knew that he and Paulellen were equally fond of Sam.

'Indeed. Indeed,' Sam laughed. 'Right, I'll get going.'

But almost out the door Sam appeared to have a change of mind and turned back. 'One other thing. The mail …' He looked to Creed.

'Indeed. I dare say, I doubt it will bring us any closer to proving the identity. The most we might expect to garner from the original is whether the villain is a good forger or a bad one!'

'Now you have it. And I wouldn't give anyone the satisfaction of thinking you were eager to meet it off the mail car, if you get me?'

'Touché, you know me well!' Creed laughed. 'I suppose you're right.'

Nonetheless, no sooner had Welply left than tendrils of ivy began to work their way through Creed's mind again. Paulellen, looking distinctly more relieved than when she had arrived, told Creed she was going back to resume her Friday visit with Dorcas and Marie.

'You're sure you're feeling well?' she pressed him before leaving.

'Of course, of course. Go, go.' He threw his arms up dismissively.

And then she was gone.

Despite his assurances to Sam and Paulellen, Creed found that rather than reopen the shop he had picked up his pen, dipped it in the inkwell and begun writing again to the newspaper, albeit at the risk of further tangling himself in the web of the anonymous spider.

*

A small piece in the *Examiner* of Monday 27 July smote Creed's heart: 'Our Macroom Correspondent must excuse us this post; nor can we refer to the matter again, until we have something tangible to act upon.'

LÚNASA

AUGUST

7

After the Calm, Must Come ...

August brought severe thunderstorms to Clondrohid and Pádraig watched helplessly from the door of the rain-soaked cabin as the torrential downpours flooded the ridges of their potato garden. Micilín's wayward children trampling a few plants around the edges was the least of their worries now. A warm humidity hung in the air, almost tropical by local standards, freakish in its nature and as badly timed and unwelcome as anything could be.

Behind the threshold, the earthen floor had turned to mud. Síle and Diarmuidín spent most days sitting on a pile of stones stacked up like a blacksmith's altar behind the door with but a wisp of straw between the stones and their nakedness. It was the only way to keep them up off the damp ground. Soaked in what dripped down from above and what seeped up from below, there wasn't much point in their wearing clothes, only to drench through repeatedly, catching what passed between the roof and the floor. The children looked pale and sickly and Pádraig's only consolation was that they weren't cold.

Tired from the heat and from eating so little for nigh on two months now, Pádraig worried at the discernible lack of spirit present among all in the cabin, himself included, characterised by a despondency in the children and a growing silence between himself and Cáit.

A week and a half into the month, though rumours of the failure where digging had taken place had begun to reach Pádraig's ears, he could not bring himself to share such talk with Cáit. And no doubt aware of the same rumours through her daily interactions with other women at the spring, she had not raised the subject with him either.

They were still surviving on boiled cabbage, milk from the Críodáins, and what little else they could scrounge, and Pádraig's anticipation of seeing and enjoying the treasure that lay beneath the muck of the drills now turned to trepidation. His fears were not helped by the superstition that accompanied the whispers: another of the Críodáins' labourers had remarked to Pádraig that 'no sooner has the word crept into an area that the disease has come again than the blight itself follows immediately behind'.

And yet, there was still no sign of it in Doire Liath.

8

DEAF SUMMER

In honour of the occasion that was the feast day of the Assumption of Mary, 15 August, Creed had closed the pawnshop for the day and, having attended the Saturday morning meeting of the Poor Law Guardians at the workhouse in his capacity as correspondent to the *Examiner* on its proceedings, made his way directly home and went to his study. There, he had centred himself at the bureau and was slowly but methodically preparing himself to write.

From the pocket of his coat he plucked a notebook, split its pages, and laid it to one side. He took out some blotting paper and settled it neatly to his left. Between the two he placed a clean white page and straightened it neatly. Everything around him was quiet and peaceful.

It made no sense.

He uncapped the ink bottle, then lifted the instrument in his hand, but found himself adrift, staring out the window, where, among the branches of a tamed wild cherry tree at the centre of the small garden, sparrows flicked and deflected glimmers of sunlight in all directions upon rapid wingbeats. Bouncing from one bowing limb to another, the birds flew in and out of the frame, inducing in him a state of mind that felt like dreaming.

The only sounds that penetrated the thick glass were the highest shrill peaks of the birds' gay phrases, seemingly made while they bent the tips of the longest, thinnest branches. It was as if silence was the tree itself, whose leaves, like tiny hands, trembled and conducted the ripples of a mute breeze.

Everywhere, above, below, and around, was abundant deaf summer, overgrown and fat.

How could it be that two such opposite truths could co-exist? Creed was perplexed. The statements he had heard that morning were as polarised as the competing ideologies of ignorance and sympathy.

And here it was before him again: the plenitude of nature at that very moment, in contrast with the inescapable want. Lowering his head, Creed squeezed his temples between the fingers and thumb of his free hand. Worried the wellspring of emotion might overshadow his clarity, he wondered if it was too soon to write. But the situation was not going to change. Nor would his feelings diminish.

Thup. Thup. Thup. The tip of the pen rose and fell, over and over, like a tap infrequently dripping, until, at last, he could bring himself to admit his thoughts and allow the ink to speak.

All in a flurry he felt a drain, as if his mind were emptying its contents down a pipe, as the nib, at his command, haemorrhaged a squid-black liquid that flowed gushing into the valleys and ravines it was carving, irrevocably changing the landscape of the arid white page at the end of his arm, just as around him the world was being altered and its future rewritten by the events that were unfolding on a gargantuan scale. His gaze darted back and forth, referencing the shorthand of his notebook as he went, scribbling violently.

When he stopped, the bleeding pen, released, lay prostrate in the gutter of the desk flute.

Creed dropped his arms either side of the chair and blew out a deep breath. The writer within him took the duty of his position very seriously. His responsibility to inform the public through honest renderings of what he saw and felt, while yet remaining impartial, was no less a burden than it was a conundrum – and one with consequences at that.

In the past he might have revelled in castigating those who his post demanded be held to account, but more recently this idealistic approach was revealing those consequences, and those who disliked what the writer Creed had to say saw no boundary between that one and the other Creed he considered himself to be: a character without malice and with good community spirit and an interest in all things intellectual.

Inevitably, over time, the writer had grown in confidence, so that mere reporting had evolved into opinionated letters to the editor. And for the most part, save for the recent *soirée* fiasco, the paper – the *Cork Examiner* – did not refuse his ink.

It was the meticulous element of his personality – the one that liked routine and order – that also enjoyed writing, documenting and structuring his environment. But Macroom was a small town, and as an opponent of his had once warned, 'A small town will be an uncomfortable place for its resident critic.'

'You don't need to openly thwart people, Cornelius. No matter how much they deserve it.' Paulellen had said this in the wake of another controversy earlier that year. 'There are ways to represent your views without inviting trouble.'

At this, Creed had promised her he would strive to walk a more graceful path in the future. 'I do have to speak my mind, dear. Otherwise what is the point? But if it be your wish,' he'd responded with a little sarcasm, 'I will endeavour to be less reckless in my delivery, moving forward.'

'That's all I ask,' she had replied.

Shaming the likes of Henry Swanzy, the rector of the Established Church in Macroom, was not likely to improve relations with his critics, but in spite of promises, Creed *had* to follow his instincts, and this day his intuition told him that a member of the clergy requesting an increase in payment for his services as the chaplain of the poorhouse under such incredibly stricken circumstances as those of the present was an abhorrence and something the people of the parish, nay, the people of Cork, Dublin, even London (all of whom the readership of the *Cork Examiner* served to inform), ought to be made aware of. The fact that Creed and Swanzy both served on the Relief Committee and had to work together frequently was irrelevant. Swanzy's two positions ought not be confused.

Creed folded the letter into its envelope and priming his arm again wrote the portentous words across the front: 'The Editor, Cork Examiner, Patrick Street, Cork.' Flipping the packet over, he took up a stick of wax, melted its tip over the burning candle, sealed the lips of the wallet and left it to set.

With the sharp scent of the oozing resin still arresting his senses, Creed stood, pushed in the chair and, leaning on its back, gazed down at the paper envoy.

It would be time to leave soon. He still had not eaten.

But had he set the tone right? Given the significance of the events, had it suitably portrayed his feelings? The shock?

Hurriedly he pulled out the chair, about to sit again.

'Cornelius, have you not heard me calling you? We don't want to be late for Mary's do. You haven't forgotten?'

Paulellen poked her head through the door just long enough to finish the sentence and then was gone again.

'Just a moment!' he shouted back.

Creed pulled on his coat and closed the door behind him, leaving the room to its familiar silence. The single red eye of the wax seal stared up from the desk, unflinchingly. It would keep its contents intact.

Macroom, 15 August 1846

The time is at length arrived when all are convinced, the potato is irreparably gone. No experiments, no suggestions, no artificial process can avert the decree of Heaven, as I believe it to be.

Last year there were fortunate exceptions, but this season proclaims indiscriminate equality; the Lord and the peasant are sharers in this dreadful visitation. 3 halfpence per weight (21 lb), I saw a large cart of potatoes sell for yesterday here, nor were they of one farthing's value per weight.

To instance any particular place is absurd, for no garden can claim exception, at least in this locality. Then each landlord should help the government, and in doing so he will thereby relieve his fellow being. If each owner of the soil but followed the example set them by one such in our district (Robert Harned, Esq. of Deelas, near this town), who last week called together his men (of which there are many), gave them food and money, and told them 'Want for nothing during this scarce season,' what little difficulty the government would have in providing feasible works for the starving and unemployed Irish people.

In consequence of a resolution put on the books, relative to the respective salaries of John Henry Colthurst, Esq. and Rev. Henry Swanzy, one the revision officer, and the other the Protestant chaplain, who both were seeking for an increase of remuneration in their district capacities, a large meeting of the Guardians of this union took place at the board-room today.

The result of these deliberations was, that in room of augmenting the payments of any of the officials of the institution, the board felt themselves called upon, on account of the universal potato failure and other circumstances, to discuss the propriety of instead, reducing the salaries already granted; in which conclusion they all (I believe) unanimously concurred.

C.C.

TOMORROW

A few fields away from Doire Liath that same afternoon, Taidhgí Críodáin and his brother Con were breaking up work earlier than usual as the bad weather set in. The one parting word of an anxious Tadhg was 'Tomorrow'.

'Tomorrow is Sunday,' his brother reminded him.

'Monday so,' he said.

Though all were desperate to see what lay under the ground, out of a kind of deference to their keepers, those labouring men working and living on the Críodáins' lands at Doire Liath, Corra Liath and beyond had, up until now, respectfully awaited the nod from the brothers before daring to go at their own sods. And now that the ill wind had brought forth whispers of the failure to their quarter, no man wanted to be the first to dig, lest he be the one to discover the bad and bring upon himself the blame of them all for the lot. But that evening Pádraig made up his mind that he could not wait any longer. *Probably, I won't be the only one,* he supposed.

If he waited until after Monday, it might be another week before he'd get a day to turn his own garden. In the morning – he decided – he would brave the weather, come weal or come woe, and try to salvage whatever had survived the downpours and the storms.

A Mathematical Problem

'How old am I?' Feigning disbelief, Creed repeated the question put to him and passed his coat to his friend Pat O'Riordan, their host.

'My daddy is a hundred years,' added the small child who'd asked the question. Delighted to have made him laugh, she smiled up, stretching her knitted hands the full length of her arms.

'How many fingers have you got?' Creed answered playfully, enjoying the first feeling of lightness that day.

'What little dotes.' Paulellen, with a smile, handed her coat to Pat too. The three girls were clearly enjoying the job given them of greeting the guests. 'Thank you, Pat.'

'Delighted ye made it along. I think your sister is inside, Paull.'

'Oh, she came? I'm so pleased.'

'Yes. Sam will be along soon too, I hope.' Pat gave a knowing wink.

'I hope so too.' Creed's wife winked back, careful not to spoil the surprise for the children.

Creed, understanding that Sam, being a baker, must be bringing some confectionery along for the occasion, offered his own quip. 'What'd be the use in having a Welply for a brother, if he couldn't take care of that end of things?'

'Exactly, Con,' said Pat.

Paulellen opened her eyes wide at her husband, as if to say he might be making it too easy for the children.

'Now. Come on in, the pair of ye.'

'My God, Pat, they're all getting so big.'

'Well, never a dull moment, I tell ye. That one'd buy and sell ye.' He tilted his head down at the cheeky girl as they passed through the door.

'Ah, she's the apple of your eye, isn't she?'

He mouthed a silent 'yes' at Paulellen, but playfully cupped his hands over little Mary Ann's ears and steered her head left and right, forcing a 'no', which made them all laugh.

Ellen, one of the other sisters, had already burst through to catch up on the fun inside. 'Say hello, everybody! The Creeds have arrived.'

'Hello, all!' Paulellen returned the greeting amid the shower of hugs and kisses that followed.

'Happy birthday, Mary!' Creed said, taking Mary's hands and kissing her cheek.

'Thank you, Cornelius.' Mary, the subject of all their adoration, blushed a little, betraying only a hint of the age-old history they shared.

'Happy birthday, Mary. You look absolutely radiant,' Paulellen gushed with audible affection.

'Thank you. We're so glad ye could join us. Even though I knew nothing about it…' Creed watched on as Mary gave an almost obligatory pretence of embarrassment and welcomed his wife into the enclave of women seated at the centre of the room. As Paulellen got settled, he felt himself being absorbed by the guard of men hugging the walls not far inside the parlour door.

The din of conversation and laughter was immense, with children running and squealing between and around the two groups.

'Well, that was something else this morning, Con. How will you tackle that?' Creed's great friend James Welply, a Guardian himself who'd been at the meeting, greeted him with a question that intuition told him was a continuation of the men's conversation prior to his arrival.

'Actually, I've written it up already, James.'

'Oh, is that right?'

'I sometimes think to form an account while all is freshest is the best approach.'

'Time waits for no man,' said the ruddy-cheeked Cornelius Murphy, a farmer and another notable Guardian.

'Man often waits for time, only to find it has passed him by,' Creed responded.

'Too true … too true.' Pat smiled, taking a sup of his drink.

The other men muttered their agreements, applauding the wisdom.

'Well, if truth be known, 'twas weighing heavily. I thought it best to oust the heathen before coming out to a hooley, though I'm not sure I managed that exactly,' said Creed.

'The man is yet to be born who is capable of that feat, I dare say.' This observation was made by the neatly shaven Daniel Lucy, like Creed a Repealer and another Guardian.

'Indeed,' Con Murphy agreed.

'I mean, the contents of the other items on the agenda were all damning enough on their own.' Pat led the charge. 'But that resolution … Right; Colthurst: he's a landowner. You'd expect as much from the likes of him. But Henry Swanzy – the rector – and head of the so-called Established Church in the town …'

'His proposal to increase his own stipend was beyond belief!' exclaimed Daniel Lucy.

'It was, Dan. And you saw it yourself. And you, James?'

'I can't say I'm surprised, Pat.' As ever, James, the most articulate public speaker among them, was calm and understated. 'He *is* the treasurer of the Loan fund, after all. A lending institution that functions on interest and advantage.'

'He'd have found good company at the Temple, with the money-changers,' Pat joked dryly, then interrupted himself. 'Jacob O'Riordan! You go easy. He's only small.' All at once, Pat had turned his attention to his boy, and Creed was disappointed not to hear the other's reactions to James's strong words. Pat was split between being a participant in the men's conversation about the great and the good of Macroom, a good host, and a supervising father to the gang of children, who were getting more physical by the minute.

'I hope to God your brother gets here soon, James,' Pat pleaded, gamely attempting to restrain one of the boys.

'So, you say you wrote it up then, Cornelius?' Con asked.

'I hope Swanzy got his due column space!' laughed Dan.

'Now, Mr Murphy, you're no stranger to the editor's column yourself,' James told a smiling Con.

'Impartiality; dispassion; objectivity,' Creed announced, 'all are important tools to the correspondent but, at the same time, it would be remiss to omit such important matters as those we witnessed today. The people of a town should know the strengths and weaknesses of the leaders of their community.'

'Well put, Cornelius Creed! Well put,' Dan said.

'But I hasten to add, Dan, as you too well know, all submissions are subject to the discretion of the editor, available space on the day of publication, and so on and so on.'

'All government relief measures officially ended as of today. At least in terms of the current channels.' James changed the line of discussion.

'But now that there's been a complete crop failure, Russell's new government will have to step up, surely? It'll be a baptism of fire for them,' Con said.

'I tell you what, men, whatever about Robert Peel – Russell might be O'Connell's new greatest nemesis,' added Pat.

'And O'Connell his, yet!' Creed smiled inwardly at Dan's enthusiasm, knowing that he dreamed of reviving the great days before Clontarf.

James nodded his head. 'Now you have it. Peel at least was doing a damn sight better than this dishonest Whig crowd.'

'You'll have no argument from me,' Creed told his cup. 'The gravity of the present circumstances, all told, is truly beyond imagination.'

'Frightful,' Dan's voice dropped as he moved his thoughts from O'Connell to the impending crisis.

At that point, one of the women shouted across to the men from the stove, 'Anyone for tea amongst you lot?'

'T is for Temperance. I'll have drop, please, dear Elizabeth. How are you?'

'Fine, Daniel Lucy; here you go.' Elizabeth approached with a scalding pot that Creed watched with some anxiety.

'I'd go another sup,' said Pat. 'Where did I leave my …' He looked around.

'I'll get another cup,' Elizabeth offered.

'Here, let me get it.' Mary attempted to get up.

'Mary Welply, don't be foolish. We have it covered,' Elizabeth said. You relax now, Mary! Every other day of our lives will do just fine.'

Pat's quip was greeted by a multitude of 'ooos' and 'boos'.

'Oh, you big charmer, Pat O'Riordan,' another of the women shouted over.

'You'll pay for that, Patrick,' James told him, in a drawl full of implied knowledge of his sister's character.

'Brave words,' someone else threw in.

'Pouring the tea in front of everyone; I saw him earlier.' Mary addressed the other women loudly. 'Thankfully most of *my* "every other days" are behind me now,' she added with a smile.

'Good woman, Mary Welply!'

Pat was laughing hard now, and, hiding his head in the cup at his chest, he took the jeers in his stride. 'I'll stay quiet.'

'Oh, by God ye will,' and 'I would if I were you, Pat O'Riordan' followed.

'Touché,' was all he added. Pat's graceful withdrawal had regained him just a small bit of respect from the feminine quarter, Creed thought, and endeared him to all.

'Speaking of O'Connell …' Con brought the conversation back to ground after the laughter settled. 'Any news from the association, Dan?'

'Not much. More of the usual rumours about his health and it not being so great.'

For the sake of the occasion and their peace of mind too, Creed was aware that all were straining to avoid addressing the subject of the absolute catastrophe before them. But it couldn't be avoided for long and inevitably the topic came around in time.

It was perhaps unsurprising that James, the most outspoken of them all, was the one to grasp the nettle. 'Did anybody hear about the meeting at Cork Mountain, or go to it?'

''Twas cancelled, I believe,' said Dan. 'Pressure from the clergy – to stop the labourers inviting trouble on themselves, I suppose. There were placards being put up in every parish and at markets all around the place, not to attend. Five thousand were expected to turn up before that.'

Pat nodded. 'By God, that was some letter, though. I got a lump in my throat, the way they signed it at the bottom: "The Distressed and the Hungry".'

James glanced at his sister and then back at Creed. 'Who could blame them, though, wanting to gather and protest at the way things have gone for them. 'Tis unprecedented. I mean, the partial failure last year, that was bad enough with only a quarter of the crop affected. But before anyone could get back on their feet again, this happens … a universal failure one year later. I don't know …'

Dan took up the theme. 'There's not a parish in the whole of the country that'll not be brought low by it. What was it you said, Con Murphy, in nine cases out of twelve, the early crop is diseased?'

'Diseased extensively,' Con answered. 'In some cases, entirely unfit to be utilised.' While most of the men were the owners of businesses in the town, Con was a farmer and would know better than them all. Creed felt the shadow of these words in his heart.

'Good Lord.' Dan ran a hand over his jaw. 'And only a few weeks ago it never looked a finer crop.'

'By all accounts the earlies are rapidly going into consumption. And God help us, the crop was already to be short, from the effects of last year.' Again, Con spoke with disheartening authority.

'Aye, and that's not to mention the shortage that'll result again to next year's … but the effects of the two of them together … ah.' Pat shook his head in disbelief.

Creed was listening intently but had lost the desire to contribute, drifting away with the sadness of the prospects.

'The earlies will be exhausted long before the late crop is dug, whatever about the quality of that.' James put down his half-finished tea.

Con shrugged. 'The Apple is practically extinct and that's the most remunerative of the three.'

'Daddy. How can you dig apples when they grow on trees?' Jacob, who Creed believed to be only six years of age, had been listening in on the men.

'Jacob! How long have you been there?' exclaimed Pat, and, when the boy looked downcast, added more gently, 'That's a question for a farmer, young man.'

'What about it, Mr Murphy?' It was Dan who saved Pat from the discomfort he clearly felt at discovering the boy eavesdropping on a conversation of the most harrowing nature.

'Well, you see, young man …' Con nobly answered the call. 'The Apple is one of the three varieties of potato we farmers grow across the country. Do you know what the other two are called? The Lumper, and the Black Cup.'

'Oh …'

'Good boy, Jacob. Say thank you to Mr Murphy.'

'I will, Daddy. Thank you, Mr Murphy.'

'You're welcome, young Master O'Riordan.'

'Now run along and play, like a good lad,' Pat told the boy.

Creed had been drawn out of his trance by the whole endearing transaction but waited until the boy was out of earshot to share what had been on his mind. 'A hundred-and-thirty-one thousand acres is the estimated extent of ground planted with any and all varieties of the potato in the realm of Cork. Of this area, it is estimated – from returns already made on the crop – that no less than one hundred thousand acres' worth are totally destroyed or will be ere long.'

'Heavens above,' sighed James. A glance at the others revealed looks of astonishment and shock.

'A good yield, on an average year, it is supposed,' Creed continued, 'would realise about ninety sacks, weighing two hundred pounds each, per acre. The loss then, of sustenance, for man and beast in the county of Cork alone, will amount, it would appear, to the sum of eight hundred and forty-four thousand, two hundred and twenty-one tons.'

Paulellen, keeping an eye on Cornelius after the glumness of his mood all that day, and in general of late, spotted the obvious change of atmosphere among the men. And she was not the only one.

'I wonder what's going on over there?' Mary Collins, James Welply's wife, whispered to her.

'Daddy!' One of the girls shouted from another room. 'There's someone at the door.'

'I'll get it. Excuse me!' It seemed to Paulellen that Pat was pleased with the distraction, and she took the opportunity to lead the group elsewhere. 'Did anyone hear the news of the Ladies' Anti-Slavery Society meeting in Cork? They're seeking contributions to send to their Boston counterpart in time for Christmas.'

'Come out of that land!' Daniel Lucy said, quoting O'Connell, Paulellen knew, who was also a renowned abolitionist, and the hero of Frederick Douglass. 'At the next meeting of the association we should raise some subscriptions, gents.'

'Hear, hear!' Creed said, along with the rest of the adults.

'Speaking of O'Connell,' Mary Collins said, 'it was his birthday only last week. Isn't there talk of making it a national day in his honour, every seventh of August from here on?'

'Right!' The door to the hall burst open as just then Pat came back in, this time leading the girls who carried trays of sandwiches and confectionery cakes. Behind them, and shepherding them all through, was Samuel Welply, Mary's other brother. He held the door open when Pat could no longer reach.

Paulellen felt the air of expectancy that grew as Pat O'Riordan, with his three girls and the boy, Jacob, around him, drew closer to his Mary.

'Our dear, darling wife and mother, Mary!' Pat commanded the room. 'We have brought your dearest friends and some of your dearest loved ones together today, to honour you, on the anniversary, of your … most significant birth date so far.' Pat finished with a cascade of words, to Paulellen's amusement, as well as the rest of the room, to judge by the claps, cheers and whistles.

'I know it seems extravagant to be throwing a hooley in such times as these, forsooth, but it's not something we do very often, and, well, we couldn't let it pass without doing something to show how much we appreciate and love our dear Mary.'

Creed's heart gladdened at the men's soft cries of appreciation for Pat's tender speech, as Mary, sitting at the centre of it all, clapped an open hand over her heart and wore again her familiar, sentimental look.

'And maybe, ironically, you know, maybe 'tis even *more* appropriate at this time, to celebrate, and to make a fuss of our loved ones, family and friends and not take things so much for granted and such. Anyway, I'm rambling now. Would anyone else like to say a few words?' Pat looked to one of the older girls.

'Thank you, Pat, and thank you to our four *beautiful* children.' Mary pulled the two youngest towards her and kissed them.

'I'd like to say a few words,' little Mary Ann shouted, then fell shy when she suddenly had the attention of the room. Pat whispered in her ear to prompt her again. '*Breithlá!*' she shouted, then listened closely with her ear on his lips again. '*Sona … Duit.* Happy birthday.' She clapped with glee.

Creed managed a smile as everyone cooed and Mary's eyes welled up with tears.

'And Mary!' With a loud voice Pat attempted to refocus a room that he perhaps felt was disintegrating. 'In case you're feeling a bit guilty about us eating cakes, Sam distributed some bread amongst the poor around the square today, to try and ease all our consciences, but as we all know he does that regularly anyway.'

'Sam. Thank you! You're a great brother.'

'You're welcome, sister. Of course, you're an O'Riordan now, but you'll always be Mary Welply to me. And may I just say on behalf of the Welply clan, as someone who has known you all your life, since you were a spanking new babe in arms, you honestly don't look a dawn over forty-nine.'

'Oh! Unforgiveable, Samuel Welply!'

'Right!' Pat shouted, clapping and wringing his hands. 'Who's for sandwiches and cake?'

'I'll help!' Dorcas, Sam's wife, got up.

'I'll help too, Dorcas.' Paulellen jumped to join her sister.

Cake and tea broke the groups into smaller conversations. It wasn't long before the floor was cleared and dancing followed. The stomping of all sizes of shoes kicked up a dust and made sure the boards were stuck fast.

Like most of the families present, many of them merchants in the town, the O'Riordans were a good station above the average Catholic family of the district in terms of their visible prosperity and they lived relatively comfortably by those standards.

Even Creed, who liked to think he cared little for the trappings of wealth, was impressed. He was all too aware of the relative affluence surrounding him, seeing, as he was, their house through the eyes of someone who all that day had been thinking of the conditions that the poor of Macroom were wont to endure and imagining what lay ahead for them. Much like his and Paulellen's own house, the O'Riordans had actual floorboards; a second floor; a slated roof; a stove; fireplaces; numerous rooms; bedsteads; a pump for clean water; a kitchen table; utensils; delph; glasses; cups; a sideboard; windows with glass in them and curtains; an eight-day clock; changes of clothes; and all manner of trinkets and relative luxury. It was comparative opulence.

The real centrepiece for the O'Riordan household, however, was the piano that young Kate was presently invited to play for her mother. Without a qualm, she sat in front of it and evidently enjoyed performing very much for everyone.

'This girl is such a bright intellect,' Creed told his neighbour, James. 'She's just been telling me all about her reading of …'

'Shush, pay heed,' Paull told him.

'Oh!' He covered his mouth, before lowering his hand again a little. 'The possibility of youth,' he whispered to James.

The whole room was in thrall to Kate's playing and Mary beamed with a pride even brighter than the shine of the Spanish mahogany casing that amplified the sound of young Kate's nimble fingers dancing above the ivory keys.

Samuel and Dorcas's daughter Charlotte, who the Creeds stood for as godparents, recited a poem next, in honour of her aunt. All of the children's talents were displayed in turn and throughout the evening each was encouraged to converse with the visiting guests.

'I didn't know you played the piano too, Kate; that was most impressive,' Creed said.

Pat winked at him as if to say, *I told you.*

'Did you teach her that too?' James asked. 'It pays to have a headmaster for a father.'

'Oh, I can't take any credit for that one.'

'He pays for my lessons,' added Kate.

Pat and Creed laughed at the honesty of the revelation.

'Mr Creed?' she asked, to his surprise. 'Do you know Latin?'

'*Et linguam populi,*' Creed answered. 'The language of the people.'

Kate giggled nervously, perhaps caught off guard by Creed's instant response, but it was clear to him that the wheels of her mind were turning.

'*Ita, possumne te adiuvare?*' Creed, feeling himself her new mentor, added, 'How can I help you?'

'*Salus populi suprema lex,*' she fired back, having regained her confidence as quickly.

'It is indeed, young woman!' he exclaimed, bowled over by her quoting of Cicero and the relevance of the sentiment within.

The guests continued to mingle, until eventually it was time for the four O'Riordan children to retire and some of the older children among the other families took younger siblings home. From there, the evening was the realm of the grown-ups: to reminisce and bask in the gentle company of their longest-held and dearest acquaintances.

A more earnest mood took the room now and with the summer evening's light all but gone, they were down to the flicker of candles.

'Pat, give us an aul' song there, would ye?' called Sam.

'Ah, now – it's Mary's night, so I won't subject anyone to the torture. But maybe Mary herself might?'

'Oh, stop now, stop!' Mary protested.

'Nice diversion,' someone shouted to Pat.

James smiled. 'Go on, Mary.'

To Creed, Mary was the picture of grace. She had paused in thought but was evidently reluctant to share her mind. 'I'll try to think of something. Pat, you do one first.'

'Come on, Pat.'

'Don't let your beloved down now.' The men cajoled him.

'I tell ye what, I'll give ye a yarn.'

'Good man.'

'Right. This miser, who always volunteered to go around with the hat when there was a collection for anything ...'

'We know a few of them around here.' The quip flew up and its owner pointed to Creed.

'Go along, Dan Lucy, ye blighter! How dare you take my name,' Creed addressed his accuser.

'Wait, wait.' Pat appealed for hush, then continued. 'This fella, the miser, he's suspected of sparing his own pocket all the time … hiding behind the safety of the hat, do ye see?'

'Go on.'

'Anyway, one day, he overhears…' Pat stopped briefly to laugh himself at what was coming. 'He overhears a chap making a comment about him to the same effect, and says he, "Other gentlemen throw in whatever they think is proper. I don't ask what *they* put in. Charity is a private matter," says he, "and what *I* give is *nothing to anybody else*."'

'Ha ha, brilliant!'

'There you go – short and sweet.'

Pat is playing to the gallery, Creed thought.

'Now, Mary,' one of the girls pressed her.

'Ah, I'm still thinking.'

'Come on, Mary.'

'Take your time, Mary, don't be coaxed.'

Paulellen looked across at him. 'Con, you tell them your one.'

'Paull!' Creed answered, in surprise. 'The realm of the witticism is hardly my natural domain.'

'Come on, ye louser, it's for Mary's sake!' Pat said.

'Tell them that one, the money digger,' Paulellen pushed him again.

'Oh.' Creed cocked his head and covered his eyes to pluck up courage. 'Very well. A labourer is, eh, digging, on a retired spot, when an inquisitive American Yankee comes along.'

Creed clasped and rubbed his palms together as he'd seen other performers do. He felt awkward, but tried it nonetheless. Then, feeling too out of place, he put his hands behind his back again.

'Yes?'

'Have you heard this?' he asked.

'No! Go on.'

'Right. Right. "What are you digging for?" the Yankee asks. "Money," the labourer replies. "Ooh!" The Yankee hurries away and naturally enough duly broadcasts the fact among the curious in such matters. And before long, a few more spectators are gathered around the labourer, making a small crowd. "We're told you're digging for money," one of them enquired. "Well, I don't dig for anything else, and if you all want some you're welcome to join in too." "Oh, thank you," the man said. "Have ye had any luck yet?" another asked. "First-rate luck!" says the digger. "It pays very well!" "Oh grand!" said they. And no sooner than he'd said it, but the four around him had their spades in the ground and all thanking him for the invitation too.'

'Right. Keep going,' Pat said, half laughing, whether at his awkwardness, or at the wit, Creed was not sure.

'So off with the coats. Tup. Tup.' Creed pretended to spit in his hands. 'The sleeves went up. All looking forward to their share of the riches. *What a generous fella,* they're thinking, shovelling out pile after pile of earth, until at length they're tiring, and one of them – stopping to wipe his brow – asks, "When did you last get money?" "Saturday night," says the labourer. "Saturday night?" the enquirer says, scratching his head. "At night time?" "How much?" another asks. "Four-and-a-half dollars for the whole week.""

'Aw, jaykers,' Pat laughed, slapping his knee, not realising Creed had yet to reach the punchline.

Creed continued and raised his voice for the final ascent. "'Yes," he said, "six shillings a day is the regular price all over town.""

'Wo ho!' It was Con's turn to laugh, somewhat prematurely.

'And with that the visiting loafers dropped their spades and vanished,' Creed finished and threw his hands up to signal the definitive ending of the tale.

'Ah, very good. Very good,' Pat said.

A polite yet large gulf of silence followed. It was an obvious anti-climax to his efforts, but Creed didn't take it too personally. 'Well, I did say I wasn't a great purveyor of the hoax.' He could see they were humouring his less-than-natural joke-telling skill and consoled himself with knowing that he had given Mary some time to gather her thoughts, which was, after all, the main objective.

When eyes turned from Creed to Mary, she clearly knew she'd put off her performance for as long as she could. 'If I must so …' she finally said, 'I'll try this one. Pat, you'll help me if I lose the tune, won't you?'

'I will. I will. Go on.'

'Ahem.' The room quietened as Mary composed herself, searching for the air in her mind.

In that moment, Creed admitted to himself he was secretly a little jealous of Pat and still as enamoured with Mary as he'd ever been as a young man. But at the same time, he somehow found it liberating to see her so settled and happy with her quaint young family around her – something he could never have given her the way Pat had.

Then, in a voice as sweet, as innocent and as pure as any songbird Cornelius Creed had heard through the window of his study that afternoon, with her head perfectly still and her gaze focused on a distant point somewhere far away beyond everything they could see, Mary opened her mouth to sing:

'Tis night – all's still save yon bright stream
Which now as 'neath the sun's light flows
The little birds in silence dream
And flowerlets on their stems repose;
The moon smiles on that gentle tide –
That tide's the calm and crystal Lee
List, o'er its waters gently glide
Sounds of the sweetest melody.

Oh! Is't not sweet love? Here to stray …
At this still hour of the night
When moonbeams on the waters play
And stars are glistening so bright
Sometimes we dream of joys that shine
Beyond the skies away,
But oh! What bliss, more like divine
Than here love! Here to stray.

'Alone …' She paused, lost, and looked to her husband.

'Alone, with …' Pat spoke. 'Alone with happiness and thee …'

Mary nodded in confirmation, singing to him, holding his gaze, almost certainly out of love more than in thanks for his support. *Perhaps the two are the same thing*, Creed wondered, but it was captivating to watch.

Then Pat, as if to scan the ceiling, or the sky beyond it, joined her in refrain for the last line of the verse: 'Upon the banks of sparkling Lee …'

'For by the moon so chaste and bright.' He stayed singing with her now, as looking to each other, but without sentimentality, their eyes locked. It was true, Creed thought, that they were the same thing. Their gaze was far more effortless and natural than mere romance: it was utter comfort, trust and mutually accepted dependence. Freeing, he imagined.

And by the silvery stars that shine
And by thine own blue orbs of light –
Thy love-lit eyes, yes thine!
I know no joy – no greater pride –
No purer, brighter ray.

Mary broke her husband's gaze and lowered her head with a smile, perhaps embarrassed – Creed fancied – at how lovingly she appeared now. She sang to her shoes and, bringing her toes together, seemed fidgety, with her porcelain concentration broken for the first time.

Quietly, Pat faded off as the end of the verse seemed near, allowing her to finish alone:

Of tranquil bliss than by thy side
Of bridges thus to stray,
Here on the moonlit banks of thee,
Thou lovely – lively – laughing Lee.

Mary gave a small laugh of relief and looked around.

But no one was prepared to laugh with her yet. The short void, by its breaking, made clear that there was barely a sinner present who was unmoved. Not by the song alone, or just by its singing, but by the tenderness displayed between the two; neither of them very green in years, and yet very much united and in love. *This might yet be the sweetest point in their married lives.* Creed wished it so for them. *A healthy young family half reared; still the seeds of possibility around them, were it not for the danger of the ominous new circumstances.*

It seemed to Creed that all present were moved by the culmination of collective joy within that moment in time and by the warmth of their togetherness in that house: friends and loved ones sharing the best of what they had, and were.

He observed a sense of peace among them all, in spite of the contrasting sadness he knew they would inevitably witness in the near future, something that the events of the morning had emphasised; a sadness that he feared would affect them all and mark the lives of their children in some shape or form across the span of the generation to come.

'Now, children, you're supposed to be in bed.' There was a commotion on the stairs as Pat spotted the oldest girls earwigging from the stairwell, kept from sleep by their excitement and the gaiety of an evening that was rolling on without them.

The merry father made a light-hearted gesture to the guests. 'It's a special occasion, I suppose. I'll let them away with it the once,' he shouted, loud enough for the children to hear after they'd scurried up the stairs.

'Mary, that was really gorgeous. I've never heard it before.'

'It's very nice, isn't it, Con?' She deflected the compliment gracefully. 'I'm not sure where it came from, but it's not that old, I think.'

While Creed stood there, hesitant, Dan came up, hat in hand. 'Listen, if you don't mind, we've to be up for Mass in the morning. So we're going to call it a night and leave you to it here.'

The same sense that it was time to depart was widespread and one by one the guests thanked their hosts, said their goodnights and left, until at last it was the Creeds' turn too.

'Listen, Mary, Pat …' Creed took Mary's hand and looked at them both. 'That really did my heart good. Thank you. Thank you both. You are wonderful, dear people. Individually of course, but a very special couple too. And your family are, might I say … well … you are raising the very finest of young men and women. I do hope you know that.'

'They're a gift, each one of them,' Paulellen said over his shoulder.

'Thank you, Paull,' Pat said.

'That means a lot, Cornelius. We think they're very special too,' Mary said.

She was clearly moved. But worried his directness might embarrass her and with Paull watching on too, Creed withdrew his affection and changed the course of the conversation. 'The care and attention you spend on each of them, Pat – and not just Kate, who is very, very bright – it's undeniable and plain for all to see. 'Twould give anyone a spark of hope in the darkness of the world we inhabit right now.'

He shook his lightly clenched fist near his heart as he thanked them again, before he and Paulellen bade their hosts goodnight.

*

They hadn't far to wander through the streets of Macroom. The O'Riordans' house was down the east end of Castle Street and it was a straight path west from there to the square for Creed and Paulellen. But Creed was in no hurry to end the pleasant feelings of the evening and, the air being so nice to take, they stepped slowly as they went.

Gripping his arm as they walked, Paulellen began a tentative conversation that caught Creed by surprise.

'Do you ever wonder, Con?'

'Wonder what, dear?'

'What it would have been like if we'd had a family of our own?'

Pulled out of the hypnosis he'd been enjoying – focusing on the rhythm of their feet tramping the cobbles – Creed took a long breath and deliberated on how best to answer. A horse could be heard neighing within the car house adjoining one of the shops further up the opposite side of the street.

But in the absence of an answer, perhaps afraid of the silence, Paulellen sought to clarify, and elaborate. 'I know it's beyond our understanding. And I don't regret anything. I know we have a comfortable life. I just … hearing Pat saying those lovely things to the children. Like "you've to be up for Mass in the morning" or seeing the joy on Mary's face when the girls carried in the trays. You know? Sometimes I just wish we could have had some of that.'

Creed listened calmly, still open to an answer that might come to him, but in just as little of a hurry to force such an answer as their feet – ambling over the darkened stones – were to reach home. *Surely she knew how he felt. She could not have forgotten. They had talked about this years before. It was not that he did not want children. And although he didn't long for them like she did, it was not something they had any control over.*

Had she seen the longing in his face as he watched the O'Riordans, coveting their closeness and affections; how he had looked at Mary when he talked to her? The faint, residual feelings of the boy within him? Remnants of the still raw but innocent history that he and Mary quietly shared since childhood days. He had been in love with his schoolfriend's sister. Mary likely did not even remember. But it wasn't anything Paull needed to concern herself about. It was just a layer of paint, buried under the many layers of paint that covered the walls of his memory. Like the sign above his shop that, through its own lifetime, had been painted over and painted over, with names, titles, fresh colours and new lettering, the old never to be seen again, but each still supporting the layer above them all the way to its present incarnation.

Paull did not need to know about that. He couldn't remember if he'd ever told her about his former feelings, but perhaps she sensed it, or something like it. Either way, he was confused. Logic told him there was no enduring problem in his and Paulellen's relations. Heart had no bearing on the reality – it was neither feelings, nor wishes, that governed the reality of their being a childless family.

But Creed, as her husband, instinctively knew he must strive to understand, regardless. It was the least he could do. *He felt for his wife, that she was still suffering in this way. It was clear now that she must have been carrying these thoughts all along.*

'Of course, dear, I wonder too. Perhaps not as often. It might be different for a woman who would long to be a mother. The instinct to nurture is …'

But he had no idea. He heard himself attempt an offering. But he could never know the lingering lack of fulfillment, the feeling of something missing, that a woman has who so desperately wants to have a family, but who for some reason, known only to her Maker, is not given to be a mother, despite her ever kind and nurturing nature, her endless supply of love to give to a child; the will and prayers of a saint for God to answer, until one day she knows it will never happen.

He did know that for those reasons Paulellen was always the subject of a quiet pity among her female friends and her sister. But perhaps saddest of all, she pitied herself.

She soldiered on, because she had no choice but to, yet life had put a stone in her shoe that gave her a limp.

Creed was not always on the list of those who pitied her – only at times like this when she spilled over and it became obvious. Perhaps he was too busy with his business, his writing and his meetings to appreciate the depth of her sadness. On the other hand, a sustained sense of pity was not conducive to a marriage of equals.

Creed did like children. Quite a bit, even. He was often surprised at how well he could relate to them. Especially bright children. He had been genuine and sincere in his praise of Kate that evening, of all the O'Riordan children, and of Charlotte. And he was as genuine and true to his feelings when, nearing home that night, he told Paulellen, 'I would like to have had children, Paull, and especially because I know how much you would have loved them. A child's light is the light of the world, to be held up high, for all the world to see by it. But it wasn't fated for us to have a family of our own.'

'I know,' she answered softly.

Somehow it shortened the distance between them.

11

THE CUTTING

Pádraig awoke to the same sound of rain he had heard all too often of late. Rain that at first might have been the crowning elixir to bring the crop to its bursting peak, but rain that had not stopped, at the peril of washing it all away. Boggy soil did not need much water. The idea of the raised beds was to keep the soil around the tubers well drained.

He lay still, face up, alive to the relentless dripping. Inside, the drops that wound their ways through the mess of old thatch fell more slowly than those blanketing the hills in a constant hush.

'Will it ever let up?' Cáit whispered beside him, awoken by Diarmuidín suckling her.

Pádraig wasn't certain if she was referring to the rain or something else, but he didn't answer. For the same reason that he hadn't climbed to his feet yet. Because there was no reason to.

He had no answer and it was easier to just lie there. Arrow-straight, and still, he fell in and out of sleep repeatedly, sometimes aware that his wife was awake or asleep, and of the children between them.

Each time he reopened his eyes it was still coming down. Nothing changed until suddenly he realised it had stopped. Without thinking, he rose to his feet, and somehow, a small but certain hope rose with him. Perhaps it was just an old feeling from childhood; the ingrained expectation of harvest times with his father and the family.

Maybe, just maybe, he thought, inspired by the tiny seed of faith within. Maybe he was far enough up the mountain for Doire Liath, and their plot, to have escaped it. Maybe they were far enough up the hill for the drainage to be better, favouring their garden over the better cultivated land down on the flats. Maybe, even, the endless rain had conspired to blast and wash away whatever pestilent thing it was that threatened to obliterate their chances of getting back on track, their health and all they had endured besides.

Cáit, still lying with her back to him, twitched awake. As she turned her neck to glance at him, Pádraig, hoisting the makeshift galluses up onto his shoulders, met her eyes, then took his spade outside and closed the door, concluding an unspoken agreement not to waken the children with their talk.

Out in the air, Pádraig was amazed to find the whole mountain enveloped in a fog that prevented him seeing further than ten feet distance in any direction.

Around the side, with the spade put leaning against the wall, Pádraig shivered as he relieved his bladder by the half-washed-away dung heap. Buttoning his trousers back up, he turned to survey the panorama of the drills. While his eyes adjusted to the blearing light, he took up a drink of rainwater out of the overflowing 'in' bucket, gulped the most of it down, flung the last drop aside, and cast the cup back into the bucket.

At first Pádraig thought his eyes were playing tricks – the fog, or some class of frost, appeared to be clinging to the flattened stalks too. But it wasn't cold enough for frost. He picked up the bucket and with it and the spade trudged hurriedly to the westernmost ridge at the end of his ground, where, with the mud sucking at his feet, he pushed the tool into the earth and began pulling swathes of the black matter aside, trying not to damage anything in his haste.

One, two pulls more – the soft, ink-black squidge lay back and revealed the tops of a marble-sized cluster of specimens. Pádraig dropped the spade and knelt in the muck to claw them out but found the top of the cluster was all there was. His hands barely recognised the weight of the infantile things. He plunged his fingers in deeper, sure there were bigger lumps hidden at the centre of the group, but there was nothing.

The feeling of something that wasn't there. The absence of what was expected.

Confirmation of his worst fears. It sent a shock through him. As he moved along to each plant with similar results, a knot grew around his guts and began to tighten, clenching and squeezing its fist. But something was worse: the same brown spots that had appeared last year were visible on some of the leaves and stems. And a smell … he hadn't noticed it until he touched them, but now, disturbed, it took to agitating his senses. An acrid, damp smell. Frantically, he began to race along the ridges, desperate to save what he could, dunking them into the bucket to wash off the grey, web-like fur wherever it appeared. Everything he found, so much less than he expected, was either dwarfed or damaged. Hardly any were whole and mature.

For most of the day, and even when the rain returned, he kept going, scooping out the pitiful buds, soaked to the skin in mud and wet, stopping only when Cáit brought him a plate of boiled cabbage. She looked out on him from the door with a face full of pity and tear-stained cheeks, helpless to do anything for him, or herself.

*

When finally he had done all he could for the day, Pádraig carried the bucket in and handed it to her. The tin handle clamoured on the side as Cáit took it from him and turned to the pot, visibly trying not to react to what she saw. Not even one whole bucket had escaped the corruption of the disease.

Pádraig sat on the floor, his head turned away, unable to meet the faces of his family.

'Daddy?'

'Síle, you help me put these in the pot,' Cáit told her as, filled with anger, he slowly began to remove his saturated clothes and put himself near the fire she'd lit both to dry him off and to cook whatever he brought in.

When the potatoes had been in the pot long enough, Cáit lifted the first few out and into the plates. They were so small she could fit three at a time into the table-sized spoon, and she served the rest up amid a deathly silence. They ate in the same silence, but for the continuous drift of rain outside, and the sounds of thunder breaking in the distance.

*

Some hours later, as the children slept, when the day had softened and Pádraig's anger had begun to thaw, perhaps sensing the change in him, Cáit spoke.

'Is it gone?'

With the same silence that had characterised the eating of the meal and the morning before it, he didn't speak at first. For some time he stared into the fire. The words were stuck somewhere. He knew he owed it to her to not act like this; to acknowledge that they were in it together. But his jaw was as hard as flint. He felt like stone all over.

It was an effort to make his lips move at all. At first, they just opened wide enough to allow his breath through. When he tried to speak, nothing came. Just a guttural stop and another breath. His head moved from side to side, his chin rubbing itself in his upturned palm.

'I'll do more tomorrow.' The words finally escaped, but scarcely louder than a wheeze. He knew he would be working for the Críodáins then, but it was all he could muster for the moment.

Cáit lowered her head. It wasn't a response either, but it was a form of acknowledgement. She too had to be dwelling on the frightening aspect of what stood before them and how they would survive it. But she was just as exhausted as he was and not long behind the children in finding the solace of sleep.

12

THE CUTTING – II

The world had never seemed so quiet, or still.

To Pádraig, it was as though everyone, everywhere, had suddenly stopped what they were doing and had fallen silent in contemplation.

A sense that time had slowed down, sucked taut into the moment, came over Pádraig as he lay staring into the dying fire not far from his head, and at Cáit's sleeping face, lit up on the other side. They had seen harder times before. All they had ever known was hardship. But this would be different.

His generation had been raised on the older people's talk of times that came before – of other failures – when hunger and sickness came on the people.

But Pádraig and Cáit – their generation – the younger people, all of them well accustomed to hardship, always took the talk as just that – something in the distant past that the old people talked about. Something that would never happen to them. Not now. Things were different back then. That was before Emancipation.

But lying here on the floor, after the digging and all he had seen … it seemed that those times had come again and were upon them now. Something had just happened that was not easy to understand.

All in a flicker, Pádraig had the profound impression that nothing would ever be the same again. Of utter disaster. That '45 had been a mere warning.

Not much had visibly changed yet. But something had been set in motion that would bring untold destruction and pain upon his family, and the people all.

Who will be left standing when this is over?

One thing was certain – many people were going to suffer. Without assistance, droves of the poor, already on their last, would not survive. All around him was a sea of people on the verge of catastrophe and it was as if a giant wave was readying to wash countless multitudes under. Hunger. It had come last year and announced itself, an unwelcome visitor. But now it said it would stay.

Before too long, the cold would come too. And if all that the older people described was to be again, then not far behind either would be sickness and disease. Together they promised to cut a swathe through them all. Feeding first on the old and the lame. Children next.

Pádraig squeezed his eyes shut with fright. *My mother and father – God bless them – they're out of harm's way, above, safe from suffering. But now 'tis us will be in the line of the storm. My family … my wife … our children. Me! We will all be in the path of deadly peril now.* Cáit, in the light of the fire before him, was still the girl whose father he had made a promise to.

Pádraig had always felt that his proposal had been a small disappointment to Uilliam Ua hOiscín. He had sensed a sadness in the man as they'd received his blessing. And though quietly then, Pádraig had understood the reservation in practical terms: Ua hOiscín would surely have worried that marrying a labourer might mean a tough life for his daughter. It would be less of a struggle for her, surely, if she married up. To someone with land. But farmers and people with land wanted dowries … and married other people with land. Pádraig knew they both knew that; Muintir Buaćalla and Muintir Oiscín, they were the poor, who met and were paired off at fairs and dances. Simple people who had nothing to lose and married for the fun and frivolity of attraction, then threw themselves at life and worked to make a go of it. They took whatever the future brought and did the best they could with what they had.

'You're sure this is what you want?' Pádraig remembered the man asking his daughter when they'd gone to him at the homeplace and stood before him, asking his permission.

''Tis, Father,' she had replied, glowing with happiness and hope, and with possibility in her eyes.

'I'll do everything I can to make her happy, Uilliam Ua hOiscín,' was the promise Pádraig had made her father there and then, in hope of reassuring him, 'to give her a good life – and make sure she doesn't have to struggle. We'll make a home together and raise a strong family.'

Uilliam Ua hOiscín had been gracious in granting his daughter's wish, despite his sadness.

'You're an honest young man,' was the compliment he had given his son-to-be. *But what would he say now?* Pádraig asked himself.

Looking across at Cáit, Pádraig foresaw the struggle he had thought he could save her from. Uilliam, in his wisdom back then, had perhaps anticipated what Pádraig could not yet see, being still deceived by his own youth – one that had tricked him into believing he could be the exception. That he could keep those promises. And for a while, even after the rocky start, when they'd come to Doire Liath, it had almost seemed possible that he *could* live up to them.

But up until that point, all their married life had been a struggle. Not to get to a place where they might prosper. That was a far-off horizon. Just to get to zero, as they knew it. Balance. Equilibrium. However hard that would be. That was the goal.

And they had almost got there, Pádraig thought, staring into the embers between them.

They had survived the impossible. They were gone to the roads and came back. They got a chance and took it. Human kindness and the will of God had saved them from the brink and helped them back to their feet. They'd settled here in this place. A cabin of their own. A foothold from which to climb their way back from the abyss. They had worked and worked to eke out an existence one day at a time, fasting and measuring, measuring and stretching, one day, then another – holding out until the all-promised harvest would come: a harvest of their own, that with God's help would take them out of the way of harm.

We had a bad year the first year. But we persevered and we got through it. Me and you, Cáit. And our little ones. We can't have endured all that for nothing. We can't have survived it to fall now, not like this. God must have willed better for us.

Only weeks ago, he had been all but certain they would finally have their reward and the climb would level out for them. But where yesterday there had been a glimmer; where in place of their destitution had sprouted fat, green leaves, heavy and laden with the bounty that would nourish them back to health; the verdant green shoots of their hopes, come to life – where all that had lived … now, he feared, was nothing.

It was all but gone. For them and for all their kind.

No matter how hard they had tried, how often their prayers had gone aloft, how silently they had suffered – however gracefully they had endured their degradation, however patient they had shown themselves in the long absence of their dignity, heedless of the bellyfuls of pride they had swallowed in place of the basic sustenance their own land should have been able to afford them in abundance, and irrespective of how long and how low they had pushed their faces into the cold wet muck … now they were being beaten back down the long hill.

Down you will go. Lower. And lower still. Suffer more. And be gone. He could almost hear the words as they rolled off the devil's tongue. The husband, the father, the child, the brother, the man. All the Pádraigs within him stared into the same abyss.

Digging that day, he had gone down every avenue in his mind, mumbling, searching. *What is going to happen to us now? How can I get us through this? What are our options? How much can I save out of the ground? If I can save some, how long will they last? What then?*

But a realisation struck him now. *It's not just for the winter we'll have nothing to eat. In winter, you survive off the harvest of the summer and the autumn. It lasts six months, followed by scarcity in summer. Summer is when you have nothing left, even when the harvest is good, and you run the gauntlet of the lean months, living on cabbage and not much else. That means from here forward there'll be a whole year with no food!*

Pádraig's head throbbed and he heard the uneasiness of his own breathing. *But in spring you sow the seed potatoes that will be harvested at the end of next summer to get you through the year after that. And what seed can there be left to plant come spring next year, if there is so little to save now? There will be nothing! Or almost nothing ...*

So even if, by a miracle, we survive a year without food, the following year there'll be nothing again. How can you live for two years without food? We wouldn't survive a week.

His mind bent, trying to see a way forward. He pictured them scavenging, foraging, begging in desperation, fasting, living on scraps and whatever handouts they'd be lucky enough to scrounge. Eating anything they could find and exhausting themselves walking the district in search of charity.

We have nothing left to pawn save the possessions we can't do without. Who could we borrow from and not leave in a worse position? No one will lend out a ha'penny now, because anyone who's not a fool will be holding on to everything they have to see themselves through. Who can you beg from when everyone is failing?

We won't be able to beg from one another because we'll all be starving.

Who will save us out here in the wilds? Us and the rest of the poor scattered across the hills and bogs of the whole of Cork. The helpless wretches living in holes in the ground the country over, like those clinging to the land in the skelps beyond Doire Liath ...

How much more can I salvage out of the ground? He tried to focus on himself again. *Whatever is saved will probably have to be eaten before it turns bad.*

Diarmuid Ua Laoghaire. Could I bring myself to be a burden on him again when the time comes that we're desperate enough? They have a servant boy. But they have mouths to feed too, and, sure, how will they live with nothing to eat? They've the grass of seven cows, but what good will that be to them if they lose their land too? The cows'll be distrained in place of the rent, if they don't sell them first themselves, or have to eat them.

Who'll manage to pay the rent now? Every farmer from here to England will be turned out and evicted. And in the meantime, if they start feeding the paupers, they'll be in a skelp too.

Taidhgí Críodáin and his brother will be as stretched as us, with rent to pay on three hundred acres and nothing growing for them.

Surely the landlords will have to help us now … If they don't, they'll have no one to work the land for them. There'll be no one left to pay the rent then. O'Connell says the only reason they leave us alone on the land is that they can find no one else to get the value out of it like we can. We who'll live on nothing and give them a rent for the privilege.

The government. Will they have to assist the people now? All their talk of food depots and public employment … But even if they do give relief in Macroom, that's six-and-a-half miles away. If I have to be away in and out of there I'll be famished walking all the goodness off myself.

Rev. Kyle, the Protestant rector beyond in Clondrohid. He's a kind man, they say, but you'd have to be at death's door to take something from under the steeple. He'll be giving out bread if it gets bad enough but how many mouths could he feed under the circumstances? He'll be overrun with them jumping at him to kiss the Bible.

I wouldn't dream of it and never have yet, but … steal?

When the children are screaming with pain from the hunger and wasting away from want and it's them or the fat sheep in the field below – a creature, getting fatter and fed better than God's people all around him. Then ye might think about it, he told himself. *But if you're caught you end up transported or, worse, hanging at the end of a rope. And then where would they be? They'd perish surely. Cáit a widow … The children orphaned … or with a different father even. Perish the thought!*

The faces of his brothers and sisters and cousins and the memory of his parents all flashed through Pádraig's mind. He thought of Cáit's people too. *Could they abandon the country where her parents were still alive? A country where the brothers and sisters of us both are still living?*

God save us ... but we might be all dead this time next year if we stay. Could we leave the place where the poor are trodden into the ground and left for dead, or worse: to rot and starve until their bones are bleached white in the sun? We could, surely!

Anyone with the sense or the wherewithal to get out will quit the country now if they can ... will run while they have the chance. But us? Right now, there is no clear way. If we could go now, would we go?

Tomorrow.

But how could we go now? What can we sell? Nothing. It's too late. Think of a way!

We're stuck.

Think of a way! For now, at least, we're stuck. If we don't go now, it'll be too late to go anywhere.

The poorhouse. God in heaven! It was beyond contemplation. *But what if we have to consider it? How long can we last on nothing before we have to consider it? How could we even contemplate going in there? They give you food, but they pull down your cabin. And they split you up! A fate lower than an eternity hungry on the road.*

But no matter how low they were now, they were a long way from there, he tried to assure himself. *That place is probably overrun with paupers now anyway.*

What will we eat after we exhaust whatever we save? Sorrel. Watercress. Sloes. More cabbage. Nettles. Charlock. Meal, if they give any out. Blackberries, if we make it to the end of next summer and don't die of some perishing disease in the meantime ...

Then winter again. Nothing grows in the winter.

'What is your plan for us now, God?'

*

On Monday there was no mist or fog. The brown spots were much easier to see now.

From the hilly field below the cowshed where he met with the brothers and the other labourers that morning to begin the dig, Pádraig could see more farmers abroad, digging their own fields and scurrying about, with presumably the same results.

He had to keep in with Taidhgí Críodáin and said nothing of his experience the day before. He wished he could have stayed home to concentrate on his own plot, saving as much as he could, but if he didn't support the farmer by whose grace he had a cabin, they might not have one at all.

The rain came intermittently.

*

One day after that, and the day after that one, the disease progressed, until the small tubers had begun to turn soft and black and he could squeeze their rottenness like a pulp between his thumb and fingers.

The long rains he had hoped would be the spurn of the pestilence had instead washed the virulent spores that had come and landed on the leaves down along the stalks and into the soil, where the decay-causing fungus attacked the roots and the potatoes themselves.

Within another day, the foul smell of an entire season's worth of food, putrefying all around them, was the final herald of ruination and the seal on any remaining doubt or hope.

There was enough in the pot that night to knock the edge off the empty feeling in their stomachs, but within half an hour of eating, one by one, Síle, then Cáit, and finally Pádraig too, all felt the griping pains of 'the cutting' in their guts. Diarmuidín, still suckling, was the only one spared the awful cramps. Little Síle fell asleep crying and rubbing her tummy as Cáit stroked her hair and tried to hum a lullaby over her. She hummed for some minutes after the moaning had stopped, until there was only the steady breathing of a tired child in sleep, and the sounds of her stomach churning, the bubbling of its gases moving around inside her.

13

GEOMETRY

Having already graced the columns of the *Cork Examiner* with articles twice that week, Cornelius Creed was pleasantly surprised to find that, albeit five days after its composition, the editor had seen fit to publish another of his submissions. Perhaps they had felt it was important to prioritise his account of the recent Guardians' meeting in Wednesday's journal. But in consideration of the dark weeks gone by, they must have felt it appropriate, he thought, pleased with himself, to afford their public the relief of a lighter note from their regular Macroom correspondent in the form of a personal and tender letter that he had hoped from the outset would lift the hearts of its readership.

Returned to the shop, he shouted up the stairs: 'Paull! You have to see this!'

TO THE EDITOR OF THE CORK EXAMINER

Macroom, 15 August 1846.

Dear Sir,–

Enclosed you will find a problem given to the public for solution by a child (as I may term her), of 11 years old. She is the daughter of Mr Patrick O'Riordan of this town, by whose incessant and paternal attention to her educational progress, she has become (what she really is) an extraordinary and ornamental little member of society. 'Tis scarcely credible, when I assert, she not only has an excellent knowledge of Arithmetic and English Grammar, but also Orthography, and is well initiated in the rudiments of Latin, together with the greatest facility of accommodating a large party in dancing by her musical performances on the Piano Forte.

Knowing that I occasionally communicate matters to the Cork Examiner, this pretty, little, and young aspirant to Geometrical distinction, requested modestly of me to present her compliments to you, and beg that you would insert her proposition in the next number of your inestimable newspaper,

Faithfully yours,

C. CREED

GEOMETRY

Through two given points, to describe a circle such that the rectangle or ratio of right lines joining another given point to its intersections with a circle given in position and magnitude shall be given, or such that the triangle formed by the common chord and straight lines, connecting its extremities with a given point, shall be equal to a given space.

And shew the pure Geometrical analysis and composition of each case within the limits of the third book.

14

QUERY

S tiffening his collar on the morning of Saturday 22 August in preparation for his recording of the meeting of the Poor Law Guardians at the boardroom of the Macroom Union Workhouse, Creed reminded himself to pack his latest notebook and the stack of freshly sharpened pencils he had cut the evening before for the exigencies of the task.

Though by now long used to the ritual, he had never yet managed to shake off the underlying feelings of inferiority and intimidation that he felt entering that room an outsider – a barely tolerated observer amongst the entitled ascendants of the wealthy landed class and the power-wielding elite of the district.

At the Relief Committee meetings, which took place in the same room on Tuesdays – Creed pondered as he walked – he was not only the public witness on behalf of the paper, but an active participant with a voice and a part to play in the proceedings and the decisions of its workings. Among the Guardians, however, he was required to be mute – and invisible. To be censored and voiceless was to him anathema.

Intellectually he felt himself a match for any one of their number. Inferiority did not burden Creed in the slightest. It was the imbalance of power. Were it the case that intelligence, or proactivity, had a bearing on who could attain the position and title of 'Guardian' – and thereby grant one a say on the urgent matters concerning the population of the district, and the application of the Poor Law as it affected them – then perhaps half the current body would be replaced, he imagined. But as a mere merchant, and more to the point, a mortal not commanding sufficient capital to compete with the uppermost privileged members of the barony in the realm of material assets – regardless of how immorally they chose to run their estates – Creed was precluded from having a voice among them. Without that ingredient – property enough to be liable to the poor rate specifically – he could neither qualify as Guardian nor ever really command their respect.

There were exceptions, and as Creed entered the boardroom and hung up his hat he was relieved to see his friend James, the foremost among them in his mind, already seated. James Welply did command their respect, even if he had to wrestle it out of their hands on occasion. There were others that Creed would place in this category too, such as Dan Lucy and Pat O'Riordan, but James Welply, the younger brother of Sam – Creed's closest childhood friend – was set apart from the bulk of the Guardians: he had a backbone, and moral fortitude. And he had capital! James ran one of the most successful businesses in Macroom, ran it well, and had business interests all over the district, as far off as Skibbereen, the city of Cork and beyond.

'Hello, Cornelius.' James pulled out the chair beside him.

'Ah, James.' Creed, with a hand in front of his face, attempted to shield himself from the blinding light of the late August sun flooding the room. 'You'd think they'd have called an expert draper in to tender for this room when they were fitting out the building, wouldn't you?' Creed said as he settled the chair beneath himself, feeling unusually relaxed and jovial in his friend's company.

'Well, in the three years since it was opened, I've never got the call,' James answered under his breath with a wry grin, 'but there are very few frills at all on this bare, plain building. The courthouse will make a nice change on Monday.'

'Indeed.' Creed responded with foreboding in anticipation of the event to which James referred: in what augured to be a feverish meeting, to be held before the public, the leading figures of the district were to address the emergency of the reappearance of the potato disease in Macroom. 'One meeting at a time please, James,' Creed joked as Edward Ashe's changing posture told him that the one before them was about to start.

'Gentlemen, I'd like to call this meeting to order.' Edward Ashe, the acting Deputy Vice Chairman, spoke from the presiding seat at the head of the giant T-shaped table.

Creed – having already untied the strap around his leather toolkit, unfurling its contents onto the green baize surface of the space before him – unhinged his bound notebook to the latest clean page and readied himself with one of the square-leaded, wooden pencils in his right hand.

Upon the chairman's request, having breezed through the regular housekeeping and the calling of the 'state of the house', Mr James Burdon, the rather obsessive clerk to the board, as Creed thought him, prepared to read a circular from the Poor Law Commissioners, in the form of a questionnaire that it seemed had been serviced on every union in the country.

'If you'd be so kind, Mr Burdon, when did this circular arrive?' Edward Ashe wished him to preface the reading with some context. Creed admired Ashe for his even temperament but was wary of his ambition – a man who seemed always to be driven by a desire to ensure the long-term advancement of his own gains.

'Tuesday, sir,' the clerk answered.

'Thank you, Mr Burdon. Please proceed.'

'Yes, sir.' Mr Burdon began by clearing his throat, as he always did – happier, it would appear, with his nose buried in the account books than addressing an audience. '"Poor Law Commission Office, Dublin. Dated August thirteenth, eighteen forty-six:

'"Dear sirs. With reference to the circular of the Poor Law Commissioners of the eighth of December last and a set of queries that accompanied it relative to the potato crop and matters connected therewith, I am directed by the Commissioners to state that they are not desirous of troubling you to send any more answers to those questions ..."'

'Thank goodness for that,' Ashe interrupted, to the mild amusement of some present. Creed, who did not count himself among them, took the gathering of such information very seriously, but allowed that at this point in time it was natural to divert those efforts to the examination of the present calamity.

'Sir?'

'Never mind.'

'Shall I continue?'

'Please, Mr Burdon.'

'"The Commissioners, however, would be glad to be furnished with answers to the questions herewith enclosed, and request that you will lay them before the Guardians. The Commissioners trust that the Guardians will be good enough to answer these questions as early as they may find practicable. – I am, Sir, your obedient servant, et cetera. et cetera. Arthur Moore, Chief Clerk."'

Calling to his mind the act of shuffling cards, Creed observed Mr Burdon swapping the order of the two pages within his grasp, one from below the other, before he cleared his throat once more and carried on. '"To the clerk of the Board of Guardians of the Macroom Union. Queries: one. Has the potato disease reappeared in your union? Two ..." Shall I read them all, Mr Chairman?' Burdon asked, nervously seeking the steering hand of leadership.

'Yes, let's hear them all before addressing them, Mr Burdon.'

Creed lifted his head out of the notebook and cast a glance at the interaction then returned to listening, pencil poised.

'Very well, Mr Ashe. "Two: if yes, in how many electoral divisions, and which, has it appeared? Three: in what electoral division has it not appeared? Four: what proportion of the crop has been affected in your union? Five: for how many months' consumption would the healthy portion of the crop supply food? Six: what proportion of the crop on workhouse land is found diseased?" That is all.'

'Thank you, Mr Burdon. I propose we submit our answers as a

priority, given that Cork's and Tralee's responses have already made the newspapers this week. We appear to be quite behind the others.'

'Certainly, Mr Ashe. If I might clarify the circumstances,' the clerk asked, clearly more at ease having regained his seat. 'Lest there be any fault perceived at our end, we are one day behind Cork in receiving mail as a consequence of geography. I've mentioned that we took receipt of the circular on Tuesday. Our board obviously sit on Saturdays here, whereas Cork meet on Mondays, being also the same day they would have taken receipt of their questionnaire. As a result ...'

'Point taken, Mr Burdon, thank you. Moving on – just to confirm, gentlemen, I believe we are unanimously of the opinion that almost the entire crop is destroyed. Unless anybody here has changed their mind with regard to the parish they represent?' The Chairman put the question to the room.

'Agreed.' 'No change.' The chorus of male voices briefly filled the air, offering predictable responses, though disheartening in the extreme. Creed shook his head as he scrawled on in silence.

'Unanimous.' Ashe concluded. 'Thank you, gentlemen, I propose a resolution be passed directing the clerk, Mr Burdon, to answer the foregoing queries in pursuance of that opinion and in accordance with the reports from the several electoral divisions of this union, sent in by the Guardians of each.'

'Hear, hear.'

The motion was passed unanimously, recorded Creed.

'Mr Burdon, have you received reports from every division?'

'I have, Mr Chairman.'

'Very good. I would expect the other questions may be answered as a formality.'

'Mr Burdon, has the last question, with regard to the workhouse garden, been answered?' asked John Pearson, the resident landlord of Mountcross, in Clondrohid. Burdon proudly remarked that as he was aware of the particulars of the questionnaire in advance and as his daily position at the workhouse presented him with the opportunity to prepare for the discussion, he had already taken the liberty of enquiring on the matter.

'Very astute, Mr Burdon. Perhaps we should just go through it now, and be sure all are satisfied? There are only six questions, after all.'

'As you wish, Mr Chairman. The first query, again, is: "Has the potato disease reappeared in your union?"' Burdon leaned over the document, pen at the ready, Creed noticed at a glance.

'Yes. As agreed,' Ashe reiterated.

'If yes, in how many electoral divisions …'

'In all?' Ashe deferred to the board once more.

'In all,' was the collective response.

From the other side of the table Creed could hear James Burdon repeating the responses to himself as he wrote them, his hanging jowls giving the words a slovenly tone.

'In what electoral divisions has it *not* appeared?

'None?'

'None?' Ashe relayed the question aloud.

'Correct.'

'For how many months' consumption would the healthy portion of the crop supply food?'

An inconclusive discussion followed, heightening Creed's frustration at not being permitted to offer an opinion, having recently made his own calculations on the weight of potatoes required to sustain a human adult male for six months. He scribbled on, endeavouring to instead focus on his practical purpose.

Cornelius Murphy offered an estimation Creed hoped was a conservative one: 'The question is difficult to answer; the crop may yet afford subsistence for a month, but even then, it will be unwholesome and patternless at best. In some districts it is now totally gone.'

'Could you enter that, Mr Burdon?' The sitting chairman recommended Con's summation, evidently considering it faithful to the mood of the meeting.

The clerk did not answer, but Creed, rebuilding the sentence in the notebook before him, noticed with a sideways glance that Burdon was writing too, nodding his head from side to side as he whispered the words.

'And finally, the question as to what proportion of the workhouse potato garden is found diseased.'

'Yes, Mr Burdon, what *was* your finding on that?'

'I estimate it at three-fourths.'

'Are all in agreement that Mr Burdon's calculation is sufficient?'

'Agreed,' came several calls.

'So be it.' The chairman confirmed the accord as Mr Burdon officially logged his own answer.

'Thank you, Mr Ashe.'

A formal resolution then put to the board by John Pearson was seconded by Daniel Lucy. Dan, who was the proprietor of Lucy's Inn on Main Street, was another school friend of Creed's. 'Trustworthy, dependable Dan' Creed and his friends called him for his quiet but constant nature. But other than socially and at the Guardians' meetings, Creed happily had cause to maintain his friendship with Dan Lucy via the Relief Committee and Repeal Association meetings too. Pearson and Lucy's resolution was passed to the effect 'that the clerk of the union take the earliest opportunity of affording the information required, on behalf of the Guardians, to the Poor Law Commissioners'.

The agenda then moved to that of interviewing paupers seeking admission and other matters with regard to supplies and the running of the house, but having business to attend to elsewhere, on this occasion Creed whispered an adieu to James and availed himself of the opportunity to take an early leave of the meeting. His exit was conveniently timed to avoid the trauma of witnessing the sorry applicants who would petition their woes in front of an oft-times hard-hearted gallery. It had always disturbed Creed that since the cost of running the workhouse was levied upon the Guardians' own estates – ironically, the criterion of their qualification for the position – it was thus in their own interests to keep those costs to a minimum. To his mind, this inevitably had to affect their approach to granting such admissions, and he could not bring himself to watch the process dispassionately. The conflict of interest was astounding, he thought to himself once again, as he descended the stairs and passed the mendicant queue, keeping his head low lest he might feel an extra pang of guilt upon recognising a face or two of his customers among them.

15

RESOLUTIONS

Two days later, as he pushed his way through the dense crowd blocking the entryway to Macroom Courthouse on Barrack Lane, Creed felt himself enveloped by an air of tension and expectation that pervaded the gathering. It was growing oppressively and was more palpable by the second with the addition of those still descending. By the looks of things, this was but the overflow, with as many already inside as could be seen without.

'Please ... Excuse me ... Thank you. Excuse me ... Excuse me ...' By the time he had made his way up the room, there was an earnest sense of getting down to business at the bench.

The occasion for such a comprehensive gathering of the gentry, the clergy, and a distillation of the peasantry of the barony upon one holy spot was – as the newspaper had advertised it – 'to consider the present state of the potato crop in the district and to devise such means as would relieve the labouring population during the emergency'. Everyone of means and influence and of a position to be deemed affected, or effectual, in the matter had been invited, though as per usual not everybody of that description appeared to have turned up.

The absence of at least one prominent figure was noticeable to Creed, but of no great surprise to any of those present, he supposed. The Honourable William White Hedges, resident landlord of the town, had been absentee since June. But still, there was a significant turnout and once the hullabaloo had passed and the participants separated from the crowd it was possible to ascertain who was in attendance.

Having secured as unobstructed a position as was possible from which to perform his duties – yet instinctively feeling as though his task was to be of an unusually trying extent on this occasion – Creed, sensing the imminent onset of the proceedings, began, as frantically as his wrist would allow, to capture as many as he could of the most influential and significant of those present.

Looking around, he took note of Captain Wallis of Drishane, who was to chair the meeting; Reverend Mr Holland; the Reverend Mr Burton, parish priest of Ballyvourney; also Edward Ashe; Thomas Coppinger, and John O'Connell, both members of the Relief Committee; William O'Driscoll, solicitor; Daniel Lucy, in his capacity as Guardian; John Woods, Turquy; Timothy Murphy of Mount Music; the good-humoured school teacher Pat O'Riordan; John Hassett; the quietly benevolent Henry Minhear of Carriaphooka; the Reverend Robert Warren, Rector of Camaway, whose reputation was sadly sullied and tainted by his association with the intolerable Massy Hutchinson Warren, his brother, thankfully absent on this occasion; to Creed's dismay, John Borlaise Warren, Massy's only slightly less unbearable cousin, also a Justice of the Peace and resident of the imaginatively named 'Warrensgrove' – 'Borlaise' was sure to cause at least some trouble in his namesake's absence, Creed thought; Father Thomas Lee, P.P., Macroom, who'd married Creed and Paulellen fourteen years before; Murphy of Ballyverane, whose first name Creed could not call to mind; John B. O'Sullivan, barrister, Cochrane; Henry Brown, Brownway; John Goold of Prohurst; James Burdon, Clerk of the Union; the Reverend Kirchoffer, of Ballyvourney; the Reverend Mr Somers Payne; the Reverend Mr Henry Sadlier, Rector of Inchigeelagh; and, of course, the Reverend Mr O'Kearney, parish priest of Aghinagh, the tireless crusader for his poor who seemed never to miss a gathering or an opportunity to speak on their behalf.

The number was made up mostly by clergy, Guardians, Relief Committee and landed proprietors. There were numerous other gentlemen Creed thought consequential, but aware that the *Examiner* would only permit column space for so many names and that the addition of each one more would be at the expense of the body of the article he satisfied himself that, by now, he had collected more than enough. Those he most felt for, as the room was called to order, were the poor themselves, who had packed themselves to the rafters above and below.

Downing his instruments to make himself more comfortable in the cramped space, Creed leaned sideways to confide in his neighbour – once again the indefatigable James Welply.

'If there were half as many ratepayers here as there are clergy, we might have a chance of achieving some meaningful results.'

'The truth,' James said, keeping his voice equally low. 'And if the crowds were anything to go by ...'

'Quite so. At least they're showing up to make their position heard.'

'No sign of he who sits on his seat, actually sitting on his seat, as per usual,' James mocked.

'God forbid!' Creed came back in earnest. 'He might get bedsores if he were to actually sit on it.'

From his vantage point along the side wall Creed now saw Captain Wallis nodding left and right along the main bench, then signalling to one of the committee members who struck the wooden disc of the gavel.

'Good morning. Thank you, gentlemen, and apologies for the circumstances. This meeting was convened by the Relief Committee, who appointed myself, Reverend Mr Sadlier, Reverend Mr O'Kearney, John O'Sullivan, solicitor, James Welply, Reverend Mr Payne, Edward Ashe, Timothy Murphy, and Cornelius Murphy to form a sub-committee, the purpose of which was to draw up the resolutions to be adopted here.' Creed felt quietly proud at hearing James's name called out, and at being alongside him as he was essentially held up for his good intentions.

'We have agreed the motions, which will be submitted to this meeting, and it would give much pleasure to hear the observations of any gentlemen in reference thereto.

'Reverend Mr Sadlier, would you care to read the resolutions?'

Accepting with a nod, the minister of Inchigeelagh parish, a tall man, whom Creed admired for the even-handed kindness of his charitable endeavours, stood and began to speak. 'The following resolutions have been adopted unanimously by a committee representing every class of society, and I feel truly gratified to share that I never saw any gentlemen more unanimous in their anxiety to do what is best for the welfare of the public, without regard for their own interests.'

It seemed a promising opening, Creed felt, as the tip of his pencil scratched and tore the surface of the pregnant silence among those up the back, anxious for clues as to their fate.

'Resolved. That we deem it our first duty to express our warmest gratitude for the measures judiciously and timely adopted by the late government, to provide against the distress with which the country was threatened during the season now drawing to a close, and our conviction that, were it not for these measures, famine must have desolated our land, and multitudes must have perished from hunger.

'Resolved. That, though fully convinced of the impolicy of too frequently resorting to extraordinary measures in order to provide labour for the working classes – which can only prove a temporary relief – yet given the present occasion, when from every parish and every ploughland, without exception in this extensive district, the report of the complete failure of the potato crop and consequently the awful prospect of the total destitution of the lower class, has been laid before us,' – here Mr Sadlier paused to clear his throat, disturbed, Creed supposed, at necessarily having to speak so plainly in the sight of those he was referring to – 'we cannot avoid urging Her Majesty's government, in the most respectful but energetic manner, to the necessity of adopting such extensive measures as shall give abundant employment to the labouring classes in every locality and also of adopting similar measures for introducing into the country an ample supply of foreign food, to those found so successful on the late occasion.'

The general silence persisted unbroken, as at this point Creed rested his hand, realising it would be easier to request a viewing of the resolutions from Henry Sadlier after the meeting and to copy them at his leisure.

'Resolved. That we conceive the most useful works in this district, and those which would afford the most immediate relief, would be extensive lines of road through every part of it, where required, and especially through the more remote and mountainous portions of it, which, though attended with heavy expense at present, would prove a permanent benefit to the country.

'Resolved. That we would respectfully recommend Her Majesty's government to take into their serious and immediate consideration the policy of affording every encouragement to all persons engaged in the cultivation of land, by giving as extensive employment as possible, via drainage, and every other available improvement which, with many other advantages, will have the effect of bringing the means of honest subsistence into every locality, thus averting the serious inconvenience and evils arising from large collections of people.'

Sadlier took a breath to gather himself once more and, sighing, dropped his shoulders, clearly moved by the heaviness of the text he was tasked with delivering.

'Resolved. That, being fully convinced that the potato crop will not yield a supply of food for six weeks, and that of the worst description, we earnestly solicit the government to make arrangements for commencing these works *immediately* … to anticipate, and as much as possible to provide against the universal distress which otherwise is certain to be felt not merely for four months, as on the late occasion, but for nearly the entire year.

'Resolved. That with a view to cooperating with Her Majesty's government in their laudable designs, through a system of public works, to avert the horrors of famine from the land, we fully recognise the justice of the principle that every individual deriving any interest from the land, more particularly the absent proprietors, whether owner in fee, intermediate landlord, rent-charger, mortgagee, or judgement creditors, should submit to an equitable and proportionate reduction of their claims, in order to enable the occupying tenant to carry on their usual farming operations, and afford food or remunerative employment to the labourers.'

'Hear, hear,' a lone voice half-heartedly threw forth from the back.

'Resolved. That, sympathising as we do most fully with the working class in all their trials, we desire to impress upon them in the strongest manner, the importance of husbanding with the greatest care their resources, however limited, and the duty of submitting patiently to this threatened calamity, reminding them that the experience they have had during the last trying season should cause them to look with confidence to the Gracious Providence who hitherto has supplied their necessities, and hope that every measure, which human prudence can devise for their relief, will be adopted by the government of the country, and that the same liberality and the same personal exertions, which were extended to them during the past four months by a large portion of their more wealthy neighbours, will again be cheerfully exercised on their behalf, should occasion unhappily require it.

'Resolved. That we respectfully suggest to both landlords and tenants to bear in recollection that the large breadth of ground which the corn crops will occupy next year – in consequence of the smaller crop, *if any*, of potatoes – will require a larger quantity of seed for that purpose.'

Henry Sadlier, looking almost pale with the oppressive heat, thanked the court and retook his seat, as the chairman spoke.

'Thank you, Mr Sadlier. Gentlemen, the floor is open.'

Payne, raising a paper aloft, signalled his desire to speak. 'I beg to propose those resolutions for the adoption of the meeting.'

'I beg to second the resolutions,' said someone else.

'Hear, hear!' came a murmur of voices from the midst of the bench at the sight of progress.

Next to come forward was Burton, parish priest of Ballyvourney: 'Mr Chairman, I consider the present a time when every person who has a voice to give expression to his feelings should make himself heard and understood.'

'Hear, hear!'

'If I may say, being the pastor of Ballyvourney, and Townadrummond, I am the representative of as large and as poor a district as any in the County of Cork. It is my belief that every man from the landlord to the farmer is called upon to come forward. I don't think we ought to mince words on the matter. From what I have lately observed, unless the landed proprietary – those who derive the fat and marrow of the land – immediately afford assistance, I think the people will endeavour to right themselves.'

'Hear, hear!' Tremendous applause and cheering erupted, causing Creed, by now scribbling furiously again, to brace himself and throw a sideward glance to James, uneasy as to where the growing tension might lead.

'I tell the chairman that the district I live in cannot hold out long unless it receives relief,' Burton went on. 'The people are famishing.'

'Hear, hear!' Again a few voices, though not so many, applauded.

'Consider, gentlemen. Consider!' Burton repeated more loudly, to surmount the sudden murmurs. 'I am bound to tell you that they have not sufficient food to last not alone six weeks, but one fortnight, and the food they are at present using is totally unfit for human beings.'

'Hear!' The crowd rose again, but Burton, eager to finish, interrupted, stifling their approbation. 'I shall conclude my observations with one remark: I think the gentlemen of the county are particularly called upon to enforce the necessity on the farmers of husbanding their corn, to store it up and not sell a single grain of it.'

'Hear, hear!'

'And the only mode of doing that is by not calling on them for the rent!'

'Hear!'

'But directing them to keep the corn for their own use, and the sustenance of the labourers under them.'

'Hear, hear!'

Burton was now fighting to be heard and, gesturing with his hands as he re-entered, he brought the room to quiet again in time to pass the floor. 'Unless they adopt this course, their resolutions will be of no avail and their application in other quarters completely useless.'

'Mr Burton.' John B. Warren stood immediately to address the priest. 'You made use of one observation which, in my opinion, requires qualification.'

'Never trust a man whose eyebrows meet in the middle,' James uttered beneath his breath to Creed.

'Indeed,' Creed agreed, recognising the new voice without needing to look up from his notes.

'Only one?' Reverend Burton answered, inciting his accuser to more.

'You said if the gentlemen don't come forward to assist the farmers they will "right themselves". Do you mean you would encourage the farmers to take the law into their own hands?'

'I would not! And my observation applied to the labourers.'

'I do not think the farmers are called on to forgive a year's rent, Mr Burton. If they don't get something, they'll be as badly off as the labourers.'

'Hear, hear!' A number of the gentry among the bench signalled their agreement with Warren.

'I do not wish to dictate what you are to give, Mr Warren. But I again repeat that unless assistance is afforded, and that speedily, I, personally, fear the consequences.'

'Oh, my word … this is unprecedented,' James Welply whispered to Creed.

'Extraordinary!' Creed stole a moment from his writing to cast his opinion on the radical speech. 'At last, someone is piercing the boil!' he exclaimed, clasping his hands briefly around the pencil.

O'Kearney now stood again. 'Mr Warren, I know of no gentleman who would be further from sowing the seeds of dissension than the Reverend

Mr Burton. He is a minister of peace, a lover of peace, and a man of peace in principle. He knows it is his bounden duty in conscience to observe the laws of the country. Without those laws it is impossible that law, order and regularity can be maintained. What Mr Burton supposed is only a possibility or a hypothesis.'

Father Lee, parish priest of St Coleman's and the pillar of his community, now stood to speak. 'I think it's best that the resolutions should be read *seriatim*.' Creed appreciated the use of Latin and was very much in agreement that they ought to consider each resolution at a time.

'With respect …' Rising again, O'Kearney nodded his approval to Father Lee – one parish priest supporting another – 'it's an unusual course to have the resolutions read and passed *in globo* without giving the meeting time to reflect on their object. Naturally, we have heard them read distinctly by the Reverend Mr Sadlier, but I think we should have time for reflection.'

As Creed expected, the Reverend Mr O'Kearney was intent upon speaking his own piece, and would make full use of the privilege to do so.

'No man can deny that the potato crop is entirely gone from east to west. To be sure there is some employment now, and there will be for a short time, but at the end of the harvest there will be a large quantity of labour thrown on the market, which must be met, or I am of opinion that though the people are peaceable and quiet, if driven to starvation they will be forced to reflect on the first principle of nature.'

There was an instant surge of disturbance in the courtroom, but O'Kearney was not finished.

'In the district I have under my charge I cannot imagine the misery, want and destitution that will ensue among them. The usual employment – digging potatoes – will be done away with, for the farmers must plough up their ground. Therefore, the state in which the labouring population will be placed within a few weeks will certainly engage our attention. It is imperative for us to be prepared for such an outcome.'

'Hear, hear!'

Despite his apprehension at the scene, Creed could not fault the priest's utility in raising valid points. And much to the concern of some of the bench who looked to be quietly agitated, the gallery was clearly on the side of the priest from Aghinagh, every bit as much as he was on theirs.

'I, for one, think the plan proposed by Lord John Russell should be more extensive and more calculated to relieve the wants of the people. The late government, under Peel, did their duty manfully, uprightly and honestly, and extended relief in such a manner that not one man starved amongst us. It is most desirable that the present government should follow the principle adopted by the late government and adopt the plan acted on by Sir Robert Peel.'

'Hear, hear!'

Along with the crowd, whose noise was becoming constant, a good deal of the bench now seemed also to be on the side of O'Kearney. 'As to the disposition evinced … I think that by the landlord conceding to the tenant, and the farmer in turn forgiving a portion to the labouring division of the community, I would have some hope for the country. However, I think it best, as Father Lee proposed, that the resolutions be put *seriatim*, and not passed *in globo*.'

Here the bench made a noticeable effort to get some results underway, and over the half hour that followed the first four resolutions were adopted without controversy. But for the fifth, Timmy Murphy begged leave to second the resolution and stood to speak. Timmy, with whom Creed was on friendly terms, was a farmer of intelligence who cultivated a tract of land at Mountmusic – his property a few miles from the town – with scientific application.

'If I may share with you gentlemen – I have two acres of potatoes dug. And I may say frankly they're not sufficient to feed the few persons I have cutting my corn. In my opinion it is necessary that the government must act. But at the same time nothing can be done by the farmers unless they are upheld. And the sooner the landlords come forward, the better. The people cannot hold out long, and unless they can, there will not be peace in the country.'

'There *will* be peace in the country,' Borlaise countered. 'And it is better we let the resolutions pass as they are.' True to the proximity of his relation to Creed's least favourite Macrompian, John Warren had at last begun to show his horns. Creed was sorry to see Timmy Murphy the object of his incivility, and was almost relieved when he quickly retreated, too gentle a man to be taking on the spite of the Warrens.

'I only wished to impress on the landlords and government to come forward, sir,' Murphy answered.

'When the landlord depends upon the tiller of the soil, he should come forward, liberally or otherwise, to assist the people during such a calamity. Self-interest should dictate to them *the necessity of doing so.*' Henry Minhear's entrance came as a welcome diversion to Creed and, along with a 'Hear, hear!' from the bench, received a prolonged applause from the room. *And deservedly so*, thought Creed.

'That's my cue.' From beside him, James Welply gave Creed a brief warning, then rising, begged leave to be the next speaker, which was granted.

'And in so *doing*,' James continued with O'Sullivan's theme, 'I aim to demonstrate the utility of its being carried out to the fullest extent. I have told my tenants not to thresh or sell an ear of their corn.'

James's statement was greeted with cheers amongst the laity, who clearly felt that at last someone was willing to offer more than mere words.

'There is not one man in this court who could more safely enforce the rent from his tenants than I, for many of them hold under me for one-third less than the real value of the ground. But if I were to desire them to sell the corn and pay me their rents, next year they'd come under some of the harpies who would very likely make them pay "cent per cent" for the seed.

'We ought to increase the cultivation of the corn in consequence of the failure in the potato crop and it therefore behoves every landlord in the country to recommend their tenants to keeping the corn.'

Creed was glad of the cheers that greeted the words of his friend. He struggled to contain the pride he felt at witnessing the model example and had to clench his fist beneath the table to remain collected in his efforts to record the scene.

'For my part,' James continued, 'I did not come here to seek popularity. I am here alone on motives of humanity. I came here in the spirit of the observations expressed by the Reverend Mr Burton, and I am not ashamed to say it.'

More unequalled cheering rose to the vaults.

'I'll give you an example of the state of the country. I was recently out shooting on the mountain of Gurtnaheina and went into the house of a most substantial farmer, that of Patrick Collins. I requested some potatoes for dinner.'

James had the crowd's attention for wherever he wished to lead them and looking left and right as he spoke – unaided by notes, prompts, or scripts – was an orator as confident and composed as any Creed knew in the barony.

'There were about five weights of potatoes put down,' he went on, 'and out of that quantity there were a small number selected for my own use. Out of that I ate three. But shortly after, I tell you gentlemen, I was seized with a griping and of pains I could not name.'

A large section of the court erupted in laughter, as James earnestly gripped his stomach in demonstration, but there was a noticeable solemnity amongst many of those in the gallery.

'Gentlemen, you might laugh, but I can assure you this was no subject for laughter,' he continued, a pointed finger solemnly reinforcing his meaning. 'I tell you – if any of you witnessed the scenes I did, you would not be laughing. It was a cause for deep regret, and not one of laughter.'

Cheers turned to a sorrowful serenity that hushed the crowd, yet a couple of the gentlemen not so far from his own position who would count themselves among James's detractors – John Borlaise Warren in particular, Creed noted – wore unconvinced, if not altogether patronising, smirks.

'I hope this example won't be thrown away by the large landed proprietors and the holders of property,' James began to close his offering, 'and I would consider that if they did not do their duty on the last occasion, they have double duty to do it on this.'

As James regained his seat, innumerable cries of 'Hear, hear!' were echoed by a shout of 'Let that be your example, gentlemen!' sent up from the throng, sealing, for Creed, the depth of admiration the crowd felt for his friend's asseveration.

'Well done, my friend, well done,' Creed muttered, slapping James's thigh beneath the tumult of the cheering.

Once again taking exception, John Warren rose to respond, buttoning down his jacket and looking down his nose at James, the air around them quietening as he did so.

'Gentlemen. Mr Welply there used an expression which I consider to be incorrect. And that is an advice to the farmers that they should not thresh their corn.'

'I admit to having said it and I consider it my duty to have done so.' James, in responding, rose to only half his height, and retook his seat as quickly. Warren remained standing.

'You see, gentlemen, I would think that a person like Mr Welply, who has been accumulating money from year to year, is quite different from persons depending on a landed property.' Warren tapped the table with his knuckles to emphasise the sentences, clearly attempting to hide his growing annoyance beneath a playful guise of gentility.

'Mr Welply might make his tenants a present of a year's rent, but what would the landed proprietors do if they were not paid their rents? The reason I speak on the subject is that it has spread through the county that the tenant should pay no rent. If the landed proprietary do not get part of their rents *they too* should starve or be driven into the poorhouse as well as any other.'

'Perhaps that wouldn't be a bad thing!' someone shouted from the back, to the glee of the gallery. But the matter, and Warren's representative intentions, were not something to take lightly, Creed was very sure. They were, in fact, rather dangerous.

'I'll tell you what a bad thing is,' Warren responded. 'In my opinion it's a bad thing to inculcate the principle amongst the tenants that they should pay no rent. For if the landlords don't get something, they cannot exist.'

'Hear!' came a few ardent shouts, demonstrating that not everyone present was on the side of the tenants, or of James's opinions. And Creed knew that however great the cheering for the cause of the poor, when measured against that for such statements as seemed to be in their opposition, the influence of opinion would – sadly – not be measured in volume alone.

'I give Mr Welply every credit for forgiving his tenants,' Warren concluded.

'My thanks to Mr Warren for his condescension,' James responded, standing again to answer. 'Mr Warren has told me that I have for years been amassing money and making it. I wish to thank him for reminding me of that too. But he can trust that I made every penny honestly and kept an upright character and reputation all the way.'

'Hear, hear!' Spontaneously deciding there was no room for the appearance of impartiality on the side of the just, Creed let his caution slip and shouted as loudly as he could.

'And I can also assure him I would sooner go back to the old trade again than distress any poor tenant under the present circumstances.'

As unbridled cheering filled the courtroom, Warren, seeming to sense the impatience of the chairman – who looked poised to close the meeting – with one arm raised, pushed for a last bite.

'If I may have leave to ask one more question,' he insisted. 'And let me see what Mr Welply's answer to it will be. Suppose he had no trade to go back to,' he eyed his subject directly, 'and got nothing from his tenant. Could he still afford it?'

'I pledge you my word,' James stood, resolute and as bold as he pleased, 'not one of them would go to bed fasting, so long as I had any other resource to fall back on.'

Warren sat down again, shaking his head, apparently believing James to be telling a falsehood, or that he felt his foe would find himself unable to stand over the same words in time. It was a statement that was certain to prove a tall order, Creed had even to admit to himself, as he joined in the cheering that supported the claim. But however bold a declaration it might be, so far as he was concerned, it was worthy of their applause on its courage and intention alone.

Captain Wallis, having regained the room, waved the next speaker in: Mr Hore, who proposed the last resolution of the day. It was seconded by Pat O'Riordan, at which time the chairman again took the opportunity to intervene and concluded that with all the resolutions passed, the business that was going to be achieved for the day had been addressed.

'Thank you for your cooperation, gentlemen.'

As they broke from the table – much to the inconvenience of the many officials struggling to gain the exit – Creed was pleased to behold the large number of individuals who crowded the front of the bench and lined up to shake James Welply's hand, in turns.

'God have mercy on you, you're a dacent man,' an old pauper in rags, resting on a stick, told James, gripping his hand and shaking it firmly. 'A friend of yours, Mr Creed? I have new respect for you.' The old man, supposing of the answer, did not await confirmation.

MEÁN FÓMHAIR

SEPTEMBER

AND DAILY RISING

Snatching glimpses of the grandeur as she worked, Onóra, looking up, caught sight of a long rail of polished wooden pegs that ran along the wall above the height of her head – for hats, she recalled – and a line of coat hooks that followed underneath. The stone fireplace at the far end of the room was as tall as a man and big enough to crawl inside. While the boardroom provided a certain distraction from the daily drudge and the squalor of the women's dormitory that, since lately submitting herself to the mercy of the workhouse she had found herself resigned to, it was somehow a daunting reminder of both how far she had fallen and how far she had ever been from a life of comfort.

But how different the room seemed to her now from the one other time she had been inside it. She remembered having been so nervous then that – overwhelmed, crying, so preoccupied by the questioning and the intimidating focus of the Guardians around the table who ogled and peered at her, referring to her like an object, as if she wasn't there – she had not noticed half of what she was seeing now.

'All in one direction!' the matron barked, snapping her back to attention and correcting the grain of the table's green material with rough, brute sweeps of her hand. 'Like this,' the loud woman instructed, twice more digging in abrasively with the heel of her hand, backed by her heavyset upper body.

'Yes, Mrs Horgan.'

Yet even under pressure – steadying herself with one hand and sweeping the surface with the wide handleless brush that occupied the other – Onóra found it almost intoxicating to burrow her fingers into the plush green pile of the surface. It was a strange smell, somehow … new. Everything smelled new.

'You.' Orchestrating the paupers in preparing the room, Matron shouted to another of the three girls she'd plucked out of the women's dorm that morning.

'Yes, miss.'

'Go down to the kitchen at once and see what's become of that other silly clot I sent for the water.'

'Yes, ma'am.'

'And make sure it's a jug of *cold* water she brings up, for heaven's sake – not hot water like that other imbecile of a man fetched last time.

'Cold water! For drinking!' she shouted after the girl, simultaneously opening out the cast-iron windows and fanning herself and then the air to relieve the room of a close, balmy heat.

'When you're finished with that …' Matron redirected her orders to Onóra once again, '… push all the chairs back in, evenly spaced. Like this.'

'Yes, miss.'

'Don't dawdle now, girl. We don't want the Guardians landing in on the sight of you sorry creatures now, do we?' Her eyes bulged as she spoke.

'No, miss.'

*

Finding himself the first to arrive at the empty boardroom that morning, Creed had time to settle himself within the solace of his own thoughts. Sitting alone at one side of the table, about to lay out his portable writing kit, he pushed his fist to sweep out a lone telltale hand mark from an otherwise pristine tabletop – it had been left by one of the pauper servants, he presumed – and taking in the obscure shape of the giant table, supported beneath by the huge metatarsal foot at its centre, he found himself tracing a series of thoughts back through his mind, to the peculiar and amusing circumstances surrounding its genesis, and how it had brought him to take up the position of correspondent for the Guardians' meetings at Macroom Union.

One of the very first meetings the newly formed board had convened here – in January of 1843 – had in fact been to agree the size and shape this very table would be, when infamously, after discussing and agreeing on the odd design, the new Guardians had taken a vote on whether the seats around the table should be hard-bottomed or soft-haired. The tally of that vote, published by the *Southern Reporter and Cork Commercial Courier* – being one of the two other newspapers that served the county of Cork – had resulted in a division, with 'final numbers leaning heavily in favour of hard'.

Creed had not been present in the room that day, but he had seen the article. Everyone had seen the article!

The *Reporter* had made a spectacle of the meeting in its columns, concluding with a comic portrayal: 'The division having been cheered loudly by the Hards – the business of the day was proceeded with.' He could still picture the text.

Creed often boasted that had it been he who was 'in the room' for the *Reporter* that day, he might well have treated the article just as his contemporary had done; that in his opinion the writer for the *Reporter* was justified in his appraisal of the events. But at any rate, he had heard, the Guardians were so incensed at the conduct of both writer and editor, that – for ever more, they maintained – no representative of the *Reporter* would cross the threshold of Macroom Union on their invitation, and, very shortly after, Creed found himself responding to an open call for a 'reliable, professional, literate person, in the Macroom area … welcomed to apply in writing to the Clerk of the Union, for the position of corresponding with the *Cork Examiner* on the meetings of the Poor Law Guardians of Macroom Union Workhouse.'

How proud he'd been of the achievement then, on his becoming the successful applicant!

He had kept the page of the newspaper, a souvenir, for some time and recalled now that running alongside the advertisement he'd read for the position that day had been another submitted by the clerk that put to tender the fitting out of the entire – then unopened – building, taking up half a page.

Creed's encyclopaedic brain could still summon the detail pertaining to the boardroom in that tender:

> 1 Table, to be made of White Deal, free from bad knots, 4 feet wide, in two lengths of 12 and 8 feet to be placed in the form of the letter T; top to be 1½ inches thick, covered with green baize, to stand on 5 inch turned oak legs, set in about 9 inches from the edge of the table, framing to be 5 feet by 1½ inches; to have ¼ inch oak bead fixed around the edge, riding ¼ inch above the top, to prevent the wear of the baize.
>
> 1 large Elbow Chair, and 23 plain ones.
>
> 2 Hat Rails, with pegs, 20 feet long each.
>
> Fender and Fire Irons.
>
> Umbrella Stand.

But however farcical the workings of the board had been – Creed thought, as the room was now filling up around him – even in the face of the widespread poverty that already pervaded in 1843, the comparatively trifling days of the Guardians' choosing of furniture for the boardroom were long behind, the general state of the country since having plummeted to the level of the crisis they currently beheld: a national emergency.

'Good morning, gentlemen ...'

Presiding over affairs this morning it would seem – as he had done that notorious day in January '43 – was Edward Ashe, as per usual performing the duties of Deputy Vice Chairman in the absence of the Honourable William White Hedges, resident Lord of the Soil, owner of the town, and of Macroom Castle, where he actually resided when he was not *in absentia*. It was a disgrace, Creed mused, that the man with most power to effect the events of the district had the least interest in doing so. But the local population, Creed included, were so accustomed to his playing truant by now that – tired of complaining about it to no good effect – hardly anyone passed much remark anymore and took it for granted that William White Hedges was not to return soon in any meaningful way.

Looking up from the table to witness his last-minute entrance, Creed was dismayed to discover that also present this morning would be *he* who Creed was wont to refer to as *the eternal thorn in the side of the reasoning man*, Massy Hutchinson Warren. Creed found himself repulsed at the sight of Massy removing his hat and laughing jovially with one of the other Guardians as they hung up their accoutrements; likely laughing at someone else's expense. What Massy H. Warren lacked in the realm of intelligence he made up for in abundance with moral repugnance and a lack of responsibility to anyone or anything other than himself and his own interests. Whether in matters related to the running of his land; or as a flag-waving member of the Muskerry Yeomanry; or as the proud descendant of the Warren and Hutchinson family lines, his ignorance was displayed everywhere. Be it administering to his position on the Macroom Race Committee or in entering his own horses in pursuit of the beloved silver cup and plate he coveted feverishly, wherever he went, he spread his intense arrogance and churlishness. But worst of all, where Creed was concerned, Massy as a Justice of the Peace seemed to treat whichever poor specimen of the paupery who unhappily found themselves to approach the bench of his court with the same dangerous contempt and maleficent joy that he – with the instrument of his beagles – took in exacting suffering upon any poor fox he could find the time to pursue. His ruthless reputation was well earned and one he liked to uphold, as Creed knew all too well from experience.

In the official capacity of a bystander, Creed should have no direct cause to engage with Massy at a Guardians' meeting, but it was still with a mild sense of relief that he perceived his friends James Welply and Daniel Lucy coming late through the door as the final seats were taken and proceedings got underway.

The pleasantries voiced and the state of the house announced at two hundred and eighty-four paupers, it was requested that the board be brought up to date on the matter of the much anticipated Labour Rate Act, details of which had been circulating in the papers that week.

Ashe stayed sitting to address the room: 'Gentlemen, I am sure it has not escaped any of your attentions that notices bearing details of presentment sessions have been published for numerous neighbouring districts of the county in the papers this week, under the stewardship of the Lord Lieutenant, Henry Labouchere.'

Noises in the affirmative, carrying a mixture of apprehension and renewed hope, were heard around the table.

'As a matter of interest,' Edward Ashe added, 'in my role as secretary of the West Muskerry Relief Committee, I myself wrote to Labouchere on the seventeenth instant, apprising him of our circumstances in general. I did, in fact, receive a sympathetic reply as of Monday last, the details of which are not relevant here, but suffice it to say that the same sympathy has not effected any change.'

Grunts of disappointment followed.

The man who had entered the room laughing with Massy, William Garde Browne, another Justice of the Peace and one of the three principal moneylenders of the district, was the first Guardian to speak. 'Imokilly; Ballymore; Kinnalea; Orrery and Kilmore; Kinsale; Fermoy; in reality, near any and all districts you care to name, but ours, have been given a date, Mr Chairman.'

'It is, no doubt, frustrating at the least, Mr Browne. I believe we are all in agreement that immediate measures of relief are necessitated by the circumstances. I would like to throw the floor open to addressing the pitfalls of the present state of affairs as we see them. But first, while we're on the subject of presentments – let us discuss and evaluate the likely outcome of the sessions, presuming a date of confirmation.'

Patrick Ronayne of Castleview, raising a pencil aloft, was given the nod as Ashe sat back, inviting him to speak: 'Based on the fixing of the neighbouring districts, as already publicised, it will be highly unusual if a notification of our own does not follow in a matter of days, having already been somewhat delayed, and for no obvious reason we are aware of. I think it's safe to assume it can't be far behind.'

'Hear, hear,' a few voices murmured, but none imbued with any great passion.

'Very well. Let's presume Mr Ronayne is correct for the moment. Can we be more specific about when the actual sessions *might* take place once announced?' Ashe asked.

'I suspect once announced, there will need to be ample time given applicants to prepare proposals. So not before the fifth.'

'Thank you, Mr Burdon. The fifth of October at the optimistic end then. And a conservative estimate?'

'Should be no later than mid-October, or the results will be disastrous in the meantime.'

'October the fifteenth. Three weeks from now.' The chairman chewed his jaw pensively as heads were shaken and breaths taken in apprehension. Creed shuddered at the thought of what another three weeks would bring.

'Our next question. How long after the actual presentments take place – wherein presumably some applications will be approved – before works are likely commenced? Mr Cross?'

'It's hard to predict with any amount of certainty of course, but we should allow some time for general bureaucracy. Even when granted, all decisions are sent back to the Board of Works for ultimate approval. After that, each project must still be passed by the county surveyor, who sends men out with equipment to strike lines and whatnot. Even at a hurried pace, all of this will take time.'

In the murmurs and gestures of worry, Creed felt a palpable air of impatience and frustration growing in response to the observations being put forward.

Philip Cross next moved to speak. 'I don't wish to trample our hopes, gentlemen, or retard this progress, but what are the chances of *anything* actually being passed when we've been sitting here since April and have not managed to get one significant project of employment off the ground through the same bureaucracy?'

'It's been a lot longer than that, with respect, Mr Cross. But a valid question nonetheless. Mr Lucy?'

'Thank you, Mr Chairman. I think a few relevant points from O'Connell's recent public commentary on his understanding of the new Act might be of some benefit here.'

'Very well, Mr Lucy, do you have ...'

'I have a copy here, Mr Ashe,' Dan said, opening his paper-wallet.

'Please ...'

With Massy in the room, this was sure to make sparks fly, Creed anticipated. But he hoped Dan would be allowed to shed some light – by courtesy of the Liberator himself – on what Creed also felt was a fundamental document.

'With particular reference to the various objects requiring critical analysis ...' Lucy began to read aloud.

'*Must* we hear the drivel of that man?'

Creed shut his eyes as, true to form, Massy finally broke cover, exhibiting the extreme impudence that typified his character.

'If it will better inform our understanding of the situation we're facing into, Mr Warren, I think we should consider any knowledgeable opinion. If O'Connell knows anything it's the law.' Lucy's response to the barbed interruption was unwavering.

'A show of hands.' The chair put the issue to the room. 'Very well. Proceed, Mr Lucy.'

'Thank you, gentlemen. The Act provides –' As Lucy began, Warren huffed, and noisily assumed a reclining posture to toy with his cravat '– that the Lord Lieutenant, upon being informed of the existence of distress in any district, shall, by proclamation, direct and require an extraordinary presentment sessions for such district. This is mandatory upon the presentment sessions: they are bound to meet on the day mentioned in the proclamation and they will be guilty of a violation of the law if they do not meet upon that day.'

'Yes – I'm sure when we have a date that will be no issue!' Warren could not contain himself.

'Secondly: the presentment session having met, they are *bound* to make presentments for public works within their district. This clause, also, is mandatory. It would be a violation of the law if they were to refuse or neglect making such presentments.

'Thirdly: the Lords of the Treasury are bound to advance all sums of money, without specified limit, to the amount necessary for the works included in such presentments.'

'Hear. Hear.' This was met with general approval.

'Fourthly: the Board of Works is bound to put into execution the works so presented for, without any delay.

'That is an abstract of the operative part of the statute, as far as relates to public works. There are also provisions for the repayment, by instalments, of the money to be advanced for those works.' Dan appeared to be justifying his skirting of parts of the document and his hurrying to the next relevant section, perhaps feeling the pressure of the obvious criticism, Creed guessed.

'The repayment is not to commence until the next year, eighteen forty-seven, so that the landlords are – by the Act – left all their resources for the present year, untouched by the payment of any rate.

'This next section is perhaps the most important,' Lucy insisted. 'Let it be recollected – O'Connell says – that if they so refuse or neglect, the existing distress in the district will remain not only unrelieved and unmitigated but naturally increasing in intensity and severity. This will be so strong a pressure upon the presentment sessions, it is not likely they will anywhere refuse to grant presentments, and by such refusal leave the starving labourers without relief. But, supposing any presentment sessions do so refuse, they are subject to legal compulsion as well as to punishment …'

From the yawns and wandering eyes Creed began to perceive around the table, he supposed that ennui was already setting in, and that there were others at the table perhaps not quite as appreciative of the importance of what they were hearing. But Dan continued to quote O'Connell's enumeration of the legalities.

Edward Ashe, on the other hand, perhaps feeling too warm, the comfort of the presiding chair having the side effect of being the closest to the large fireplace, stood and walked to one of the two large windows overlooking the public entrance to the building directly below.

'Let it be recollected,' Lucy emphasised, 'that the *one thing* wanted at present is *food*; that the pressure for food is immediate; that the supplying of food cannot be postponed without the utmost inhumanity – nay, cannot be postponed with safety to any class.'

'Hear, hear!' James Welply alone seemed to respond in spirit.

'Food the people want, and food it is the duty of everybody to provide for them, as well the government as the landlord: in short, everybody, having any means whatsoever. The government plan suggests the mode of obtaining food is by earning wages; such wages to be paid for the execution of Public Works.' Lucy punctuated the speech with his fist as if tapping an imagined nail with an invisible hammer, while with hands behind his back still at the window, Creed sensed that Edward Ashe's attention was adrift.

From the position of his own chair, Creed could not see what Ashe was looking at below the sightline of the window, but he could hear the commotion of the gathering paupers outside vying for entry and likely being delayed by the porter until the Guardians could interview them. Where order, patience and quiet shame used to characterise the small numbers who sought admission, of late – by the activity out front, if not by the numbers within – Creed had weekly perceived the increased acceptance by the poor of the workhouse as a possible avenue of relief and found himself wondering now, as Ashe likely did too, what hellish sights the house would be forced to behold in the depths of the dark winter that surely lay ahead.

'... no plan can be of any value to meet the present horrible emergency but a rapid plan – there is no time for delay or postponement. The penalty of delay would be death – in fact, deaths innumerable.'

Evidently realising he had read well past the point of relevance, Daniel Lucy stuttered and stopped, perhaps surprised that no one other than Warren had interrupted him. 'Mr Chairman?'

'Thank you, Mr Lucy.' Ashe, coming back to the room, also returned to his chair. 'Very well, gentlemen. It seems we just have to await our date. In the meantime, the floor is open. Suggestions, concerns, options, thoughts – Mr Welply?'

'Thank you, Mr Chairman. I believe we must earnestly direct our attention to the necessity which now exists for establishing depots.'

'Hear!' said Creed, slapping the table, to the consternation of his neighbours. He had momentarily forgotten his place and found himself relieved that his peers, and Massy in particular, who must have been practically sleeping, had rather politely not taken the opportunity to diminish him and put him in his place.

James, meanwhile, likely in an effort to protect his friend from just that, left no time for interruption and hurriedly proceeded with his analysis. 'We are all well aware of the absolute want that prevails at this moment arising from insufficient food and employment. This has proved to be especially true in remote districts where the food of the poor may fall into the custody of a small number of merchants monopolising the substance. Although expressed rather conditionally within the act, I noticed that they made provision for depots in certain scenarios. I would like for us to put forth a proposal on the matter.'

'Thank you, Mr Welply. Could you find a seconder and draw up a resolution?'

'Certainly, Mr Chairman.'

'If *I* may propose a question, Mr Chairman.'

'Yes, Mr Pearson?'

'Can anybody say – given that we've never before had a total failure of the primary daily article of food on which millions depend – what viable alternatives, whether home-grown or from abroad, are open to us?' John Pearson, an industrious landowner, was one of the two representatives of the parish of Clondrohid upon the board; some parishes only had one, while Macroom itself had four. Pearson too volunteered for the Relief Committee of his constituency, which had recently merged with that of Macroom's, causing Creed to have found himself in collaboration with him there of late.

Cornelius Murphy, one of the wealthier Catholic farmers, was a studious man whom Creed also enjoyed a friendship with and he was the first to express what Creed knew would be an informed opinion in response. 'According to the estimates of those most competent to form a sound opinion – and I refer to the *Mark Lane Express* here – with the exception of hay, which is abundant and of excellent quality, the gross amount of food raised in the whole of Ireland, and England, for man and beast, is unquestionably considerably below what is likely to be required before another harvest can be gathered.'

'Hear, hear!' several voices weighed in, their energy apparently provoked by the mention of the venerated publication.

'It's even possible that imports would have been required if the potatoes hadn't been attacked by the fatal disorder of last year,' Murphy added. 'But I think it rather a plain fact that the wheat, oats and barley crops of this country are by no means equal to the return of the potato crop we're accustomed to.'

'What worries me is this.' Edmund Boyle took the floor and stood up as only some of the members tended to do when speaking. 'In what market and in what corner of the Earth are we likely to find a supply abundant enough to meet our deficiency? A deficiency not caused alone by a diminished yield of a particular description of grain, but by the total annihilation of a hitherto stalwart article of human food, which placed millions beyond the rise and fall of the price of grain.'

'Yet, Mr Boyle, perhaps we should concern ourselves with what applies to us locally,' muttered Robert Nettles, a mostly despised entrepreneur with railway interests whom Creed found to be as acerbic and unpleasant to handle as his name suggested.

'This is universal, Mr Nettles; we are but one link in a long chain.'

Nettles ... one link ... chain... Creed – back to taking notes after the break Daniel Lucy had afforded him by the quoting of a long, already widely published article – was again with his hand a-flurry to keep up with the main points of discussion and wrote on as Boyle leant forward, hands on the table, his glasses off, to eye his fellow Guardians and continue his droll prognostication.

'I, for one, feel it is pertinent to make ourselves aware of what circumstances are unfolding upstream from our position and will manifest themselves consequently as our own symptoms further on. The harvests of Europe have been miserably deficient this year and the price of grain has been considerably raised as a result of those same deficiencies. I speak of France ... of Belgium ... both of which, by their heavy orders, have already materially raised the price of corn all over the Baltic. So, then you might say America is the answer, as it was last year. But those other European nations will meet us in the market, with the advantage of that increased demand, and realise a large profit by the general distress.'

'Thank you, Mr Boyle, very profound. Mr Ronayne?' Ashe passed the floor from one to the other.

'I agree with Mr Boyle. It might be well for the people of Ireland did the increase stop there, but so long as there is the true spirit of trade to influence the Irish merchant and corn broker, they too will naturally seek to make as much by the sale of that commodity as they can, not only to make a profit, which is their fair right, but to recoup the inflated cost they must purchase their wares at.'

Henry Minhear now interjected. 'The work of hoarding up large quantities of grain is already going on.'

Creed longed to join in with the mutters of disapproval that now broke out once again, but having escaped lightly once already this day, resisted the urge and took to a private reckoning instead: *how shallow are the morals of humankind when the desire to fill one's coffers is stronger than that of helping those in distress.*

Yet even I am guilty of that to some degree, he argued with himself, but reasoned in his own defence that he, at least, was the provider of a service.

'Those who lost by the depression of last year,' Minhear, a large holder in Carrigafooka, whom Creed noted for his abacus-like brain, prophesied, 'will exert themselves to meet their losses, by the profits of this season.'

As the discussion went on jumping from one Guardian to another, Creed pondered on the fact that Ashe, who described himself mostly as a middleman, was keeping decidedly quiet. But he was not *only* an agent on occasion. He was also a moneylender and, as an active member of the local committee for the coming line of the Cork to Macroom railway, an astute businessman. In fact, there was not much in terms of the business of making money that he wasn't involved in. But most relevant in this instance was that Ashe was the principal *Corn Merchant of Macroom,* as the sign above the large store on Castle Street openly declared. Yet he evidently didn't care to pass much comment on corn merchants turning excessive profits right now, Creed thought, as James was speaking again.

'Individual fortunes will be desperately struggled for, to the misery and destruction of those whose hard-earned wages will scarce suffice to provide themselves and their families with a single meal a day.'

As he scribbled on, listening with one part of his brain and writing with the other, Creed became fixed upon a certain hypocrisy: not only Ashe but a number of other men around the table were indeed the potential profiteers of the exact situations they were describing. None present was likely to speak about the obvious, but it was becoming ever clearer to Creed. A student of words, he found himself curious at the tension that lay between the obvious and the unsaid. And if it wasn't for the fact that he could just as easily be labelled a hypocrite for doing so –

being a pawnbroker by trade – Creed would, he reasoned there among them, have elected to write up his thoughts and send them off to the editor, post haste.

But he allowed himself to wallow in the irksome feelings nonetheless. It made him superior. These men, the Guardians, were trusted to administer the Poor Law throughout the district, but also to set the rates to pay for it, at the expense of their own estates. By such reckoning, the poor could only benefit so far as the Guardians would tax themselves and their estates. And it was all deemed to be acceptable by the lawmakers, the Poor Law commissioners, the government and the gentry at large. Theirs was a class-led society. That was nothing new to Creed. He did not accept, however, that those with such an enormous financial interest at stake should be the ones to formulate and implement policies to alleviate the growing catastrophe.

Creed found his heart beating excitedly faster when Dr Crooke, the ageing medical examiner of the workhouse, who had been listening throughout but had yet to make any contribution, now raised his hand. The elderly man had the habit of saying something of practical value on the rare occasion that he did speak.

'Gentlemen, if I may – we have talked of presentments, but not of how works will be conducted if and when presentments are granted.

'I have had time to examine the circular published on the seventh of September and have found it to be pickled with clauses and conditions. The language of the letter is indicative of a rather plain intention to make the recipients of any funding work damned well hard for it.'

'To my mind, the language is designed to merely discourage any opportunism. That was how I perceived it, Dr Crooke,' the chairman spoke.

'I believe it is more than that.' Dr Crooke shook his head, frowning. 'Let's be plain, Mr Chairman, there are precious few unions who would find themselves in the enviable position of being merely opportunistic at the present moment. No, I fear the government will be seen to say all the right things in making gestures of relief. But behind the public facade, they are going to make it as difficult as possible and unions will lock horns with officialdom. Mr Burdon, do you have the document to hand, please?'

'Of course, Dr Crooke. Let's see ...' the clerk said, fumbling through his papers. 'Here it is.'

'Thank you.' Dr Crooke held his glasses and studied the document briefly, to Creed's relief, some of his faith restored at there being any utility to the other speakers.

'Yes, here ... "the Relief Committee will not, as heretofore, be authorised to issue tickets for employment on the public works, but should furnish lists of the persons requiring relief to the officers in charge". He searched for another passage. 'Elsewhere ... "are required to abstain from giving higher wages or demanding less work than on government works". And ... "the sale of meal to persons who have no other *means* of acquiring it *at the prices of ordinary years*". How can that be seen as relief when they have *no* means? But it's one condition after another.'

Creed was heartened to see that the majority of the Guardians uttered their endorsement of the Medical Examiner's summation. Yet the chairman was practical in his response.

'I'm afraid we need to be mindful of time, gentlemen. But we'll make a note to continue this again, Dr Crooke. Mr Welply, have you ...'

'I have the resolution here, Mr Ashe.' One honourable man to follow another in closing the day's proceedings, Creed was pleased to see; he readied himself to record his friend's introduction to the resolution.

James, a fair-haired man, had now lost most of the growth on top of his shiny scalp. Creed remembered him as a boy, younger than him and Sam. Industrious and strong-willed even back then, James stood holding a paper and began by offering a justification. 'All this is to say that depots are the key, which will act as a check on the uprising tendency of the markets. Should prices rise higher than would realise a fair profit to the trader – so high as to keep one meal from the mouths of the hungry – in theory, the doors of the depot would only have to be flung open to purchasers for one day, to depress the prices to fair standard.'

*

Cork Examiner – Monday, 28 September 1846

MACROOM UNION

At the weekly Meeting of the Guardians of this Union, held this day, which was numerously and respectably attended, the following resolution was adopted –

'RESOLVED – That as there is no appearance that employment under the Board of Works can be in operation for another month at least in the Barony of West Muskerry, the proclamation not having yet been issued, it appears to this Board from the great destitution that prevails, consequent on the failure of the potato crop, that several families would famish before that period, and to prevent such awful consequence, and to preserve Peace in the country, we respectfully and urgently request of his Excellency, the Lord Lieutenant, to order a sum of Two Hundred Pounds into each parish of the barony, which, with additional subscriptions, would enable those families to procure food at a reduced price, so as to sustain life until employment comes into operation; and we again strongly recommend the establishment of a Depot for the storage and sale of food in the town of Macroom, which is the centre of a very large district, in order to correct the enormous Prices to which the food has already arrived, and which is daily increasing.'

By Order,

JAMES BURDON, Clerk of the Union.

Macroom, 26 September 1846.

17

On the Last Day of September

On the last day of September word spread among the poor of the district that there was to be a gathering in Macroom. Not of the elite. Not of the landed class. This was to be a coming together of the labouring poor of the entire union, or most of them.

Contrary to what the gentry feared upon hearing of its initiation, the aim of the meeting was not to display a show of force, nor threaten any other sinister purpose, but simply, by presenting themselves to the leading officials of the district, in a peaceable display, to say: 'We are here'; 'We are suffering'; 'What is to be done for us?'

Nobody knew who had called the meeting. It just was. The word had begun somewhere, then travelled out from the source and was passed from place to place, one labourer to the next and one home to another, until that mysterious, all-too-rare occurrence came into being, where the poor unified in their determination to change the course of their fate. Then, in as primitive and as ancient a rite as anybody knew, bonfires were spontaneously lit across the hillsides, from one end of the barony to the other.

Speculations on the assembly's purpose, when the news reached the hills around Doire Liath, were second only to a feeling that it must be a peaceful gathering. It was common knowledge that demonstrations and gatherings of any kind, even peaceful ones, were strongly discouraged by authority, and that all were illegal as a rule, but the gravity of the situation was exceptional. The ubiquitous sense that the winter ahead was to be the hardest they might ever have faced urged every man, and every family, to put their survival first and to 'take the hills to Mahomet'. If ever there had come a time for them to band together and let their voices be heard, this was it.

Language was no barrier and by Wednesday evening there was scarcely a soul in the barony of Muskerry, east or west, who had not heard of the meeting. All were sure that such a show of solemnity would bring the authorities to see the situation as they did and would result in their judiciously coming to the aid of the people.

Pádraig, in his travels, had first heard it from a man east of Cahireen, but by the time he'd got back to Doire Liath, Cáit had got the talk from Caitilín Pruiséal, in the bothán behind the ridge.

'What are you doing, Daddy?' Síle asked.

'I'm just taking a bit of the fire outside, little one.'

'Can I come outside and see?' she asked, curious at the novelty of the action.

'If your mammy wraps you up. Put the blanket on our daughter, *a bhean bheag.*'

'Come here to me, Síle,' Cáit called her.

Outside, the dusk of a September sky was burning a fire in sympathy, as below the hills, far off into the distant plains below, the orange and red dots bestrew the darkened ground like the stars that would soon fill the sky above them.

Standing beside Pádraig as he nurtured the embers beneath the pile of sticks and the dry grass of the summer he had plucked in handfuls from the ground around them, Cáit held Diarmuidín rolled up in her shawl, as Síle caught her breath and marvelled at the sight.

'Why are the fires outside, *a dhaid?*' she asked her father.

Pádraig, standing up, watched the grass catch and begin to smoke.

'We're going to light up the sky, Síle, so that God will see us.'

18

A Cupful of Milk

'I'm going to take the children inside, husband. It's getting cold. Come on, Síle,' Cáit said taking her hand. Pádraig nodded, but stood firmly with his hands in the pockets of his heavy short trousers. With the low fire still burning beside him, he was preoccupied, surveying the landscape nearby.

'Are you coming in, Daddy?' Síle called back to him, walking with Cáit.

'In a little while, pet,' he responded over his shoulder, then turned to see Cáit with the hood of her shawl now up, almost at the door. 'I might call to Diarmuid Ua Laoghaire,' he added.

She stopped and looked back at him, staring a moment as the breeze tossed the air between them. 'That's a good idea, husband.'

Having been the beneficiary of profound generosity at the hands of Ua Laoghaire, Pádraig held the man in such high esteem that he dared not call on him without good reason; he had promised himself only to do so on an occasion when he might make himself a useful friend to the man. Sensing this to be such an opportunity, Pádraig left his fire and strolled down the hill to begin the short walk across to Liscarrigane.

They were so close in distance that from the western end of the ridge Pádraig could see the Muintir Laoghaire house just a few fields over, down on the flats below. It was far enough away that a stone's throw would not reach it and if you tried to send a shout across it would not carry; respectable enough a distance, Pádraig felt, that one was unlikely to see the other unless it was intended. So it was with purpose that when he'd reached the threshold Pádraig rapped his knuckles on the door of the little whitewashed house, then waited for a response.

With a creak of the hinge, the youngest of Ua Laoghaire's sons opened the door and invited Pádraig in out of the darkening, dusky light.

'*A Phádraig Óg.*' Ua Laoghaire half-rose to greet him, extending a working hand after rubbing it clean on the thigh of his trouser. 'Come on in.'

'*Bail ó Dhia oraibh*, Diarmuid, Siobhán,' Pádraig said, removing his cap and nodding to each of his hosts.

'Ah, Pádraig, welcome in. It's well to see you,' Siobhán, the woman of the house, spoke.

'Sit, Pádraig.' Ua Laoghaire motioned for Pádraig to join him.

'*Go ra' maith agat.*' Pádraig accepted and sat on a hard chair.

'How are the little ones?' Siobhán asked.

'They're fine children,' Pádraig said softly, with affection. 'But ...'tis hard times.'

'That is true, surely,' she agreed with a look of concern.

'And all within?' Pádraig strove to return the kindness.

'Ah, sure ...' Ua Laoghaire cocked his head, censoring his own speech.

'Sure, 'tis the same all round. But we're managing,' the woman answered.

'Would you bring Pádraig a sup of milk, Siobhán?'

'Oh, where's my manners?' she said getting up from resting on her knees.

'Thank you, Siobhán, but I'm fine without it.' Pádraig impressed his wishes upon her as much as politeness would allow. He hadn't come for that – the opposite, in fact.

But she was gone before he finished, saying, 'It's no trouble.'

When Siobhán had left the room and the two men were alone, Ua Laoghaire intimated what was plainly obvious and pushed the conversation to reach its meaning – not out of rudeness, Pádraig knew, but because he was a practical man, of few words, who did not bother the next man by moaning about something he could do nothing about.

'I'm sure you know of it already, Diarmuid, but I've come to share talk of the gathering that's to happen in town on Saturday next. You might have heard already?' Pádraig repeated himself nervously, getting the words out, already observing an absence of enthusiasm from the listener.

Instead, Ua Laoghaire tilted his head in such a way that both confirmed he had heard of the meeting and at once gave Pádraig the answer to the question he had been about to follow with.

'Will ye go yourself?' Ua Laoghaire asked Pádraig, before it was asked of him.

'I will, *A Dhiarmuid Uí Laoghaire*. Every man who's able is going, besides.'

His host left a knowing silence and from it, Pádraig deduced, Ua Laoghaire was decided not to be among every man.

'I was going to offer … to walk with you,' Pádraig said.

'Ah …' Ua Laoghaire began, cocking his head lightly, ''tis a good thing you go, Pádraig.' The older man's tone was one of affection, but he turned away and watched the stick in his own hand as it poked at the fire, bridging the holes in their speak.

As Siobhán returned and placed the drink on the ground next to his foot amidst the silence, Pádraig tried to guess at the complex response, but was at a loss for the riddle of it.

'Thank you, Siobhán.' he said, and took a sup to be polite.

With Ua Laoghaire quieter now the conversation turned briefly to talk of the disease and how they'd both experienced it. But shortly after, determined not to overstay the welcome, Pádraig gave his manners and begged to leave them to their evening in peace.

'Thank you for calling, Pádraig. It was good of you to think of me.'

'Don't mention it, Diarmuid Ua Laoghaire,' he answered. But approaching the door, Pádraig felt a need to say something more, and turned back. 'Some day I hope to repay your kindness … properly,' he added, punching out his cap.

'Now!' Ua Laoghaire, cocking his head again, firmly stopped the talk. His expression was one of thanks, while seeming to say that there was no need to thank him, but it had been the only Christian thing to do.

Siobhán insisted that Pádraig take the can of milk along with him. 'Give it to the children if ye won't drink it yourself,' she said, handing it up to him.

'I suppose they'll be very grateful. Sincere thanks to you both,' Pádraig smiled as much as he could.

'God be good. And here ...' she said, passing him a blanket.

'Mrs Ua Laoghaire,' Pádraig protested more formally, but in vain.

'We can spare it, Pádraig,' she pushed it into his grasp. 'It was Margaret's fetch, but at her age now she doesn't look for it.'

'Awh ...' Pádraig tutted. 'You're awful kind people.'

'It'll be getting cold soon, especially up on that hill, with the winds and winter coming,' she told him.

He had come with the aim of proving he could give something back, even if it was only the gesture of news. But once more Pádraig had been disarmed by their generosity.

'Wait,' Ua Laoghaire said, and perhaps inspired by his wife's example rushed out the back, returning moments later with half a sack of oatmeal.

'Diarmuid Ua Laoghaire, I only come to talk of th–'

'We know, Pádraig.' Ua Laoghaire closed his eyes and waved Pádraig's pleas away, while Siobhán reassured him. 'Look after those children.'

'Thank you. We will. I won't refuse your kindness. God bless ye all.'

'*Go mbeirimíd beo slán ar an am so.* May we live safe again this time,' said Diarmuid, as they closed the door and left him with arms full.

Making his way across the fields in semi-darkness, Pádraig took large steps, trying to get home while he could still see where he was putting his feet, eager to get the extra blanket onto the little ones.

The last of the dying fires across the landscape were but glowing sparks now, flickering below a twilit sky whose amber streaks and pink-hued bleeds were fast sinking into the depths of a charcoal slumber.

Pádraig wondered again about the strange reaction Ua Laoghaire had given to his talk of the meeting. But these were melancholy times and each man would have to plot his own course through it. Ua Laoghaire must have had his reasoning.

The kindnesses of Muintir Laoghaire embarrassed him. Pádraig felt uncomfortable accepting the many gifts they gave him. He couldn't help but feel it put him further in their debt – a feeling he had hoped to diminish with the visit. He now hoped it hadn't seemed he'd come with one arm longer than the other, expecting something. Deep down, he even asked himself whether that had, in fact, been his real motive. He wasn't fully sure of the answer. In a way, all things were true.

But no matter which way he turned it, their generosity was God-sent. The nights were beginning to get much colder and Pádraig knew they would need every scrap of food and every source of warmth they could lay their hands on to beat the winter.

DEIREADH FÓMHAIR

OCTOBER

19

GREAT GATHERING IN MACROOM

On the morning of Saturday, the second day of October, stepping out into the dewy autumn air, leaving Cáit and the children huddled beneath the blanket, Pádraig set off for Macroom. He was not walking alongside Diarmuid Ua Laoghaire as he'd imagined, but he did not have much time to feel lonely in his footsteps. By the time he'd reached the road at Clashmaguire he had loosely fallen in with two other men and before long their small group had been absorbed into a larger stream. With a sense of belonging within the careworn mob that continued to grow in number all the way, Pádraig marched towards the centre of the barony, until, approaching the head of noon, he was but one soul among a mass of between three and four thousand beings that descended upon the town. Apart from the rare sight of a woman and child whose husband was unable to come, the gathering around him appeared to be wholly made up of the labouring men of the district. In many cases that was an older son present in place of an ageing father, but all were the family members likely to be the most capable of work among a household, when work was to be had.

As Pádraig had expected, he saw not a single sign of weapons, or tools of any kind, among them. Bringing their physical presence alone and led by one or two individuals – men unknown to him, but who seemed to have the confidence of the gathering – they entered the streets. The atmosphere amongst the lot was one of quiet desperation. With the signs so easy to see that severe want prevailed among all, Pádraig had a sense that each knew what the other was experiencing, and a strong sense of unity in their plight was present. He recognised a face here and there and knew some other men from Clondrohid, but sharing the earnest silence that hung over the group he kept to himself most of the way until, wedged closely together as they passed through the streets, he broke a long silence to enquire of a stranger who'd seemed to be beside him for a long time, 'Where are we headed?'

*

Having assembled at the Boardroom of the Union earlier that morning, the Guardians had begun their usual Saturday meeting, though it was plainly evident to Creed, seated within their midst, that to judge alone by the inordinate number of Guardians in attendance, the occasion promised to be anything but ordinary.

Yet in spite of the circumstances, the routine business of the board had to be processed as a matter of course, and looking down at his notebook preparing to write more, Creed's eyes fell upon the main details he had recorded thus far, wondering on the comparative utility of any of it in light of the imminent events. His notes contained the names of those Guardians present and the State of the House, called by Mr Burdon at three hundred and five paupers. This figure, he'd noted, had been introduced as being almost the same as that of the corresponding period the year before. This contrast had been the cause of some debate between James and William Garde Browne, with James proposing that the recent increasing prejudice of some board members against admitting paupers too freely was the only possible reason the numbers could be as low now as they had been then. A moot point – the argument had achieved no conclusion.

Under the title of 'Extraordinary Business', below a brief note on 'discussions on contractors declared for the supply of various articles of consumption for the house', Creed now finished a line, as Mr Burdon announced his having received 'a gratuitous stock of books, for the use of the workhouse school'.

'Yes, I think we can deal with that at a later date. I'm sure all are agreed that there are more pressing matters requiring our attention today?' Edward Ashe pushed on.

'Hear, hear!' came several voices.

'Anything else, Mr Burdon? You appear to have something on your mind.'

'Admissions, sir?' the clerk replied.

'Admissions?' Ashe seemed uncharacteristically ill at ease, realising, Creed supposed, that there were still more such 'ordinary' matters to be dealt with before they could grapple with the unspoken presence that unnerved them all and had the entirety of the board on edge. Every member present knew that despite the government's widely known, and sometimes heavily enforced, policy of strongly discouraging such behaviour under any circumstances, the poor of the district had decided to gather *en masse*, and were expected to arrive within the town imminently, at the risk of who knew what outcome.

'I suppose we should proceed with our admissions as per usual,' Ashe said and gestured reluctantly to Mr Burdon at his left. 'Bring them in.'

'Very well, sir.' Burdon left his chair and the porter, notified, was sent to bring up those awaiting admission. The porter could be heard to respond to Mr Burdon, saying that it seemed there were not many applicants today, supposing most had been distracted 'by the larger events beyond'.

'Are there any?' Ashe called out to Burdon on the landing.

'Two forthcoming,' Burdon answered.

This was the part of the board meetings Creed found most difficult to endure. He was not required to report on the admissions of individual paupers and therefore almost squeamishly avoided witnessing the process. He had good cause to feel conflicted: as a pawnbroker, he had often witnessed the slow descent of customers over numerous visits to the shop until, having finally reached the slump of their trajectory into degradation, they crossed his path once more in this room where for the first time he would hear the back story he had hitherto been shielded from, as they revealed the intimate details of their sorry circumstances to the Guardians in a desperate plea to be shown the mercy of the workhouse. As bad as that was, it was a worse thing, he felt, to witness when – dependent on the number of applicants on any given day, regardless of the suitability of a person, or what heart-rending level of woe their plea contained – the Guardians might have already reached a quota and would reject as many as they had admitted as a matter of practicality. But admissions being typically the last item on the agenda of the Guardians, on a usual day Creed might well have left at this point. Today, as they awaited events yet to transpire, he knew he must sit tight, accepting that he should learn something from the experience.

The first of the two applications, a young woman Creed did not recognise but judged to be of ingenuous appearance, was brought into the room by the porter and stood within one of the triangular bays of the T-shaped table, therefore being equally visible to all. The porter then left the room and the woman was invited by the clerk to speak: 'Miss MacDonagh. Unmarried. No children. Please state your case in brief.'

The woman, a delicate young thing, but pretty, if barefoot and ragged, her voice shaking, told the board: 'I am labouring under a complaint of the chest, which has left me unable to work. My parents are dead and the family home has been taken from under me by the bailiffs.'

The patriarchs of her fate debated her eligibility and ogled for proof of her suitable destitution, looking her up and down.

'I note Dr Crooke has already refused this application on a prior occasion?' the chairman inquired of the clerk, in accordance with the paperwork he held before him.

'That is correct, sir. On the … twenty-sixth.'

But Mr Ashe, seeming more to be taken by the woman's impoverished charm than concerned with medical criteria, Creed quietly thought, was happy to question her further, despite the doctor's evaluation.

'So, you have been several times in the hospital before but have always left cheerfully on convalescence, young lady. Would that be a fair assessment?'

'I have, sir.' The woman answered nervously and bowed her head under the inquisition of such ordinary men as must have seemed to her to have God's powers over life and death. 'I am eternally grateful to the house for its mercy, kind sirs, and wish only to stay until such time as I am back to the full of my health and able to earn my survival.' She stuttered through the line she had obviously rehearsed, but managed it eventually.

'I see no reason why she should not be admitted,' Mr Ashe proposed over the rim of his glasses. 'With respect, Dr Crooke, would you be willing to review your earlier assessment?'

'I am satisfied that Miss MacDonagh is suitable for admission on this occasion,' Dr Crooke relented across the table.

'Any other objections?' asked the chairman.

Creed surveyed the table in search of any signs of disapproval, but the invitation brought no disagreement. All were apparently satisfied that the woman was endowed enough with poverty and devoid enough of hope, her clothes adequately frayed and holed, her feet, hair and skin sufficiently marked by squalor.

'None? The application is granted.'

Creed, among others, sighed with relief as the young woman was led out. 'Thank you, gentlemen,' she said in tears, shuffling as she went, as if attempting to hide her bare feet.

William Crooke, the magistrate, next wished to propose the admission of 'an idiot boy', whom he personally introduced after thanking the porter for leading him in.

'I found this boy in a state of exhaustion near to my own residence at Derreen. His mother was a mendicant and died in the Kilmallock workhouse, leaving him there.' Creed presumed it would be hard to convince some of the Guardians to accept an applicant who had left another union, even if that union was in another county. Kilmallock, he reasoned, was near to fifty miles away, in Limerick. The ginger-haired boy, who was approximately sixteen years old, and by his level of cleanliness in clear need of some looking after, stood now in the same spot the young woman had occupied.

'Why did you quit that place, young man?' William Garde Browne asked, without delaying for further introduction by Dr Crooke.

'I did not wish to be … so far from my own place,' was his reply, and one that sounded lucid and clear. Slowly turning his head from side to side, however, with a stare that swung like a pendulum, looking at no one in particular, he appeared to be locked in a world of his own and incapable of communicating consistently on his own behalf. Creed found it hard to predict how the board would vote.

But before any more discussion could be had on the boy, a bustle was heard on the stairs outside the room and, the door being opened to them as the boy was encouraged to stand back, another group of men arrived and presented themselves to the chair. Creed was pleased at the sight of Father Thomas Lee leading the group.

'Please excuse the interruption, Mr Chairman, and gentlemen Poor Law Guardians. I wish to humbly present a delegation of the Macroom Relief Committee. With the inclusion of myself; Reverend Mr Barry, curate; Mr Michael O'Connell; Mr Matthias Ryan' – Father Thomas in his floor-length, daily robes, so well worn as to be frayed through at the elbows, gestured with an open hand to introduce each delegate he named as a matter of formality – 'and already present amongst you today of course your own resident physician of the house, Dr Crooke, and naturally Mr Creed, your correspondent. We respectfully wish to urgently offer our support in the interests of a combined effort to address the exigency of the crisis that threatens to overwhelm the district.'

Owing to the significance of the gesture, the chairman rose to speak. 'Thank you, Father Lee. Under the circumstances, I should think we shall dispense with a vote, and welcome your delegation in the spirit of your suggestion.'

'Hear, hear,' the board agreed loudly, amid a grave resolve to get down to work.

'Please make yourselves comfortable, gentlemen,' the chairman said and reseated himself, as chairs were pulled out and the incoming men began to settle themselves.

As they did so, Creed was saddened to overhear Edward Ashe quietly confide in the clerk, 'I should think the boy ought to be sent back to the Kilmallock workhouse, Mr Burdon. We have no facility to debate the matter further under the circumstances.'

'Yes, sir, Mr Chairman.'

At the same moment as the clerk arose from his chair to call the porter and escort the boy out, one of the delegation from the Relief Committee who had not yet taken his seat interrupted.

'The gathering is upon us, gentlemen.' It was Matthias Ryan, the apothecary, who had seen something out the window, and a dirge of chair legs rubbing the floor launched a scramble for the dormers to gauge the threat. Creed, climbing a chair to attain a view, spotted a crowd of boys running towards the gate. Ashe, who must also have clearly seen the multitude advancing up the avenue to the entrance below, shouted for Mr Burdon. 'Have the porter close the outer gate immediately!'

'How many is there?' a voice asked.

'A great many, and more coming,' was the answer amidst a growing atmosphere of anxiety.

Moments later, apparently having received Ashe's instruction from the clerk, the porter was to be seen below attempting to roll some huge stones into place against each fold of the gate instead of simply drawing the iron bolt across.

'What is he doing?' Ashe shouted. 'He'll be too late … It's too late.' He rubbed his hands over his face in the light of the window.

All in the crowded space at the sills fell quiet, it being clear that the crowd had reached the gates before the porter had managed to close them properly. He had run inside, leaving no impediment at all to their breaching the main door, with the exception of the abandoned boulders. But remarkably, as Creed and all above gazed down upon them – helpless to do anything either way – the mob stopped there, finding no one had come to receive their wants.

In the absence of anyone making any sense of the situation, Creed heard himself speak: 'Father Lee … you are the one man they are most likely to listen to. A man of God, and one of their own, if you'll pardon the phrase.'

'As you say, Mr Creed, of course.' Father Lee agreed without hesitation and filled his chest with a necessary breath of courage.

'Well said, Mr Creed,' Mr Ashe followed quickly.

'I'll accompany you, Father,' James added.

'And I,' Creed also volunteered, as the priest and his curate had already begun to filter through the open door and down the stairs. Following James out of the room, Creed caught up fast. But upon reaching the ground floor, it was discovered that due to the porter's incompetency, the gathering was by now pressing against the iron wicket gate within, and although quiet, dozens of men were earnestly staring Creed and the others in the face, with each group seemingly as frightened as the other.

'Please, gentlemen! Be calm and we will open the gate,' Father Lee shouted as he pulled the wicket back; and in doing so he bravely used himself as a barrier between the anxious mob and the hopelessly unprepared troupe behind him. Creed, among that troupe, felt strangely apathetic in the face of the apparent danger, at the same time coming to the awful realisation that with one poor judgement on either side, those at the front might be crushed by the weight of the crowd behind them. Looking at Father Lee in the stillness of the moment, Creed cognised the profile of his white, clean-shaven face as the mask of apprehension. But the priest's posture displayed self-assurance. That, and the all-respected collar, Creed estimated, were their best hopes of commanding the attention of the multitude facing them, who, all told, were behaving as calmly and as peaceably as could have been hoped for when one considered the awe-striking depth of the number he had seen from above moments before.

'The Guardians and a deputation of the Relief Committee are at this very moment *in situ*, discussing what can be done on your behalf.' As – stepping forward – Father Lee spoke, those before him respectfully moved back, allowing him to take up a position upon the step of the outer doorway. 'I tell you earnestly that we are doing all that is possible for your relief. I know it is hard to hear. But you must be patient.'

The priest paused long enough for the crowd to respond, whether intentionally or from a lack of initiative Creed was uncertain, yet there appeared to be no spokesperson for the other side, nor any apparent message they wished to have heard. At least not a verbal one, Creed surmised. Looking into the withdrawn expressions of those who occupied the front of the gathering, he was amazed that they just stood there, saying nothing, having come so far. As a man of words, it was hard for him to understand the methodology, though at length he inwardly remarked that silence itself is sometimes the most powerful statement.

'Here beside me is Dr Crooke, a magistrate of the county, who is come out to impress upon you the necessity of obeying the law. For the man who violates the law is an enemy of the people – and an enemy to the relief of the distress which has driven you here.'

Father Lee seemed to recognise that this was no time to mince words and that in the interests of their own safety, if nothing else, the crowd must be convinced, in the starkest terms, to desist from any rash action. Creed agreed wholeheartedly, but on some quiet level – more on the side of the poor – almost wished they would do something bold to further their cause. Whatever that was, however, he did not know.

'We'll not violate the law, Father Lee …' someone was heard to shout. Others cried out in support of the statement, at last breaking the skin of their silence.

'All the gentlemen you see around me here,' the priest gestured, 'are exerting their interest for you.'

From behind, the darkness of Lee's stiff black soutane heightened the odd shape of his silhouette as he stood upright with one hand blocking the afternoon sun from his brow. Within the hallway, his voice boomed and reverberated thick and full, as without, his power was being mostly absorbed by the first few rows; without the benefit of a roof to amplify his cadence, Creed assumed it must have been hard for anyone further than five or six lines deep to make him out clearly.

'The government have sent a proclamation for holding a session to procure employment by giving works.' Among the crowd, a few attempted a sporadic cheer with whatever enthusiasm they could muster at these claims, clinging to any hope. But some were either unconvinced or too feeble, and remained despondent.

'They have applied to keep depots for provisions, either in the parish or in the neighbouring parishes, which would be the means of affording relief to every one of you.

'But for God's sake … let there be quiet, and order, and regularity amongst you. I expect one thing from you, that every one of you will return peaceably and quietly to your homes.'

'We will, Father,' was the return of some representative voice, speaking on behalf of the pitiful, ever-submissive poor.

Lee looked behind, gesturing for anyone else who wished to speak to come forward, at which point the tall William Garde Browne stepped out, having somehow found time to collect from the rack on the way down the beige top hat that matched his clothes. 'I am happy to share the news, men and boys, that Mr Treacy, the county surveyor for the Board of Works, has been about the country this last week, and he is ready to commence works immediately in this locality, to the tune of four thousand and seven hundred pounds' – to this came a more substantial, if laboured cheer from some – 'which will have the effect of making you prosperous again.'

But inspired by the less vigorous response to Browne's second statement, which was met with some disgruntlement as well as silence,

Creed imagined that the larger share of the crowd considered the sum inadequate for making any man prosperous for too long.

'Four thousand seven hundred – that will make all of us prosperous again?' was heard, almost as an echo within the dense body.

Further back, just loud enough to be heard up front, a labourer shouted, 'Some people have brought their families here!'

This remark, seemingly unrelated, quickly underlined to Creed the fantasy of Mr Browne's rhetoric. It pulled things sharply back into perspective and the crowd soon made it obvious they weren't to be won over so easily.

'People are living on cabbages in Ballyvourney,' another shouted.

'I assure you,' James answered, taking the place of William Garde Browne, 'that no effort will be spared for your welfare. The Relief Committee are here to propose to the Guardians that as at Cork, there will be a meal provided daily at the workhouse to those who would otherwise lack the sustenance for life. But I will second Father Lee, and ask you to please be patient. Allow us to act as best we can on your behalf.'

'Thank you, Mr Welply.' Father Lee again took over. 'If you must stay, please do so peaceably, so we can continue the meeting on your behalf. Your presence has been felt. We thank you for listening to what we've had to say.'

The priest, having turned away, shepherded the delegation before him back towards the staircase. 'Thank you, gentlemen.'

Creed, convinced that the authoritative stance had almost certainly had the desired effect, watched with some relief as the crowd began to withdraw.

When, back upstairs, the meeting had regained its composure in the boardroom, Lee, having been thanked for his careful handling of the situation, sought to reintroduce the same formal proposal to the Guardians as had been raised on behalf of the Relief Committee delegation before the disturbance had taken place.

'Mr Chairman.' Father Lee, seated at the end of one of the giant table's three limbs, stood to speak. 'Having already exhausted my breath somewhat, I wonder if the board would be opposed to my nominating Mr Creed to speak the part of the Relief Committee's proposal?'

Mr Ashe, directly facing him, seemed a little taken aback. 'Well, it would seem highly irregular, Father Lee, to have our correspondent ...'

'I only wish it on the merit of his being a significant voice of the Relief Committee, Mr Ashe, and as one whose hand was an equally significant architect to the proposal in question.'

'Very well, Father Lee. Of course. Mr Creed?'

Well alive to the slight upon him as Ashe sat back and joined his hands with an air of superiority, Creed felt that he ought not dignify the implied suggestion that, a mere servant to the Guardians – as Ashe might have him – he should somehow be prevented from administering his part as a member of the Relief Committee. And rising from his chair now in spite of the insult, Creed considered that it had suited Ashe very well to hear him speak not half an hour before, when upon the crowd's arrival at the gates all else *but* him had seemed at a loss as to what to do, and he had been the only one among them to evince an initiative. It was, in fact, his duty to stand at the juncture of the two bodies that his presence was common to and invested in, and from there promote the spirit of their shared interests. Ashe, being also a member of both organisations, was perhaps a shade envious, he imagined, and might have wished to take credit alone for the distinction. But Ashe had been absent from the Relief Committee meeting on Tuesday last, the twenty-ninth, when the proposal Creed now held in his hand had been drafted.

'We have come at the behest of the Relief Committee, Mr Chairman, to call attention to what is already known to each of you here – that being the frightful distress existing throughout this barony – and to make it known that we add our support to the demand for extraordinary measures, as well as to solicit yours.

'The feverish anxiety of the public mind; the total absence of public employment; the prices of provisions. We are induced by such things to adopt the very unusual course of waiting upon you, the Poor Law Guardians of this Union, to consider the enlightened plan now being undertaken by the Cork Guardians: that being, that persons in a state of extreme destitution receive at the workhouse either a breakfast or a dinner, daily ...' Creed spoke the sentence aloud, then stopped a moment, to allow the gravity of the proposal be fully absorbed ... 'We conceive that such a mode of relief is not against the letter, but to be truly in accordance with the spirit of the Poor Law, which provides that *no person shall die of starvation.*

'On Wednesday last we witnessed something like that of the spectacle you all saw just now; men and women coming long distances into our town to make their presence felt ... what in the world could induce this? There are thousands now awaiting with deep anxiety the resolution to which your board will come. It is *impossible* for us to conceive that level of distress. The board is relieving up to four thousand persons at the present moment – I am sure I need not place such facts before you – but I would impress upon your minds in the name of the starving hundreds outside and the tens of thousands beyond, across this district, to come to their rescue at least during the time before the public works can be brought into operation.'

Resting his papers before him, Creed now leaned his knuckles on the table, spreading his thumbs wide for balance, and, feeling the importance of the moment, spoke from the heart, making eye contact with each man around him as he did so. 'I entreat you to seriously and earnestly reflect, gentlemen, that it would prevent those consequences all of us would deplore. In conclusion, on the Relief Committee's behalf, I thank you for the kind manner in which our delegation has been received here today. Thank you, gentlemen.'

'Hear, hear!' Members of his own delegation and Guardians unanimously commended the proposal, as Creed resumed his seat, feeling a flush of satisfaction.

'Thank you, Mr Creed,' Father Lee commended him on behalf of the delegation, while James, Pat, and Dan repeatedly rapped their knuckles on the table in a gesture of exceptional respect.

As Creed listened, the other members of the deputation went on flattering and shaming the Guardians into action, urging the absolute necessity of both establishing some form of emergency relief and sending a strong letter of remonstrance to the government, yet again requiring the establishment of a depot. But doubtless the Guardians needed neither shaming nor urging. The thousands who thronged the streets were surely sufficient proof of the disastrous situation that prevailed.

'But what has induced them to come?' Ashe interrupted the nuanced discussion, perhaps to bring their focus to a conceptual level. 'It may seem an obvious question, but it still warrants discussion. Was it something specific?'

'It's because expectations were held out to the people that their condition would be improved,' Father Lee replied. 'It is to express their belief that food and employment should have been forthcoming by now. We all strongly hoped those promises would be realised, but as the presentment sessions are not due to sit for another ten days, and it will require at least eight or ten days more before lines can be laid out … I really don't see how upwards of forty thousand people, each and all of them under our care and protection, our guardianship dare I add, can hold out until then without food.'

'Hear, hear!'

Dust circled and spiralled in the faint yellow light at the centre of the room – the last squeeze of September's warmth, brimming over the lip into October. The blown plate glass of the windows gave a distorted view of those insectile beings that aimlessly drifted in and out of their unusual conglomeration below, and Creed, feeling the waxen skin of his freshly shaved jaw, remembered pondering a similar scene through the window of his shop some months before, only then it had been perceiving but a handful of creatures on the square. Now it concerned the poor of the whole district.

'On behalf of the board,' Pat O'Riordan said, rising with the apparent intention of concluding the proceedings, 'I propose a resolution: that one hundred pounds be placed at the disposal of the Relief Committee; that the board enter into a subscription; that we solicit external assistance with a view to the establishment of depots.'

'I will second the resolution,' Dan added.

'Thank you, Mr O'Riordan,' Ashe acknowledged, 'but how do you propose this should be supported in the short term?'

'The money could be raised on the book and levied upon each district afterwards,' offered James.

'That is quite illegal!' Massy Warren argued bluntly, speaking for the first time. Amid the industrious proceedings of the day and the larger body than usual, Creed had barely noticed his presence and was frustrated now to see him predictably putting himself in the way of any meaningful progress.

But the chairman too argued against the measure: 'It would only embarrass the commissioners, and time and money would be wasted.'

'With respect, Mr Ashe, what care a starving people about the commissioners' embarrassment?' Dan Lucy fired back passionately.

'If I may say so … I tend to agree with Mr Lucy's and Mr Welply's assertions. And I would assert that there can be no greater test of destitution given the people than to walk miles to the workhouse and back again for a single meal,' said Father Lee.

'But the system would be wide open to abuses,' Massy Warren contended.

Creed watched the subsequent wrangling with growing dismay, conscious that hundreds and hundreds were still standing outside the workhouse gate, suffering. Exchanges continued between those desirous of urgent action and those more concerned with the law and the perception of their decisions among the authorities, until at last Dr Crooke stood and, digging one fist into a hip beneath his open waistcoat, peering out over his glasses, brought the discussion into focus with a proposal: 'So long as we have the means of feeding every poor creature who comes, God forbid we should refuse that assistance. However, instead of bread, oatmeal should constitute the relief; it will last longer in their stomachs.'

'And the applicants should eat it in the yard ...' William Garde Browne interrupted. 'I suggest that persons arriving at eight o'clock should not be fed until nine or ten, to prevent abuses by those who would undertake to travel to another union in the same day and receive food there as well.'

'Very well ...' Dr Crooke said with a frustrated sigh. 'I therefore propose the following resolution: that a meal of stirabout be given in the yard of the workhouse to such destitute persons as may apply for it, until public works commence, but that the applicants be required to remain two hours on the premises before their wants are supplied.'

'I second that resolution.' James stood, adding, 'But may I urge that we act upon this resolution with immediate effect? There are hundreds within view, who I believe you'll all agree with me have likely not broken their fast this day.'

'Hear, hear!' The room appeared to be reaching a conclusion.

At last, Creed thought, feeling that with the persistence of those conscientious speakers present, the beam was finally being tipped in the right direction, and it was James who might just have managed to sink the balance.

'I wish to point out that my electoral division would not benefit at all by this resolution and it is unjust that we who are liable to an equal share of the rate should be missed over by this proposal. I mean, is it rational to suppose that a person would travel all the way from Kilmichael or Donoughmore and back to get a single meal a day? Nigh on ten or twelve miles each way, on foot?'

Cornelius O'Connell was pulling the board's attention back to a point he had earlier passionately attempted to address, but which had been disregarded entirely. O'Connell was a solicitor reputed for often taking a lighter approach when representing crown prosecution cases against the poor at the courthouse. Creed respected O'Connell greatly but regretted that he felt the need to hold things up further at this moment. But he knew that O'Connell – who rolled a pen between his thick-fingered hands as he protested in a heavy country accent – was perhaps right: 'While I concur on the principle, I feel compelled to dissent.'

'It is a very particular situation that may never again occur.' Mr Ashe sought to tie the matter up.

'And will be of a short duration,' James agreed, adding with a wringing of his hands, 'Gentlemen, please. Are we to keep those people waiting while we refuse the possible in search of the perfect?'

'Ill-thought-out measures will do more harm than good, Welply. I think the ramifications are prohibitive.' Massy Warren, almost feline in his tones, seemed to relish James's desperation, although Creed had to reluctantly admit that in adding another point, he appeared to have a well-reasoned opinion on this occasion. 'A man leaving the remote parish of Ovens, getting a meal and walking home would be hungrier when he got back than he was when he'd left,' Warren added, laughing childishly.

The heat of the crowded room was beginning to carry the musty scent of some of the old suits and Creed felt himself loosening his own collar, wondering if the proceedings would go on much longer.

'Gentlemen, we must move to do something, as best we can, for as many as we can. I am open to other solutions, but I don't hear any. We are restricted as I see it, by the law, from a comprehensive solution that the opening of depots would resolve. We must request of the commissioners that restrictions are eased to take in the needs of all, but in the meantime let us not be paralysed entirely.'

Creed breathed a sigh of relief at Ashe's having finally come around to his senses and began to move his pencil to record Dr Crooke's resolution, by now put forward from the chair thus:

With the following amendment – that the Poor-Law commissioners be requested to sanction the opening of soup shops in every electoral division of this Union, where an application may be made for same, with the object of affording food to such destitute persons as may apply. That, in the meantime, at the Union Workhouse, a meal be given to any persons producing a ticket from the clergymen, stating their residence, and that the electoral divisions be charged accordingly.

The resolution, it was decided, would be put to a vote by the Guardians alone, and the deputation, invited temporarily to leave the room, withdrew gracefully with the exception of Creed and Dr Crooke, who remained in their respective roles as related to the board.

The visitors occupied the wooden landing separating the boardroom from the clerk's office, as Creed observed the Guardians to take the vote *in camera*. 'All in favour?'

A sizeable show of hands responded in the affirmative, but was it enough, wondered Creed, fully aware that he himself had no vote, while the chairman would have an extra, deciding vote, in the case of a tie.

'All against?'

A similar number raised hands in dissent. But when the result of nine to eight in favour was counted as decisive, James shot a look of triumph at Creed who tightened his fists and felt his eyes widen with delight in passing the same look to Pat and Dan amid the cries of approval that surrounded them. The rush of euphoria that Creed felt unleashed within him was almost too great to contain. So moved by the result, he realised how unaware he'd been of the strength of his feelings on the matter and now sought to hide the overflowing emotion in the wagging tail of his pencil's capturing of the moment. But behind the glasses his eyes were watering. All the tension seemed now to have been worth it. It felt like a remarkable victory – that the day had turned full circle from the very real threat of upset he had earlier been practically in favour of to the poor having now been given a chance. And to him, that the crowd had essentially brought it about through their own initiative was inspiring.

While Massy H. Warren and some of the others who'd voted against the resolution wore their disapproval begrudgingly, Mr Burdon, sitting to the left of the chairman, recorded the result unaffected. Father Lee and his associates were then invited to rejoin the room, whereupon Creed took great joy in documenting it being finally arranged that such of the crowd still remaining outside the gates and scattered through the town, as were extremely destitute, 'should be admitted to the yard ... and that each receive half a loaf of bread, as sufficient oatmeal could not be procured'.

'Gentlemen, I hereby call this meeting to a close. Thank you all for your patience. Our thanks to the visiting gentlemen. Mr Lee, may we leave you to acquaint those outside with the decision?'

'Of course, Mr Chairman.'

The room prepared to disperse and Mr Burdon was asked to call the staff of the workhouse to order, in preparation for the imminent distribution in the yard.

'Mr Lee,' said Ashe, 'perhaps you might give us a ten or fifteen-minute head start, to get ahead of the confusion? And Mr Burdon, please make a note too, that when you next have the time, you might also put out a tender for an urgent supply of oatmeal.'

'Yes, sir.'

Creed – who had decided to remain behind with James, Father Lee and his curate, Father Barry, until all the Guardians had left – found himself appreciating that even though Ashe had been against the resolution, he had yet fulfilled his duty to the letter without prejudice or spite.

With the room suddenly quiet and emptied of the weighty matters that it had just contained, he could now hear the gentle murmur of the crowd outside, still awaiting news of the meeting. On the instruction of the matron, a young pauper woman, one of the inmates, stood at the door holding it open for them. But only when he had decided that time enough had passed for the Guardians to clear the workhouse did Father Lee set out down the stairs to address the crowd from the same step he had stood on earlier, with the curate, James and Creed in his wake.

'Thank you for your patience. The board have come to a decision. I am pleased to relate that you will all be admitted to the yard shortly, and there given something immediately to relieve your hunger. There is to be a daily allowance of stirabout here to the most destitute, on production of a note from your priest.'

The crowd seemed almost shocked and did not react to the news as quickly as Creed had expected. 'What will the poor children do, who can't walk to the workhouse?' one voice was eager to enquire.

All around him the crowd stayed silent, clearly intent on learning the answer and Father Lee, perhaps lost for words, lowered his head, and mirrored the same silence.

Creed could not help but feel the force of the objection, nor, it seemed, could anyone else present. There was an air of disappointment directed towards the small group who had worked on their behalf, against the odds, to secure the decision. But it was of course an understandable reaction, and even if disappointing for James, Father Lee, Father Barry and himself, Creed knew it was perhaps a sobering reminder that the extent of suffering was beyond anything any of them could imagine, and certainly beyond the reach of what their limited efforts could affect.

'There is no panacea, I'm afraid,' Father Lee said with a hint of unconcealed sorrow. 'We are doing the best we can. Thank you. Please wait here until you receive instructions that the yard is open.'

With his curate in tow, Father Lee left the step and began to make his way through the crowd in the direction of the town along the avenue of the workhouse. Fearing that some had already started for home, believing no one had come to their aid, Father Lee would naturally want to ensure that the news would reach the greater number of the poor creatures in time, Creed reasoned, and, alongside James, feeling it his duty to observe the proceedings, followed the two priests out. Creed was happy to be among the small party – even if it was now somewhat diminished in its elation – to bring the good news to more of the huge gathering of the district's poor. A ten-minute walk took them to the square, where, at the castle gates, they stopped to address the scattered crowd, who were sitting or lying prostrate in every direction for hundreds of yards.

Amidst a profound silence Father Lee addressed the multitude once more, some of whom began to move towards him to hear better, though all were clearly tired and in poor spirits. 'As promised, the Guardians and the Relief Committee are attempting all within their power to bridge the gap while we await the government measures to come to your aid, as they surely must do.

'It has been arranged in the meantime that anyone sufficiently destitute will be provided with half a loaf of bread at the yard of the workhouse in the course of the next hour.'

More of the crowd began to stir on hearing this.

'Beginning tomorrow, and until such time as the sessions can afford some public employment, for those, again, destitute enough to apply, a meal of stirabout, or oatmeal, will be given daily inside the yard of the workhouse. We ask of you all to please, after you go there, peaceably return to your homes.'

Creed noticed how the message was passed among the crowd by those who had 'the Béarla' to those who spoke the native tongue alone. Within a short time, the majority proceeded to filter out of the square towards Castle Street in the direction of the workhouse across the bridge and heeded every wish of the authoritative cleric.

'I shall leave you here, gentlemen. It has been a long morning,' the priest told Creed at last, visibly exhausted himself.

'Agreed, Father Lee. A long week,' Creed added, acknowledging the work they had put into drawing up the resolution leading up to the meeting.

'We can but continue to do the best our energies will permit, gentlemen,' James said. 'Although it might seem a thankless task, we have achieved a great deal this day.'

'Agreed,' said both the priests and Creed.

And at that the group splintered, with Creed setting off against the flow of the crowd towards his shop on South Square, as the priests headed east along Castle Street for St Coleman's, and James for his home behind them on North Square.

Amongst the crowd, Pádraig, weary and by now feeling faint, walked in step, like so many others, contemplating with mixed feelings the news that relief would be issued daily from the workhouse. After waiting all afternoon wondering if there'd be any benefit, the immediate release from anxiety, in anticipation of some food being given only a short walk away – a small but tantalising reward for his journey, and a somewhat encouraging token of what he hoped would be the assurance of some security from starvation in the weeks and months to come – was only tempered by the reality that it was going to be a long and arduous trek home, not to mention a physically demanding daily slog to get to the workhouse and back from Doire Liath.

The half-pound of bread, when he eventually got to the top of the queue, felt so small in his hand that he had to agonise over how much he could afford to eat, with Cáit and the children present in his mind.

The hunger was immense and Pádraig struggled to hold himself back from the urge to attack and to wolf down the bread as quickly as he would be able to swallow it. Many around him appeared unable to resist that urge and tried to satisfy the hunger immediately upon receipt of theirs, some almost gagging as they attempted to swallow gulps of the dry matter without a drink to aid in the process.

Determined to hold out as long as he could, Pádraig put the half-loaf in his pocket and holding the jacket tight under his hand, lest any preying eyes were watching him, turned to join the many others already fed as they set out for home.

It was almost completely dark at the hour he neared the cabin, bone-weary, his pockets containing very little more than they had carried when he'd set off that morning.

20

The Rhythm of Relief

In the middle of the small cabin, Pádraig sat up and propped himself against the back wall. His head flopped forward repeatedly above the buried embers of last night's fire, as with some effort he struggled to waken his senses. Steadying himself upon one hand pressed into the floor, he probed and scratched his face, neck and chest, then swung up the tattered cap that had fallen off his face during the night and slapped it onto his head.

The light of an hour-old sun poked juvenile fingers through the gaps above and below the door and sounds of a virgin morning competed for his dozing attention, as working ahead of its brain, his body performed its habitual and ancient functions unbidden. A yawn, a stretch and a shudder coincided to shake loose a fart from his bowels in crude reply to the natural world outside. The sharp pain startled him and caused him to groan. He was in poor condition and grave discomfort, still adjusting to the new routine.

Rising early was not foreign to Pádraig, but for most of the last month, since Taidhgí Críodáin had ploughed everything up and the work with him and his brother had all but fallen away, there had been little reason to get up early, and he had got used to being idle. The last seven days, however, had seen him trekking in and out the long haul to and from the Union in Macroom to receive outdoor relief. The accumulation of those seven days' efforts to get there and back were proving a shock to his system and, surviving on so little while taxing his body for all it could give, he was finding it harder than usual upon waking to clear the fog around his brain.

This was the first day he could afford to set off a little later, but even still he was finding it hard to get any further than just sitting up. The capital lure of hunger had got him this far, but the actual reward of a meal was so far off in distance and time that he felt almost no incentive for instant action. Seeming more urgent in that moment, the need for heat and sleep were conspiring to pull him back down again and again and appeared to be winning, until suddenly, without the awareness of any sentient decision, he found himself standing outside again, splashing the dung heap and shivering in the brisk air in the grip of another yawn.

'Relief will be administered from eleven onwards starting tomorrow morning.' Pádraig recalled a pauper translating the announcement for him as they'd poured out of the yard the evening before. Tired as he had been on the way home, his brain had taken that news to mean he could rest longer this morning, and readying to set off once more he realised with some dismay that he was now late, meaning he would be longer in the queue, longer hungry and later getting home.

'Now, Diarmuidín, come on up, little wispeen.' From a standing position, Pádraig bent down and strained to lift Diarmuidín out of Cáit's arms.

'Shhhh, husband. No need to waken him.'

'Don't worry … it's only myself I'm talking to. He won't waken a while yet.' Pádraig struggled out the words.

Cáit, still half rolled over and curled up, kissed little Diarmuid and reluctantly released him into Pádraig's hands, who turned and stepped through the squeaking old door with the sleeping boy on his shoulder.

'Ah, she'll be fine,' he said quietly after a few minutes. 'She wouldn't be able for the walk … But one of us has to go … and carry you … She could never do it … Says she could, but … and what use would I be here, sure?' Pádraig set off, talking to the child who he had positioned astride his shoulders. It *was* mostly himself he was talking to, trying to clear the cobwebs of his still sleepy mind through the act of conversing out loud.

'There's still a bit of the oatmeal left … from Muintir Laoghaire …

'Tis lucky we're getting the bit now abroad ... me and you. That'll cover herself ... and little Síle ... while we're away to get the bit in town ... There was about a stone in it ... originally. It dwindles fast surely ... even on one feed a day.'

Catching his breath as he walked, Pádraig allowed the rhythm of his footsteps and the sounds of whatever was crunched underfoot to break up and disarticulate his sentences, imagining that Diarmuidín was listening or soaking in his thoughts, even if not aware of their meaning.

'We'll have to figure out something else ... when that's gone ... but there's not enough to bring home, that's for sure ... And how could I carry watery soup ... all that way? ... Six-and-a-half miles! ... And holding you up on my head ... Please God the works will start up soon ...'

Pádraig trudged on, calculating, measuring, sometimes trying not to measure the walk: how much ground he'd covered, how far was left to go, how many yards to cover and bends to turn, how many fields, skelps and little both"ans he was yet to pass, roads to cross, paupers to acknowledge, or ignore, townlands to name, how many miles he would cover over the week to come, or in a month like this. He tried every method he could conjure to distract himself from hunger and the discomfort and fatigue.

But it was better when he managed not to think at all; not to feel the weight of the sleeping child on his head and the strain of keeping a forced posture for long periods of time, so that little Diarmuid wouldn't fall off. At one stage or another Pádraig had tried every different way to carry Diarmuidín – across his shoulders, around his waist, upon one shoulder, then up on the other.

'Six miles ... six-and-a-half.' Any distraction was a good one. Sometimes measuring *was* good. *One section at a time. Just walk to that next big oak sticking up over that corner of the road. Then we'll be closer by that much.*

'Maybe, if I get stronger, I might bring Síle some time ... leave you at home ... She's heavier, though ... She'd like to come ... "Mammy ... where are Daddy ... and Diarmuidín gone to?" she probably asks ...

The main reason I bring you … and not Síle all the time … – and God bless Father O'Brien in Clondrohid for ours – … families who've tickets … they're allowed half measures … for children who go along … and you … the baby … you're light enough carried … It gives your mother a break too … still nursing you at her breast … Sure, she's not eating enough … to nourish herself even.

'No … Síle is much heavier… and over thirteen miles … the extra weight'd really add up … She'd scoff the lot.

'Anyway … the bit of cream … Máire Ní Críodáin gives us … off the milk for you every once in a while … that's a bit of good … but you need to be eating something solid now … especially as you're a bit on the small side and not well … Your eating's not what it should be.

'Ah, yes … a bit of real food! … I'll keep bringing you … to get the bit at the union … we'll get you built up strong again … grow the baby out of you.

'Up there on my shoulders … the air is good for you as well … And I get a bit extra betimes … It's an awful long way for you to be going … your mammy says … But what choice have we got? … 'Tis only for the while, I told her … At some stage they'll have to open the works … There's been talk of it for so long … Maybe they didn't take it seriously … last year … But now … huh … nobody can deny it now … They'll surely never allow so many people suffer.

'I'd nearly put money on it … we'll hear of something starting up any day … in Clondrohid even! … Then we can quit this nonsense … walking miles … for a stomach full of watered-down oatmeal … 'Tis very hard … to carry a sleeping child on your head … Even a small one … but a heavy one … foof! … You're much lighter when you're awake … holding yourself up … balancing … If we didn't live so far north now … and west … If we'd be still in Carrigaphooka … or Inchinlinane … the journey'd be near halved … maybe halved … But the tension with Aindrias … your uncle … things were half said … You could tolerate it for a while but … 'twas getting too much.

'And then … poor little Mary … ah … We needed to go somewhere … stand on our own … a fresh start … But sure, how could we've known this was going to …'

Away off in the distance, Pádraig suddenly heard the pealing bell of the union house. It was small, but high-pitched and rancorous enough to travel its pangs a great distance.

''Tis as invisible … and far-reaching as hunger itself,' he told Diarmuidín. 'But maybe it's telling us to stop here … a little while … We've missed getting to the top of the queue anyway.'

With a grunt, Pádraig lifted Diarmuidín down over his head and tried to loosen the cramped muscles in his back and his neck.

For those who'd started out on their journey earlier that morning it made no difference, but Pádraig likened the hammering of the bells to a lure, reaching into the lanes and stirring the town-dwelling hungry from the relative comfort of their own tired old straw. He knew that many, already wakened earlier by hunger, were by now long queuing at the gates of Macroom Union. They'd be pouring into the yard by now, jostling for position as the servers struggled with the giant, cast-iron pots of liquid.

Before relief had existed, the bell told starving paupers beyond in their abodes that the inmates of the workhouse were better off than they were, getting meals three times a day. But its sound now, which probably carried three or four miles distant, Pádraig fancied, would be tugging on the sleeve of anyone in range who knew hunger well.

As he drew nearer his destination, the sight of an odd pauper here and there became almost normal, despite the alarming state of the creatures.

Another half hour later, as he bounded down the Sop Road with Diarmuidín on his shoulders, one half of the huge effort Pádraig's day demanded was almost completed. Reaching that point had already become a landmark moment in the routine. The Sop Road was the long main road into the town and there were no more turn-offs other than the one for Macroom Union itself.

But by now Pádraig was very aware of a limp, a hardening of the muscles around his hip and his overtired legs. He had set out feeling stiff, eventually warming up to a stride in the middle of the trek, but along the final stretch it had completely tightened up again. On top of that, he was wet through with sweat from his scalp to his chest and itching from the heat of the little body wrapped around his. But Pádraig knew it could not have been any easier for Diarmuidín. The poor mite must sorely have been feeling the effects of the journey too, he thought, suffering with his little hips spread so unnaturally wide up there for so long. Except to cry and struggle to right himself, Pádraig had realised, Diarmuidín did not yet know how to express his discomfort. When *he* was wet through, the child was wet through, and that they would be stopping very soon could have been no comfort to Diarmuidín.

The bell had long stopped ringing, replaced by a quiet hush in the distance that grew as he walked, until it became the gushing waters of the Sullane somewhere beyond the far side of the road. The sound of the river alone brought some relief to the thirst that had mounted since the last stop they'd made to drink from a stream running into the Finnow.

But within view of the turn-off, a growing sense of chaos and a repulsion at the sight of other paupers mixed with his own instinctual, hunger-driven compulsion to hasten him in his steps. Converging with the others – whose movements seemed to Pádraig like those of flies drawn to waste – made for a tense and dissonant nausea within him, as mingling and moving among the influx he walked up the avenue towards the complex of buildings a hundred yards or so ahead. He was now but one of the many that formed a tightening scatter of destitute beings lucky enough to have a ticket to receive relief at the yard, but unlucky enough to need it.

Yet Pádraig reasoned that this – access to food, without the terror of having to commit his whole family to the clutches of the institution – was probably the least frightening amount of contact any poor soul in need of it could have with the workhouse.

Inside the densely crowded men's yard, commandeered by the Guardians for the purpose of distributing the relief, Pádraig, and Diarmuidín above him, was directed to the back of one of the queues, and there amid the noise and haste began a long shuffle to the front. The initial frenzy had been diffused and, albeit slowly, the lines were moving.

21

Sleeping Illusion

'**M**ale adult paupers, the yard's usual inhabitants who break stones here during the day, are being treated to a temporary change of scenery. Some are breaking stones in the boys' yard, with the greater number distributed to other outdoor parts of the grounds; the workhouse gardens and the yards for the idiots and the sick – you'll have seen those situated between the infirmary and the death house at the back.

'There are just too many people to fit in one place at this point, and we can't have the inmates mixing with the outdoor paupers.'

Warren Crooke, the doctor of the house, had received and accepted Creed's request to lead him on a tour of the facilities, as one of a series of correspondents answering a call by the *Examiner* to report on conditions across the county.

'How many outdoor paupers are daily dependent on this new relief, Dr Crooke?'

'There are approximately a thousand individuals in and around the yard, give or take. But many more besides who would wish they could get in.'

*

Three-quarters of the way up the queue, Pádraig, hearing voices in the Béarla behind him, observed some other paupers straining to see the men in their midst as if gazing upon some strange beings from another land. He had no sense of what they were saying, but as the expression of a more curious pauper in front said they were of no consequence to him, he stayed looking ahead with other thoughts on his mind.

He was exhausted, and by now it had been almost twenty-four hours since he or Diarmuidín had last tasted food. The claws of hunger were exacting their torture, stabbing and twisting within, and anxiety came in their wake. The sensation of being so stricken that he did not even recognise hunger; of not knowing if he was being overtaken by the fear of his mind; of feeling so frenzied that he might collapse on the spot; of being eaten alive from the inside. The general maddening that rendered him incapable of coherent thought was practising its reckoning once more. His eyes bulged; his brain throbbed from the thirst; his mouth was parched and dry; his heartbeat quickened and his feet were sore and torn up from the stony road. Irritated by the heat and the sweat that soaked through his rough old clothes, the skin of his midriff itched constantly. His body trembled from the exertion of having walked thirteen miles since his last meal as the boy who'd been on his shoulders for every step of the way now pulled at his hair, every bit as agitated, tired and hungry as he was.

'*A Dhiarmuidín! Éirigh as! Cuir uait!*' Pádraig shouted to the child and slapped up at his leg to quieten him down, then felt guilty when the boy began softly to cry.

*

'What benefits – beyond keeping them alive – do you think the relief affords for those who receive it, doctor? Is it of good nutritional substance?' Creed asked the tall, elderly man alongside him as they began to walk again.

'A very valid question, Mr Creed. Although it is keeping them alive, its only real utility is as a temporary measure for those who cannot source food elsewhere in the short term. Most of these creatures, particularly those walking great distances, are now borrowing more from their reserves than they are putting back in. As you might imagine, the effects of such an ever-diminishing return on a body's health can only give one result.'

'Have you tried the substance yourself, Dr Crooke?'

'Well …' the doctor laughed under his breath, apparently caught off guard by the question. 'If it was pleasant to eat, that would be something, but I expect it's quite bland. The best that can be said is that it's warm and voluminous.

'Ultimately, the cooks have to stretch what resources they have to their limit. But serving something appetising is naturally not the highest priority on the list of the Guardians, the government or the Master here. In fact – and I fear this must be said off the record – I can personally attest that the Master has it written and pasted to the wall of his own quarters: a reminder, lest any erratic pang of sympathy should ever penetrate his decorated bosom, that "Inmates are to be worse fed, worse clothed, and worse accommodated than that of the lowest peasant outside the walls of the workhouse." This is the prevailing ethos of the Commission.' The doctor raised one hand as if to absolve himself of any culpability.

'I've heard that,' Creed responded, still writing, and arching his brow in amazement.

Although many of the points he and the doctor discussed were items both men were already privy to and abundantly aware of, Creed knew they were operating on the understanding that what was stated here was for the benefit of the reader who was likely hearing it for the first time. But some facts *were* new to him, so that he was finding much of the doctor's knowledge to be informative.

'Sadly, there is not much danger of achieving such an ideal, however,' Crooke went on. 'The architect of the current Poor Law himself even admitted as much a few short years ago upon concluding a tour of the country to investigate the condition of the poor of Ireland: "The standard of their mode of living is unhappily so low that the establishment of one still lower is difficult" was the statement, I believe.' The doctor enunciated the quotation dramatically. 'Of course, it didn't stop him trying.'

'What was his name if you please, Dr Crooke?'

'George Nicholls. Poor Law Commissioner.'

'Give back your tins!' a woman standing beside a table shouted as she noisily stacked empties in a soaking basin. 'Give back your tins, please. Thank you. Over here. Yes, here. Thank you.'

*

After he and Diarmuidín had sucked, licked and pawed every last drop out of their borrowed vessels, Pádraig turned away to seek out a gap amongst the row of fed bodies now slouched against the outer wall of the yard. Slumping down and lowering the boy into his lap, he grabbed at the sides of his neck to relieve the cramping there once more.

With the beast of hunger put to rest for a while, Pádraig was able to sit back and observe his surroundings. The interior of the complex he had seen so many times from the outside was even bigger than its foreboding and terrifying façade promised it to be. But Pádraig was more preoccupied by the sight of so many of his own kind reduced by desperation to taking scraps to stay alive. It was even sadder and more heartbreaking than he could have imagined. They moved about slowly, dishevelled, drunk on the stirabout, conserving what little energy they had.

The spectacle of suffering humanity on display was, all together, very hard to see. And this was just the yard! God only knew what the other sections held.

Pádraig tried to imagine what was inside the buildings and pictured paupers in the last stages of their agonising descent toward death, bundled in together, coughing and moaning, each a stranger to the next. *They must be even worse off than the saddest looking paupers out here in the yard. You'd surely have to have given up all hope before you'd commit yourself to that. How could anyone put themselves at the mercy of such a fate?*

If any wisdom had come from the experience of seeing what was behind the gates of the workhouse over the previous seven days, it was that Pádraig was sure he never wanted his family to find out what was inside. It was one thing to come in and out of the yard in the same day just for the relief. It would be another thing entirely to abandon the last vestiges of independence, your home and your plot, however small, to abandon yourself to this.

The yard before him read like a cross-section of all the poor of the barony: able-bodied men like himself – labourers – for whom no work was to be had; decrepit old men, not long for the world and devoid of joy or comfort. *What a sad end for a soul to come to. Winter will surely take them.* There were young women who, save the poor existence they were obviously enduring, still looked vital enough, even a pregnant one or two. Others skinny and frail, lying down, so reduced that it seemed extraordinary that they could have even crawled there; boys, approaching the age when they should be out learning the ways of the soil, now feeble, listless and emaciated; children of all ages, from the most tender of years to the edges of adulthood, many of them clearly suffering and deficient in all a body required to grow healthily. But whatever their differences in age, or levels of deterioration, the whole lot were brought together by the commonality of dire want. Those not among the already fed – who lay along the walls, drunk on the elixir of the estranged substance called food – bore either a look of irreconcilable vacancy or the mad stare of ravenous animals.

A shadow passing before Pádraig turned out to be an old woman leaning on a black stick. She stooped and began to lower herself into an empty space beside him. Even she would have to wait out her two hours on the hard ground before being allowed to leave, he thought. She barely managed to make it to the ground without falling on top of herself. *How can the older people, unable to make the journey here, be surviving outside?*

*

Completing what had been a slow lap of the yard, Creed listened, testing his faculty for note-taking on the move, as Dr Crooke continued to reel off facts and figures.

'Oh, indeed. Under normal circumstances – if such a thing exists within the bounds of the workhouse system – the rule set out by the government is that any able-bodied pauper capable of manual labour must be employed for at least ten hours a day in return for the privilege of nourishment. The irony is astounding. The Guardians have forgone that rule in this instance but it still applies to the inmates.

'Irrespective of the weight of its consequences, the enforcement of this standard, within, is the charge of the Master. But if things keep going as they are, it will soon be impossible to keep with that regulation. In every respect the wheels of the cart are coming off. For the first time in its short history, the number of Macroom Union inmates is fast approaching the designated capacity of six hundred persons. It is not hard to imagine what horrors will follow.'

'The trend is a national one, I'm afraid,' Creed offered.

'You are quite right, Mr Creed. And what is worse is that the alarming numbers do not appear to be levelling off. The sum capacity of all union workhouses established across the island is a figure you may be aware of?'

'Not as yet, but please do inform me of it, Dr Crooke.'

'It is, at this moment, ninety-one thousand, one hundred and sixty: a figure which is barely equal to one per cent of the national population. The government refuses to abandon the illusion wherein the *status quo* maintains an equilibrium or fixes *itself*; that crop failure is not an unheard-of occurrence; or that the population of the country has not exponentially catapulted itself to almost triple what it was one hundred years ago, leading many to predict such a happening as this.'

'Indeed,' Creed responded, suitably impressed by the staggering insight and the doctor's ability to articulate it.

'The workhouse system does not provide for such an eventuality as a failure of the potato crop. It is simply designed to cater for the everyday poor. And as though their numbers were in the minority at that!'

*

Nestled in the hollow of Pádraig's embrace, Diarmuidín was by now drifting in and out of sleep. *He's sleeping much more than is normal for a child his age.* Pádraig heard Cáit's words in his mind. He rubbed the boy's hair, studying his breathing. To him, sweet little Diarmuidín looked very like Cáit in his features, but Cáit said he reminded her of Pádraig's mother.

Turning his head to one side, resting his cheek on Diarmuidín's head, Pádraig watched the old woman stirring in restless sleep and imagined his mother in the same situation. He found it painful and still couldn't talk about her death – the grim end she'd had troubled him too much. But at least she would never have to endure this.

Suddenly Diarmuidín erupted in a spasm of coughing and momentarily woke himself, as well as the old woman. But he cleared the loose phlegm off his throat with a rapid jutting of his larynx, snuffled, and dozed back off again.

Pádraig worried for Diarmuidín. He had been in delicate health for some time now. The cough appeared at times to improve, but seemed always to come back worse again. It was so ever-present that sometimes they didn't really notice, or pay much attention to it. But thinking about it now, Pádraig could hardly remember when it had not been there. He recalled his own father saying of his mother that it was 'a bad sign to have a cough all through the summer'. And with winter not far off now, the damp and cold would be hard enough for a healthy body to deal with, let alone for a poorly nourished infant.

But there had been other worrying signs that not all was well with Diarmuidín. Pádraig and Cáit didn't have another little boy themselves to measure him against, but compared with how fast Síle grew when she was a baby, he was still very small and slight. His teeth, still new, sometimes bled at the gums. They were still coming through, his little teeth, but Pádraig couldn't remember seeing blood in Síle's mouth.

It was when he'd been trying to get Diarmuidín to eat a little mouthful of oatmeal scooped up on his finger one day that Pádraig had noticed it

– the red and pinkish streaks through the substance as he drew his hand back from the baby's mouth. It didn't look to be coming from any one place, but generally around the rims of his tiny new teeth. Cáit thought it was a bad sign, and Caitilín Pruiséal, in the cabin behind, had told her she should take him to the woman with the charms in Cahireen.

'I don't want some aul' hag foostering at him,' Pádraig had insisted. 'Anyway, my teeth bleed all the time,' he'd added, trying to dissuade her with some convenient reasoning.

'So do mine, but it's not natural for a baby,' Cáit had instantly replied. 'Yours probably bleed because you're forever sticking those pipes in and out of your mouth.'

But the most worrying thing for them both was that the little boy's appetite had dropped off too and he wasn't suckling as much as he should.

With the sun in his face and Diarmuidín snuffling against his chest, Pádraig closed his eyes to bask in the relative feeling of relaxation ... as full as a sausage, warmth on his body and no need to move anywhere for a while. Of all the stages of his current daily existence, this was about the zenith. He knew it would be a tough walk back, mostly uphill, on tired legs, with no more food to look forward to for another twenty-three-and-a-half hours. But for now he could rest.

Listening to the boy's breathing, Pádraig began to drift. The gentle wheezing had levelled off into a kind of contentment, against a backdrop of sombre clamour: the sound of empty tins thirty or forty feet away, clanging to the instructions of the kitchen staff; paupers moaning and grunting; bodies lifting themselves up and dropping themselves down; children and babies crying sporadically; the repetitive shuffle of feet coming and going, up and down along the wall before him, beside him.

Before long, Pádraig entered a dreamlike state, one that was broken only by the occasional falling of his head, or a new burst of Diarmuidín's coughing. He was walking along a crooked path that stretched away for miles ahead and more behind ... Away off in the distance the horizon was broken by low, pale mountains yearning for the sky despite an ominous dark cloudscape. But among the lumpy tussocks of wild grass on either side of the road sat rows of the sick and everyday poor, coughing, and moaning, sometimes stretching out an arm, tin in hand, calling for assistance. Their mouths moved, but the babble was quiet and indecipherable save for the faint hint of cries and woe.

'Daddy? Daddy?' Rocking on his shoulders, Diarmuidín was animated, and shouted excitedly as they walked along.

'*A bhuaichillín – ó, mo chroí … A Dhiarmuidín bhig*'. Oblivious to the onlookers Pádraig patted the leg hanging down over his shoulder, in love with his little boy.

'Look, Daddy.'

Among the crowd on the left side, Pádraig saw they were passing his mother, Mairéad. She wore a worried expression and was shaking something, mumbling concerns. Pádraig Óg, beside her, turned to make eye contact with Pádraig, who couldn't seem to stop his own forward motion. His father's old, wizened face revealed nothing. Pádraig's mother was rocking on her folded legs as he passed her. She did not look up though he wanted her to. The road continued to talk to his feet as Diarmuidín urged him forward, steering the animal with his knees and hips like a rider on a horse. Pádraig tried to keep sight of his parents, but they were drifting away behind. The walls around them, hemmed with paupers, resembled those within the union. Tins were stacked to the ceiling and an old woman stirred the meal with a black stick.

New voices neared from behind, conversing in the foreign tongue, winding around each other, planning, deciding. He turned to examine them as he walked on, but with the glare in his eyes he could not make them out. A man, and another man, one older. Somewhere ahead of them, by the fire, Cáit was sitting on the three-legged stool, combing Síle's hair.

*

'They just lie about like this for a time after they've been fed,' Dr Crooke said, looking down at the paupers along the wall as they strolled by, Creed listening with his head in the notebook, 'but if we were to turn them directly out after feeding them, they would lie about on the road, or in the town. We'd have even more complaints, of course. People don't want to see them, but they're everywhere. In fact, it's nigh on impossible to avoid seeing them.

'The board are aware that some paupers are travelling great distances – up to sixteen miles a day – to receive relief in the yard. We did, for the first week, have them arriving at eight and nine o'clock, when they had to, in line with the policy of the Guardians, wait a minimum of two hours before being fed, but …'

'An absurd policy. If you don't mind my saying.' Creed worried that he'd overstepped the mark. Though he and Dr Crooke were both on the Relief Committee, the doctor himself was still a Guardian after all. But he found himself reassured when Dr Crooke expressed his understanding.

'Of course, Mr Creed. The aim was primarily to prevent abuses; such as paupers being fed here, then being found to be receiving relief again in some other part of the barony on the same day. But with that out of the way, there was still the problem that some were so loath to spend a moment longer than they had to here that they would leave immediately afterwards and make a spectacle of themselves beyond our bounds, as described.

'Thus, it was decided to confine them to the yard on the other end instead: before allowing them to set off again. Of course, even if their feelings were otherwise, and they wished to stay, or to sign themselves in, it would scarcely place them in a better position, unless additional accommodation is to be effected somehow. There are at present five hundred and fifty-one inmates within.'

'Just forty-nine places left, then,' observed Creed.

'Officially.' The doctor seemed to be implying that the numbers at the workhouse would not be kept to six hundred.

'And do you suppose those places will be taken soon, Dr Crooke?'

'Perhaps even by tomorrow,' his companion acknowledged. 'At any rate ... it was felt, upon reflection, that it would be more humane to feed them upon arrival, their hunger being so severe.'

'Indeed.' Creed was sceptical that this had been any part of the motivation for the change but, accepting that he did not manage to attend every single meeting, took it for granted that the advantage to the paupers was likely a convenience the Guardians had merely embraced.

'The system only changed on Saturday, but improvement has been instantaneous. And there have been some other convenient side effects.' The doctor walked in long straight strides with hands clasped behind his back as Creed ambled alongside, studiously perched over his pencil, stopping every so often to finish a sentence.

'Could you elaborate, please, doctor?'

'Certainly. The hot food acts as a kind of a soporific and afterwards, while they are obliged to remain in the yard for a period, there are far fewer squabbles. This way, they tend to sleep it off and wake up just in time to face the journey home.'

'But in a strange way ...' Creed wrestled with whether to speak his thoughts or not, but decided to risk them. 'I myself have reported on many meetings at the boardroom, as you well know. And it would seem to me that ... well ... would it not be better if the hungry *were* seen in the streets, so that their numbers and their true condition were more widely appreciated? I know that seems counter to ... but it might have the effect of a call to action.'

'One could only hope, Mr Creed. The policy has already been effected, of course. But something must be done to relieve the pressure, or who can say what the consequences are likely to be?'

'Concerning the Relief Committee, Dr Crooke. For the sake of the readership I am obliged to set my own position as a member aside and to ask without prejudice: is it your opinion that the committee is functioning adequately?'

'I understand, Mr Creed. The Relief Committee do what they can, although to be frank, bureaucracy tends to retard progress at times. This is merely my opinion, of course, but it is my experience that there are among its members those who wish to be heard and have their own interests represented above those of the poor, which is, of course, entirely contrary to the function of the committee.' Creed was delighted to hear someone else echo his own feelings.

'But the overall efforts of the body must, and do, come to *some* good. As you are well aware, in addition to the judicious and humane resolve of the Poor Law Guardians in giving such extensive relief as you see here today, the exertions of the Relief Committee are currently directed to providing meal at a reduced price. And approximately eleven hundred tickets have been issued to the heads of families, entitling the holders to receive Indian meal at one shilling and sixpence a stone, while other private vendors demand from two shillings to two shillings and tuppence a stone ...'

'Oatmeal, I believe, is now priced at twenty pounds a ton!' Creed couldn't help exclaiming.

'Of course, the cost of every article is daily increasing.'

'Well, Dr Crooke, speaking of the very same Relief Committee, I'm due very soon at the weekly meeting. I'm most grateful to you for your time and instruction. I'd happily listen all day, but the committee won't find itself to be any more efficient if its own membership is loose in its punctuality. That said, I hope that getting this information to the public will be a worthy reason for any delay of mine. I should have liked to do this another day to avoid the clash, but the *Examiner* has requested this with a certain urgency.'

'My pleasure, Mr Creed,' the doctor gestured a bow. 'If you should require it of me, I am available at any time. I'm afraid I myself cannot attend the Relief Committee meeting this day, however. I have my hands full at the infirmary.'

'Of course, Dr Crooke. My sincere gratitude for your time and indelible expertise.'

'I'll walk with you back to the main building.'

'Thank you, doctor.'

Moving freely, feeling somewhat unburdened, though he'd only carried his satchel of paper and writing instruments, Creed now became aware of the din of hundreds of bodies stumbling about, joining and leaving the queues, all of its accompanying sounds blending into a sandpaper grit of ethereal noise, amplified and echoed by the large stone walls that skirted the yard: those of the main building; the infirmary; the kitchen and chapel building; and the outside perimeter wall through which the visiting paupers came and exited by a small gate.

The doctor led him through the grounds and left him at the back of the entrance building, whence he found his way through the reception rooms. Creed was conscious that he had just reversed the experience of an inmate entering the building upon admission.

He navigated himself around a line of paupers seeking entry and heard the porter explaining to them, 'You'll have to come back on Saturday, when the Guardians are sitting.'

Knowing so well the procedure, Creed climbed the stairs unattended and knocked upon the door of the boardroom before letting himself in.

'Good afternoon and welcome, Mr Creed.' Edward Ashe greeted him from the head of the table.

22

The Art of Truth

On Tuesday, 13 October 1846, Cornelius Creed left the shop in the direction of the courthouse on Barrack Lane, in anticipation of its being the focal point of the crisis in Macroom that morning. Besides the poor themselves, an assemblage of magistrates, landed proprietors, gentry, clergy and anyone who was anyone from across the barony of West Muskerry were set to converge upon the building, and to bear witness or take part in what every meeting, conversation and quiet hope over the past month had built up to be the solution to everybody's woes: an extraordinary baronial presentment sessions. When not extraordinary, the sessions were a bi-annual sitting of the grand jury, to consider 'presentments': proposed works, or grants for the construction or repair of anything from roads and bridges to lunatic asylums, the primary purpose being to raise money for a variety of local public works by means of the county cess, and now the Poor Law rates. The *extraordinary* presentment sessions had been arranged and publicised for every barony in Ireland at the behest of Henry Labouchere, Lord Lieutenant of Ireland, who it was said was greatly feeling the pressure to relieve the crisis, and on this occasion the purpose of the sessions was simply to provide emergency employment in the extreme.

The unusually large attendance of the labouring poor of the district too was such as might be expected when it was their fate that hung in the balance and naturally when it was they who had no other means to alter its course; the many thousands of them existing on the precipice of starvation.

Every parish in the union was to be represented and among the almost sixty men of influence, Creed took a seat alongside his dear friend James Welply.

When the crowd had settled, Captain Wallis gave the signal and the secretary read the instructions of the Lord Lieutenant, with reference to what means were to be adopted in connection with the Labour Rate Act. During this reading, Creed observed the crowd as something of a large organism trying to find comfort in a small space. Though it was made up mostly of men, with some women and children among them, he reasoned that they were as still and attentive as they could be under the circumstances. The appointed secretary having finished and the proceedings having got underway, Creed groaned internally at the sight of Robert Fitzgerald demanding the floor to ask whether 'other sessions might be held for the purpose of receiving applications for drainage'. Fitzgerald was the owner of some miserable land north of Macroom and always the first in line to grasp at government funds when the opportunity arose.

'Such is my opinion,' was the reply of the secretary.

'Can tenants apply for presentments under the Drainage Act?' a voice shouted from the gallery. Creed looked to where he perceived its owner to be situated. 'Hello, sir. I'm here.' A respectable-looking farmer waved his cap. 'My name is John Hanna.'

With an interest more in the procedure than in the answer, Creed turned to see the response of Wallis in the chair. What happened next, he reasoned, would answer an important question: whether a spectator's intervention would be tolerated and his question considered.

'I am unable to say, but I would recommend that all should apply, and then leave the government to decide.' Creed was satisfied that the proceedings were going to be fair and amenable to interjections.

Fitzgerald, jumping in again, left no time for anyone else from the crowd to speak. 'If someone succeeded in getting a presentment for drainage, could he – if he thought proper – afterwards allow the matter to drop, without proceeding further?'

An air of consternation had begun to grow around the bench at the wasting of time on what appeared to be a self-serving and pestiferous question, before they had even got into the flow of the more urgent matters. But the secretary sought to diffuse the discontent.

'I see no reason why not. Thank you.' He pushed on, despite other attempts at interruptions. 'I wish to draw your attention to two paragraphs in particular, within the instructions. First, the presentment sessions will estimate the sum which it may be necessary to raise off the barony for the purpose of affording employment. And second, they will also ascertain the proportion of such assessment which, according to the last Poor Law evaluation, may be chargeable upon each electoral division – if the whole be not included – in the barony; and they will obtain for this purpose, from the clerk of each Poor Law Union, a copy of such valuations.'

It did not surprise Creed that Massy Warren was the first to respond. 'I have made a calculation of the amount that would be required to support the people for three months.'

Nor was it unexpected when James leapt to his feet for a moment to interject, 'Three months is by no means sufficient!'

Massy Warren countered, 'I recommend the utility of voting for a sum sufficient to support the people during a three-month period, but certainly no longer.'

'Three months would be completely useless,' James reiterated, 'considering the obvious destitution of the population.'

This was lauded by all, especially the onlookers, with loud cries of 'Hear, hear!'

But Massy, sticking stubbornly to his position, arose again: 'I would advise the meeting to consider the propriety of adopting works under the Drainage Act at the risk of swamping the barony with useless roads.'

This was greeted by uproar, and cries of 'Sit down, sit down!'

James, on his feet again, attempted to surpass the argument. 'It will probably take up to four weeks after any presentments are granted before any employment can actually commence. If we do not grant sufficient on this occasion, great distress will ensue while the machine is being set in motion again.'

Creed concurred with James's reckoning and was pleased by the overwhelming level of cheers that greeted the statement.

'We all know that six months cannot elapse without misery and famine and we are equally aware that we will not see provisions arrive in the country for at *least* six months.'

This time, among the general approbation along the bench were cries of 'You are wrong, sir.'

Undeterred, James continued. 'I maintain that before that time, no foreign supply to affect the circumstances of the labouring poor can be procured. I earnestly advise the gentlemen present to deliberate seriously before adopting any resolution restricting the relief to so limited a period.'

James was cheered once more as he retook his seat.

'I am as ready as any man to uphold the population of the country, but I do not understand the point of granting works, which will occupy six months and certainly swamp the barony.'

Creed felt a certain satisfaction in observing that Massy was not doing well to win over the crowd, who hissed with disapproval. But he knew that Massy wasn't trying to. The vengeful face of the yeomanry's latest generation in Macroom – and a JP to boot – was one that was used to being the villain, and more than comfortable with the disdain of the poor. It justified his hatred for them.

'I don't see why we shouldn't avail ourselves of the Drainage Act,' Massy Warren continued, his pointed face glowing with something like defiance. 'The results would likely be of permanent advantage and it would afford general employment.'

A new voice, that of Massy's brother, the Rector of Camaway, Robert Warren, now entered, proclaiming, 'If the works do not commence before the expiration of four weeks, this meeting is of no use. Therefore, we shall require government to pass them. A meeting took place in this town lately, and instead of sending food the government sent bayonets!

'I'm so happy to say that the people were pacific and the bayonets unnecessary. But are the people to starve?'

'No, no!' came from the effusion of shouts that gushed from the crowd, along with 'We are determined not to starve!'

'Are they to be left without food or employment for four weeks?'

The courthouse erupted in terrific noise.

Leaning on his knuckles to extend his tall, thin body to its maximum height and speaking with the impressive voice that years of sermonising had honed, Robert Warren continued: 'There are no provisions in the country, and immediate action is necessary. Today is Tuesday. If possible, the work ought to commence by next Monday.'

Whatever about Massy Hutchinson Warren's disregard of the power of public opinion, his brother the cleric, taking the completely opposite tack, was whipping the crowd into frenzy and winning their popularity.

'Ask Captain Gordon,' a voice shouted.

'I would not apply to Captain Gordon,' Robert Warren fired back, resolute. 'The government is the party to call on.'

'There is a maxim amongst moralists,' Reverend O'Kearney of Ahinagh stood to say, 'that deems the safest course is best. But when the government exercises so material a discretion in the selection of works, these sessions must place the people beyond the reach of starvation. I contend that a period of three months is by no means sufficient to relieve the prevailing distress. No less than six months will suffice. In relation to the present Labour Rate Act, I consider it the worst measure ever introduced for such purpose by any government. I for one would much rather see the people engaged in the drainage and reclamation of land; in sub-soiling and adopting improved systems of agriculture. But when no other work is available, it is necessary that the people be employed under the circumstance, to afford them a means of subsistence.'

Robert Warren did not sound as though he welcomed the interruption. 'I recommend the gentlemen present abstain from speech-making and proceed practically to business, by passing largely the works of necessity and utility. That is the only course that will save us from destruction. Otherwise, we cannot resist the torrent of misery and distress that now envelops us.'

'Hear, hear.' Many members of the bench appeared to be quite distressed in the presence of the crowd and their lively, vocal participation.

Creed watched with interest as the gallery grew louder and wilder by the minute, hoping the dignitaries would find it hard to escape their responsibilities under such popular scrutiny.

Stepping out from among the crowd Creed noticed a small boy, clearly upset and covering his ears from the tumult as his father led him crying towards the door.

'Should we sanction employment for three, or six months?' the secretary enquired of the bench, but as it became clear that some of them did indeed want to limit obligations to three months, the volume of angry noise among the crowd made it difficult to keep order.

Beads of sweat were visible on his high domed forehead when Massy, refusing to let go of his position, stood again, interrupting the vote. 'I believe three months to be sufficient, and I demand a poll to that effect.'

By now the onlookers had found their full voice and the shouts of 'Sit down!' eventually led to a great cheer as Massy Warren, shaking his head in denial, gave way and resumed his seat with a careful adjustment of his coat tails.

'You have your poll!' A voice from the back stood out among more hissing and booing.

'Quiet, please – quiet, please,' the chairman requested and regained sufficient order to put the question of three months or six months to the vote. A big cheer, in which both Creed and James joined, greeted the victory of the longer term.

The next aim of the meeting, Captain Wallis called, was to reconcile the level of the grants against the baronial rates, in anticipation of which Creed threw a doubtful look to James. Having looked intently over the figures in advance, Creed knew it was bound to be a most troublesome task for the bench to come to agreement on anything near the necessary amounts, even without the added pressure of the crowd.

'I recommend a liberal expenditure,' O'Kearney spoke again. 'By my estimation, in any portion of the population, and especially in the remote parishes, three-quarters of the people are in need of being supported by the money that public works would afford them. Out of a thousand head of population as a base example,' he explained, 'seven hundred and fifty individuals would be in need of that support. Seven hundred and fifty divided by five – the average number in each family – gives that a hundred and fifty families would be supported. Now, all this is on the presumption that in each family there is also one male physically capable of engaging in active employment.'

Massy, who seemed to be at odds with every view but his own, challenged the accuracy of the priest's statement. 'Your estimate of the proportion in need is much too large.'

With a shake of his head and a glance at Creed, James rose once more. 'I suggest that we should commence with the parish of Macroom, and allocate to it the full valuation, which is eight thousand five hundred.'

'Eight thousand even,' Jeremiah McCarthy, a visiting Justice from Cork, objected. 'The Poor Law valuation amount is eight thousand and that is the sum that should be allocated. Mainly for the purpose of complying with the mandate of government. In their allocation of that sum, it was not to be considered by any means granted, for less might answer, but they had pledged themselves to eight thousand pounds if it was required and not to the additional five hundred that Mr Welply proposes, which must necessarily fall on our own shoulders.'

"Tis quite unnecessary to go into the valuation at all!' Massy shouted, leading Creed to wonder why he'd even bothered to attend, if not simply to cause anarchy and upset the whole scene.

'Unless you comply with the instructions most of the applications will fall.' Wallis reprimanded Massy, then again struggled to steady the ship amid the disorder that followed his outburst. 'For mercy's sake, be quiet!'

Another of the newer members of the grand jury now spoke for the first time – a well-dressed man whose use of some inventive language caught Creed's attention. 'I propose that the sum that's necessary be the one granted. I see no advantage in coming forward with specious pretexts of humanity when people are starving.'

'What is that man's name?' Creed whispered to James.

'John Herrick,' James replied, leaning in but remaining focused on the proceedings. 'Belmont. Counsellor,' he added.

With a calm expression, seemingly unaffected by the rowdy gallery, Herrick, given closer scrutiny by Creed, was a man who looked to be in his thirties, confident and unaffected. Creed wondered what the man's impressions of their proceedings would be and if, coming from the other side of the county, he must be attending many of these regional sessions. An impression of a connection with the sea was created by the dark blue frock coat stretched wide over his shoulders.

Many other members of the bench, hitherto silent participants, now seemed moved to have their say and such a diverse range of figures was presented to the assembly that Creed found himself becoming more and more agitated until, at last, he felt it necessary to speak his own piece. It seemed to him as if everyone else gave way and even the gallery became somewhat less rowdy, as he stood, and heard someone whisper, '*Examiner.*'

'As collector, I can prove there are ninety-seven unemployed labourers on Holland's Lane alone – just one street in Macroom – the implication of which fact is that the most exaggerated figure so far proposed must still be a modest one in real terms.'

McCarthy, rising, stared at Creed, and proposed: 'Six hundred men for six months at one shilling a day will require five thousand pounds and I move that be granted.'

Creed shook his head and stood again to answer. 'You vastly

underestimate the crisis faced by the labourer. Clearly, you have not thought to include the number who'll shortly be put out of employment by the farmers who haven't work or means to continue them.' Passionate in responding, he strove to speak calmly.

Confusion reigned as the gallery roared as one, 'That's right!'

'The population of Macroom is nearly five thousand,' a body protested.

The chairman, Wallis, amid a tumult of increasing chaos, put McCarthy's motion forward, announced that it was carried – though Creed could not believe that it had been – and moved proceedings to Ballyvourney.

'That's not enough for Macroom!' a voice shouted. 'Go back to discussing Macroom!'

'If we go back to Macroom we won't be done for the night,' Massy Warren shouted back, to be greeted with more hisses and cries.

'Give it up, Massy! Give it up!'

'I care not for your hissing. I am here sworn on my oath. And I'll do my duty though you hiss me to my house.'

Great noise swelled up at Massy Warren's combative stance, which was evident in his pose as much as in his words: feet planted, angry eyes bulging with bitterness, his face searching for a target among those who were hissing.

'On Thursday last,' Lee stood to speak, the respect for him bringing instant restraint among the crowd, 'a poor man died of starvation in this town. We'll stick to Macroom for a month if we have to!' Lee's summation had the effect of doubling the uproar that had preceded the restraint.

'Good gracious, what a scene!' the secretary uttered to those around him on the bench, clearly disturbed by what he was witnessing.

'Macroom is decided!' the chairman shouted, to cries of 'No!' that rang out in the back.

'There is much more poverty and much more distress in the town of Macroom than in any other place. I call on you to reconsider Macroom,'

Lee insisted, amid the greatest confusion and noise from the crowd.

It took several minutes, but Wallis eventually restored the session to something of a reasonable atmosphere, only for Robert Warren to utter loudly to the bench, 'For God's sake, let us out of this! I propose every presentment be passed *en masse*, then let them go to the Board of Works for control.'

Warren's suggestion elicited the most rowdy and conflicting response yet. Voices made insinuations of 'connections' and 'unfair motives'. Creed was unaware of what brought such a response and threw his hands up at James with a puzzled look.

Robert Warren looked stung by what was being shouted and Creed listened attentively to him when he spoke, quiet having descended once again. 'I believe, I may say amongst those who know me, I attach no importance to the accusations being expressed against me in this room today. But on the recommendation of the magistrates present and to avoid further confusion, I consent to withdraw the motion.' He took his seat again amidst more yelling as Creed heard him to say, 'Anything at all for the sake of peace.'

More pandemonium ensued and the quick withdrawal of the statement led Creed to wonder if Robert Warren might have had something to hide after all. There was no reason to believe that the Rector was anything like his brother, or *any* of his villainous relatives, yet that oft-heard phrase of local renown did spring to mind: 'there's no such thing as a good Warren'.

Creed's own feelings were ones of dismay and a sensation of being invisible. His statement of fact, so relevant to what the presentments ultimately sought to accomplish, had been summarily disregarded, swept aside at best. The image of a fallen branch spinning away in a fast-flowing river was somehow conjured up in his mind and he found himself battling with familiar feelings of inferiority amidst what he suddenly remembered was the realm of the nobility and the local rich and powerful.

When compared with the bewigged and gowned majority across the bench, most of them decorated with one title or another, he was essentially a layman of little importance. On the merit of his standing in the community, his right to speak was tolerated, but brushed off regardless, and realising his sphere of influence was limited to the realm of the observer yet again, he found it convenient to have to concentrate on stenographic fidelities.

Without any clear gesture to cause it, and though silent beside him, Creed could sense the pity of his friend. Or perhaps, he realised, it was more that he himself was embarrassed by the idea that James would pity his being ignored. He was angered by the situation: angry at himself for not being able to achieve the confidence of the bench, and at them for being so miserly and fickle with it.

Yet Creed knew that he did have power, if only indirectly – the power to affect what had happened in that room and beyond it. His influence lay in the perception, and in the recording, but most of all, in his relating of the events within to those who were not present; and there were far more who would *read* about the event than were present in the room. In a strange way his power was even more significant than that of the bench. For there was truth, and there was the art of retelling it.

As he listened to men of considerable means deciding upon the fate of thousands of their fellow citizens, Creed could almost see the words seeping up and blotching into existence across the cotton paper of the *Examiner's* broadsheet, running off the printing press in black text as soon as they had been uttered. His hand scribbled viciously, pulling lines of speech out of the air and planting the seeds of sentences into the bed of his notebook, one cursive letter at a time, to be harvested later by a thousand readers and fed to the public mind:

> The secretary discharges throughout this appalling scene the part of the Greek chorus. The observer makes reflections, and occasionally suggests attention to points of form and matters of prudence; but, as in the Greek tragedies, is entirely disregarded by the principal actors.

Rev. H. Swanzy: There are 450 unemployed people. (Increased uproar.)

Mr Massy. H. Warren: My calculation of the unemployed in the parish of Macroom.

Mr J. E. McCarthy: 600 for six months, at 1s. a day, will be £5,000. Now, I'm satisfied that £4,000 be granted. (Yells.)

Mr R. Warren: And I second that. (Dreadful confusion, at least ten voices addressing the chair.)

Father Lee: It must be at least £5,000. I propose £5,000. (Tremendous shouting.)

Chairman: Does Mr Robert Warren second it? (Cries of 'To be sure.')

Mr R. Warren: Anything for a quiet life. (Great shouting.)

Rev. D. O'Kearney: What's the population?

Father Lee: 4,734 according to Pigot's map. (Uproar, confusion and the chair insisting to move on, that £5,000 was agreed to.)

Secretary: We'll now take up Ballyvourney. The poor-law valuation of this parish is £5,740.

Chairman: And the population 4,456.

Mr M. H. Warren: I propose you grant £3,000.

Mr McC. O'Leary: And I second it. (Yelling.)

Father Burton: You must grant £4,000 at least. (Tremendous shouting.)

Mr R. Warren: Oh, very well. Give it to them – give them anything. (Shouting.)

Chairman: Well, £4,000 is agreed to. (Great shouting.)

Mr McC. O'Leary: If you do that, you break your arrangement with Macroom. (Tumult.)

Mr J. E. McCarthy: There is industry and a healthy population in Macroom, far from what there is in the mountains. (Shouting.) I know Ballyvourney. I know the rude mountaineers. They would be honest if they had enough to eat; but God only knows what they may be when starving. (Loud shouting.)

Mr Fitzgerald: Take the opinion of the Relief Committee as to the wants of the parish. (Shouting.)

Counsellor Herrick: I think that £4,000 will be required.

Mr M. H. Warren: I move that £3,500 be granted. (Uproar.)

Father Lee: There is much more poverty and much more distress in the town of Macroom than in any other place. (Great confusion.) I call on you to reconsider Macroom. (Tremendous uproar.)

Chairman: Macroom is decided. (Cries of 'No'.)

Mr Welply: As the principle applied to Macroom has not been carried out you are bound to reconsider Macroom. (Shouting.)

Father Lee: l am ready to prove that last Thursday a man died of starvation in Macroom. (Awful uproar.)

Chairman: A poll is demanded as to whether we reconsider Macroom. (Great tumult.)

Mr M. H. Warren: I shall press my motion. (Groaning and yells.)

Mr Colthurst: It is all nonsense to press any matter here – see the confusion around you. Give it up, Massy – give it up. (Tremendous yelling.)

Chairman: We came here to serve the people, but we shall not be allowed to do so. I'm quite useless here, and shall, therefore, leave the chair. (Increased tumult.)

Mr R. Warren: Hear me – hear me for a moment. I shall now bring this scene to a close. There is but one course we can adopt, and that I propose, that the Presentments be passed en masse. (Great cheering.) The devil a thing else can be done here.

Mr Colthurst: I second that – it is the only course left us. (Great uproar.)

Mr R. Warren: Hear me – do hear me for a moment. (Great yelling). See what a scene you have here today – look around you. Is it not utterly impossible that we can go through these applications dispassionately – that we will be permitted to consider them calmly or quietly? For God's sake then pass my resolution, granting them all, whatever they may be, and leave them to our guardian angels – the Board of Works. (Great shouting.) I move that the applications pass en masse. Does anyone second me? (Shouts, 'We do.')

Mr McC. O'Leary: I second you with all my heart. (Tremendous shouts of 'All.')

Mr Welply: No! We must do our duty. And we must act now.

Mr R. Warren: If you carry that you may go home to your dinners – if you reject it prepare to stop here for a week. (Yells.)

Chairman: Who's for passing them all? (Tremendous shouts of 'All.')

Mr R. Warren: Mr Secretary, bundle them all up, and cut away as fast as you can. (Great uproar.)

The Chairman, Secretary, County Surveyor and Captain Gordon, it being half past four o'clock, here escaped from the court amidst great uproar.

23

A Mountain Is in Labour

*B**ang. Bang. Bang.*

Forcibly pulled from a realm of relative peace to one of confusion and disappointment, Creed mumbled to himself. 'What?'

Bang. Bang. Bang.

'Yes! Yes. I'm coming.' Shaking his head, he clicked his tongue in irritation and hurried to dress.

'Who could that be, Con?' Paulellen moaned.

'God knows. Don't they know the law has changed?'

Bang. Bang.

Feeling his way down the stairs, Creed tightened the belt of his dressing gown, shouting ahead of himself, 'It is now prohibited by law, as per the regulating act of September the fourteenth, for a pawnbroker to take any pledge before the hour of seven in the morning.'

Unsure of what hour it was exactly, but acting on the supposition that it was not yet that hour, he berated the mystery assailant as he crossed the shop floor to open the door.

BANG! BANG! BANG!

'What in the name of God?' Creed fumbled with the lock and yanked open the door in anger, only to be blinded by the October morning sun. Shielding his light-sensitive eyes with a hand over his brow he perceived a boy below him.

'What do you want, young man? Are you aware of the ungodly hour?'

'The baker, Mr Welply, sent me to bring you the early paper, sir …' The boy handed a folded copy of the *Cork Examiner* to Creed. 'He said there's an important article in it, one you have to read.'

'Oh! Right. Ah … Just a moment.' Creed stepped over to his counter and returned to hand a farthing coin to the boy, hoping to make amends for his impatience.

'Thank you, sir.' The little hand took the coin carefully and scurried away.

'What page?' Creed shouted after the boy. But looking out, blinking, he could only see the black soles of the child's feet vanishing into the distance. He closed the door, but, realising it was too dark to read inside, turned back to open the blinds and scan the print in the half-light that filtered in.

As usual there was almost nothing but advertisements on the front page, but having checked just in case, he immediately turned the periodical over. The rigid sheet resisted with a thunderous crumpling, until, got under control, he spotted the wide circle Sam had noosed around the relevant article.

'Jesus, Mary, and Joseph.' Creed took off his glasses, cleaned them on his nightshirt and returned them to the bridge of his nose. With the print magnified through the bifocals, his eyes focused earnestly on the report. To the sound of the stiff paper popping as it settled around his fingertips and the ticking of various clocks on the wall to the left of the counter, he drew his breath and held it in anticipation of what he thought the article would say; then, letting it out again, he began to whisper the words to himself:

QUASHING A PRESENTMENT SESSIONS

Mr Johnson, the Grand Jury Secretary, has received a reply from the Board of Works in answer to his letter conveying the result of the late Macroom Sessions, held under the Labour Rate Act.

The Presentments passed at those sessions, and sent up, have been annulled on the plea of informality.

'Dear God!' Creed gasped.

> It appears that in carrying the Presentments, the instructions contained in
> the circular of the secretary of the board were not complied with; they should
> be considered strictly with reference to the 9th and 10th Victoria …

Leaning on the counter, Creed read the words again in disbelief, his attention jumping erratically from one phrase to another, trying to process information with a mind and senses that but moments before had been in the depths of sleep. This news, dramatic and jarring as it was in its delivery, was as confusing as being ambushed by a pot of water. His mind was awake with the shock, but he couldn't see, or think clearly through, the meaning of it yet.

He tried again, reading more slowly, breaking it up in case he was missing something fundamental.

> … has received a reply … from the Board of Works.

He went back further:

> Mr Johnson, the Grand Jury Secretary, has received a reply … from the Board
> of Works.

Then skipping forward again he kept being drawn back to the same sentence at the crux of the text.

> The Presentments passed at those sessions have been annulled …

Annulled?

> Instructions contained in the circular were not complied with.

Damn! The knot in Creed's stomach tightened as he threw his head back, jaw still agape. *What instructions exactly?* He spoke his thoughts aloud to himself: 'It doesn't matter which. Hardly any instructions were complied with at all. I've been saying it all week! Everybody has been saying it.'

He charged up the stairs, talking to himself, resolved to tackle it all to right at the kitchen table. 'How could anyone have thought they'd let this go?'

In the week since the sessions had taken place, Creed had been monitoring the national press as well as some of the British papers. The latter had been bombastic in their criticism of Macroom's magistrates and cess-payers for the manner in which the sessions were conducted and for the scenes that resulted. Each publication, whether Irish or British, had peppered mocking descriptions of the proceedings with their own brand of scorn.

He pulled his chair in under himself, then covered his face, trying to regain his clarity of thought. *They're going to make an example of us. What in God's name are the poor masses of this district supposed to do now? Are they to be sacrificed? The ass sent into the wilderness after the high priest has symbolically laid the sins of the people upon it?*

Is this because of the gathering of the poor in the town weeks ago? A backward attempt at punishing the Grand Jury for putting the problem back on the government, when they passed everything at the sessions and left it all to the Board of Works to sort out? Maybe both?

Surely under the pressure of the crisis there have been other sessions conducted under high tensions and with controversial results. We cannot have been the only ones.

Does 'quashed' and 'annulled' mean the decision is final, and irreversible? Will they re-hold the sessions? Good God, will we have to go through that all again and wait for weeks more without any intervention on behalf of the poor godforsaken people? Surely either will mean hundreds of deaths, if not thousands!

Creed swung his glasses by one wiry arm as he tried to imagine what the future would look like in the weeks to come. What would his eyes see? He rubbed the length of his face, into the hollows of his eyes, where his fingers settled for a moment before sliding over his cheeks and down to his jawline. As his hands let go he released an exhausted breath and all at once his sense of hopelessness turned to anger.

This is abandonment! The suffering this decision wilfully permits ...

The thud of footsteps in the other room pulled him out of the trap of his mind and back into bodily awareness. Paulellen was up and about, probably wondering what had kept him so long. It was nigh on the hour they daily arose anyway by now.

'Who was that?' She appeared behind him and rested her chin on his shoulder to see what he was reading.

'Bad, bad news …'

'Oh, no?' she said and, spotting the headline, sucked a breath into a backwards gasp.

'Sam sent a boy over with the first delivery.'

'What does it mean?'

Creed shook his head from one side to the other.

'Is there anything we can do?'

'I don't even know where to …'

'Oh, dear. I'll make a cup of tea. Come on, get dressed, dear. You'll have people knocking soon.'

'I shall. I shall, you're right.' He found himself still staring at the page.

'Sam didn't send over a loaf of bread with the paper, did he?'

'What? He did not. Funny, that!' The talk of food snapped him out of the spell at last.

'You'd think that's the least he could do, sending over news like this …' Paulellen's voice faded off as she passed from the kitchen to the bedroom and the back room.

Creed went to the bedroom to retrieve his clothes, only to realise that he must have been in a world of his own and that she had already carried them from the bedroom and draped them over the chair for him.

'I was looking for those clothes,' he said as he wandered into the kitchen.

'I told you they were behind you. I think I'll go out and get some bread.'

'Are we out?' Creed asked.

'Well, there's not enough for the day.' Paull hesitated. 'Why do you suppose Samuel sent that article to you so urgently? What does he expect you can do about it?'

Creed contemplated the question without speaking and shook his head once again. 'I expect he just wanted to get the news out through some responsible channel. Maybe because I'm on the Relief Committee … It's hard to know. Maybe he wants me to let the committee, or the board, know. I mean, at this hour … you are right, it's pointless to contact anyone this early, even the Guardians.'

Back looking at the paper, Creed spoke to the topic before him and gestured to some imaginary figure in the room before noticing that Paulellen, his only real audience, was undressed and had begun to put on suitable clothes for the outdoors. He found himself momentarily confused and distracted by her still-beautiful figure.

'Oh,' she shivered. 'It's going to get cold again soon. God help those people out in all weathers.'

Although he was still struck by seeing the profile of her body through her shift, Creed's mind was in motion now. 'Exactly. I just can't understand how they can be so blatantly cruel … and wilfully ignorant of the consequences that will undoubtedly follow this decision. What do they expect the labourers to do under the circumstances? You cannot condemn the poor for taking the only natural option open to them in the mode of self-preservation – to gather, peacefully as they did, without any malicious intent, and appeal to those local officials whose duty it is to represent them. To be heard and noticed above all else! Are they supposed to just die quietly? And without seeking any assistance in the hour of their greatest want?

'And that assistance, I propose, from a government that is failing them at every step? Which would be the greater sin of the two. Ugh!' Creed threw up his hands. 'They have done nothing wrong. There is no actual law against assembling peacefully so far as I'm aware.'

Paulellen rubbed his shoulders. 'I'll be back in a few minutes. Do you need anything while I'm out?'

'I do not, thanks, dear.' He patted her hand as it slid off his shoulder.

'Right, so,' Paulellen said, crossing behind, leaving him to the paper, and his thoughts.

You could almost expect this from the government who are removed from the reality; they don't see what's happening down on the ground. And they also have the entire population of the poor to deal with. But as for the so-called high-up members of the community here, entrusted with the responsibility of looking after the interests of the poor on their own doorstep: some of them couldn't care a fig if the poor all perished and silently disappeared.

It was clear to him that for some of the cess-payers and proprietors of the district, their only interest in being on any board or committee representing the destitute was to limit the extent of the taxation on their own estates, and even to be paid a salary while doing so. Massy H. Warren, who made no attempt to conceal his disposition – no matter who was present when he exposed it – was more driven by self-interest than anyone. The added status of his being a Justice of the Peace gave him a mistaken sense of having licence to do as he pleased. To Massy, Creed thought, this whole crisis was nothing more than an inconvenience. And now with his beloved silver cup gone and the races at large having been postponed, he was aggrieved beyond belief and hell-bent on taking out his frustration on anyone who tried his patience. That it would have been grossly disrespectful to go ahead with such a prize as forty-one pounds in plain sight of a people starving was obvious to everyone else but him.

Just over one week ago – the day prior to the presentment sessions – a meeting of the race subscribers had taken place at Williams Hotel, where Massy had publicly lampooned one of the race stewards, John Hawkes, for standing up and saying he refused to take part in the race on the moral grounds that 'it just would not feel right ... in the middle of a national calamity'.

Having considered Hawkes's stance, the cup subscribers had voted almost unanimously to join with him and had postponed the plate race until the following November.

Even now Creed had a bitter taste in his mouth from witnessing Massy's subsequent vociferous attack on John Hawkes. Witnessing Hawkes's embarrassment had been as disgusting and as grievous a scene as anything Creed could remember. And to think that Hawkes was Massy's own father-in-law!

As the meeting had come to a close, somebody had applauded John Hawkes for his honourable stand and most of the room signalled their agreement with a simple 'Hear, hear.'

But Massy Warren had evidently been feeling a weight of indignation accumulating on his back, and this was the final straw. His subsequent outburst brought the room to a standstill.

'What utter nonsense! What do you think this will achieve? Do you think this man, a lowly steward, a butler for want of a better word, do you think his "refusal" to uphold his position will make any ounce of difference to those paupers out there? You are as pathetic an imbecile as he is who listens to him. You flatter yourselves.

'Tell me, John Hawkes – do you really believe that by not allowing a few horses to run across a meadow, the poor people of this barony will be saved? Do you? It will change nothing. All you will have achieved when you see how *pointless* it is,' Massy shouted as he packed his belongings, 'is the knowing that you have deprived an innocent few of a harmless distraction from the constant misery they bring upon us. And worse still, that they will have starved and died *anyway*, and your stopping the race won't have done a single thing to change that. You sanctimonious fool! Good morning, gentlemen.'

The remaining subscribers had been left speechless at what they subsequently agreed was a shameful response to such a noble gesture. The steward, alas, had been a vision of humiliation.

'Mr Hawkes … John.' Creed had caught the small, inoffensive man on the way out. 'Massy Hutchinson Warren is right on one count – stopping the races will not save the poor of our district. So treacherous is to be the season ahead that nothing save the intervention of Providence can do that now in the vast majority of cases. Even if the presentment sessions prove effectual, they can only hope to attenuate the suffering somewhat. But with the exception of the obvious party, every other person in that room shared your view, and commended you for it. Your motives, and the principle … the showing of *some* solidarity with the poor; should it even be found that all other efforts come to naught, that is still what will have mattered, sir. The gesture was a noble one. You have my admiration.'

'Thank you, Mr Creed.'

'The entire meet was postponed by a year! And it was unanimous! That is proof it was the right thing to do.'

'That's very kind of you, Mr Creed. It gladdens my heart no small amount, and brings me some stillness of mind.' Hawkes was clearly still shaking.

'And it *will* make a difference, John. In fact, it already has.'

'I hope you're right.'

'Go home now, and sit yourself beside a warm cup of tea. Do you hear?' Creed had told Hawkes, gripping his shoulder, and smiling kindly upon him.

That the reputation of the one dissenting exception was that of an uncharitable, self-serving narcissist had not needed to be communicated, and, after all, Creed had to be careful not to say anything that might come back on him later. Family politics were a dangerous area to meddle in, but so was anything that had to do with Massy Warren.

Afterwards, Creed, as his self-imposed duty dictated, had written the incident up and sent it to the *Examiner*, not alone for the satisfaction he felt in exposing Massy Warren, but because Hawkes's actions were the kind that would set an example. *The power of a single good deed is potentially boundless* – Creed knew this to be a singular truth. His own standing on the side of right was the least he could do, both in his role as a correspondent and as a race subscriber himself.

He told himself it wasn't revenge for the *soirée* affair, and it wasn't. He was just doing his job. There was no proof at all that Massy Warren had been the one to attempt Creed's public assassination, though his suspicions still led him to believe it was almost certainly so. He was sure everyone else suspected it too.

Creed was well aware that Paulellen worried that her husband was becoming obsessed and consumed by the growing rivalry between himself and Massy. She told him as much and frequently.

'You need to just ignore that man, Cornelius. He seems to know how to goad you like no one else. You shouldn't indulge him. That only provokes the bully,' she had said, and not without some wisdom, he had to admit. But she had not seen his poisonous character at work, nor his behaviour at the meetings where his own self-interest was always put before any other consideration.

'There you are – you haven't moved.'

Creed's reverie was broken by the return of his wife. 'Oh. You're back.'

'Do you want a hot sup?' she asked, feeling the pot, and evidently sensing it was warm enough poured some into his cup without waiting for an answer. 'I'll make some oatmeal, and toast.'

Paulellen was a soft-hearted soul who was always mothering him, and through the extra tension of the unravelling crisis even more so. He wasn't affected more than anybody else, certainly. The situation was weighing heavily on everybody in one way or another. It was inescapable. But in a selfish way that comforted him, he knew he was the focus of her care. She responded to his needs in a way that told Creed she could daily see how much it all was pressing on him. And although his own worries were trifling when compared with those of his customers, and those on whose behalf he endeavoured at the Relief Committee, he found it gratifying to know that someone else noticed.

'Well? Any revelations? Or what's to be done?'

'A mountain is in labour and it has brought forth a mouse,' he muttered.

'What, dear?'

'I mean … the scale of the impending famine, and how little the

204

government response. But in answer to your question, the secretary and the Grand Jury will have to study the circular, weigh it against what took place, and see what can be salvaged from it. Or decide if the sessions will have to be held again, but I doubt anyone will want to risk another fiasco – the government included.

'It's not much to go on, really, but listen to this: "It appears that the instructions contained in the circular were not complied with", and later the article says "they should be considered strictly with reference to the ninth and tenth Victoria". This refers to laws made in the ninth and ten years of Victoria's reign, this year and last. So there is possibly a grain of hope, however meagre, and miserly, that something can be saved through formality.'

It wasn't as though he could do anything directly about the quashing of the presentments himself, and in the meantime it still spelt disaster for the wretched flocks of people awaiting delivery from the jaws of starvation, but where there was a hope that *anything* could be done, it had to be grasped.

Creed, suddenly alert, active and purposeful, began to put on his shoes.

'What are you going to do?'

'I don't know yet, dear. To begin with, I suppose word must somehow be got out to the poor to save them from panic and from doing more harm to their plight by disturbing the peace. This …' he banged on the circled passage with a finger, 'this is only bound to cause alarm, and stress in the extreme.'

*

Creed spent the rest of the daylight hours visiting friends and associates, members of the Relief Committee and the Repeal Association, discussing the finer details of what the annulment meant, and generally preaching the word that they had to keep the people from gathering at all costs.

He visited Father Thomas Lee, Daniel Lucy, Pat O'Riordan, Matthias Ryan, Sam and James Welply, even Val McSwiney. That evening, having been encouraged to do so by Lee, he undertook to be of service once more where he felt he was of most use to the community, and set himself writing a piece to the *Examiner* appealing on behalf of the inhabitants of Macroom. But it would not be to the government directly, and not to the Lord Lieutenant. If it was to them alone, they would pay no heed at all. Nor could it be just another letter to the editor, were it even attributed to a member of a Relief Committee. Ashe, as chairman of the Committee, had publicly written to Labouchere only weeks before, and while the letter was acknowledged, and the Lord Lieutenant's response published repeatedly in various editorials, it had been officially just that, an acknowledgement for the sake of appearances. Nor would Creed address the poor alone, whose word travelled faster from person to person.

Instead, he wrote to all three together.

The official all-seeing eye of the government, he was sure, would take more notice of being publicly addressed in the sight of all. The alarm of the poor had to be prevented from catching hold at all costs, and yet the potential threat of the same might delicately be used to attract the attention of the powers that be nonetheless. The news of someone appealing on behalf of the poor would in itself be a message to them and would travel among them. And beyond its obvious functionality, being controversial and engaging enough to its readership, the editor – Maguire himself – would appreciate the tripartite approach.

The difficulty lay in finding language that steered a course between further exciting the fears of the public and the need to impress upon the government the desperate realities of what lay ahead if the sessions could not be recovered.

Into the small hours, Creed sat advancing the letter by candlelight and on Thursday morning, with the benefit of a proper night's sleep, he re-examined the piece. Satisfied that he had polished it sufficiently, he sent it on the mail car in hopes that it would make Friday's publication.

The following afternoon, however, he found himself disappointed to discover that his letter was merely acknowledged via a note in the columns of the *Examiner*, to the effect that

'C.C.' (Macroom) – too late for this post. Our Dungarvan correspondent shall be attended to.

But on Monday, to his belated satisfaction, the full article appeared.

THE EDITOR OF THE CORK EXAMINER.

Macroom, 22 Oct. 1846.

Dear Sir – the unwelcome intelligence communicated to the starving people of this district, by the *Examiner* of yesterday, under the heading of 'Quashing of the Presentment Sessions at Macroom', created the most fearful alarm amongst the labouring classes, and distrust in any effectual government relief this awful season.

The suffering population of this town and its environs had set great example to the world, by their patient endurance, for a very considerable time, until driven to despair by the total absence of the intervention of the Legislature, in averting the frightful and impending national calamity; day after day they had contemplated meeting solely for the purpose of exhibiting their numbers, in the hope that the local Relief Committee, and other gentlemen, would draw the immediate attention of the Government to their most deplorable condition. This at length, they resolved to accomplish, and after they had assembled, in large but peaceable numbers, in the town, returned to their respective homes, quite satisfied with the promise of the Roman Catholic priest, Rev. Fr Thomas Lee, of Macroom, and other gentlemen, that ere the lapse of many days, they would get plenty of food and employment.

It is unnecessary to remark what time elapsed between the application to his Excellency, for the calling of those sessions, and the issuing of the proclamation; but I believe everyone is aware that the intervening period was unusually long, as if to try the forbearance and mock the more than unprecedentedly severe privations of the eagerly expectant labourers of this proverbially tranquil country. But the time at last arrived that was to put an end to their long and silently borne hardships; but alas! the moral certainty that they entertained of immediate succour has now but tended to augment that cloud of opacity, which had already encircled their hearts. I am no alarmist, but I much fear this town is doomed to internal convulsions ere long, unless the most prompt measures be adopted to render some practical assistance to the famishing and emaciated inhabitants who have been, and now or ever are decreed to look directly into the face of starvation and its concomitant horrors.

C. C.

24

IMPROVEMENT OF THE BRIDGE

W ith the exception of two consecutive days late in the month, when a stubbornly painful hip had caused him to turn back during the attempt, for the previous twenty-four days Pádraig had walked in and out to Macroom Union, barefoot and exhausted with Diarmuidín on his shoulders, covering thirteen miles a day – each time for the life-sustaining privilege of a single pint of oatmeal stirabout. On Wednesday 28 October, for a different reason, he left Diarmuidín at home and made the walk alone. That morning he walked half a mile further than usual, and, passing the turn-off for the workhouse, became one of many labourers to converge at the foot of the town, where, rumour had it, improvements to the west side of the bridge had been scheduled, to provide emergency employment for the famishing poor of the district.

Like Pádraig, many of the hundreds who'd turned up had left their homes much earlier that morning to try their luck at being one of the eighty men it had been announced would be employed at nine pence a day. Others among the crowd, also like him, had heard of the plan as recently as the day before at the yard of the union, while behind the circulation of the news there was talk that some had already secured their place, having somehow got their names onto the official Relief Committee lists in advance, be it by straight or crooked means. But the entire enterprise having been rubber-stamped at the eleventh hour, Pádraig hoped there would still be a number of places to compete for.

He had arrived with time to spare and stood observing the crowd growing larger as they waited for the officials to arrive. From a distance, as Pádraig had approached, each of the paupers had appeared to be uniformly dressed from the shin to the head in short trousers, waistcoat, over-jacket and hat, and all in shades of black, brown and grey. At closer range he'd realised there were many other random swatches and flecks of colour amongst the gathering. Each outfit was, in fact, a one-off arrangement of tattered patches and holes and it was easy to guess that – just as was his own habit – many of the wearers likely slept and lived in their clothes day and night. The fact was so apparent in some cases here that it was hard for him to imagine how the clothes could be reassembled if they had to be taken off. As for shoes, most of the other men had none either.

The other oddity was the prevalence of a large number of military jackets and coats among the labourers. For the most part at least, Pádraig knew this was not a clue to their past occupation, but merely a consequence of what was practical, warm and often available from the pawnshops.

As he stood comparing his own ragged clothes with those of the men around him, wondering how he himself appeared in the eyes of his equals, someone up the front at last took charge and spoke to the crowd. The selection process was beginning. Pádraig tried to push his way forward through the confusion as a flurry of names were being called out by more than one voice, some of them barely audible.

Men around him jumped and shouted in response, sending ripples through the huddle when they heard their names, or thought they'd heard them: erring on the side of bursting forward, even when unsure, lest they might miss their place.

'Ned Brien Swiney!' someone called.

'That's me.' A man near Pádraig jumped forward.

It was hard to see what was happening at the centre, but the system of choosing who was to be given work did not seem an entirely mysterious affair. Numerous overseers and Relief Committee members were handling the process. The larger men and louder candidates appeared to be the popular choice. But with all those in charge operating simultaneously in this task, at the same time that the lists were being checked off, it was hard to know who to approach, or how. Pádraig – appreciating that he was thinner than his usual self – was on average, he estimated, as strong a man as most on display and among the more youthful of them. But pushing himself forward to be heard was not his nature, and finding himself in the middle of a mêlée being conducted in a foreign tongue did not inspire him to immediate action. Then as quickly as it had started, it was over. The crowd were told to disperse and the group picked were being herded in the opposite direction.

The bulk of those rejected set out for their homes, some near and some many miles distant, he supposed, without so much as a morsel for their trouble. Pádraig lingered, waiting a while, desperately hoping that one of the men chosen would drop out, or that some small quirk of chance would fall in his favour. There were others around him who, also lingering, seemed simply unable to face returning home so soon, empty-handed. One man repeatedly asked for 'the lend of a shovel or a spade'. His pleas fell on deaf ears.

It was a strange representation of the reality of things, that in the midst of a shortage on an unprecedented scale, among a gathering of hundreds of men competing for the handful of jobs that might make the difference between their families surviving the winter and not, many had not appeared to be over-zealous or competitive in the act of vying for a position. The fact that they had shown up was proof that they were not idle by intention, but, as Pádraig had witnessed elsewhere, resignation and indifference had lately come to characterise the expression of many of those who had been struggling for such a protracted period.

Regardless of age or strength in reserve, that they all held relatively equal shares in destitution was plainly obvious to Pádraig, himself included. But the difference – he warned himself to remember – was that between those who pushed and those who hesitated, was a line that might divide those who would fare better from those who would fall behind.

Pádraig softened any disappointment he had in himself with the fact that he was lucky enough to be still in possession of a ticket for outdoor relief. Save that there would be one small portion of sustenance less at home now – with Diarmuidín getting his feed from the reserves of the oatmeal Muintir Laoghaire had kindly given them, as opposed to receiving it at the yard – for Pádraig, the thirteen-mile round trip was not yet a total loss this day. Giving up at last, even as a few others waited on in hope, Pádraig walked off in the direction of the Union Workhouse not far away. On the way home he weighed up in his mind whether or not it had been the right decision to have tried his luck at the bridge. But he'd have had to come this far for the relief anyway, he decided. At worst he had a lighter walk home for one day, and had gained an insight into the process. As he walked, Pádraig wondered how he might get his name onto one of those lists.

25

An Outdoor Pauper

I t being a Saturday, Onóra once again found herself enjoying the weekly break she had come to look forward to: that of being taken out of the women's dormitory to service the boardroom in advance of the Poor Law Guardians' meeting. Though relieved that she never actually encountered the Guardians themselves in performing this task, she still had the domineering ways of Martha Horgan, the matron, to endure, who treated her and the other pauper servants as though they were brutish animals with no intelligence.

On her knees, Onóra rubbed the tart, earthy-smelling paraffin wax in circles onto the already immaculate surface of the wooden floor that ran in wondrous, conflicting patterns, like arrowheads flowing against each other on the flat plane of a wooden river, each rectangular block showing off its unique grain of golden threads, glowing in the light, and reflecting through the polish. It was a refreshing change from the putrid smells and cold bare boards of the crowded women's dorm and Onóra flared her nostrils, drinking in as much scent as she could absorb for another week.

'When you're done with that, carry that bucket of cold ashes down the stairs and spread them in the garden,' Matron barked at her and went on pushing in the chairs around the giant table.

'Yes, Miss.'

'If the gardener isn't there to supervise you, be sure not to dump them all in one place on top of something.'

'No, Miss.'

'Then go down to the store. Refill that one with coal, and this one with timber,' Matron said, pointing.

'I will, Miss.'

'You know where the store is, don't you, girl? Beside the infirmary. Ask the gardener, or any of the staff if you're lost. Now away with you. Go on.'

'Thank you, Miss.'

Getting up, on the pretence of needing something to lean on, Onóra rested her hand upon the surface of the table, intent on stealing just one drag of her fingers through the soft green pile – a sensation she had come to look forward to so much each week.

'D ... D ...' Matron struggled to utter a word – rising on her heels, her eyes almost popping out of her head, she yanked Onóra's hand away as if she might be about to set the table alight. '*Don't* get any of that polish on the baize!' she shouted, dusting off the table with numerous slaps of the cloth in her hand.

'Sorry, Miss.' Onóra recoiled and, cowering, scurried away around the table towards the fireplace, as Matron bent down to the level of the surface, checking the baize for any grease. Carrying her life in her mouth in fear of another scolding, Onóra, going to her task, turned her head to glimpse the door she would escape through and perceived another pauper woman who had arrived carrying a tray bearing cups and a large jug of water. The woman, older than Onóra, was dressed in a white calico cap and wore a long blue linsey-woolsey frock over a flannel petticoat. It was one of the paupers from the older women's dorm and the fact that she was wearing a workhouse uniform, which the house had run out of before Onóra had come in, spoke to the fact that she'd been here a while.

'Just over there,' Matron directed the woman. 'In the centre. No. Just ... yes. That'll do. And where's the other jug?'

'Coming, Miss,' the older woman said, trying not to spill a drop as she lowered the tray carefully onto the table.

'Hurry up. They'll be upon us soon. You too, Miss Waters.'

Onóra, who'd been waiting for the woman to clear the exit, now picked up the heavy wooden buckets and struggled away under the weight.

'Yes, Miss,' Onóra answered at exactly the same time as the other woman and for a moment they shared a glance. Passing behind the woman as she left, Onóra spied the two large letters, 'M.U.', embroidered into the back of the woman's frock. Understanding that they stood for Macroom Union – emphasising that the clothes were the property of the house – Onóra felt a strange sadness, and wondered at the comparative lack of value the union seemed to place upon the inmates themselves, the old woman and her too.

Downstairs, passing through the yard, feeling more like she was carrying a bucket of stone to the garden than a light bucket of ashes, Onóra spotted the man known to the inmates as O'Brien, the Master. O'Brien was notorious for his heavy-handedness and though Onóra herself had never had any interactions with him, she thought him every bit as formidable an old turnkey as the paupers had described him.

Dressed in a military outfit as he stood now at the centre of the yard and wanting only a cocked hat to make him look as ferocious as he clearly wanted to seem, he was a man, Onóra sensed, who saw himself as the centre of the world. Hugging the walls as she went along, seeking to make herself invisible, she wondered if O'Brien knew he had the nickname 'lantern jaw' amongst the inmates, earned for his habit of extruding the under-bitten rake almost at random. The empty bucket felt as heavy as the full one, Onóra thought. But with the benefit of the regular meals, she definitely felt stronger now than when she'd come in.

*

O'Brien was supervising the dishing up of a meal that he alone in the yard knew to be one of the last servings of outdoor relief they would administer at M.U. for the foreseeable future. Just the day before, Mr Ashe had confided in O'Brien that he believed relief would be terminated as a matter of formality. Ashe, as a member of the board, was, in theory, superior to O'Brien, but in fact O'Brien considered himself more than Ashe's equal. He was, of course, answerable to the board, but having been let off more than once when charged with using excessive force – at one time for 'whipping one of the pauper children severely' – among numerous other infractions, O'Brien was confident he had the board for his puppet, there merely to prop him up, as the necessary gears of a machine that, ultimately, he was operating.

It was a standard procedure of the workhouse to have ex-military men serve in the position of Master – men accustomed to enforcing discipline and daily routines, just as he was: the barb at the end of the whip. O'Brien knew what was expected of him and took pride in his role. As usual, that morning he had dressed to intimidate. But despite the many tasks of his gruelling routine, for the special occasion of this particular date he had expended yet a little more effort.

Today, he wished to make a special impression. For the paupers? Never. For his staff? Heavens, no. For the visiting board members? Most certainly. As he stood upon the spot, O'Brien expected the Guardians – mostly plain-looking, unremarkable businessmen – to begin arriving through the side gates of the yard at any moment in ones and twos, as per their usual custom of avoiding the front entrance, where they might be plagued by paupers seeking admission and access to relief.

His timing was perfect and as soon as the first of the Guardians appeared, O'Brien moved across the yard to take up a conspicuous position, from where he feigned surprise at the fortuitous location and timing.

'Ah! Good morning, gentlemen.'

As John Pearson and Francis Woodley turned to him, O'Brien bowed slightly, making an effort to smile as he did so with hands clasped deferentially behind his back.

'Mr O'Brien.'

The two returned the greeting but carried on towards the main building, through which they would gain access to the entrance building from the back.

'Miserable lackeys,' muttered O'Brien under his breath, and he turned to look for the next, as through the gate came a portly, stunted-looking figure who passed at a quick pace with a huge folder of papers under his arm.

'Ah, Mr Burdon.'

The rubicund clerk appeared almost startled by the address, but carried on like a locomotive that did not want to slow. Amused, O'Brien knew that Burdon, eager as ever to get to the boardroom, was not one for social interaction, especially when in the course of his duties. The clerk to the board existed in a state of absorption, buried in the inner sanctum of his meticulous paperwork.

One at a time, over the space of seventeen minutes, fifteen gentlemen passed through the gate making the short cut across the corner of the yard to attend the weekly meeting of the Guardians, whereupon, the last of them having arrived in, the door was shut and their business conducted under closed session.

Fifteen seemed something of a paltry turnout by their usual standards.

O'Brien was mildly disgusted and cracked the bones in his neck before thrusting out his jaw and starting back towards the building himself. At two minutes after ten, it was past time for him to visit the sleeping wards of the male paupers and see that all had been cleared out, ventilated and duly cleansed. None of the Guardians had paid him much attention or even slightly acknowledged the formality of the singular occasion, but he had not given up just yet. He had lingered longer than he should have, to the detriment of his own time-keeping, but there would be another chance to catch them on their way out later.

*

Almost two hours on, at ten before the head of noon, having disposed of certain duties, O'Brien returned to the yard and found the relief lines in full swing. With bodies belching, and hungry paupers gulping down the liquid faster than their mouths could stop to taste it, the yard was awash with outdoor paupers desperate for their manna, or drunk on a full stomach of it.

Having arrived late, the queue Pádraig and Diarmuidín were in seemed to be moving at the pace of a snail and inwardly Pádraig vowed never to find himself at the far end of the proceedings again.

He had never seen so many in the lines, or so much activity in the yard, with many hundreds already fed and lying on the ground enduring their obligatory three-hour post-meal detention. But while it could certainly fit more people, Pádraig had learned from talk overheard in the yard that the buildings themselves were, for the first time, nearing full. *And winter has not even arrived,* he thought. Though he could not bring himself to even consider committing his own family to the workhouse, he realised that for any family who *were* in such a position, as of this day the option was no longer open to them. Pondering the fate of such families, he shuffled and inched forward one foot at a time to the ever-present sounds of sloppage, receptacles colliding and dunking ladles until, with the scent of the meal growing ever more intense, Diarmuidín on his shoulders became agitated, and Pádraig was feeling his bowels churning and rumbling ever louder in anticipation.

Nearing the top of the queue, Pádraig became aware of a commotion, when, about ten places behind, an old man suddenly collapsed. Some of those nearest the man attempted to help, but evidently concerned by the prospect of losing their places – as Pádraig was – their responses were limited to meek noises of alarm. But a break in the order of the queue and some heads spinning about in confusion were enough to send ripples through the line with the indication that something was wrong, and within moments the entire yard – up until now bustling with the industry of relief – had stopped to follow the groans of the man, whose struggle to regain his breath echoed off the huge walls.

'Somebody help him!' an old woman cried out.

'SILENCE!' A broken shriek rent the air. Its owner, the Master, bellowing, sounded as though he had torn his throat asunder. Pádraig felt his hair stand on end and saw that the shout had almost frightened the life out of many of the paupers around him.

'Take him out!' the Master shouted. It was as if he were more concerned with not having a hair out of place in his yard than with the health of the sick old man, as two of the workhouse staff scurried into position, trying to gather him up.

'Where will we take him?' one asked.

'OUT! OUT! OUT!' the Master shouted, an outstretched arm and whip extended, punctuating each word for full effect.

The two men half carried and half dragged the unfortunate creature away, still gasping, and likely about to expire, Pádraig thought. But whether he would be taken to the infirmary or dumped in the street was a mystery.

'Back to it!'

With a blind nod of his head – the whip returned to its latent position behind him – the Master ushered the staff behind the serving tables to resume, causing them to jump into action again with renewed vigour, the pace considerably stiffened.

Pádraig, with Diarmuidín above him, reasoned that he could have done nothing to help the man who collapsed, but felt guilty at realising he had been as disinclined as everyone else to leave the queue, and recognised that his behaviour was increasingly driven by hunger, apathy and exhaustion. Holding the can he had picked up at another table before him, he was at any moment expecting its weight to change with the dull, muted ring of a large dollop of oatmeal when, out of the corner of his eye, he noticed a young woman walking from the direction of the sheds in the far corner of the yard. It was the way she was struggling under a burden that caught his attention. With a loaded bucket in each hand she was hugging the wall and walking towards the main building behind him, when the Matron made to cut her off.

Pádraig was much too far away to hear what passed in hushed tones between them but it was clear that she was being admonished when the Matron pulled one of the buckets from her and, changing the woman's course, marched her across the yard by the arm, bringing them within earshot.

'Where were you all this time?'

'I told them I had to report back, miss, but they said they needed help with the servants in the infirmary … they ordered me.'

The path of the two women had them on course to pass behind the serving tables just up ahead of him when, appearing and reappearing between the bodies of the servers and the master, Pádraig – conscious that he was reaching the head of the queue – caught a brief sight of the younger woman's face. It was only a half-moment's glimpse, but it was enough, and he knew it was her. Onóra! Cáit's sister!

At that exact moment, the weight of the can shifted suddenly in his hand, so that he almost lost his grip on it. Pádraig's mouth swung half open, ready to shout, as the server plunged a half ration into the second can, for Diarmuidín, and he felt the same shift in his other hand.

His instinct was to call out to her, but he knew better and somehow stopped himself. Given what had occurred only moments before, any utterance would surely have come to disaster. Onóra was already in trouble with the Matron. The Master of the workhouse was bearing down on the slightest crack in the skin of apparent order, and if Pádraig had shouted to her as he wanted to, all hell would likely have broken loose. Who knows what kind of trouble he'd be getting her into? He himself would almost certainly be ejected from the yard too, making a whole day's journey pointless.

'Move on,' the server grunted. *Oh, Onóra! What are you doing here?*

'Move on,' the server grunted again. Pádraig, preoccupied, only faintly noticed the woman tapping her ladle on the side of his can, until suddenly she made a sharp chop at his arm with the instrument. The smart to the bone of his wrist brought Pádraig quickly to his senses, and he met the server's fearful expression just in time to notice the Master glaring at him. Pádraig turned away as fast as he could with the weight above him, trying not to spill the contents of the can. In the flurry of thoughts storming his brain, he struggled to conceive a way of finding Onóra again. How had she ended up here? Was she an outdoor pauper too? Or an inmate? It had looked as though she was being brought inside. Would she be here later, tomorrow, another day? And how had he missed her before now? He'd been in the yard almost every day for a month. Had she been here all along, under his nose? Stepping away, he turned back in hopes of sighting her again, but among the shifting bodies moving at random it was hard to see anything, and when they cleared, she was gone. What did this mean for Cáit's family? How was he going to tell her?

Suddenly aware of the child's restlessness at the sight of the food, the sensations of hunger rushed back to the fore and, raising the first can to his mouth, Pádraig guzzled down the lion's share of the contents. When only about a quarter of the tin was left, he handed it up to Diarmuidín and started on the half measure. Diarmuidín plunged his little arm in, scooping out what remained stuck to the bottom. He reached in repeatedly, painting the substance onto his tongue as Pádraig concentrated on catching any drops that went awry, then burped and handed up the remains of the half ration for the same purpose. A few moments later, having ensured that Diarmuidín had cleaned out every last finger of liquid, Pádraig approached the table to give back the vessels, but stopped again.

Onóra hadn't seen them. But maybe it was just as well. Who knew how she might have reacted?

'Cans?' someone barked at Pádraig, still adrift.

'Cans!' The collector banged two empties together, gathering his attention.

'Huh?'

'Return your empties,' the collector shouted as an old man nearby looked to Pádraig and then at the tin in his hand. But as the pauper pointed to the table as if to say *I'd return those if I were you*, from his left Pádraig intuited the imposing figure of the Master suddenly lurching towards him, apparently moving with some purpose. Restricted, with Diarmuidín on his shoulders, Pádraig braced himself, as, looming nearer, the shadow seemed to sprout wings from behind its back. Trying to balance the weight as he pulled away, Pádraig dropped the can in his left hand. The tin clanged and bounced off the cobbled yard and the imposing footsteps grew imminently louder until, blinded by Diarmuidín's leg, Pádraig felt a glancing impact and the dense wool of the man's jacketed shoulder against his. It felt like the Master had deliberately collected him on his way past, but Pádraig was relieved to realise that he was apparently not the intended target after all, and bending low to gather up the noisy can rolling on the ground before him, he heard the aggressor speak behind him.

'Mr Nettles,' said the Master in a calmer voice, altogether different from the one he had used to address the suffering recipients of relief not long before.

The cans returned, Pádraig moved to join the resting paupers along the wall for the mandatory time remaining. A trickle of well-dressed men was beginning to emerge from the building beyond and clearly had the Master's attention. A diminutive gentleman he was talking to was wearing a pair of enormously large-heeled shoes that – judging by the Master's expression – he'd have been happy to lick clean, for whatever it was he wanted out of the man.

*

'A bit on the short side today, Mr Nettles?' O'Brien smiled at the lead Guardian.

'Excuse me?' came a rather curt reply, causing O'Brien to realise he had perhaps chosen an unfortunate arrangement of words.

'The meeting, Mr Nettles.' he added hastily.

'Indeed, Mr O'Brien.'

As the others emerged, O'Brien began to count off the Guardians, but lost hope with each one that any of them had noticed the significance of the date, least of all Edward Ashe, who declared that he was in a hurry and did not even slow down to indulge him.

One and two at a time, they brushed him off and passed through the gate until Daniel Lucy, a middle-aged man of annoyingly fresh complexion and green eyes, was the last to leave. Lucy but barely acknowledged him at all, and that was it – O'Brien had had enough. Fully vexed, he stormed off in an apoplectic huff.

'Fourth full year of service to the day, and not a solitary note of congratulations or thanks from a single one of them – ingrates, the lot of them!' he grumbled to himself as he turned on his heels.

Passing out the gates and wondering on the strange behaviour of the Master, Daniel Lucy was unsurprised to notice that at half past noon there were still a thick stream of paupers arriving to join the queues. Turning left down the sop road toward the bridge he was particularly struck by the fragility of a woman being supported by her three children as she walked. She did not look old enough to be as feeble as she was, and Lucy was fully sure that without support she could not have stayed on her feet. Out of something of a caring curiosity he passed deliberately close and sadly confirmed what his eyes had told him, but more: he now doubted she would even get as far as the queue. An emptiness filled her gaze and Lucy shuddered at the almost ghostly remnant of someone who had surely been an able mother to her children not too long before. *What is to become of these people*, he asked himself, shaking his head sorely, *when the board's decision is effected?*

*

The Guardians having all vacated the boardroom around him, Creed finished up his notes and retrieved his hat from the long rail. He looked around the empty room, disheartened at what he had just seen enacted before him.

No sooner than could be heard the ring of the pawnbroker's heel on the last stone stair, Matron, with a small cluster of pauper servants behind her, once again hurried into the boardroom and began issuing orders to prepare the room in reverse. Not willing to see the heat of the coal go to waste, she began by ordering one of the women to shift the burning embers into the fireplace of Mr Burdon's adjoining office. He was in there already, and would be working for most of the rest of the day.

'Nelly!'

'Yes, miss?'

'Gather up those coals and transfer them into the clerk's room.'

'Onóra! Put the jug and all those cups onto the tray, and get them back to the kitchen.'

'Yes, miss.'

'And don't go missing this time, or I'll take the whip to you, girl.'

'No, miss.'

By now making his way through the outside corridor that ran between the boys' and girls' yards, over the wall to his right Creed could hear the ringing and splitting of the rocks where, temporarily relocated to accommodate the outdoor paupers in the male yard, he pictured the mix of full-time male paupers in with the boys, sitting on the ground in their hundreds, breaking stones; the thankless price of their daily keep. The slam of a door at the other end of the next hallway he entered coincided with the Master returning from the kitchen to his apartment carrying a bowlful of what Creed presumed to be O'Brien's own allowance of the gruel he'd been supervising the distribution of, to eat within the privacy of his own quarters.

Passing O'Brien's door as it closed with a bang, Creed continued inside the main building until, exiting at the other end, he stepped into the male yard again. This was the long way out. Ideally, he thought, one would have simply walked down the stairs and out the front door. But by the same reasoning – that they might be obtruded upon by the more desperate paupers queuing out the front – the Guardians and gentlemen involved with the business of the board were encouraged to leave through the rear, where the paupers in receipt of relief would be more docile and less bothersome.

Passing the effluent privies in the corner of the yard, although he resented having to endure the inconvenience of the extension to his journey, Creed realised that he welcomed the opportunity to witness the actual 'state of the house' for himself. It was to the benefit of his writings and ultimately those for whom he wrote that he should perceive these things, and in some strange way, it was a privilege.

Nevertheless, relieved to be escaping the oppressive air that pervaded the buildings, heavy with the malodorous nox of the cesspools and drains that were struggling to function under the weight of the growing population, he crossed the remainder of the yard with the book beneath his arm, avoiding lines and sidestepping paupers until, approaching the gate, he stopped to observe one, and to consider what the outdoor relief had in fact been supporting. Below his gaze, half propped up against the wall with a tattered cap over his face, lay a sleeping pauper with a small child comatose upon his chest. The dishevelled creatures looked as though they'd been dragged into the yard. It was with pity that he considered them – the rawness of the father's calloused, cut and filthy feet; the tattered patchwork of materials arranged to make the clothes on both; the unkempt and dull, roughly shorn clumps of hair; and the grazed, careworn and scarred, bone-protruded joints of underweight limbs exposed to the elements. The owners looked exhausted, malnourished, unwashed and as though they had been in that neglected condition for some time. *How unconscionable,* Creed thought, *that, unknown to these poor objects, this is the last relief they will receive for some time to come.*

*

On 5 November at Codrum House, Edward Ashe took delivery of his morning papers, toasted bread and coffee, whereupon he discovered an article that featured his name. A practical man, undisturbed by hostile press and public opinion, he brought the hot brew to his lips and sipped it carefully, squinting through the steam. The only aspect of the article that surprised him was that it had taken an uncharacteristic four days for the report to appear:

TO THE EDITOR OF THE CORK EXAMINER

AN OUT-DOOR PAUPER

SIR – I believe no one will venture to quarrel with me when I assert that the bona fide and most substantial relief afforded since the enactment of the pauperising and abominable Poor Law, and its sinecure offices, was in the out-door relief recently given in the yards of workhouses. At least, I would say, for my own locality, that no person who would witness the consequent joy of the parties getting food in this way, would be instrumental in stopping this real and inexpensive channel of charity; but, to their disgrace be it told, nine of the Guardians of yesterday's Board peremptorily refused the continuance of any further aid to the not only famishing, but actual dead-alive hundreds who visit this place daily, and who, it is admitted, are wholly unable to procure a morsel of food elsewhere ...

The members who attended yesterday's meeting were Patrick Ronayne (Chairman), Richard Coppinger, Henry Howard, Edward Ashe, Daniel Lucy, Cornelius Murphy, Timothy Murphy, Messrs Nettles, James Boyle, James Foley, John Pearson and Francis. G. Woodley Esq.

Mr Ashe moved, and Mr Robert Nettles seconded, that the out-door relief be discontinued. But Mr Lucy, starting up, said he had a motion to put before the Board, which Mr Ashe said was illegal, for want of previous notice. Mr Ashe added that some people wanted only popularity in thus acting, which Mr Lucy said he despised.

After some further remarks on either side, Mr Ashe put his motion, which was backed by nine of the above – Mr Lucy with warmth observing that if left in a minority of himself, he would urge the necessity of the adoption of his own resolution that followed, and which was supported by Messrs Cornelius and Timothy Murphy, the Chairman acting neutral: –

Resolved – That a meal of the above be continued for one week more at the yard of the Workhouse to such destitute persons as will apply for it, and that they remain three hours in the yard, as few public works have as yet commenced, and very few labourers are employed – Daniel Lucy. Cornelius Murphy.

This is the resolution of as pure a poor man's friend as ever lived – one who is connected, by purse and personal exertions, with every public institution of charity in this town – one entirely above the motives attributed to him by Mr Ashe – and who would not fill the offices of D.V.C. to the Board of Guardians, and Secretary to the Relief Committee, and regard their functions as a mockery.

The Rev. Mr Lee says this outdoor relief has checked the commission of many crimes hitherto but he would not for a moment undertake that the starving multitude will pursue a similar course in future. What was it? £2 8s. per day to relieve and keep life in ten hundred fellow beings? Not altogether amounting to one pound for each of the parishes in the Union per week!

A poor woman (with young children) on her return from this poorhouse meal yesterday, was so debilitated, that she fell in Sleaven, and died in a FEW MINUTES! Another victim to Russell Legislation!

Before I close, perhaps it would not be amiss to ask you, or rather Mr Treacy, whose duty it is – why our Macroom Bridge was not proceeded with? 'Tis really strange, and suspicious too, why the work that was the first opened should so suddenly be stopped. Conjecture will have it, that local parties, for selfish motives, have influenced the authorities in charge. It ought and must be satisfactorily accounted for.

C.C.

Macroom, 1 Nov. 1846

SAMHAIN
NOVEMBER

26

EMERGENCY WORKS

Wood on wood and the sounds of chair legs rubbing and jutting across the floorboards above signalled a transfusion of amenities from one room to another, when, owing to the growing urgency, the Macroom Relief Committee met at the Union Workhouse on Saturday morning, 7 November, in spite of the obvious realisation that such an event would clash with the regular weekly meeting of the Guardians. As, naturally, the boardroom was already occupied, it was simply decided that the Committee would situate themselves in the adjoining clerk's room and Creed climbed the stairs between the two just in time to witness Mr Burdon – having left his ever-constant position at the side of the chairman – orchestrating the groans of the furniture and shifting into various disappeared nooks and crannies the extraneous piles of papers that cluttered his desk, demonstrating throughout the whole procedure an air of pride over the comparatively cramped space he called his office.

'I shall leave you to it, gentlemen. Please make yourselves at home, or as comfortable as you can.'

Creed managed a smile and thanked Mr Burdon, who closed the door after himself.

He had never paid much attention to the clerk's room before, he realised. A generous space for one man but made to seem very small by the addition of a few more bodies, the room had not much to recommend it in the way of fixtures or features. Apart from the small writing desk and fireplace, taken as granted, there was but one large book press and a couple of shelves, among which the minutiae of the inner workings of the M.U. were housed. It had been into the large press that Burdon had stuffed most of the papers.

Creed found himself to be focusing on such trivialities in an effort to ignore the apprehension he had been experiencing in the lead-up to this, the second meeting in the space of one week with Massy H. Warren at the helm, serving in the position of Deputy Vice Chairman due to Edward Ashe's finding himself lately too preoccupied with business elsewhere to commit fully to the position. In anticipation of the tension, Creed had been coaching himself, and had arrived with a certain resolve in mind to pass around whatever obstacle he might encounter at the meeting with the ease of water poured over a rock, and to view Massy Warren himself as an object, such as a floating cloud passing by, unattached to his own material sphere. But the incoming object of Creed's focus as the meeting began was an unusual guest whose participation he saw as a welcome distraction.

Given his chequered history as a representative of the Board of Works and the less-than-united sense of feeling towards him among the gentlemen of the district, the reception for Captain Gordon, who brushed off the arms of his military jacket as he settled himself, was bound to be a fiery one.

Michael O'Connell opened for the Relief Committee. 'I would like to put a question to Mr Gordon.'

'Yes?' Gordon answered, still fixing his chair as though bracing for an assault.

'Can you please clear up an important matter for us and state what the position of the Board of Works is with regard to employment for the poor of this district? We have been led to believe that each unemployed labourer is to get work at once.'

'From where, or from whom, has that claim emanated?' Gordon asked with a provocative nonchalance, during which speech Creed could not help but find himself distracted by the expansive and ostentatious moustache the man insisted on keeping.

'Well, the *Cork Examiner*, for one.'

'A falsehood, insofar as I am aware.' Gordon spoke abruptly, and without emotion.

'And have you anything to add by way of information, Mr Gordon? With respect, my question was in relation to the position of the Board.' Given the life-and-death implications, and Gordon's ignorance of them, O'Connell was already flushed with anger.

Creed sympathised with O'Connell's fury, but felt it necessary to intervene and steer their guest towards being of some use to the committee. 'Mr Gordon, you'll forgive us if we appear rather passionate this day. As Mr O'Connell has pointed out, there have been rumours circulating and we must be able to understand the position of the Board, to know our own ...'

Nodding, Gordon interrupted. 'I am here at the behest of the Board of Works, and as such it is my duty to dispel those rumours. The position of the Board, as you know, is one of being committed to providing assistance to all districts suffering under the present calamity. The situation, in terms of this barony in particular, is – or has been – slightly confused by virtue of the complications arising from the recent presentment sessions.

'Beyond that, unfortunately I know no more than you, gentlemen, and I am also awaiting news on the matter.'

'Mr Gordon,' Reverend Mr O'Kearney was the next to confront the visitor, 'a period of almost two months has elapsed since both the magistracy and the landlords of this barony, without distinction, unanimously signed a requisition imploring the government to provide immediate and general employment for the famishing people, and unequivocally acquainting them that if apathy or indifference continued to characterise the conduct of their representatives, they would not be responsible for the consequences. The failing of the presentment sessions is only the latest in a series of mysterious obstacles.'

'Mr–?'

'Reverend Mr Denis O'Kearney, parish priest of Aghinagh.' Massy, appearing to be taking his role as chair with impressive seriousness, vouched the name of his interlocuter to the visiting delegate, who no doubt was unaware of the identities of most of his opposition.

'Mr O'Kearney,' Gordon gathered himself, 'the law has changed significantly in recent months, with the introduction of the Labour Rate Act, and, I believe, this has made the status of earlier applications irrelevant. But with regard to your other comments, I must remind you that the position of the government is that they *do not* and *will not* respond to threats or coercion. I would think that rather plain.'

The increased agitation of the bodies that filled the small room at this answer was abundantly plain to Creed, and emphasised further by numerous members indicating a wish to speak.

'Gentlemen, please,' said Massy Warren. He gestured to O'Kearney who, protesting that he had not yet finished, had raised a hand.

'My apologies, sir, Mr Gordon. I believe you misunderstand me. It is not my intention to make threats, but merely to acquaint you – as a representative of the government – with the gravity and the reality of the situation here. Let God forbid it.

'Gentlemen, I would like to remind Mr Gordon that the population of this barony is considerably over forty-six thousand persons, almost the entirety of whom are, or rather were, dependent on agricultural pursuits for their subsistence.'

'You needn't, Mr Lucy, but thank you. That does not, however, bear on the point that there will be no advantage to any of those persons who demonstrate at this time. Quite the opposite,' Gordon said, giving portent of some sinister event.

Listening on, Creed fancied he recognised the views that Gordon was representing. They were, he believed, derived almost directly from the Lord Lieutenant, Henry Labouchere – Gordon's ultimate superior a few mouths further up the echelon – whose position in relation to numerous demonstrations of the poor across the country recently, had just been published in what was, to Creed's mind, a rather paltry and infuriatingly patronising manner. As he recalled:

> The Lord Lieutenant, fully sensible of the patient endurance which has marked
> the character of the people of this country under great privations, faithfully
> trusts that the assurance of his unceasing anxiety to alleviate their distress by
> every means in his power will tend to allay excitement in their minds, and prevent
> those numerous assemblages, which, while they create alarm in the minds of
> many, can effect no advantage to those who join in such demonstrations.

The difficulty for Captain Gordon, Creed supposed, was that here was a man, a decorated military officer, temporarily relieved of his formal duties and sent off to what he no doubt considered an unholy, backward outpost in the middle of nowhere, there to populate the unenviable position of administering to a chaotic rabble of hopeless peasants in the middle of a providential disaster. Creed stared at Gordon and likened the level of enthusiasm he was displaying for the position to the amount of excitement one could expect from a mounted stag's head sleeping on a hunting lodge wall. The captain had answered the summons of the Relief Committee to speak on the part of the Board of Works, but Creed now came to the realisation that if the committee did not ask the right questions of him, Gordon would not feel inclined to volunteer any more insight than he had to.

Father Lee next attempted to penetrate the captain's lack of concern. 'To the best of your knowledge, Captain Gordon, has there been any response from your supervisors in relation to correspondence from the Grand Jury Secretary on what will happen next with the "quashed" presentment sessions?'

'I can only suppose that the response will be a direct one, Mr Lee. I would propose that the committee look to local endeavours, until you hear otherwise. The most I can guarantee is that I will consult with the secretary of the Board of Works.'

'And how soon might we expect ...'

'I would hope to hear back within the week.'

'Thank you, Mr Gordon.' Massy Warren looked ready to release the captain, who it seemed it was pointless to question further. 'If no one else has anything for the gentleman?'

Rising from his chair, Gordon issued a sigh of relief and collected his hat from the table in front. 'Gentlemen.'

'I would like to bring something to Mr Gordon, if he might permit us to trespass on his kindness a few moments further …'

'Captain Gordon. Mr Coppinger.' With the opening and closing of a hand, Massy seemed both to introduce Coppinger and to offer the lingering Gordon the choice of whether or not to accept another question.

'As you wish.' With visible reluctance, Gordon took his seat once again, but this time held onto his hat and slapped it temporarily into position beneath his armpit, indicating his intention to not stay long.

'Thank you.' Coppinger pulled out a newspaper from the documents in front of him and pointed it in Gordon's direction, tapping its end once on the table. 'This is yesterday's paper – Friday, 13 November 1846.' Gordon flared his nostrils but Coppinger was not hurried.

Stephen Coppinger, a man Creed considered to be one who reserved his opinion for when he had something intelligent to say, was the owner of the land behind the castle grounds bordering the river and the bridge of the town, and someone he admired as having a benevolent soul for the poor.

'There is an article in this paper,' Coppinger addressed the entire group as he spoke, 'under the heading "Public Distress", detailing a band of about three hundred famished labourers who, in the worst possible state of destitution, presented themselves upon the mercy of the workhouse in Middleton on Monday last. Now, getting no satisfaction there, they were obliged to go away disappointed, but fortunately were the recipients of some admirable charity within the town there afterwards, when a few individuals gave them some money to procure bread.'

Creed, familiar with the account, divided his attention between Coppinger and Gordon, who now stared unblinking at the floor as if his mind were somewhere else altogether.

Coppinger went on to reference the words of the paper: 'The writer states this is the second demonstration of its kind the town has witnessed, and adds that "unless the powers interpose to stave off death from the poor population, there will be many more such".

'Mr Gordon,' Coppinger continued, folding up the journal again and now tapping it, but also intermittently raising it to wave at Gordon as he spoke, 'these gatherings are becoming more frequent across the country. We had one in the town here ourselves, as you may know, at the beginning of October. I for one would not be astonished to hear shortly of similar and greater multitudes openly rising and scouring the country over. In fact, it is my belief that this illustrates just what we're likely to become accustomed to in our own district if something is not done to afford some relief soon.'

By now Gordon's eyes were ready to open fire upon his opponent, and might actually have done so if indeed they had possessed that ability, as Coppinger, proceeding to drive his point home, returned the burning glare: 'And might I say, Mr Gordon, I suspect it will do neither *you* nor your superiors any favours to have occurrences such as these showing up in the papers and highlighting the exact regions in which public works are uncommenced or stalling for one reason or another.' Stopping abruptly, Coppinger dropped the paper and removed his glasses to the breast pocket of his coat while the other committee members made tentative noises of support.

'Now, gentlemen, we are not here to rebuke the captain.' A half-hearted Massy Warren alone came to Gordon's defence, leading Creed to wonder if it was an added insult on his own part. But having made up his mind that Stephen Coppinger's passionate but barbed plea was either the best way to provoke Gordon into action or the very worst, Creed now watched with great curiosity as, in the silence that invited his response,

Gordon took a moment to breathe out a long, ominous breath, before renewing a cold stare upon his critic.

'Mr Coppinger,' Gordon let the name hang in the air before continuing, 'would you presume that I do not keep up on the contents of the newspapers, or stay informed of those events which concern my post within the region? Feel no need to reply, the answer is quite plain.'

Some human passion at last, Creed thought.

'I am in fact, Mr Coppinger, in regular communication with Mr Benson, over the whole of the county of Cork, with the inclusion of the Imokillys. But I will thank you for your condescension nonetheless. As for the gatherings, and the potential for more; I believe I have spoken to the matter of threats and coercion already this day.'

'Will that be all, gentlemen?' Gordon readied his hand on his hat once more, as stubbornness met stubbornness in silence.

'Thank you, Captain Gordon. I believe that will be all for now.' The chairman released him properly this time and Gordon wasted no time in brusquely reaffixing his strangely shaped hat.

'Then I shall bid you good day.'

Once Gordon had cleared the room, Creed sensed an air of determination among the remaining occupants, who readjusted their chairs to absorb the extra space.

'Well, you heard it yourselves, gentlemen,' said Father Lee. 'It falls to us to come up with a solution that will somehow bridge the gap. I believe we must presume that the government will not intervene. At least certainly not in the short term.'

'I would like to make a suggestion.'

'Yes, Mr O'Connell?'

'I propose that we form a sub-committee, to which I'd volunteer of course, the purposes of which would be to approach the principal householders of the town with the aim of gathering private subscriptions to ignite emergency works immediately.'

'Hear, hear.'

'For how long should we propose to support such an endeavour – that is my question.'

'If I may,' Creed offered, 'Mr Lucy proposed at the last Guardians' meeting to provide for "one week more". Now, that resolution was voted down by the Guardians, but that is not to say we cannot adopt the same principle. We may or may not receive news from Captain Gordon one week hence, but the propertied are unlikely to engage with a longer period of support either way. Therefore, I propose that we work off the basis of one week. If in such time we need to address the issue again, then we will deal with that as the occasion arises. And ...' Creed added, fomenting a brief suspense and sending a smile around the small table, 'if we begin with the gentlemen next door ...'

'Ah. That is very astute, Mr Creed.' Father O'Kearney was amused.

'We could then, of course, also look to the gentlemen and merchants in the immediate vicinity of the town,' Creed added.

The plan agreed, Massy Warren read out the names of all the gentry of the town likely to contribute.

'Very well, gentlemen. Shall we see what we can muster, and meet back here in one hour?' Warren proposed.

Pleased with how well his personal approach to the meeting had worked out so far, Creed found himself wondering for the first time whether he might actually have found a point of balance in his having to engage with Massy Warren on a regular basis.

The last thing addressed before the room dispersed for the hour was to agree on a wage for the emergency labour, which settled on eight pence per day, as per the Board of Works standard. 'Hear, hear!'

*

On reconvening that afternoon, with Creed having diligently approached his neighbours and made a contribution of his own, Massy Warren made a note of the promises and announced that £10, 3s and 7d had been raised, to which the committee members then added some of their own contributions.

Quickly making the calculations for the sake of exigency, Creed informed the committee that they could now employ 'one hundred and ninety-nine men for one week, with some small change left over'. But he had barely finished his sentence when Stephen Coppinger, impressing Creed immensely for the second time that day, announced that he was happy to increase his own contribution 'so as we might round it up to two hundred beings in total'. A hearty 'Hear, hear!' was shared once again at the result, and finally it was agreed that the following morning at five a bellman would be sent around the town of Macroom to announce the opportunity of employment.

'Oh!' Creed held up a finger, as the first of the chair legs rubbed the floor again and all were on the cusp of rising from the borrowed furniture. 'There is *one* other matter ...'

Creed had, hitherto, been unsure as to whether he ought to make such an announcement, and had planned to deliver it on Tuesday next: but inspired by the spirit of community that had been achieved throughout the proceedings, and taking Massy's rather amiable mood into account (where previously he had worried that having being absent from the last race committee meeting, Massy's coming to learn of its latest decision might provoke his anger) he decided to risk it and take full advantage of the good will.

'Of course, Mr Creed,' Massy anticipated, 'the last item on the agenda is the appointment of a new chairman.'

'Not quite what I had in mind, Mr Warren, although there is that. No, I have some other good news I thought might further bolster the occasion.'

'You do?' Warren replied in a haughty but curious tone.

'It has been requested of me to acquaint the committee with the result of the assemblage at Williams Hotel, of Tuesday last, in connection with the Macroom Races.'

Massy, sitting back into his chair, suddenly looked like the old Massy Warren, and assumed a more foreboding countenance.

'The subscribers of last year's races,' Creed continued, 'as Mr Warren will know, have adopted to forgo a plate race this year, in consequence of the general distress. And a resolution was passed by the stewards on Tuesday for the funds held over since last year, amounting to forty-one pounds, to be released and soon handed over to this committee …' The tiny clerk's office grew loud and clamorous in response to the news, forcing Creed to rise above the excitement in finishing, '… to utilise as they see fit, in the interests of the poor of this district.'

'I am opposed!' Massy Warren shouted and slapped his palm onto the table before him.

His blunt statement brought the atmosphere into a wintery temperature as quickly as it had previously risen, to the obvious surprise of all present.

'Opposed, Mr Warren?' The room had fallen completely silent, as Creed voiced his horror. 'On what grounds?'

'On the grounds, Mr Creed, that I am unaware of such a meeting, or of such a resolution.'

'Then that is no grounds at all, Mr Warren.'

'As chairman,' Warren insisted, thumping the desk again, in a manner that put Creed in mind of an insolent child who was used to getting his way, 'I oppose!'

'You are joking, sir! Surely? When through the discretion and economy of the committee, such a sum might afford very considerable relief to those we commit to serving as a committee? We have just agreed to employ two hundred men for a week at a cost of a mere ten pounds in subscriptions – that is demonstration enough of what difference a fourfold sum would realise. It is rather unaccountable that a member of this committee should object, on the basis that he is *ignorant* of such a resolution. Try as one might, Mr Warren, one can no longer *be* ignorant, when one has been informed – as you have been by me, the envoy of that committee – of the very resolution.'

Creed was boiling inside and, aware that his passions were getting the better of him, realised there was never going to be a suitable time to deliver this news. He did not care that Massy Warren was likely doubly incensed: in the first instance, at learning that the Race Committee had *officially* decided to forgo his beloved plate race without having informed him personally; and in the second, at having to receive the news in front of the rest of the Relief Committee, as he chaired it, from a lowly upstart he openly considered unfit to pick the tar off his shoes.

'As chairman, I *oppose!*'

'Mr Creed!' Father Lee intervened, positioning an arm between them, as Creed now found himself standing face to face across the table from a seething Massy, whose sheep-like eyes, locked with his own, seemed to be filled less with hatred than with a surprising look of fear. Behind his own anger Creed sensed that Father Lee, knowing the politics of the town and likely fearing the potential consequences, was attempting to shock him out of saying something he might regret, as well as to censure a situation that might escalate further, and likely to only Creed's detriment. 'Perhaps we should bring this up for discussion again when the chair has been passed.'

Reminded that the position of Deputy Vice Chairman would have to be voted on again at the end of the meeting, Creed calmed himself and resumed his seat as Father Lee attempted to change the course of the discussion.

'Mr Daniel O'Connell MP, I hope, will be in receipt of a letter from me in the coming days, which I posted just this morning, informing him of the destitute condition of our people and earnestly recommending him to afford his assistance on Tuesday next, the occasion of the Fermoy deputation. I have sent a letter of a similar nature to the government authorities at Dublin Castle.'

'Hear, hear.' Though cognisant of the words that Lee was speaking as the Committee lauded his initiative, Creed was adrift on a cloud of apoplectic disgust, from the vista of which his mind raced through multiple understandings of the confrontation that had just taken place, each one leading to a potential avenue of righteousness through which he was determined to guide his foe if the debate were resumed. At a glance Massy appeared to be equally distracted, as the workhouse bell rang in the background, signalling the paupers in the yard to go back to their accommodations.

'I think we ought to take that as a sign to conclude our business, gentlemen,' Father Lee suggested.

At this point a knock upon the door, which immediately opened, revealed Mr Burdon, the clerk, signalling that the Guardians' meeting had finished next door.

'Mr Ashe, myself, John Warren and Daniel Lucy are now available to join the meeting if it might be of any value so late?' Burdon asked gingerly, only partly visible to Creed through the door. 'Of course, if it's a hindrance ... but the board room is now free, so we could conclude the meeting there.'

'A brilliant idea, Mr Burdon.' Father Lee seemed to decide for the group and nobody argued, perhaps agreeing that the air of the clerk's room had become too oppressive to further achieve anything meaningful or indeed to accept any more bodies. As they moved from one room to the other, the cloud of anger Creed had been floating on now changed to be one of surreal tranquillity – but he was passing through emotions as rapidly as the chairs being returned across the hallway. When they'd resettled, with Massy Warren now at the head of the grand table, Father Lee, perhaps again thinking to the least controversial result, brought the Committee back to its obligatory task. 'Mr Warren, I believe the chair is due to be passed.'

'Quite so. I would like to propose the principal resident of the town, the Honourable William White Hedges. All in favour?'

'Aye,' was the ubiquitous reply. Creed raised a lacklustre hand and uttered his concurrence. It was the usual merry parade, which Creed found to be increasingly ridiculous given that Hedges was away indefinitely. Instead, it would be better to just recognise that Hedges would never attend and decide who would chair in his stead.

'Unanimously carried.' Massy, happy as could be in the seat of power, gestured for Mr Burdon to record the decision, to Creed's renewed indignation.

'In his absence, as we have no particular indication as to when he might return, we must call on a suitable member of the committee to preside in his stead.'

Massy's voice took on a gleeful tone as he delighted in turning the screw. Creed knew that Ashe did not want the position, meaning that the next eligible candidates were magistrates, of which – at this sparsely attended sitting – Massy was one and his cousin John Borlaise Warren the other.

Clenching his jaw, Creed decided that he cared not a jot what the outcome was to be. It was almost certainly a foregone conclusion, and he would simply have to endure the motions. Blinded as he was with outrage, he could see no further than getting free of the meeting, to clear his head elsewhere.

At the other end of the table, Massy confidently surveyed all those before him and awaited a nomination, which eventually came from Edward Ashe. Creed knew that Ashe was unaware of what had taken place next door but, given his close ties with the Warren family estate, felt sure that he would have proceeded exactly the same way regardless.

'I nominate the Messrs Warren as the next eligible candidates.' To Massy's obvious delight, Ashe had moved to ensure that he was not in the running himself. 'Any objections?'

Creed raised a hand.

'Just a general objection, Mr Creed, or something specific?'

'Comprehensive!'

'Then I accept.' Massy's grin was only marginally restrained.

'John?'

'I accept.'

'Good. Then I propose we save the trouble of a vote and agree to share the duties.'

'Yes. I think that'll work fine. Would you care to conclude the meeting?' John Warren asked.

Massy nodded his acceptance, again turning to the clerk. 'Messrs Massy H. Warren and John Borlaise Warren; moved to sharing the duties of the chair, Mr Burdon.'

The clerk nodded too as he silently recorded the proceedings, untroubled and unburdened as he was by the desperate weight of conscience and politics, Creed mused, if only to distract himself, until his legs would be given leave to carry him from that room as fast as he wished they would. And presently they were.

'Thank you, gentlemen. We shall convene on Tuesday the tenth.' Massy straightened his papers upon the table before him as Creed kicked out his chair and was first through the door.

He fumed down the stairs ahead of everyone else and once outside darted the street with the tip of his unopened umbrella, cursing Warren, and mumbling as he went. *In the clerk's room Lee stopped me from uttering anything by which he must have supposed I might cause myself great trouble. But in the boardroom he pushed to re-elect the position of acting chair, when it must have been obvious that Massy was going to be voted back in. Was he just trying to occupy us both until the meeting had passed?* Ultimately Creed could only conclude that Lee had sought to shelter him from inviting the wrath of Massy H. Warren upon himself. For the priest surely knew as well as Creed did that Massy was a spiteful and dangerous man, who would have loved nothing more than to be thwarted further by someone far below his own standing, as he saw it, and to have, for the object and focus of his general dissatisfaction in life, a man to dismantle and goad, for his own twisted enjoyment. Creed, still seething, assured himself that he was not intimidated by Massy and in that moment it was finally true. However reluctant he *had* been in the past to admit to himself that he was intimidated, he had always made a point of rising above such self-created restraints, and had nevertheless stood firmly on his own principles. But not any more. Cornelius Creed had tip-toed around Massy Warren for long enough.

*

'Damned ignorant waster!' Creed burst through the door of the shop almost knocking the bell off its swing and shivered with cold as he removed his drenched coat.

'Is there something wrong, Mr Creed?' French, concerned by his employer's apparently catastrophic mood and the consequences it might have for him, instantly vacated the stool behind the counter.

'Forty-one pounds,' Creed muttered as he hung up his coat, the saturated wads of his long, silver hair clumped together by the heavy rain, which he'd apparently forgotten to ward off with his umbrella. 'A miserable inconsequence of a sum when compared with his wealth, and all the estates and fortunes of the Warrens going back to Cromwell's distribution of the plundered lands of Ireland.'

'Sir?' A vision of the three black balls that, until relatively recently, had sat atop their slender iron spars above the square for over forty years flashed in French's mind as he gazed upon the man now standing in the doorway behind Creed. Those severed heads and the fact that they had stayed up there for so long were testament enough to the latent power of the yeomanry and the willingness of Warren and his ilk to wield it in all its gruesome force.

After the assassination of Warren's grandfather, Robert Hutchinson, in '98, those accused of the crime, hunted down the county over the span of almost a year, had been brought back to Macroom and subjected to a brutal public execution as a spectacle for the townspeople. Horror stories had abounded in French's childhood of how the hangman, who had dressed mockingly in bright green and worn a broad buff belt inscribed with the letters *Erin go bragh* had butchered and dismembered the corpses of the McCarthy brothers with apparent *sang froid* until, by the time he had raised the three heads on spikes before the appalled and disgusted crowd, even he had been nauseated to the point of removing his mask to vomit over the side of the gallows platform.

French knew that the 'H' that Massy Warren insisted on keeping in the centre of his name was no accident. It represented every inch of that power and Warren thrived upon it. But feeling his eyes to be practically out on stalks, French wondered what in hell was going to happen now that the confrontation between Mr Creed and Mr Warren had reached the doorstep of the shop.

Creed, evidently understanding that something was amiss by French's shocked countenance, spun his head around and discovered a silent Massy, who came no further than the doorstep.

'Yes, Mr Warren, can I help you?' Creed said rather coolly.

'I just wondered if there was anything you might wish to say to me, Mr Creed, now that Father Lee is no longer present to restrain you from your eloquence.'

'I have nothing to say to you, Mr Warren. I will be more than satisfied to limit our need for conversation to the realm of the boardroom, Thank you. Unless, of course, you have something you wish to pawn.'

Thomas French, who felt prouder in that moment than he had ever felt to be in the employ of Mr Creed, now discovered an urge within himself to take down the blunderbuss from the wall and blast Mr Warren into the street. He knew quite well that he would not, however, and that it was highly unlikely that the arm was even operational.

'Hear me now, Mr Creed.' With drenched hair dripping down in streams over his face, his arms concealed beneath the waxen hide of his rain-shining cloak, Massy Hutchinson Warren stood perfectly still and spoke with quiet menace. 'Do not presume to think I do not see your nature. You pass yourself off as a benevolent fellow, doing good, expending your efforts in the service of the downtrodden. But you are as you have just yourself described, Mr Creed …

'Your attempts at spreading good cheer at this morning's meeting were as transparent as the window of this shop. A window that shows you to the world just as transparently, and by your own bidding. I say it would suit you very well to see another forty-one pounds put into the hands of those innocent beings whose honour you so conveniently defend. For where else would they spend it, but to come and visit you? Cornelius Creed, the pawnbroker.'

27

The Business of God

J ust behind the south-east end of the square, the bell of St Colman's had been tolling since six o'clock, ante meridiem, its iron tongue proclaiming each hour and calling the parishioners of Macroom to attend Sunday Mass in the chapel below. But owing to the proximity of the chapel, so used to its molten soft tones were they that Cornelius and Paulellen lay undisturbed by its early calls, and awoke at their regular time of half past seven.

By the time they were kneeling facing each other on opposite sides of the bed in silent devotional prayer, Father Barry, the young curate, was bringing Mass to a close for his seven o'clock congregation.

'And so, Lot's wife', his soft voice rang from the lectern, 'was turned into a pillar of salt because she stood still and looked behind her. Thus salt, which preserves everything, becomes a striking and warning symbol to the conservators of olden times, who too stand still and look behind them.'

At Gurteenroe James Welply had finished polishing his shoes and was putting the brush back into its wooden box. He picked up a comb and, looking at himself in the silver-nitrate mirror, crossed the hair onto the flat of his head, holding it down with the opposite hand.

'Are we ready, Mary?' he called out, eyeing himself in the mirror.

'Ready, dear,' he heard his wife reply.

In and around the many lanes of Macroom, other townspeople, in the fast grip of want and squalid misery, wished they too had strength and the grace afforded a soul by the basic dignity of clothes: that *they* might enter the chapel and receive the blessing of prayer. But they daren't show themselves at the divine house now. Not in the condition they had been lowered to.

Half way between the chapel and the square, in Duggan's Lane, a young woman lay on a mud floor in a state of exhaustion occasioned by her lengthened abstinence from food; her three children huddled around the wretched fireplace, where a lonely sod of turf burned in the grate – a pathetic reflection of the kneeling parishioners who, still in the curate's thrall nearby, looked upon the glowing candles that bathed the chancel and its marble alter in amber light.

Another cabin nearer the church, consisting of the ground floor and a single storey above, was home to eight families, all members of which, too cold and tired to move, were still lying on their beds and as they had been throughout the night: completely destitute of covering. A gentle young boy among them complained that his little sister had been crying since the previous morning.

The narrow lane, barely a hundred feet long, was home to hundreds of other residents of the town, most of whom had not tasted a morsel of food that morning, or throughout all of the preceding day. Such as were able-bodied providers among them could not find employment, while others had not strength enough to crawl outside and beg, let alone take themselves to the workhouse, which had long since given up its system of outdoor relief and was by now over capacity by almost a hundred souls.

Besides the meagre flicker of heat and light that pierced the darkness of their cabins, the music of human voices that suddenly leapt from the church was the one disturbance that brought a modicum of comfort, as, within the pitch of a cast hook, the curate was distributing the sacrament of Holy Communion, accompanied by the chants of *Te Deum*. The solemn tone swelled through the building, as, one by one and row by row, the early-rising and well-to-do faithful of the parish gathered together to shuffle up the aisle of the simple church.

As the three children in Duggan's Lane listened and indulged in fantasies of being saved by the kindness of someone within the nave of the chapel and as, facing the filthy grey wall behind them, their mother hallucinated that the flickering silhouettes cast over her children's crowded shoulders were the source of the holy strains, Father Barry drained a last sup of wine from the chalice and the relief of the music ended all too suddenly. The young curate cleaned out the vessel with the blood-red stole around his neck and handed it to the sacristan.

'The grace of our Lord Jesus Christ, the charity of God, and the communication of the Holy Ghost, be with you all. Amen.'

The customary blessing ended the Mass and the church cleared in plenty of time to be reset for the intermediate eight o'clock service, to be offered by the older curate, Father Foley. The main offering, at ten, would be the privilege of the parish priest, Father Thomas Lee.

*

At the stroke of eight the bell rang again as the iron grape beat against its bronze cheek high above the heads of Cornelius, Paulellen, the Welplys and the many incoming Macrompian Mass-goers who parted the waters of assembled beggars and sinners with outstretched palms and tormented limbs outside, until finally the door of the church was closed to the last of them – an old woman who had trailed behind the flock attempting to solicit any coin that might otherwise end up in the plate. The small man guarding the door paid no mind to her cries of woe and shut it tightly to the last sliver of her face, turning her rant to soliloquy, her clear speech to murmur, so that she performed her final address to the only available audience: her fellow beggars.

'Shut the door, and that's it, is it? Oh, then, that's what I'll be saying to you when you want to pass through the gates o' heaven. It's then I'll be saying to St Peter, "Shut the door, St Peter, " says I to the dirty sinner that'd disgrace the place entirely, says I, and ye'd be asking me to let ye in … The curse of the poor and helpless cripple upon you every day you pull a coat over your back!'

Inside, the more experienced curate, sent from another parish two years before by the Bishop of Cloyne, dispensed with his opening prayers and ascended the pulpit with what appeared to be singular determination, pausing for only the briefest of moments before speaking. It was Father Foley, Creed realised, wondering at his unusual entrance.

'The souls of the just are in the hands of God ... and the torment of death shall not touch them.'

The curate's first words, spat into the air, rang cold against the plaster walls and, coupled with the unaccustomed opening, caught his flock off guard, commanding silence and setting the tone for all that would follow.

'The souls of the just are in the hands of God and the torment of death shall not touch them. In the sight of the unwise they seemed to die. Their departure was taken for misery and their going away from us utter destruction. But they are in peace, and though in the sight of men they suffered torments, their hope is full of immortality ...'

Father Foley paused, holding for what seemed like an inordinately long moment, inducing a tension that Creed found unsettling.

'Two people,' he finally resumed, 'two souls have departed ... have perished ... of starvation in the vicinity of this town in recent weeks. Many more are not far behind. God alone, we are told, watches over the hovel of the poor as well as the palace of the wealthy, and includes within his all-embracing solicitude the pallet of straw as well as the bed of down.

'But those who do his earthly work – do they too not watch over the hovel and the palace? Often have I myself, during my own ministrations in this district, when visiting the abodes of the sick and dying, heard *His* name mentioned with gratitude and veneration by those who confessed themselves indebted to his kindness.

'Many a fervent penitent has had cause to bless tears of bitter compunction. Many the heart, long seared and callous in its obduracy, has been softened by grace and, after long years of barrenness, bloomed and blossomed like a flower, liberated at last. Is this not the goal, and the duty, of the pastor and the priest?

'We all hear Him in his sublimity and wisdom, when it is fitting so for Him to speak – in the melody of birdsong, in the voice of the kind. At times we hear Him lower Himself to the simplicity of little children – speaking in artless phrase and cheerfulness, he soothes their hearts. He has made Himself all to all, so that He may not lose one soul, however humble, when the crown of eternity is at stake.

'Whether the languid form stretched upon its bed of straw, laid upon the earthen floor, emaciated by want, or stricken by terror-inspiring pestilence. Whether in lonely garret or filthy lane, it matters not to Him. They are all His children, and He hath for them a father's heart. His purse is ever open to them, and His sympathy is ever active to them until purified by many sufferings and tribulations they are borne to that better land where sorrow and weeping and mourning are to be no more. Is this not our goal, and our duty? The souls of the just are in the hands of God.

'The hopes held out to us by religion are among the most powerful sources of consolation. In every sphere of life and every department of duty its benign and blessed influence is felt, sweetening labour, sanctifying exertion, and making even the hard struggles and bitter privations of the poor not only be patiently endured but become the occasions of future glory.

'Even where the sorrow that shuns the prying gaze of man seeks to hide its woes. What affliction is there, that it will not lessen? Religion.

'That the hard bed of sickness be softened by religious sympathy; that religious charity in its most persuasive form be introduced to the abodes of poverty and wretchedness and with healing upon its wings be ever ceaselessly engaged in winning the weary and heavily laden to God. That through wise and comprehensive benevolence, that precious gift be conferred onto you, to edify you by its virtues and to be to you and to those who shall come after you a bright and shining light.

'These are the goals, are they not – and the duties of the parson and the papist?'

Sibilant sounds and whispers raced along the pews but dried up and vanished the instant the priest paused between sentences to refer again to his book. Creed found himself questioning where the priest was going. The sermon was already highly unusual in its approach: dispensing with the conventional offerings and machinations of the ceremony. *But now bringing the* established *church into the fold?*

'The souls of the just are in the hands of God. As His earthly representation, the good we teach to others is what we must first practise ourselves. To not allow that any other should outstrip us in the course, or surpass us in the field of virtuous emulation, when the crown of eternal life is to be won. To be powerful in word and in work. To seek the Maker's glory in all that we do … The walls of the Lord's house, of this very edifice, are gifted with the faculty of utterance. If ever speech is given to them, they should ring in responsive echoes to that rich voice they hear so often, and give it back in music as if by some angel's agency, as though not a sound was to be lost of that, which is so sweet and graceful to our ears. That is our responsibility as the clergy of any and of all denominations. Because the souls of the just are in the hands of God and the torment of death shall not touch them.'

'Is he talking about someone in particular? Who is he directing his anger towards?' Paulellen whispered to her husband.

Creed shook his head but kept his eyes fixed on the curate lest he miss a single word, tormented by the realisation that he had no means of making notes. He sensed that something was about to happen. But more than the question of who the priest was castigating, Creed was now weighing up the potential consequences of publishing the words of a priest in the pulpit. *It would be cardinal to divulge, especially when that priest is confiding in his flock. Of all the times to not carry a notebook!* At any rate it was far too late to begin transcribing the sermon. And were he to be seen transcribing, reporting on what the priest was saying, without permission … he would have to content himself with gathering the core of it.

All of a sudden Father Foley seemed to change course and grow dangerously passionate: 'Then rose a shriek of despair, a wild cry of mortal dread ... the clasping of hands, the hoarse voices of men. Screams of women, the piercing shrieks of the little ones, all blended together in a tremendous confusion of sounds, like the howling of a storm, the lashing of furious waves and despairing cries of drowning souls.

'The barrier of the void was trodden underfoot and there was a movement and a heaving mass towards the sea, the frightened frantically driving all before them into the tide. And the waves rolled, crushing down the helpless, covering the floor of the temple with the confused, in a tangled heap of struggling beings. Higher, louder, shriller, rose the fright!'

Paulellen flinched and Creed turned to see her blinking repeatedly as the curate bellowed on before them. The hurried footsteps behind turned out to be those of a woman ushering her children towards the doors.

Turning back towards the front, Creed's eyes found Daniel Lucy and Pat O'Riordan seated across from each other, throwing looks back and forth as a growing restlessness weighted the atmosphere and the words of the curate had begun to manifest themselves in the behaviour of the frightened parishioners before him.

'The steps led down from every side choked with the pressure of the multitude. Numbers of maddened people peered over the edge with frenzy and affright, before rushing back from its temptation.'

Foley, his fists gripped into balls, pulled them away violently from his tightly squeezed eyes, as if to tear them out, and up and down the chapel the laity looked all around themselves for some clue or reassurance as to where the tirade would end.

'And still were heard fainting! Shrieking! Hysterics! And the cries of terrified children – THESE!'

Foley stopped at last, hands held aloft mid tumult, leaning so far over the pulpit that Creed was amazed he had not come tumbling over the edge.

'These are the scenes that would result in the absence of religion ... of faith, and of spiritual leadership in this parish. These are the scenes that some irresponsible leaders within our community would yet have us behold: were they to have their way ...'

To spare the thrall his honest rage, or to oust the heathen stone lodged fugitive in his gullet. Creed had begun to think of the words he would use, composing for the newspaper as Father Foley entered again at the almost normal din of speech. But there remained a quiet tension in his voice that began again to rise immediately, and Creed fancied it was merely the calm before the final ascent as around him he felt the parishioners to instinctively brace themselves, sensing, as he did, that the curate could not have taken them so far to abandon them now – so near to the peak of that concern which plagued his thought.

'Every project of public benefit that offers a well-grounded hope of raising this country, and its people, to the state for which nature seems to have destined them, but which misfortune and misrule have hitherto prevented, must be met with the warmest concurrence. I particularly refer in this instance to the efforts to bring to fruition those projects which would provide the poor of this district with employment – life-or-death-giving employment.'

Finally, a purpose revealed.

'Though we, as men of God – regardless of religious persuasion – ought to stand aloof from the angry strife of party and the arena of political discussion, there should be no heart more alive to the country's wrongs ... for the country's wrongs are the people's wrongs, and the people's wrongs are the business of *God!*'

Foley thumped the wooden desk with his fist as he uttered the last word. 'There should be no heart that yearns more for the prosperity of the country and its people than that of the cleric. Who else can offer that consolation? Who else can represent the people, and stand for the people when government have failed the people?

'Henry Swanzy!' Foley shouted in isolation, as if calling to someone within the house, bringing all to search around them, as if the rector had actually entered. But Creed knew this was the climax.

'The Reverend Henry Swanzy, vicar of the Church of England in this town, might have it otherwise. It would seem that he would have the employment of the poor of this vicinity delayed indefinitely.'

Creed sensed utter shock as the dissonant murmurs evaporated.

'In the name of God, he must not be left ignorant of their woes. And I put it to you, that if the starving labourers of this district are in want, *that* minister should be petitioned for it, in the absence of such employment as he has been a party to impeding.'

Creed suspected that if the assemblage had hitherto been immune to the speaker's passion, with this incitement they might well have turned from peaceful congregants to seething mob, were it not for the restraint they felt obliged to hold by virtue of the house in which they resided.

The silence of the laity was once again broken, let loose like an unbridled horse released to run riot in the stalls. 'That's right Father!' and 'That's the truth' were among the discernible comments thrown up in support of the rant.

'Dear God,' Creed whispered to Paulellen. But while some of those present found it hard not to respond, most, Creed knew, would be far less inclined to follow the priest into battle, the further he rallied them.

'Meanwhile, we have men and women dying of starvation in the vicinity of this town. Falling out of their standing in plain sight. But Swanzy is not alone! So-called Justices of Peace …'

And at last it comes, Creed thought.

'Messrs Massy Hutchinson Warren and John Borlaise Warren, cousins, have been Swanzy's cronies in this cause. Two souls have already perished in this town. And how many more? Who will be next? The souls of the just are in the hands of God, their hope is full of immortality.'

The rage had now been fully aired and the whole gathering was teetering on the edge, just as Foley's gospel had prophesied. Creed watched as, with the sign of the cross, the maniacal curate uttered his final blessing.

'*Deus qui corda fidelium, defende quaesumus Domine.* The hearts of the faithful, O Lord, protect.'

And with that Foley blessed himself and the congregation, closed his book, vacated the pulpit and left the church without speaking to anyone.

Bemused conversation flooded the vaults above as the spectators stood up from their seats and queued to alight by the one narrow aisle.

'I would think there'll be some discussion to be had about this,' Paulellen told Creed as they made their way towards the door.

'My word. If ever it was to be had,' Creed answered and looked around for any of his fellow committee members, who might save him from himself by confirming the instinct that told him he should not attempt a public article on the events he had just witnessed.

'Tell me you're not thinking of writing that up?' Paulellen said under her breath, as Creed felt a tap on his shoulder and turned to behold the tall figure of Pat O'Riordan, who, raising an eyebrow, peered down at him, and leaned in to say, 'Not really one for the papers, Con.'

'To be stored in the bowels of the earth.' Grabbing his other shoulder, Daniel Lucy, closer to Creed's own height, smothered any lingering doubts.

'I know it. I know it,' Creed relented. The interaction of his friends was almost playful as they toyed with him, knowing he would have an overwhelming urge to see that dramatic sermon printed in black and white. But the matter of a clash between the churches, let alone the involvement of the Ascendancy, was serious business and he knew he would just have to accept the need for restraint.

'See you Tuesday.' Dan patted Creed on the back repeatedly, as if to commiserate with him.

'Darling gintleman, kind lady, the heavens be yer bed and give us something, if you please?'

Families and shocked parishioners streamed out the gate past the poor old man sitting under a blanket, rusty tin in hand. Much to Creed's surprise, not a sinner of those walking out before him had stopped and he reasoned that the old man must have had no idea what had taken place within or why the parishioners were so preoccupied.

'Thank you, and God bless you, Mr Creed,' the beggar said as Creed pulled something from his pocket and dropped it into the empty tin with a clump.

*

The meetings of the recently merged Macroom and Clondhrohid Relief Committee were, to Creed's mind, becoming more tense each time they met. And the cause of the fractious atmosphere on the morning of Tuesday 17 November was the proposal by Father Lee that the curate, Father Foley, be added to their membership, the timing of which, he reasoned, could not have been worse.

'May I stop you just a moment, Mr Lee.' Henry Swanzy, sitting forward, was not long bringing matters to a head. 'I would like to enquire if it is true, as reported, that I, myself, along with other members of this committee, were denounced by Mr Foley at the chapel on Sunday last?'

And all but ensuring that the meeting was to be a short and explosive affair, Father Lee, to Creed's left, went on the defensive right away.

'I do not think you have a right to catechise me relative to what any Catholic clergyman may have considered it his duty to speak of in his chapel. But bring forward your authority, Mr Swanzy. Let your author be known.'

Father Lee's white cheeks flushed with colour, and Creed, burying his nose in his journal, found himself disturbed at the potential for such confrontation as he had not seen before between the spiritual leaders of the town's churches.

'Mr Swanzy has, I conceive, acted fairly in mentioning what he heard, and in giving you an opportunity of contradicting it.' Massy Hutchinson Warren now sought fit to involve himself, coming to Swanzy's aid. 'Several communications,' he went on, 'have been made to me on the subject. But I need not tell you that my authors dare not come forward.

'Now, for myself – and I think I may add for Mr Swanzy, and for my cousin – such an accusation, if made, is entirely without foundation. It is false.'

To this, Mr Swanzy and John Warren alone concurred with a 'Hear, hear!'

Creed could not help but admit to himself that on this occasion, Massy seemed to be in possession of a compelling account of Foley's sermon, but being opposed to almost anything Massy would have to say, and still simmering from their recent stand-off, he could not bring himself to join in the approbation.

'I think Father Foley would be as incapable as any man of making a false statement.' Father Lee, intent on protecting his curate – whether blindly, or with some strategy – was for the moment battling all three alone and Creed wondered if any of the other committee members would step up to support him. It was not his own place to do so, knowing so little of the background to the events. But Massy had not finished, and now drew out something that Creed suspected he would suggest as evidence from his leather paper-wallet.

'Having committed to this page the observations of Mr Foley, as communicated to me by a person present, I beg to read them. Naturally, as I did not hear Mr Foley's speech myself, I cannot vouch for them.

'But I can say how they were understood vis-à-vis ...' he began to read directly from his hand, 'that Mr Swanzy, John Borlaise Warren and Massy H. Warren were the cause of so many being unemployed ... That if the labourers wanted food, they knew where to look for it and not to spare them. Which caused such observations as "There's Swanzy" and "There are the Warrens for you" and such.'

Lowering the paper to rest upon the table and seeming to understand the weight of consequence that might follow were such a confrontation as this not to be resolved quickly, Massy had thus far managed to maintain an unusual composure in denying his being a party to any delay in the employment of the poor.

His next words Creed found remarkable: 'I wish to express myself most eager to see every man employed.'

This was so out of character for Massy that Creed thought him quite happy, even anxious, to keep a lid on whatever it was the priest had sought to expose.

But Edward Ashe, who Creed expected might have remained impartial as chairman, especially when all had seemed to be achieving balance, now threw a new cat among the pigeons. 'I heard a similar report of what was said, and I *can* give my author.'

And if Edward Ashe's stirring of the pot had not been enough of a surprise for Creed, nothing could have prepared him for the shock of seeing James Welply, who he had not spoken to since the infamous Mass on Sunday, now rise to answer Ashe's statement.

'Mr Ashe, having been speaking to me since this discussion commenced,' James addressed the committee directly, 'it might be inferred that I am the author he alludes to. But our conversation was on an entirely different matter. I had no notion that this subject would be introduced. Having heard what Mr Foley said, however, I pledge myself that the statement read, as far as the Messrs Warrens are concerned, is not correct. As a Roman Catholic, I cannot mention what I heard said in the chapel, but I deplore – I deeply deplore – the observations that were made, the effects of which I had great difficulty in doing away with, so great was the excitement raised against Mr Swanzy.'

Creed was struggling to orientate himself within the exchanges. That James had been speaking to the chairman during the meeting had not escaped his attention, but Ashe seemed to have caught James out in some fashion. Something seemed highly odd about the way the debate was unravelling. Why, if James had not been speaking about that very subject to Ashe, would he feel the need to answer the accusation and in doing so volunteer such information freely at the risk of igniting a fuse?

Massy now spoke again. 'Although the statement may not be correct in every particular, I would wish Mr Welply to say if I and my cousin were not charged with being parties to the delay in giving employment.'

'I have given my answer,' James countered abruptly. 'I did not expect this discussion. I came here for a different purpose. But as regards the memorial, there was no reference to you.'

'What memorial?' Massy shot back. 'There was no memorial brought to me. I allude to our being in any way the cause of the poor people not being employed.'

'I did not understand it that way,' James said again, refusing to elaborate further on the subject.

The matter then seemed to be dropped, with the dust settling upon it, when Father Thomas astonishingly reintroduced his proposal for the addition of Father Foley to the committee, which, for Creed, only added to the list of strangely timed behaviour and notions he had witnessed this day. But at the obvious risk of more blood-letting, it seemed, no one seconded, and the matter was then superseded by other business.

As all returned to relative normality, Creed could not help but wonder that the timing of Father Lee's request to have the curate added to the committee was so conspicuously bad and the information given so freely by the witnesses that one might have been forgiven for wondering if the whole proposition and its subsequent confession had been orchestrated, and a benign version of events administered by the Catholic side, in collusion, to pre-empt a retaliation and lance the proverbial boil.

Father Lee could not be seen to criticise his own curate, and yet, to some extent, the sacrificial lamb had been served.

28

As He Who Has None

I exist. I am alive. I am living. I am existing. I am wet. I am cold. I am numb, and in pain. I am tired. Always tired. I feel weak now.

I can't remember what it's like to feel strong. I try to imagine what it's like to feel warm. I search for it. Sometimes I can trick my body and the cold feels like burning, stinging heat. It's a struggle to see light in this darkness. I try to picture a way out for us, but everything seems impossible. So sometimes it's better to just exist.

If I think about it. If I try to hope, try to feel hope, I only see decay. Everything looks even worse, and it's hard to find the strength to continue. To breathe. To get firewood. To walk. To speak. To go outside when I need to, for nature's work. To open my eyes when I wake up to another day of struggle and hardship. To be a father. A husband. Sometimes when I'm tired, they feel like a burden, Cáit and the little ones. And I curse myself for feeling that.

I curse myself for being a burden on them. For not giving them better. For not finding a way to get them out of this. I curse my eyes, which watch them wasting away, a day at a time.

So instead, when I can do nothing, I just exist. I exist, and I move from moment to moment, whichever way the wind bends me. Sometimes, I'm not sure if I'm alive or dead. But I'm surely alive. Because death must be easier than this.

But I exist. So long as I have a name I know I exist. I am Pádraig Ua Buaċalla.

'Patrick Buckley, Derry Leigh?'

Pádraig raised his hand. 'Over there.' A steward pointed him to the line where tools were being handed out to the men.

'Jeremiah O'Leary, Holland's Lane?'

'Yes.' A man almost as tall as Pádraig answered.

'Over there.'

'Denis Murphy, Masseytown?'

'That is I,' another pauper answered.

'In the line.'

'Ned Brien Swiney, Slevean?'

Grey clouds of night were still resisting the glowing of an emerging sun coming up beyond the horizon – a sun that ever so slowly was taking a bite of the sting out of the air. The breaths of the men condensed and fogged, and some of them blew and coughed through their hands, then tucked them back under armpits until, one by one, the shuffling line took them to the hut where Mr Barrett, assistant engineer and head of the tool department, sat hunched over, staring into a log book with pen in hand.

'Name?'

Pádraig Ua Buaćalla. That's what Pádraig heard, and what he wanted to answer. But his mouth said something else. 'Patrick Buckley.' He struggled to get around the odd shape of it, as though it were a rock too big to even fit between his teeth.

This was the third consecutive day since the long-awaited start to an official Board of Works project, and against his instincts and in spite of his remaining pride, just as with the outdoor relief back in October, Pádraig knew that to survive he would be forced – even in very tiny amounts – to learn, swallow, and speak the Béarla.

I exist, he thought to himself, as he shuffled on to the next hut. *I am Pádraig Ua Buaćalla. But even that … I am not even allowed the refuge of my name intact. They want to change that too.*

'But you are still Pádraig Ua Buaćalla,' he recalled Cáit impressing the point upon him the first evening he'd come home, bereft. 'There is no shame in bringing home food to your family. No shame in surviving. Be Pádraig Ua Buaćalla inside yourself. No one can change that. Let *them* have their honour, who let their families die around them and sink down into the grave when they still have a choice,' she had said.

And he knew she was right.

In the next hut the storekeeper gave out hammers to the men in exchange for the tickets they'd just received and they were directed by the porters to move along to the spot where they would break stones for the road. At his marker Pádraig got down on his hunkers and, as though he hadn't stopped at all, resumed putting one rock on top of the other and pounding it with the hammer so that it made a ringing crack, letting out the smell of ancient sulphur buried within. He stacked them and struck them, and stacked them and struck them again, and again, until each one fell asunder and his hands buzzed from the repetitive vibrations. Crouched over the hammer, his ears rang. His already rough hands blistered. The skin cracked. His back ached. His joints seized. Muscles cramped. And tiny exploded splithereens flew apart, cutting at his shins.

Slowly, the early dark turned to subdued November daylight and the morning air rang with the stinging of metal on stone; the groan and grumble of gravel underfoot; the choke of the spade thrust into earth; the wincing and wheezing of human beings operating the dull and crude weapons of the age-old war between man and nature. The machine of industry was warmed up and underway, insofar as it ever could be with its purveyors in such condition as Pádraig saw himself and his fellow labourers alike, akin to those Israelite slaves who laboured under the armies of the pharaoh.

Except for the shouts of the gangers and stewards ordering men to carry 'new rocks here' and to 'empty that barrow there', the men struggled on in silence, their unified muteness broken only by the occasional gasp of an injured man who, belting at the ground, had split a toe with his spade or burst a knuckle under a hammer. A man overcome with the weakness, seized in the back, or collapsing with hunger …

But gone now were those hangers-on who'd hoped to take the place of anyone who might drop out. All labourers beginning their employment had to be on site for the calling of the lists at first light and only he whose name was on a list compiled by the Relief Committee could be started.

That alone had not stopped, nor would stop, some hanging around, clinging to the hope of a change to the rules, or a change of heart. But the rain had come in, and had driven off anyone left with common sense.

It was only the third day and already Pádraig was feeling the huge drain on his depleted reserve of energy. In their own silences, he presumed, each of those around him, his mute companions, were probably asking themselves, as he was, *How long can I keep this up for?*

Stacking the next rock, Pádraig grunted. Water from his rain-soaked hair rolled down across his lips and ran off his beard at the speed of a tiny river.

When, a month ago, he had walked in and out to the workhouse for outdoor relief he had been surviving on one meal a day. Now he was covering the same distance, performing nine to ten hours of exhausting manual labour on top of it, and without the benefit of any extra sustenance. On less, in fact. All too aware, reminded constantly by his hunger, Pádraig knew that the labour was in place of the relief and would be until he was paid and could afford some substantial food. In the meantime, he and Cáit rationed what little they had to its thinnest. *This could kill a man before long,* he thought, and struck another rock with his hammer.

Pádraig had no idea when he would be paid, but found himself praying that it would be soon.

*

Over the following days and weeks Pádraig rose daily almost three hours before the birds sang. Having to leave long before they called up the dawn, he slept restlessly some nights, fearful that were he to turn up late, his place on the works might be taken or his wages docked, or that he'd miss receiving them altogether. Out in the beyonds and the wilds, Pádraig had nothing to read but the light. Knowing the shades of darkness, he could sense the hour: by how warm or how cold the embers of the fire were, how still the sounds of the night, and through an ancient sense he could not put a name to. But he knew when it was time to leave. Six-and-a-half miles he walked and stumbled through the early dawn to get to the huts on time. There he worked all the hours of daylight and stumbled back home through darkness once more to eat the one scant meal Cáit had ready for him, before – barely awake to finish it – he collapsed into sleep again as he had done each night preceding.

When he slept it was not restful sleep. Silent at the skin, perhaps, but inside him was the ringing of the hammer, clinking relentlessly as his cold hands ached and throbbed, hovering over frozen joints, shifting positions, stacking and splitting, bashing, splitting, carrying, stacking. And then he would kick and wince, waking himself with a groan.

'But at least then I know you're alive,' Cáit told him.

*

Above the pawnshop, on the square in Macroom, Cornelius Creed was dreaming too. But the hammers did not clink in his dreams. Having himself visited the works – the 'relief' that in part had been secured through his long and tiresome efforts – his dreams were haunted by the wringing of greedy hands and the corruption springing up and infesting every level of public enterprise around him, to the detriment of the famished workers.

At the next meeting of the Relief Committee, Creed stood and protested. 'It is shameful to perceive the inefficiency of the numberless and wholly unnecessary staff of subordinate officials upon the road. Is it these people we have wrestled and grappled with the government hard and long to bring employment to? Check clerks. Pay clerks. Paymasters. Stewards, and under-stewards. The list goes on and on. Half of them appear to be employing their horses while they're at it!'

His ire was greeted by a mixture of laughter and indignation, with Massy, of course, the ringleader. There were those who agreed with and supported him. But Creed was determined to be heard fully. If his words were not effectual in the arena of the boardroom, he had another place for them.

25 November 1846

Members of Relief Committees use their influence in giving appointments, entirely unmindful of how these valueless, so-named 'officers' swallow up the great portion of the scanty pittance granted by the Board of Works for rescuing thousands from the horrors of death by starvation.

The system is thoroughly rotten and wherever the fault is, the proper means ought to be applied for its remedy, instanter.

Most of all Creed was disgusted at how severely the labourers were being made to adhere to every cruel nuance of the regulations, when in principle the primary object of the scheme, as meted out so often by its architects in government, was to ensure that the people would not starve.

Over an all-too-rare social gathering for lunch with Paulellen and Sam Welply, his old friend and brother-in-law, Creed shared what was bearing heavily upon his thoughts. 'Will any person suppose a man will go to work on the public road for eightpence a day who is not in distress? 'Tis absurd to be wasting time on lists. The paranoia is frightful. I saw it for myself recently … on three separate occasions, and at different times of day, I have delivered the lists myself, one morning expressly to witness the commencement of a road. The names on the list were called to one side. But another hundred or so were told to just go home, regardless of how far they'd walked or from what part of the district. Many of them clearly in deep distress.'

'And what was the end result?' asked Paulellen, concerned.

'Well, they wouldn't go. And I wouldn't blame them for it. The consequence was disastrous, of course, which didn't help anyone.'

'Was that the one postponed?' She asked.

'It was. The opening was put off until the difficulty was overcome. But even the men who are actually employed … they're in such a weakened condition. And the ridiculousness of the principle …' Creed shook his head. 'On the one hand, the government says the primary aim is to keep the people alive – that the functionality of the schemes is secondary. But on the other, they will insist on working them to death.

'They're so petrified that the masses will become reliant on handouts that they say, "If you give the poor outdoor relief you encourage bad habits. " But, I maintain, the present system of relief is demoralising at best. Very well, I know … a month, three months, six months ago, all you heard from me was "Where is the employment?" But it's so little, and so frustratingly late in the year. You cannot expect the poor, starving creatures to be able to perform a solid day's work.

'A ten-hour day they are expected to put in. For eight pence! What man can support a family on that? The wet and cold of the season is killing them. And they've barely clothes to protect them. I know! Trust me, I know!

'Then, with the days getting shorter, 'tis only bright for eight hours at this time of the year. And when they have to quit their labour because it's dark, they're docked a quarter of a day! Where is the humanity in that, I ask you?'

Dispirited, Creed threw his napkin into his lap. 'The distress in this town is so deep and universal amongst the poor. In fact the distress is so bitter that I maintain it's difficult to say with any conviction whether the man who has work is not as much to be pitied as he who has none. Perhaps even more so!'

'But you can't take it all upon yourself, dear. Come now, you have hardly touched your food,' Paulellen gestured.

'Thank you, dear. Food!' Creed said, dipping a chunk of bread into the soup and stuffing it into his mouth.

'Beautiful bread, by the way, Sam. It gets better every time,' Paulellen said dipping her own bread in the soup.

'Ha, you're welcome!' Sam laughed.

'But food! Now there's another subject.' Creed cleared his mouth, wiped it with the napkin and, dropping it back down, began again. 'My labours don't require much sustenance, thankfully, but these men – I have seen it myself – each brings with him a small portion of griddle bread made of Indian meal. But generally, too small an allowance for even an idle man. They work until nine, when they're given half to three-quarters of an hour for breakfast by the ditch. Often, they remain standing due to the inclemency of the weather, the ground being so wet as to prevent them from doing otherwise. And in that sad position they devour the little bread they have, perfectly dry unless the rain adds some moisture, which at the same time drenches the man eating it.

'When they return to their labour again they continue through cold and rain, until one o'clock, when they're given time for dinner. Again, they retire to stand by the ditch and rest themselves, but not one of them tastes a morsel of food. No such thing as an actual dinner is to be seen among them. No, no. That luxury is confined to the officers of the Board of Works, who're being paid to sit in the huts. And alas! The men outside return to the hammer and the spade for the remaining daylight hours.

'But if and when they retire early, completely exhausted, unable to move, as I believe has happened with some of the older men – but young and apparently strong, healthy men too – they're cut a quarter of a day's wage! For their idleness!

'Oh …' Throwing up his hands, Creed sat back, adjusting the waist of his trousers, then looked to his sage old friend in the hope of answers, or if none could be voiced, some comfort at least.

Paulellen smiled sympathetically. 'Now, would you tell him, Sam – all of this stress is not good for his health!'

'I would, Paulellen.' Sam, having long finished his soup, was sitting back with one arm over his chair, and grinned as he answered, looking out over his glasses, 'But do you think it will change anything? He only listens when you agree with him.' Samuel chuckled, poking his glasses back up. Retaining his easy composure, he brought his elbows back to the table. 'How is the business doing, Con?'

'The business? Have you not had enough woe for one sitting, Sam?' Creed sighed and, half-smiling, caught Sam winking to Paulellen as if to say, *We need to get it all out of him.* 'I'm inundated with every pauper in the district, if you must know it. Pledging me – nay, selling me – rags, blankets and all that they have. All their earthly possessions, one limb at a time. My fear is that I'll never see half of them again, forsooth. And *they* know it too …'

Creed's concentration intensified. 'You can see it in their eyes,' he said, imagining himself positioned behind the counter of the shop as he stared through the food on his plate, pushing it around with his fork. 'I watch them, as I provide the terms. I say, "You have up until ten months to redeem the pledge, with accrued interest," and so on and so forth. But they look upon the clothes being taken away as if you were burying their children. And once you pay them the few pence, they can't get out of the shop fast enough. I've often found the tickets blowing round the square outside…

'The pauper has always been a frequent class of customer.' Creed looked up for a moment, then gazed off again. 'Oftentimes they'd pledge their shoes for a few days and come back for them in time to go to Mass on a Sunday. But not any more. I expect George Wiseman is the same. But ever do you think we get any praise?' *Clink!* Creed dropped the fork merrily onto the porcelain rim. 'We're the devils of all merchants, don't you know? The scorn of all … Hah! Well, you did ask!' He smiled at Sam who, laughing, now seemed somewhat happier. 'There's not much similarity in what we administer, Sam. But I suppose there is a constancy in both our trades. People will always need bread and, God help us, it seems that there will always be a class of the poor, for the rich to tread o'er the backs of, and in need of a line of credit to bail themselves out.'

Sam sat up now and, loosening the napkin over his lap, seemed ready to offer something in response. *But where would he even begin?* Creed wondered.

'Sadly, yes, you're right on both counts, Cornelius, my friend. But … the way I view it, all things must pass. That, of course, can be of no comfort to those who are squashed beneath the wheels of the rolling machine of time. But just like my bread that also rises, every empire has a limited life. Nothing has been surer since the dawn of civilisation.

'And just like the bread … every civilisation is eventually consumed by the poor.'

Creed brimmed over. 'Oh! Wise words. Wise words indeed, Mr Welply.'

'Very profound, Sam!' Paulellen too seemed genuinely impressed by Sam's remarkable wisdom, and Creed, smiling now, was even more proud of his friend for it. And Sam had more: 'In the meantime, we each can only do what we can manage. It can do no good to throw ourselves under the same wheels, Con. One day at a time, we … I, the baker, bake the bread. And you, the scribe, record the gospel.'

Creed's smile widened. He was pleased by the flattery and much comforted by Sam's counsel.

'Or …' Samuel Welply proposed, 'the baker puts bread into the mouths of the poor, and the moneylender extorts every last bean out of them. Whichever you prefer.'

'Oh!' exclaimed Paulellen.

'You …!' added Creed, getting up. 'Thus spoke the Pharisee!'

Risen out of the chair, Creed beat the laughing critic with his napkin as Paulellen squealed in delight.

'I love it when you are around, Sam,' she said. 'You always know how to cheer him up.'

*

At around four o'clock that same afternoon, Samuel Welply, not long returned from his lunch with the Creeds, found himself administering to just such a scene as they had inadvertently described, when, as if manifest by his very word, a number of the most careworn and sorry creatures the eye could look upon marched into his shop.

'Have you any bread to spare, kind sir? Lord ha' mercy we are stricken with the hunger,' said a woman, standing over her boy, both of them looking almost spent. Those now within appeared to be part of a larger group, some other members of which Welply could see through the window, scattering across the square and splintering in every direction.

'Where have you come from?' Sam asked, simultaneously handing a cloth bag to his son who had been manning the counter. Sam gestured for him to go through to the back.

'We have marched from the parishes of Kilnamartery and Ballyvourney, in hopes that someone may alleviate our utter destitution and misery,' a young woman said with her withered hands held out.

'We have children and parents at home, unable to make the journey,' pleaded the hoarse, dry voice of a man behind her.

Returning from out the back, Sam's son brought a message: 'They're already working on the dough for tomorrow, Father, but there's not much left from this morning it's so late in the day.'

'Give out whatever we have, John.' Sam placed his hand on the boy's back to reassure him. At sixteen, John was the youngest of Sam's sons and quiet, but the most even-tempered and the most like him, Sam felt.

It did not take the two of them long to exhaust what was above and below the counter and when they were getting down to the last of it, Sam turned to reach up and take down a box on the higher shelf. 'Pass out a few of these,' he told John, filling his hand with a handful of the penny-sized token coins he'd had minted, bearing the inscription *Samuel Welply Merchant Macroom*.

'The blessings of God upon ye, sir. We haven't eaten a crumb since yesterday,' one of the beggars, walking out with a penny loaf, thanked him.

'Venial sinners all, God have mercy on you!' Through the open door, Sam looked for the source of the strains and saw it was Father Lee, who, along with his curate Father Barry, had arrived on the scene, likely intent on highlighting to the paupers the impropriety of their ways. A figure in a long black robe was enough to send all the God-fearing poor upon their heels as Sam and John, now joined by ten-year-old Charlotte and their mother, Dorcas, from out the back, watched on.

'You mustn't linger here, making a nuisance of yourselves,' Father Lee told the last of the frightened souls as he stepped in over the threshold. Father Barry, in his wake, drove them too as they scattered. 'The Lord forgives you, but you will do more damage to yourselves acting in this manner than you will ever be nourished by it.'

'Father Thomas.' Sam greeted the priest affectionately by his first name.

'Mr and Mrs Welply,' Lee said by way of returning the greeting, 'I have great sympathy for them, as we all do of course.' He stood in the doorway with one hand on the frame and the other upon the brass handle, readying to close it when he went. 'But they must be discouraged, or ere long we'll have every poor soul in the barony descending upon the town.'

'They're like a flock of famished crows, the poor creatures.' The priest lingered, explaining, 'Obviously presuming that one baker could not feed them all, they divided themselves up among all six bakeries – yourselves and Magner's next door were the last to get them. It's taken myself and Father Barry some time to round them up, hasn't it, Father?' he said, wiping the beads of sweat from his forehead with the patched arm of his cassock.

'Oh, they've been to Magner's, Duggan's, Baldwin's, Cotter's. Every one. All showed remarkable generosity, God be good to them. Each of them had given out plenty to the poor souls before we were even alerted,' Father Barry said in his high, pointed voice.

'They've the poor of the town driven mad,' Father Thomas added, 'who'd probably be off on their own daily quests to scrounge the "going offs" at this stage. Anyway, most have received something now.' And with that, satisfied the burden on his soul had been lessened and his task made lighter, the priest began to withdraw, pulling the door out behind him. 'Good day to you, good people, and sorry for the trouble.'

'No trouble at all,' Sam said, raising his hand, then holding Dorcas close, as under his other arm, Charlotte pressed herself between them, in need of comfort in light of the unusual scene.

'Go on now, back to your homes. And pray for God's mercy.' Through the window, Sam heard the shout of Father Lee.

As Dorcas took Charlotte back into the house, Sam too was satisfied that, temporarily satiated, the crowd had left peacefully to wander back out towards home, or whatever home looked like to them – their desperate hovels, away in the desolate hills and rocky pastures of bog and marsh. Ballyvourney and Kilnamartery were a long way to walk from Macroom, he knew that much. Most would be hungry again before they'd even reached home, at six, eight, ten miles distant.

'We'll close up for the day, John. What do you think?'

'There's not a loaf left to sell, Father,' the boy replied.

29

Gravel in the Pot

A bhean úd thíos ar bruach an tsrutháin.
Seoithín seó, úileó leó.
A' dtuigeann túsa fáth mo ghearáin?
Seoithín seó, úileó leó.

'What are you singing, Mam?' little Síle asked, staring at the wall.

'It's the woman caught by the faeries, down by the stream,' Cáit answered. 'And she has to send for her husband to come and break the spell.'

Seoithín, seoithín, seoithín, seoithín,
Seoithín seó, úileó leó.
Seoithín, seoithín, seoithín, seoithín,
Seoithín seó, úileó leó.

Cáit sang the gentle strains of the lullaby and pulled the bone comb through the strands of Síle's yellow hair, picking out the moss and leaves she'd collected while sleeping on the floor. Cáit remembered when her own mother used to do the same for her – the way Síle sat quietly, trying to keep her head still, and the way her neck moved when the comb caught in her hair. It was just like that, but in poorer surroundings now. And now Síle was Cáit, and Cáit was her mother. *How did all that time go by so fast?*

Abair lem' cheile teacht amáireach.
Seoithín seó, úileó leó.
Agus scian coise duibhe a thabhairt 'na láimh leis.
Seoithín seó, úileó leó.

'Will they catch *us* when we go to the stream, *a mháthair?* Síle asked.

'Not a bit. It's not by our stream she was caught. 'Twas another stream far away off,' Cáit told her, combing the long strands at the back. 'We'd be too clever for them, Síle. Anyway, your father would come along and cut the chains with the black-footed knife.'

'What's ...'

'Shhhh. Don't wake Diarmuidín now.'

Cáit continued singing and picking out the debris. It amazed her that Síle seemed to be under the same spell, but the ritual had a calming effect on herself too, Cáit realised.

Nó mara dtige sé san tráth so.
Seoithín seó, úileó leó.
Beadsa im banríon ar na mnáibh seo.
Seoithín seó, úileó leó.

Cáit sang on and off all the while some days. To entertain the children and herself. To pass the time. And to banish the hunger for them. Singing brought stillness and simplicity to everything. The words and the winding airs of the old stories were often a comforting description of her own sadnesses, by those who came before her. Someone else's words about their troubles helped her to forget her own, or think less of them. That the same songs were sung all around, and had been for eons, meant she was not alone. But most importantly the songs connected her to people far away and beyond in different times. To her own people, no matter how distant they were, or how long any of them were gone from her.

'*Seoithín, seoithín, seoithín, seoithín.*
Seoithín seó, úileó leó.
Seoithin, seoithín, seoithín, seoithín.
Seoithín seó, úileó leó.'

'Now ... hopefully Daddy will bring home some new, clean straw soon. He promised me he would.' Cáit let Síle down off her knee and teased away the strands of gold thread from the comb. Opening her hand, Cáit got a picture of her mother and, longing for simpler days, she watched as the hair fell and slowly sailed down through the shades of dark and light to the earth floor below – a floor that was bare but for its partial covering of leaves and moss from the woods. New straw would take a bit more of the dampness out of it, and put something between them and the cold ground. Each day lately, Cáit had held hopes that Pádraig would bring home a fresh wad to scatter across it. But she knew and understood that he was coming home in darkness since he'd got on the works, and that before that, this long time, he'd had nothing to barter with.

If it wasn't that it was so hard to come by at this time of year, she'd go and ask one of the local farmers herself. 'Maybe we'll try a walk ourselves today or tomorrow, Síle, ha? See if Máire Ní Críodáin has a bundle of straw she can spare for us.'

'We will, *a mháthair*. But can I go and play with Seághainín and Peig Labhráis first?'

'Is it raining out?'

Síle poked her head out the door and back in, as Cáit stayed put on the three-legged stool. 'No, it's stopped.'

'Are you not cold to be staying out long in this weather?' Cáit asked.

'I am not, *a mháthair*.'

Both children had been struggling with bad chests already through the month. But Cáit knew it was unhealthy to restrict them too much. Fresh air was what they needed and it suited her to get little break when Síle went off playing.

'Right then. Go on with ye so, but just for a short while.' Part of her was just too tired to argue. But Síle was already gone and Cáit began deciding what needed to be done to keep the little bothán in order and herself distracted from the desolation.

'What do you think, little man?' she said, peeling the blanket back off Diarmuidín, who began to moan at being disturbed as she picked him up. 'Oh, *you* have an idea what we should do, have you, ha?' Cáit said opening her shawl as she put him near her breast and brushing the few bits of old straw off his cheek as he latched on in the dim light of the cabin.

'We'll get you big and strong again, like your father, and your grandfather Uilliam ...' Cáit stroked his cheek with the back of her fingers, and smiled when Diarmuidín's little blue eyes suddenly looked up and stared into hers.

He seemed to smile back, through his eyes alone, and it made her very happy. 'I'm very glad you are feeding again,' Cáit told him, and admitted to herself that Pádraig taking him to the workhouse for the relief had really helped, even though she hadn't liked the idea of the child being gone so far from her at first. Silent, Diarmuidín stared back at her, until his eyelids began to close and, feeling his suck releasing, she realised he was drifting off again.

''Tis good you're eating some real food now too, though,' she told him as he slept. 'Even just a little bit. Your poor mammy isn't as full of milk as she used to be now.' Even just looking at her own hands, she worried at how thin she was getting.

After Diarmuidín had awoken and fallen asleep a couple of times and she had swapped him to the other side, Cáit knew there was no more for the moment and she closed her shawl, wrapped Diarmuidín back in the blanket, and left him sleeping on the floor.

*

Two buckets. One for the outgoing and one for the incoming. Fresh water from the spring was the incoming, and whatever had been passed during the night, and now, was the outgoing, kept in the corner so it wouldn't be kicked over. A scoop of ash from the fire helped keep the fumes down, and the splashing too of course, until it was full enough to go out. But as it was all going to go on the dung heap outside, the smell was not the biggest concern. At this time of year, the cold helped too. It was only in summer that the flies were a bother, but even then, for the most part, the smoke from the fire kept them at bay.

Up off the bucket, Cáit let the shawl back down over her knees and, pulling up the hood, shoved her hair inside it, behind her head.

Before she ever took a step outside, the hood went up. Year-long, like all the women around, Cáit wore the black shawl covering up everything from head to foot, with a thick slip underneath to keep her warm. The hard-wearing cloth of the shawl was tattered and glazed with the salt of sweat and dirt. But so long as it kept her covered and it wasn't falling completely asunder she could scarce afford to think about not having another one.

'Now, you'll be all right there for a little while, won't you?' Cáit whispered to sleeping Diarmuidín, and taking up the out bucket, she stooped down and pulled the door behind her.

Around the side, Cáit dumped the out as high and far over the heap as she could manage, then rinsed it out a few times with what was left of the fresh, before turning towards the spring carrying the one empty bucket to refill. She walked to the sound of Síle and her friends playing off in the distance and the cold breeze whistling in around the hood of her shawl.

The spring was also a meeting place of sorts, and even in all weathers, the chance to converse with an equal was a welcome break from the monotony … if the right people were down at it.

As Cáit wandered towards the spring, she saw that Máire Rua was approaching to go filling at the same time. Cáit liked her talk. Foxy Máire was the name on her, and the name put on all the people with red hair. Máire was a tall, gentle woman, ladylike in her manners. Cáit felt for Máire because she had it even worse off than Cáit had. She could recall Máire telling her that when the blight had come to their garden – when the stalks were rotting and falling – she had spent the day looking out at it, crying, she said, and wondering where in the world they were going to get something to eat. The garden had barely a salvageable morsel left in it. Cáit had lived all of that too. But, Máire had confided in Cáit, after they'd eaten everything they had in the house, Labhrás Ua Duinnín, Máire's husband, had been struck down. 'Attacked by rheumatism' was how Máire had put it, and he'd been unable to rise from the bed since. Cáit knew Máire had described her situation that way both for her own and for her husband's dignity – and understandably at that, she thought in her heart. But what it really meant, Cáit and Pádraig had discussed, was that poor Labhrás had likely lost his will to live. It was no great surprise to Cáit, or to her husband, that many people, glimpsing the likely future ahead of them, as Labhrás surely had, simply lay down and gave up. It was hard enough to be in the situation Cáit and Pádraig were in, Cáit knew that well. But it would be another thing altogether to be in a situation where the man of the house was not only no longer capable of supporting his family but was himself another helpless dependant – for his wife to carry alone, along with her children. Cáit knew Máire had the worst of it, and lately, whenever she saw or thought of her, she could not help but think of her terrible plight and feel pity.

Almost every morning ever since the blight had come, Cáit knew that Máire, fasting, went out and travelled east to Clydagh across the hills, a distance of four or five miles. She had some relations over there who gave her a can of milk, which she carried home and put over the fire until it turned to curds and whey. She gave Labhrás the curds, and drank the whey herself. Cáit pitied her greatly, but admired her in equal measure because no matter how bleak her lot, she got up, and kept going regardless.

'Good morning, Máire.'

'Well, Cáit. How are the little ones doing? Are you faring all right, with Diarmuidín? 'Tis terrible hard times. And Síle is getting such a fine little girl, I do see it.'

'It's the hard times surely, Máire Rua. But we're taking it a day at a time. The children are faring well enough, thanks be to God. And how is Peig Labhráis, Máire? She's such a bright child. Full of the stories.' Cáit turned and squinted at Síle playing beyond in the rushy field, and at her friends, with Peig Labhráis among them. Peig Labhráis, a little older than Síle by a couple of years, was Máire's daughter, named after both her father and her grandmother.

'Oh, Peig na Croise will never be gone with her. It's telling the stories of Séadna now, she is. Every bar of her grandmother.'

Cáit was happy to see a little smile come to the face of Máire and a little relief to her troubles, however brief.

'How is that gentle husband of yours, Cáit? He's a good man.'

'He is that, Máire. He's a place got on the works now and that's keeping us going.'

'Oh, that's fine news, Cáit. God is good. And ye deserve it, the two of ye, with all the hardship you've been through. But there's tougher times ahead, Cáit. We have to conserve what we have, and be sparing with the lot.'

'I know, Máire. We're very lucky indeed. Now I don't want to be complaining … I know any family'd be glad of it.' *The truth of it is, Máire …* Cáit thought to say something of the huge strain the walk was putting on Pádraig for all the trouble it was worth, but remembering Máire was doing almost the same journey over Clydagh and back, daily, for a similar portion, thought better of it and stopped herself. 'And how are you, Máire, are you looking after yourself? Clydagh is an awful long way to be going. Surely there's somewhere nearer you can get something easier?'

'But sure, I have to take it while it's going, Cáit,' Máire answered with her head down. 'What choice have we got, but to keep on?' Cáit sensed the defeat in Máire and could see it was near impossible for her to entertain any ideas of escaping the situation as it was. It was going to require help from the government, or intervention by the Relief Committees, to save the people, or to tide them over while there was nothing to eat in the ground. Cáit kept the thought to herself, but agreed with Máire. What *could* the woman do with Labhrás laid up as he was? Even if fortune was wildly in her favour, and she and he somehow had the passage for a steamer to some foreign shore – which Cáit was almost certain would never be the case – Labhrás was incapacitated and unable for travel. Cáit found herself trying to picture how far he'd gone down in his health by remembering how he used to be out digging and laughing, leaning on his spade, a good-natured man with a trickster's humour. No one had seen him for some time.

'Máire, I know Pádraig was very lucky to get on the works,' Cáit said, 'but do you think if Labhrás could manage and maybe go and see Father O'Brien in Clondrohid? That's who got Pádraig his name on the list of the works. There's bound to be a long queue, but at least it might give him a bit of hope. It might get him up and going again.' Cáit heard the sadness in her own voice as she pleaded, attempting to waken a bit of the light in Máire. But before she'd even finished talking, she could tell by the shaking of her head that Máire saw no hope of her husband rising up again.

'It will not … between ourselves, Cáit; it'll be this until the end. Labhrás is fading …' Máire began to cry. 'He's not a young man, as you know, Cáit.'

Cáit put her hand to Máire's shoulder. 'I know, Máire. Sure, you're doing the best you can. But listen, you never know, even just the thought of it might help him regain a bit of his strength. A bit of hope is a kind thing.'

'Oh, look at me here,' Máire said, wiping away her tears. 'Keeping you standing out in the cold, listening to my woes, and you probably with the baby inside needing your attention. I haven't even put my bucket to the sup.'

Máire set her bucket filling under the fast trickle of cold mountain water spouting out of the cleft of rocks in the side of the ditch. Searching for something to comfort her friend, Cáit looked into the little stream below, which licked over the rocks and ran away off into the cold, wild, poor hills. She and Pádraig were going to see their way through these times somehow. Cáit knew that much. With Pádraig on the works and they being much younger than the likes of poor Máire and Labhrás, they were far better off than a lot of those around the parish. She didn't know how, but she decided that when the time came, however the opportunity presented itself, she would do what she could to help Máire.

'Cáit. God bless you. You always make me feel better about my troubles somehow,' said she, leaning her head over, and pulled her bucket away as the clear water neared the lip of it.

'Sure, it's not hard at all to listen,' Cáit said, rubbing her friend's shoulder, then putting her own bucket to the flow of the water.

'Well, Cáit,' Máire said, sniffling back the last of her tears and catching up the throat of her own shawl to keep out the wind. 'I have to go providing before long now and I better leave you to look after your little ones.' Like everyone, Cáit knew that someone going 'providing' was a kind word for begging. But the least that life could afford the poor woman was a little bit of pride and self-respect, Cáit thought. These were the *droć-śaoǵal*, the bad times, and people were to be forgiven for whatever they had to do to get on.

'Right so, Máire. You mind yourself, now.'

'Oh. Would you look at …' Máire Rua said and turned her feet to walk away. 'Here comes Caitilín Pruiséal. Cáit, I'd better be going or I'll never get back to himself.' Caitilín, as Máire had called her, was known to Cáit as Kitty Uí Laeire, whose husband was Mícheál Ua Laeire. They were Cáit and Pádraig's closest neighbours from the bothán behind the ridge. Pruiséal was Caitilín's name before she'd been married.

'Right so, Máire. *Slán. Slán.*' Cáit was caught now, she knew it. Her bucket wasn't full enough to leave yet and although she had the strong urge to get away and would much rather come back with her bucket again later, Kitty would spot the half-filled bucket and know Cáit was avoiding her. The closer the woman got, the more Cáit knew it was too late and she soon accepted that she would just have to talk to the woman. It was just as her bucket was nearing full and she was drawing it back that her neighbour arrived at a rush.

'Well, Cáit, how are ye all keeping?' Kitty's tone, as always, was full of pity, presuming any answer before it had even been uttered, Cáit observed. It was always as if whatever was to come back was bound to be a grief-filled response and there was something Cáit found irksome about that disposition in Kitty. It said more about her own view of the world than it did of whoever she was talking to. It seemed to Cáit like a trick. One that gave Kitty a feeling of being better than her neighbours. Cáit supposed that by concentrating on the other person's woes, Kitty aimed to distract herself – and probably her listener too – from her own desperation, however deep it was, with the result that they'd both believe *her* problems were not as bad. But on Cáit, for one, it did not work. She understood why Kitty would want to fool herself. It was the way it was done at everyone else's expense she thought was unfair.

'Hello, Caitilín.'

'Get them little ones in out of the cold, Cáit; it looks like it's going to rain,' Máire Rua shouted back to Cáit from away off, trying to give her an excuse to get away.

'I will surely, Máire,' she shouted back.

'How are the little ones, Cáit? Oh, they're such beautiful children. I do see Pádraig going away in the mornings. Has he got a bit of work somewhere?'

'Well, he's doing the bit, Caitilín …'

'Oh, isn't it very lucky ye are?' Kitty lowered her head to one side, making her face long. 'If only my Mícheáilín could get the bit of use as well. My poor children are starving up there, the crat'urs.'

'Ah, 'tis the hard times, Caitilín. God save the hearers.' Instinctively, Cáit wished her well, but she could not bring herself to see Kitty's struggles at that moment – she was too preoccupied with getting free of her talk.

'God save us, Cáit. And how was Máire Rua beyond? She was in an awful hurry there to be leaving.'

'She had to get back in out of the weather to poor Labhrás,' Cáit said, in Máire's defence.

'Poor aul' Larry is right,' Kitty said. 'He's not much use to her at all, God help her. But sure … 'Tis better a poor horse than no horse at all, I suppose. *Níorbh fhearra dhuit mar chneastacht fé d'bhonn.'* Kitty, wearing the sorrow, looked after Máire in the distance and tutted a regret. 'Cáit, do you think your Pádraig could ever put the word in, and get the start for Mícheáilín?'

'Oh, Caitilín, I don't know if …'

'He's a fine strong man for the work, is Mícheáilín. And he might be likened to return the favour some time, God willing.'

'Sure, you know yourself, Caitilín. 'Tis only by the grace of God. And Pádraig has no idea himself how long 'twill last.'

'I know,' Kitty said, intimating her sympathy, 'but maybe he'd keep us in mind, if ye'd say it t' him, Cáit. Your Pádraig?'

'Of course, Caitilín. Sure, he knows Mícheál is a good man.'

'That he is, Cáit. Thank you, girl.'

'And isn't it lucky you've only the two? Tut.' Kitty looked sorry away at the children playing again. 'Will ye have any more, Cáit?' she said, turning back and searching Cáit's eyes, with an intense stare that disturbed her.

'Well, now …' Cáit turned away.

'Don't mind me. I don't want to be sticking my nose into any soul's business, girl … but trust me, don't have more if you can help it, Cáit.'

'I know, I know. Thank you, Caitilín. Listen, I'd better be gettin' back. I left little Diarmuidín on his own.' Cáit started away, knowing that she'd never be invited to leave if she didn't take herself away.

'… because it's you who will have to keep them all fed on your bosom all the day long.' Kitty continued.

'Thank you, Caitilín. Get yourself in out of the cold, won't ye.'

'They're grand children, Cáit, so they are. Don't forget us now, won't ye?' Kitty called after her.

'Come on, Síle, in out of that cold.' Cáit shouted away up at the group of children and marched towards the house, holding her shawl closed with one hand, her other arm fully extended and the bones and veins showing, exposed as it was from the elbow down by her frayed sleeve, as she struggled with the bucket.

'Oh, Mam! Are you going to put gravel in the cake?' Síle had returned from playing to get a drink of water.

'I am, Síle,' Cáit teased. After nine days on the works, Pádraig was finally due to be getting the first wage, and in the hopes that he might be bringing home some meal from town this day, Cáit, down on one knee, was scouring out the bastible pot with some gravel. Excited at the prospect she smiled, as Síle, finishing the water, ran off again back to her friends.

'*A Chonchubhair.*'

Cáit stopped her scrubbing to listen as Síle, still within earshot, called out to the boy who was her friend, her little voice grief-stricken and with worry on her tongue. 'What are we going to do, Con? What'll we do at all?'

'What's wrong with you now, Síle?' Cáit heard Con answer, and smiled to herself.

'My *mamaí* is making a cake in the wide-bottomed pot and she's putting gravel into it. All our teeth will be broken! Some of the stones are very big. Only Diarmuidín will be all right. His teeth are still new and he doesn't eat much with them yet.'

'What ever do you mean, Síle?'

'Come and look,' said Síle, her voice drawing nearer as she brought Con, Peig Labhráis and Seáinín Philib in tow.

'What did you think I was doing, Síle?' Cáit said. 'Sure, I'm only cleaning out the pot. Now isn't your sister a silly goose?' She turned and spoke to Diarmuidín, who, attracted by the commotion, had stood himself up in the doorway.

'Will you eat some gravel cake, Diarmuidín?' Conchubhar asked the baby, as they all began to laugh.

30

GREY ARMY

'Pssst!'

Clink, clink, smatter.

'Pssst! Hey!'

Pádraig roused to turn his head.

'Did you see that fella? He went into the office. Into Mr Barrett's office.'

'Who?' another voice said.

Tap, tap, swing, clink, smatter.

Too exhausted to expend the energy, Pádraig carried on with the monotonous pounding of rock. Slowly and steadily, one at a time. *Clink, stack, clink, smatter.* Sometimes one tap, others three or four.

'It looked like the head gaffer.'

Smatter. Pick up. Stack.

'Maybe he brought the wages.'

Recognising the word 'wages', Pádraig's head spun on its post and followed the eyes of the others. But except for somebody taking horses away, he couldn't see anything.

It had been nine days since they had started on the works now, and yesterday being Friday, he'd had high hopes of their being paid – but nothing.

'I heard we're going to get the wages in silver,' one of the voices said.

Pádraig kept his concentration trained on the cabin.

'Silver, gold, dirt. It'll be all the same whatever way we get it. You can't eat any of them and we'll have to swap it all for food. But so long as it's equal to eight pence a day …'

Denis Murphy, Pádraig and Jeremiah O'Leary were now grouped together as a gang, taking it in turns, one carrying the rocks, another smashing them and another filling the barrow with a spade and throwing them up on the road. At times they took to all breaking at once, but interchanging the tasks gave their hands a break.

'What did he look like?' Denis asked, staring at the huts too.

'He was on that big horse, another two with him,' Jeremiah replied. 'But he looked very official, all dressed up in regalia. It's the big bag the others were carrying for him makes me think it might be the wages.' Jeremiah looked to the heavens as a light few drops began to fall. 'She's not going to hold, I don't think, lads.' Distant rumbling gave punctuation to his words.

Denis, squatting down, looked skyward to make his own assessment and blinked through the small drops landing on his face. 'If it keeps up like this we'll have lost four out of nine days to the weather; I'm fasting half the time and this rain is getting into my bones.'

To Pádraig, in that moment, Denis looked as poor as he sounded. He wondered how pathetic the three of them would look to anyone who cared to notice them. *A sorry, ragged lot,* he was thinking, when out of his peripheral vision, he perceived one of the stewards on a horse staring squarely at them.

'We're being watched,' Jeremiah said.

'Be the divil.' Denis Murphy pulled his head down, moving a rock as the steward turned away again.

Denis's face stayed in Pádraig's mind as, stacking the next rock, he watched the little man get up to go for more. It was a grey face, but so was everything else around them when he came to think of it. Their clothes were grey with dirt. The rocks were grey. The sky was grey. The rain – everything about the scene was miserable.

Clink, clink, smatter. Pick up. Stack. Tap, tap, swing, clink, smatter. Pádraig continued on.

'Did you lose a shoe?' he asked when Denis came walking back, carrying a rock that made his small frame bend and hunch, one lonely shoe flapping from his foot.

'No. I found one.' Denis dropped the rock and walked away again.

Through the distortion of his tears as he tried to hold in the laughter over the minutes that followed, it was all Pádraig could do not to smash his fingers with the hammer. He couldn't remember when he had last laughed at anything other than entertaining the children. He wasn't fully sure if Denis was being dry-witted or matter of fact, but that made it all the better and, either way, Pádraig was happy about it. The feeling was medicine. He felt comradeship, admiration, pity and love for the man all at once. If Denis was earnest it was funny. If he was being sarcastic it was even funnier. No matter what way he thought about it, the whole idea made him shake. It felt like poitín coursing through his blood and he soaked up the feeling for everything it was worth.

'What's wrong with you?' Jeremiah was back with the barrow.

'Ah ...' Pádraig saw no point in trying to conceal his amusement any more, but the merriment was almost spent now and he wiped away his tears, still enjoying the departing ripples of feeling, like rings that drifted out around a stone dropped into a pond.

'Are ye all right?' Jeremiah asked again, clearly confused.

'What's wrong with him?' Denis was back with another rock.

'I dunno,' Jeremiah answered, shovelling up the debris.

Pádraig was still trying to catch his breath when the steward began to approach on horseback. But just in time, another ganger blew the whistle for the 'morning suck', the early break, when the labourers without food might suck a pipe instead. The steward slowed his horse, glaring at them, then turned away, as Pádraig rose up from his haunches to walk the fifty yards or so to the ditch.

'What was up with him?' asked Jeremiah after each of them had finished eating the griddle bread out of their pockets. Nobody talked while they were eating. The luxury was all too rare at this point to be absentmindedly wasted.

'He asked me if I'd lost a shoe,' Denis answered.

Jeremiah shook his head, clearly unimpressed by the ridiculousness of the wearing of one shoe, the attempt at humour or at Pádraig's laughing at their friend's misfortune. But that just started Pádraig off on another bout.

'Did you really find one?' he asked, holding his guts, feeling his ribs through the gaping hole in his shirt. He couldn't help himself now even at the risk of the poor man's feelings.

'Are you away with the faeries?' Denis replied. 'I've been like this for about three days. I told ye, I fell asleep down by Browne's field one of the evenings a couple of yards from the road and when I woke up the other one was gone.'

'What?' Pádraig was contorted from head to foot as he choked on the laughter.

'Whist. There he is, look ...' Denis gave a flick of his head at something by the sheds.

A group of men were coming out of Mr Barrett's hut. The tall, military-clad figure in their midst was about as conspicuous as a tree in a field of corn, and was like nothing Pádraig had ever seen.

'Some get up, isn't it,' Jeremiah said.

'Gordon, is it?' Denis brushed aside the question with one of his own.

'There's two of them, you know,' Jeremiah said, staring after the group in awe.

Denis looked across at him. 'What?'

It was then that Pádraig noticed the steward on the horse reaching the group with the trussed-up figure at its centre. Barrett, dressed in a three-piece more suited to one of the labourers when compared with the soldier, appeared to be addressing the head porter, hitherto waiting on the group.

'Mr Conroy, fetch the gentlemen's horses, will you?'

'Of course, sir.'

'After you've had the visiting steward mop up here, Mr Barrett, I suggest that you send him out to Buckley's to collect the stores.' Gordon, with a moustache as thick as a cigar to top off his outlandish attire, expressed his wishes to Barrett.

'Yes sir, Captain Gordon: for the implements and tools to be utilised on road number nineteen and numbers one-seven-four and one-two-eight. I've made a note of it.'

'Inch-perfect,' Gordon answered, looking straight ahead.

'And you're satisfied that all is in order in so far as labour is concerned here, Captain Gordon?' Barrett sounded anxious.

'As good as can be expected.' Gordon nodded, if with only a slight hint of reluctance, as the porters drew up the horses beside them.

'If only the weather would hold,' Barrett said, looking to the sky. Captain Gordon was atop his horse by now, and readying to depart.

O'Leary squinted. 'Do you see the bag I was talking about?'

'I see it,' Denis replied.

'Does it look any lighter to you than it was when he came in?'

'Jaysus, how would I know … and it so far away.'

'Ah, cack,' Jeremiah muttered. 'It's a fine-looking uniform all the same. All the shiny buttons. You'd get a few quid for that, sword and all.'

'Pompous-looking battle axe,' Denis scoffed, jerking his chin back into his neck in repulsion. 'If I didn't need the work I'd run him through, and ten more like him, just to get meself warm.'

He sounded more earnest than trite to Pádraig. He rubbed his thin blue hands together, blowing into them, for they stung with the cold, and studied his elder companion, tracing the desperation of his sunken cheeks and dark, rheumy eyes.

'You have what you need, Mr Barrett?' Gordon asked.

'I have, sir.'

The horse stirred restlessly and Gordon held on to the reins to control it. 'Easy, Jess.' He patted the beast's neck. 'I must stop into Macroom for some business this morning. I leave for Cork directly after. I'll be away throughout most of the week, but I can be got at the Imperial.'

'Of course, sir.'

Gordon kicked his horse and departed, leading out his armed associates as Mr Barrett looked on and checked his pocket watch. At his command, Mr Roberts, the overseer, nodded to the steward who, acknowledging the order, pulled a whistle from his breast pocket and blew it shrilly, signalling the semi-starved, shabbily clad, grey army to get back to the task of further weakening their fading constitutions.

31

A Trail of Silver

Just in from Killarney, rattling over the cobbles, the Cork mail car crossed the rain-wet square and came to rest outside the post office on the south side. Its back wheel sloshed to and fro in a muddy hollow as the horses settled and the driver, still in his seat, picked up a bell and rang it vigorously to signal his arrival. At the same time, the guard, a woolly-bearded man with pointy boots, alighted from the cart at the rear and, ready for a new deposit, leaned on the locked well that protected Sunday's outgoing mail, collected and stored at each stop along the way.

The unhappy-looking passengers – four apiece facing out on either side of the central luggage corral – were as varied a cross-section of middle society as could be found on the top half of a coach, modelling everything from a black veil to top hat and beaten bowler, from bonnet to straw hat to no hat. But from the knee down the spattering mud had blended all to an indistinguishable gallery of classlessness.

Inside the post office Peter Williams, postmaster for Macroom, dressed the last of his dispatches with a Penny Black, shunted on the postmark for MACROOM dated NO29 1846, then continued loading the bag of mail bound for Cork, and who knows where beyond.

'Oh! Thank God, I'm in time.' A hefty woman busied in the door all a fluster and made a beeline for the counter, letters in hand.

'Now, Mrs Callaghan, I can't be holding up the mail car.'

'Ah, Mr Williams. Don't say I went to all this trouble for nothing. Is the car not a bit early?'

'On time, Eileen. But he won't be anywhere else if I've to hold him up for you.'

'I won't hold ye again,' she said, dabbing her neck for sweat.

Outside, the now restless passengers complained about the inconvenient delay, cramped as they were on the outer seats, and one of the horses whinnied and kicked its hooves to reduce the discomfort of the traces and harness. But just when Mr Williams should have appeared with a half-filled linen sack bearing the words Royal Mail, a studious-looking Cornelius Creed, carrying a bag that looked too big for him – and awkward to carry – approached the driver at the front.

'How would you like to earn yourself a shilling, young man?' asked Creed.

'Not as much as I'd like to earn half a crown.'

The answer was dry and sharp and Creed did his best to hide his outrage with professional detachment. 'Huh! Half a crown is it? You haven't even heard the task yet.'

'Half a crown. That's my price. I've to split it with yer man in the back there.'

Creed looked over his glasses back to the guard and, satisfied with the added security, decided to accept terms. 'Very well. A half-crown. I need you to take this bag to the Imperial Hotel.'

'That's not on my route, sir.'

'I'm aware of that. That's what the half-crown is for.'

'It'll be a shilling more. I'll have to walk there after I drop the car to the depot.'

'A shilling more? Sixpence!'

'Shilling. It's Sunday. There's no other cars but the mail.'

'Ch!' Creed considered himself to have an able way with words and to have no small experience negotiating over coin. But as the youth on the mail car had him beaten and feeling at an impasse, he exchanged the sound of exasperation for logic.

As he stood there, the guard returned from the transaction with Mr Williams, unlocked the hatch with the turn handle and slung the new mail sack in on top of whatever had travelled from Killarney, Tralee and Millstreet.

'Next stop, Coachford,' the driver shouted over his shoulder, then squeezed a spit out of the far side of his mouth and wiped his chin on his sleeve. 'A half-crown and a shilling?' he reiterated.

Conscious that he was running out of time, Creed shook his head, then bowed it and began talking to himself as he consulted his purse. *I could get a labourer to walk it for ninepence,* he thought to himself.

The driver sat forward, relaxed and easy with elbows on his knees and the loose reins flat and at the ready in his upturned palms. 'Take it or leave it, if you please, sir.' He looked over his shoulder. 'Everything secure back there, Mr Keogh?'

The guard uttered something inaudible as the driver made to start.

'Half a crown and a shilling. So be it. The bag is to be taken to the Imperial Hotel, where you'll ask for Captain Gordon, Board of Works.'

At hearing this, all eyes fell on the bag. The driver too was suddenly attentive, causing Creed to fear another price hike. But it did not come.

'Mr Keogh,' the driver called over his shoulder, eyes still on the bag. The guard, with one foot on the cart ready to climb on, dismounted but moved no further from his post. 'Ready for another bag!'

'Ahem.' The driver looked down at Creed.

'Oh, the fees?'

'Up front.'

'Indeed. Naturally.' Creed tried to hand up his money while wrestling with the unruly object. 'There you are.'

'What's in it anyway?'

'I believe I'll decline to answer such an enquiry, but rest assured that it's nothing that concerns you.'

It was almost certain that no harm would come to anything entrusted to the Royal Mail, although Creed had approached the negotiation feeling that a more polite discourse would more definitely ensure the safety of the bag. With this latest question, he drew a line.

'Now here is your fee as requested, up front.' Creed concluded, anxious to get shot of the conversation before he was asked any more questions he couldn't answer.

An old man on the far side was fed up. 'Is this coach ever going to move? God help us – we'll all be late, letters and all.'

'Right.' The driver, his money in hand, dispensed with further courtesy and, turning away from Creed, seemed only concerned now with the complaints of his passengers.

Creed, taking the hint, went to the back of the carriage and handed the satchel to the guard, who flung it into a space he'd cleared among the many cases and bags.

'Could it not be stored in the locked compartment?'

'Mail only in there.' Keogh was rather too matter of fact for Creed's comfort.

'The divil are we going at all?' the old man spluttered in a phlegmy voice.

'All clear!' Keogh shouted.

Creed took one step out to the side and with hand on mouth shouted up to the driver, 'Captain Gordon, Imperial Hotel.'

'Hup!' The driver called out to the nags, slapping the reins, and with a sudden start the whole apparatus shuddered into life. At that moment, the back wheel nearest Creed momentarily jammed in the rut, then skidded out of the puddle and, catching up with the speed of the other three, unexpectedly cascaded mud all over Creed.

'Ahgh! My Sunday trousers,' he gasped, realising the filth had sprayed his coat and waistcoat too. The blank-faced passengers drifted away, rocking from side to side, watching Creed as they did so. It was of only small consolation that they did not laugh or make a sport of his misfortune. None but the driver, who, glancing back at Creed, wore a mischievous grin that no one else in the carriage could see.

Soaked and holding out his arms, instinctively wishing to avoid contact with his wet clothes, Creed wandered back towards the shop, eager to change. He had no idea what was in the bag but had been sure

Captain Gordon would appreciate someone having sent it on. He hoped it was worth the trouble.

'Why did you volunteer to send it?' Paulellen wanted to know, after he'd changed into something else.

'Simply a matter of our proximity to the post office here,' he told her. 'Gordon left in such a hurry yesterday after that abominable ruckus in the boardroom, I'm not certain he even knows he left it behind him.'

'Captain Gordon left yesterday for Cork, you say? Are you sure?' Paulellen, chopping vegetables, stopped the knife to look over her shoulder. She was preparing a winter stew, Creed gathered, and he opened his nostrils to draw in the sharp, warm scent of the dried thyme.

'I'm sure – right after the meeting. And could anyone blame him?' He began to scan the paper.

'That's Captain Gordon of the Board of Works? The soldier?'

'Yes, dear.'

'I was sure I saw him walking up Castle Street this morning, towards the rectory. I presumed for the Sunday service.'

'No, dear. You must have him confused.'

'Oh.'

Gordon was a representative of the empire, and something of a prickly character to boot. But there was something Creed admired about him. Fast becoming a thorn in the side of some of Creed's own opponents, Gordon was showing promising signs that he might just shake a few of them up. Perhaps it was that, he pondered.

But besides, the charitable deed Creed had just undertaken might yet earn the Relief Committee, and the labourers of the district on the whole, a little of the man's favour. Not that Creed had calculated on the gesture costing him as much as it did.

*

'You wouldn't get this on one of Riordan's cars.'

The guard turned to see whence the remark had emanated. Although no one claimed ownership, it was clear from the other passengers' expressions that the slight had come from behind the black veil of the sullen, mourning creature, who, from what could be discerned, was in her wintering years. It was unclear, however, whether it was to the delay she was referring or to the general discomfort. And with that, the mood was set. More rain dogged the coach for the first leg of the journey and the conversations lagged. At Coachford some of the passengers alighted and for the first of three more changes, the horses were swapped too. Thereafter the weather cleared and the top coats and parapluies came down, lightening the atmosphere.

Naturally, with the coming and going of passengers, the luggage was disturbed and with no one in particular care of it, the ownerless satchel was shoved about. After Coachford it was left turned upside down so that the strap buckle became snagged, threatening to empty the contents onto the road if jolted with any force.

A foreign traveller who wished to know how there existed 'such poverty in a land of unsurpassed fertility' sought to foster a conversation with any willing speculators. 'The poor seem so badly clothed and badly fed and yet the country is most beautiful, teeming with the promise of abundance,' she said, re-emphasising her view.

After a silence left unattended by the rest of the passengers, the old man who'd spoken up at Macroom, with legs swaying and knuckles knotted over a stick, took up the lady's question. 'I'll tell ye ma'am …' He cleared his throat. 'It can all be traced to the withering effects of the Union.'

This was met with both nods of agreement and gesticulations of intolerance, with the veiled woman seeming horrified at the prospect of having to endure a treatise on such a subject.

'The chief cause of Ireland's pauperism,' the man went on regardless, 'at least in terms of the attire of the poor, is the rise of the manufactures of England. Since that started, all our women are unemployed. The poor man, out of the meagre earnings he once made, must now purchase every rag worn in his house, while his wife and daughters sit roasting their shins by the fire.

'I remember,' said he, 'when the womenfolk manufactured every item of clothing the household required ... and sold some yarn as well. But now, in our common wisdom, we prefer the English article for its cheapness and pay for what could be made at home, much better, and for far less.'

'What is your own trade, sir?' the lady asked.

'Why, I be an out-of-work tailor, ma'am.' With a brief doffing of his hat, the man demonstrated a pride in knowing his profession and in doing so revealed a small, unhealed sore atop his bare crown at which he likely scratched when in thought. 'And that is why I answer your enquiring about clothing the way that I do. As for costs, the only expense of a yard of linen to a family who've got hands to spin it is about thruppence. That includes the cost of seed and weaving. But your yard of that linen is equal to the value of three yards o' cotton or thereabouts.'

'Is that so?'

''Tis.' He nodded and opened and closed his eyes before elaborating. 'A yard of frieze, for dying and weaving, costs one and eight pence. And anyone who has worn out a coat of this description,' the man looked around, as if to invite any of his fellow passengers to challenge, or support, his assertion, 'will be able to estimate the real value of the flimsy English fabric now in general use: half wool, half cotton, which keeps out neither rain nor cold.

'But, by heaven,' the old man shook his head in woe, 'there will be nothing but hunger and misery in the cabins of Ireland until the people take a pledge to banish cotton and commence again the manufacture of their own wool and flax, which requires no capital but what they are abundantly supplied with, praise God.'

Over the clatter of the hooves, a younger woman nearest the driver, occupying the end of the seat, seemed to disregard the man's entire argument, but spoke inoffensively. 'That was all before the bad times. No matter what they wear now 'tis full of holes.'

The old man did not respond and seemed either untroubled or smart enough to stay quiet.

The topic kept the conversation flowing for a while, at one point running so high that the old man swore that some of those aboard must be the vendors of the very articles he was demonising.

'... which, granted,' he admitted, resuming his earlier, gentler tone, 'though they might be produced cheap by machinery, are still very dear to the poor people who have no money to purchase them. The poor of every other country, except the Irish,' he insisted, 'manufacture their own clothing.'

At Ballincollig the horses were changed once again and more mail was taken on. But the more talkative travellers having been replaced, the remainder of the twenty-and-a-quarter mile trip to Cork was spent mostly on a gallery of nodding heads and swaying bodies, until, at length, the meandering carriage stopped with a sudden jerk outside the Cork Post Office in Caroline Street, waking all therein.

Disembarking passengers sleepily collected their luggage as the driver signed over his coach and its contents to the inbound staff. The last bag to leave the car was the strange-looking, heavy leather case that had travelled alone for twenty miles and that was now acquainted with the shoulder of the driver who took it on the hoof and faded off through the gas-lit, smoky streets of Cork in the direction of the Imperial Hotel on South Mall.

Keogh, the guard, in whose keep the Royal Mail was officially entrusted between stops, stayed behind and handed the contents of the well over to the inbound porter of the Caroline Street depot, where throughout the course of that night, its multitude of pieces were filtered through the various departments of the sorting office, never to meet again.

*

'Aha, my drawings.' In the lobby of the Imperial, Gordon was approached by the Suisse.

'Is that what's in it, drawings?'

'Yes. When did it arrive? In fact, who dropped it off?'

'The night porter took the bag in, sir, Captain Gordon. The note here says it was ... dropped off by a coach driver from the Royal Mail.'

'No more? Does it say who sent it on?'

'It doesn't say any more, sir.'

'Hmm. Strange ... Oh well!'

32

EXALTED FLY

A s was his routine at this early hour in the office of the *Cork Examiner*, John Francis Maguire was going through the Monday letters with one of his junior editors and together they discussed what would make the Wednesday issue, his paper being an editorial that circulated only three times weekly – on Mondays, Wednesdays and Fridays – which happened to be the days the other nationalist newspaper of the region, the *Southern Reporter and Cork Commercial Courier*, did not.

'Let's put those aside. This one is too rambling. There'll be more in tomorrow of course. So these, we're undecided upon – and these here, we agree are ready to go. This one is good, but could be cut down. Keep "Fair Pay for Ballyvourney" for now, but as it's a counter to an earlier correspondence, let's watch it and not allow it drag on, or get too petty in any further responses.'

'Isaac S. Varian?' Thomas Crosbie, the young man looking over Maguire's shoulder, had started at the *Examiner* as a fifteen-year-old paper boy, but was fast becoming the protégé of his astute employer.

'He can stay,' Maguire answered. 'That's Repeal business. Right – we'll send these down to press for set up, and work on these ones in the meantime.'

*

The following evening, 1 December 1846, the printing press at the heart of the city spoke its inky truths to the cotton paper of the people's canvas and in the small hours of Wednesday morning the bundles of freshly printed journals left the floor of the *Examiner*'s premises loaded onto various carts to be transported to the towns, cities and provinces of Ireland, as well as to populate the coffee houses of Dublin and London. Appearing on the front page of all copies, one stack of which found its way to Macroom, a letter, completed its round trip to Cork and back:

TO THE EDITOR OF THE CORK EXAMINER

Dear Sir, – Having frequently written anonymously, and also with assumed names, but fearing should I adopt either course just now, more especially where I am reluctantly constrained to resort to personalities, it may serve as a pretext to any party concerned or desirous in the least to publicly refute any assertion of mine herein contained, I shall, therefore, at the foot of this hurried communication, place my real signature, confining myself strictly to facts and thereby keeping outside the power of the refutation of any individual.

Captain Gordon visited this district yesterday in his official capacity as connected with the Board of Works and attended a meeting composed of the Relief Committee and other gentlemen interested in the alleviation of the miseries of the starving poor, held in the Board room of this Union.

Scarcely had the usual preliminary formalities been disposed of, when Mr Massy H. Warren thought it proper to open a volley of grape at Mr Barrett, the Deputy County Inspector and assistant engineer to Mr Treacy, the county surveyor in this locality. Whether actuated by a feeling of public good or private malice, I am not ready to say. But at all events Captain Gordon, in the necessary protection of the character of one of his staff, said rather indignantly that he was happy to bear his testimony to the efficiency, straightforwardness and unblameable conduct of Mr Barrett; and that he would not listen to or receive any complaint against that invaluable officer, except in writing, no matter whence the charge emanated.

Mr Charles Colthurst J.P., Clonmoyle, fully concurred in every word that fell from the worthy captain and said he had ample opportunity of judging the demeanour and services of Mr Barrett and considered that no person could be better adapted to discharge the functions of the responsible appointment that excellent official so creditably filled.

It is really deplorable to witness such an attempt of stabbing at the character of a public man, who has given such universal satisfaction, and *that* in the total absence of all manner of satisfaction. The rotten and ill-working system of appointing shopkeepers and farmers to the various subordinate offices on those public roads – which is now undergoing a revision by Captain Gordon – was loudly condemned by Mr Barrett on his first arrival here, not alone on account of their incompetence, which is too obvious; but believing that it would be as much charity to give those appointments to certain persons, equally, if not more capable, whose disappointments through life and altered circumstances compel them to become the candidates for those petty situations, as to employ the famishing labourer, whose once athletic frame is now rendered attenuated, and – if I may use the word – perfectly skeletonised, by the complete absence of any nourishment.

The learned Justice, disappointed in his attack on Mr Barrett, directed his sarcasm to one of the Guardians – Mr Cornelius Murphy – simply because Mr Murphy advocated the opening of a line of road, now being made within half a mile of this town, the public usefulness of which is universally recognised, save by a few who have formed themselves into a phalanx to upset a proceeding by which near two hundred starving fellow beings are getting daily the only means by which they can avert from themselves and families the piercing shafts of death.

Like the exultation of the fly seated upon a wheel, what a dust one of these Magistrates fancies he kicks up when located upon his Magisterial throne, administering the British law to the *profanum vulgus & c,.* but here I would suggest, to his Worship, to place in a state of dormancy his justicial dominion until his return thereto, and not exhibit upon every occasion that authority with which he is only vested for the safety of the community and the peace of the country.

Another gentleman, holding Her Majesty's commission of the peace, in his opposition at the meeting to the making of this line, said he saw *my name* upon the petition to the Board of Works in favour of the opening of this work of charity, and that I had not a *perch* of land, which, in his wise way of estimating a man's competence in voting or assisting upon such occasions, rendered my signature insignificant and valueless. I beg to tell this generous personage that he stated behind my back what was not the *truth*. I have seventy-five acres of most valuable land, not three miles from this town, which I believe will enable any person who is not either wholly stultified or entirely demented to put the plain and proper construction upon the disqualifying assertion of this benevolent *justice* towards me. I should be extremely sorry to hold with his Worship that a man's worth is to be measured by the magnitude of *his* purse or the chance of birth, and should much prefer the doctrine inculcated by the immortal Livy –

    Qui sis, non unde natus sis, reputa.
    Consider what you are, not where you were born.
    Dear Sir, faithfully yours,
    C. CREED
    Macroom, 29 Nov.

NOLLAIG
DECEMBER

33

WHEN SPEECH COMES

Every evening since getting a place on the works, Pádraig found himself staggering over the threshold, feeling vacant and often delirious from exhaustion. The draining effort of walking upwards of thirteen miles a day in cold weather and putting in a full shift of gruelling manual labour on top, all on the strength afforded him by a single daily meal, was inevitably taking a huge toll on his body, his mood and his will. Having to fast on days the weather stopped the works only further depleted his reserves and nightly, upon entering the cabin, it was all he could manage to stay awake long enough to devour the one precious charge of fuel that was keeping him alive before collapsing down onto the straw and disappearing into a dreamless void.

Each morning when he awoke, sometimes with a panicked start of the legs, Pádraig found himself sitting bolt upright and the strange, recurring, terrible dream began anew.

But on Friday 4 December, two weeks and four days into this monumental test of his endurance, Pádraig was finally paid for the first time.

Before knocking off, one at a piece, each man was called into the pay clerk's hut. Inside, from what Pádraig could make out, each was being told how much he was to be paid, then handed his coin with scant accounting of deductions, and sent on his way lest he hold up the queue. Pádraig, awaiting his turn, observed the disappointment on the many faces leaving the hut before him and reasoned that, the men being mostly too tired and hungry to ask questions, the weeks of waiting and the anxiety of having to hold out for so long on nothing had knocked the fight out of them, and by and large, most of them just wanted to take whatever they were given and get home with it to their families.

With thoughts of complaining if he was to be as badly treated as some of those now muttering their discontent outside, in his heart of hearts, the closer Pádraig got to the hut the more he knew he would not make any noise. The fear of being replaced for seeming troublesome or ungrateful was enough to feed his apprehension and slow the bull of his anger, but Pádraig had the added barrier of the Béarla to trouble his confidence in asserting himself. The fear of embarrassment at not understanding what was being said to him caused the tension he was feeling in his wrinkled brow, and in the end Pádraig accepted that he would just have to resign himself to whatever he was given.

'And the blackguards know it too!' was how Jeremiah O'Leary had put it.

Pádraig left the hut with seven shillings and ten pence in his hand and between seething and feeling defeated spent much of the journey home as he had done in the weeks past: trying to remember what days and hours he had worked; counting and guessing how much he should have earned; then accepting again what he did have and estimating what could be got for it.

But after so many mornings and so many walks, Pádraig had begun to doubt his own memory. He believed that of the fourteen good days he had arrived at the line to work, he'd been rained off six times for some part of the day or another and for being late one morning he'd been told in advance he was to be docked a quarter of a day. There was also the matter of some of the men saying there'd be deductions for not working a full ten hours with the daylight getting shorter.

At eight pence a day, fourteen full days would have amounted to nine shillings four pence a man. But it hadn't, and in every case, so far as Pádraig was aware, the result had put paid to all the talk of whether or not they'd get the full eight pence regardless of breaks in the weather.

'Expectation is the father of disappointment,' Denis had said as they'd parted for home. 'We should have been wiser than to trust the honesty of the officers of the government.'

*

Even though they now had money to buy food, the next day Pádraig went to work as usual. He brought the money with him in case the weather broke, but unless they were rained off he could scarce afford to lose the day's work that the dry permitted, and would have to take advantage of every hour it was possible to earn. It was just unfortunate for his family, he thought, that while other labourers' families closer to town could send one of the children, or another family member into Macroom to purchase meal, his would have to hold out one day longer, until Sunday, when there was no work, and he could travel in for it. It would be impossible for Cáit to go. *And her feeding Diarmuidín, not to mention having to carry a bag of meal home all that way on her lighter frame.*

On the line the day was cold and windy, and threatened rain all morning. But none came.

At the ditch for the long suck, standing and sitting around in their threadbare raiments, the men in their various groups discussed and theorised what deductions their wages had met with. Pádraig could see that each man was as tattered and exhausted as he was. Grey faces. Young and old. Sad-looking eyes, under hooded, tired lids. Hair unkempt and dirty. And cold … everybody looked cold. Pádraig himself had noticed it was getting harder and harder to feel warm in his body. It was the losing of what little fat he had left, he thought, and imagined it must be the same for all the men. They were an uncared-for looking lot. But while at other times the exhaustion also showed itself in a lack of enthusiasm for talk, today, with the topic of the wages itching on everyone's lips, there was barely a soul struggling to stay awake.

'By my reckoning, eight pence a day for fourteen days should have come to nine and four pence a body,' O'Leary shared his thoughts aloud, echoing the same arithmetic many men had spoken over the day, 'but they should have made it clear we'd be stopped pay for the bad weather.'

There was no shortage of guesses as to what had been taken off for what either, but no matter what the allowances suggested, there could be no agreement on how the totals had come to be calculated, leading Denis to shout, 'You can bandy it about till kingdom come, lads, but unless you were standing over them when they did the sums in the huts, you may as well be catching smoke in your hat. There is no pattern to it at all.

'I'd say there's a few of those apprentice lads sorry now they threw in the work they had for this lark,' he followed with sarcasm, referencing the rumours early spread that the works were so easy that there were men leaving off good jobs to take advantage of the free wages.

'And the farmers' labourers too,' Daniel Spillane, a neighbour of O'Leary's from Holland's Lane, added. Spillane had come to be called 'Clench' by the other men for seeming to always be gripping a pipe between his teeth, whether there was something in it to draw on or not. 'What was it yer man said?' the gentle, wide-shouldered man asked.

'Who'd work in a wet drain for one and twopence when they can work on the public roads and stand by the ditch doing nothing all day?' O'Leary answered.

'That's right, or something like it. So much for that.' Clench shook his head.

'I tell you what, I wouldn't be too long at this till I'd be taking the next steam packet to America.' Denis was the first to broach the subject of emigration that day, though it came up often.

Pádraig lay on the ground between the men, sometimes guessing at what notions they were knocking back and forth. Naturally enough, there were others up and down the line who, like him, spoke only *an Ghaeluinn*, and through them he could generally pick up what the talk of the day was. But for the immediate sphere of discussion, Pádraig was limited to the voices of those he had been grouped with and those nearest to them, whose discussion was always in the Béarla. It suited Pádraig's nature to involve himself at his own pace. Whenever he was interested he needed only look to Denis, who spoke the tongue – if sometimes poorly – and could, in a few words, give him a rough idea of the talk. But for now, to take his mind off the hunger, Pádraig stayed chewing on a spear of grass and studied the expressions of the men, when he wasn't weighing stones in his hand and squinting at the clouds.

It might have been the tall, bent hat O'Leary always wore, but even though Pádraig himself was taller, O'Leary had always seemed a long man to Pádraig. Even now, lying on the ground alongside him, the man seemed even longer. He supposed he'd probably got that impression measuring O'Leary against Denis, who was small and weakly even from this angle. The runt of the litter, Pádraig thought. Pádraig himself was closer to O'Leary in height and shape. But he had a different colouring: there was a bit of Viking in O'Leary. The straw-coloured hair. And he loved to talk.

'Oh! I wouldn't be there just yet,' O'Leary said to Denis.

'And what's to stay here for? Sure, the country's gone to the bottom. All the way to the cack. If I'd the passage I'd be gone in the morning, I tell ye now,' Denis replied.

'Big money, though,' O'Leary argued. 'It's near a pound to go as far as London alone and that's just to stand on the deck. Then you've a wife and … sure I've six children!'

In spite of O'Leary's appeal to logic, Denis merely purveyed an apathetic silence in response, as O'Leary gave his Irish-speaking companion a glance, then adjusted his hat to make a spot for his head.

'I've a cousin in Skibbereen says they're giving assisted passage down there, and if you know someone in England they'll send ye,' a stranger weighed in.

'England? Pftt. I wouldn't take it if they were giving it away,' Denis answered in a mocking tone.

'For God's sake, Murphy, sure it's as good for us to die there as here, where we're starving and fading away, even when we're getting employment,' O'Leary argued.

'Sure, 'tis as well for us to starve and fade away here in the land of our fathers so,' Denis retorted. 'England? I wouldn't spit on it if 'twas on fire. No. America for me,' he added, putting the dagger in, even after O'Leary's earnest plea.

Back in his own world again, Pádraig was not paying much mind to the bickering between the two. As ever, they seemed to be including him in the conversation, each acting as though he was on their side of the argument. He chose to acknowledge them when it suited him, and kept to the part of the quiet, unwinnable referee the rest of the time.

'It's no wonder there's so many joining up with the regiments,' O'Leary started up again after a momentary peace.

Denis caught Pádraig's eye and scornfully reported the words, before adding, 'Oh. Go off and get ourselves blown to bits instead, is it? That's a great idea. You won't catch me doing that either. And certainly not for a foreign queen occupying my own land neither.'

'Don't worry, Murphy,' O'Leary switched the mock. 'They wouldn't take ye. Sure, what would they want with an aul' weaver from West Musk anyway, ha?' It was his turn to look to Pádraig now, trying to win him as an ally.

'Well, I'm sure they'd prefer me blown up than one of their own. But no fear.' Denis in turn grinned and appealed to Pádraig as he repeated himself *i nGaeluinn*.

'True enough,' O'Leary admitted.

Pádraig, drawn back in by both, was reattuned to their battle of wits now. Despite the depths of the low ebb they were plumbing, the dynamic of their banter, however bitter, was something he quietly enjoyed whenever he involved himself. And he was sure the same was true for each of them too.

'But you can talk, O'Leary. I'd say *your* marching days are behind ye,' Denis quipped in his musical voice, offering the same few words to Pádraig. O'Leary had no response and growled at his spade. And with that, the sound of the steward's whistle signalled that the late suck was over.

A little while later, with all back at the task of breaking and shifting rocks, Denis heard O'Leary asking a question of Pádraig: 'What about you, O'Buachalla? Would you join up for the shilling?'

Recognising his name, Pádraig squinted and twitched his head to Denis, who related the gist of the question.

Looking into the full barrow at his feet, Pádraig seemed to think a moment, then tilted his head as if to release the answer. *'Nuair a thiocfaidh an chaint don bhfiach dubh,'* he replied and walked away, pushing the wooden vehicle that squeaked as he started and groaned under the weight.

Denis stopped his spade and stood upright, smiling after the gaunt figure that was Pádraig.

'What did he say?' O'Leary asked, looking confused.

'When speech comes ...' Denis said under his breath.

'When speech comes? What do you fathom that means?'

Feeling a new level of admiration for his quiet, resilient friend, Denis answered. 'Eoghan Ó Súilleabháin, the poet ...'

'Go on?' O'Leary pushed.

'Nuair a thiocfaidh an míol mór ar an Moing.' Denis closed his eyes and enjoyed remembering something that had seemed long forgotten. *'Nuair a thiocfaidh an Fhrainc go Sliabh Mis, Nuair a chaillfidh an sagart an tsaint, Is ea a thiocfaidh an chaint don bhfiach dubh.'*

'What does it mean?'

Denis lowered his head and stared through the stony gravel floor of the world. 'When the whale will come up the Maine river. When France will come to Sliabh Mis. When the priest will abandon his greed. Then, speech will come to the raven.' Breathing out a long pass of air, Denis shook his head, and felt the welling of proud tears in his eyes at the small gift of hope. He turned back to gauge O'Leary's reaction, who too was now stopped, gazing after Pádraig O'Buachalla, understanding.

Kiiieoouuwh!

Denis thrust his spade into the earth as the rain began to patter and thick drops fell among them, blotting, turning light grey to dark.

*

That evening, Cáit watched sadly as the wearied, thinner version of the man she'd married only a handful of years before dragged himself in through the doorway with nothing in his hands once again. He looked down at the sleeping children, then back to Cáit.

'The rain never came. I couldn't afford to stop,' he said quietly, shaking his head. 'I'll go tomorrow then.' Pádraig ploughed into the bowl of cabbage Cáit had waiting for him and not long after that was asleep, before she could get a conversation out of him.

But the rain did come. Though half a day late it followed soon, as if it had been waiting for him to rest. Then Cáit, going outside in it, cut a sod out of the mossy bank of grass along the ridge. Just as Pádraig usually did when the weather got bad, she hooshed it up onto the roof, to cover the hole that let the smoke out. She couldn't reach it as easily as he could, so used a stick to flip the sod over, grass side down, which gave it grip, and stopped the muck from falling asunder and raining in on top of them.

Back inside, Cáit took off her cold wet shawl and hung it over the fire to dry. From the stool she watched the three of them sleeping on the floor, Síle and Diarmuidín nestling into their father for the warmth. But covering the hole in the roof kept the smoke inside, and every once in a while it needed poking up with a stick to relieve the air a little. If she stayed awake a little longer, Cáit reasoned, she could dry her shawl, and they'd benefit from the warmth of the fire. The nights were already very cold, so it was best to keep it going as long as possible. She'd have to bury it before she went to sleep so that it wouldn't smoke them to death.

They usually argued over whether to cover the roof or not. If it wasn't torrential she always preferred that they just put the bucket under the hole to catch what was coming in. Sometimes they had to spend so much time poking up the sod to let the smoke out that she often said they were as wet as if they'd left it open in the first place. But with no one to argue with tonight, she somehow thought it was better his way.

Sitting there alone in the quiet, listening to the hush of the rain and its dappling of the roof above, Cáit longed for the days past in the warmer months of the year, when they hardly covered the roof at all and when, if the sky was clear, they could see the stars overhead one at a time as they passed across the small opening.

Pádraig would be only working a regular amount for the Críodáins, not so exhausted as he was now. Then around this time of the evening she'd shove her feet under his leg, his back, or any part of him she could reach just to get the cold out of them. And he would curse and feign blindness at the shock, letting on he didn't like her warming up to him, but she knew it was part of the ritual.

'Mother of God,' he would say, or something in protest, 'your feet are like ice, woman!'

'They're God's angels watching over us,' she remembered saying to him one night, looking up through the roof at the stars, wriggling her toes in further to get the warmth into them.

'Is that them digging into me back?' he'd winced. 'It's more like the pokers of hell prodding at me.' And she had laughed and shushed him.

'Don't wake the children!' she'd said.

On nights like those, when they slept with the children between them, the fire would settle to a glow and a single shaft of pale light sometimes shone in through the hole in the roof, casting a soft ellipse below, so that the cabin was rarely in complete darkness. But that had been a long time since – the year before the blight, in the summer, when they had been just a whisper from the first, good harvest here in Doire Liath. The harvest that had never come.

It had felt like life was tough back then and yet those times seemed carefree and simple compared with their lives now. Cáit only had to look at the emaciated frames of Pádraig and the two children to be reminded of that. How she had faded, she thought, looking down at her own thin body, examining how much of herself she'd lost. Wrapping her fingers and her thumb around, she felt the thickness of her wrist and could not remember when she'd ever been so thin, then shivered with the cold and decided it was time to lie down. How long would it be, Cáit wondered, as she put the long shawl over her head again, and began to bury the fire, before they might see those relatively carefree days again. It frightened her to think that they might not come for a very long time.

34

WHEN SPEECH COMES – II

'When is Daddy going to wake up?'

'Your daddy has been working very hard, Síle. He needs a good rest, pet.'

'Aww ...'

'He'll be awake in a while.'

Síle, unused to seeing her father lately, whether awake or sleeping, was finding it hard not to be able to touch him and play with him, now that he was here.

'Is Daddy all right, Mammy?'

'He's fine. He's just a bit tired, love.'

Cáit was describing herself as much as her husband and rubbed her eyes, trying to wipe away the unwanted parts of her reality. If Pádraig was tired, at least he was getting a change of scenery. She was tied to the cabin and the children, day in and day out. But Pádraig wasn't going to rest today. Sunday was the only day he could afford to go to Macroom for meal.

When an hour or so later he awoke with a wince, maybe imagining he was to go off working again, Cáit offered to go in his stead. 'The children would like a bit of time with you,' she told him. In her heart she wanted to do it, for him, but behind the gesture, she wasn't sure if she could manage it.

Squinting and blinking, but drawn to the light coming in above and below the door, Pádraig sat up on his elbows, trying to get his head to work, while Síle and Diarmuidín crawled over him, craving his attention.

'Daddy, Daddy!'

'Come on, Daddy!'

Pádraig closed his eyes and let out a long groan, tilting his head back, not sure himself if it was a sigh of pain or a sigh of relief at realising he did not have to go breaking rocks today. He began twisting his neck from side to side until the words came out.

'You'd best not … ' he yawned, groaning again, looking at Cáit. 'It'll be too heavy. You'll never carry it.'

He knew the walk itself was enough of an ordeal, and that her slight frame could not hope to stand up to carrying a couple of stone of meal all that way. Then there'd be the money, and the talk, and the matter of the purchase itself. Pádraig shook at the thought of her being watched by greedy eyes, and maybe swindled or taken advantage of.

Cáit didn't argue, but he could see her disappointment.

It was unthinkable, though. What would anyone say about him if they saw his wife struggling up the road with a stone or two on her back? And him at home saving his energy. Or worse – too weak to go himself!

'You may wait a while until that rain stops anyhow before you go off again and catch yer death of cold,' Cáit barked. Pádraig heard the sting in her voice and knew she was probably annoyed at herself for being unable to do it. That was only a waste of strength. Being hard on herself when there was nothing she could do to change it. But he understood, and accepted that she'd have to blow off a bit of steam.

He knew by the smell of the air it was going to rain for a while one way or the other. He could be wet and dry and wet again by the time he got there and back. There was no point in hanging on when he'd have to get going either way; otherwise he'd be carrying it back in the dark for the whole stretch. But if only to let the children maul him another while, and for himself to feel the warmth of them a bit longer, he did as he was told, and waited.

'How much have we borrowed?' he asked her after a spell.

'Nothing,' she snapped quickly. 'Sure, who's got anything to lend anyway?'

He didn't answer. There was only the sixpence he'd got 'on time' from the gangsman Roberts the week before. But without that he'd have had no griddle bread.

'How much can we afford?' Cáit asked.

'Meal is going for two-and-six in town. We can just about afford three stone.'

'Can you get it cheaper, from Father O'Brien at the Relief Committee in Clondrohid?'

'The Relief Committee is gone broke. Is what I've heard. Anyway, you'd have to go on a Saturday to get it.' The only concern Pádraig had in his mind at that moment was whether the rain would stay gone when he'd be carrying the meal home, and if the cloth sack would go any way to keeping it dry if it didn't.

Three stone, when they'd been living hand to mouth on a diet of almost nothing but cabbage and the odd scrap of griddle bread for a month, sounded almost luxurious. The sense of relief from just knowing they'd have a stock of food for the weeks ahead was almost blissful. With the works still continuing for the time being too, the feeling was that they might be just that bit better off than the next family up here in the hills. Enough to be guaranteed survival in the short term, at least.

But somehow Pádraig was not feeling the advantage. Compared with families either side of them they were better off, yes. Compared with the town-dwelling labourers on the works, the distance he was having to walk each day was a great disadvantage. But Denis had made a strong argument that every man had his own pros and cons according to his circumstances.

'You've only two small children to feed on the same wages, when we have five and six, so you're faring better than we are there. It all weighs out,' he had told Pádraig.

These were the issues the three men discussed among themselves. Difficult matters bandied around to give each other support. Even in the best of conditions – on the works, with good wages and a small family –

nobody was anywhere close to thriving. It was simply the case that some families were surviving with more or less hardship than others.

'It was two-and-a-half weeks before the wages were got the first time, Cáit. God knows how long it'll be the next, or how much the weather will allow it from here on.'

'Surely with Christmas coming they won't delay paying ye so long again?' Cáit protested.

'Well … I wouldn't count on anything. They're already cutting lumps out of it for the shortening of the light and everything else. The point is, whatever we land with this now, we have to make the most of it and stretch it out as long as we can manage.' Pádraig was up, hoisting onto his shoulders the rope galluses he'd made for his trousers.

'It's not dry yet,' she said, referring to the rain.

'It's dry enough when it'll be wet soon again.'

'And you're sure there's actually something to buy? Is the meal store definitely open of a Sunday?'

'Course it is.'

With the last of the griddle bread in his pocket as a carrot on a stick, Pádraig followed his feet almost the entire way to Macroom before stopping to answer the weakness he could feel coming on, and there ate hurriedly in case anyone might see him, a lonely stranger, with food.

He'd left it so late before heading onto the road that he knew it would be dark again before he made it home. But by now he had the walk mapped so well that he could do it in his sleep.

Macroom on a Sunday was practically a ghost town, and a different place from the regional metropolis he knew it to be. The masses were over, and there were far fewer paupers and beggars out on the streets. There'd be no point in them hanging about in the rain and cold with no one to skin off, he supposed. Realising that everything was closed, Pádraig began to panic, second-guessing if Cáit had been right after all. Maybe the corn merchant's *was* closed. Would it really be the only thing open in the whole of Macroom?

Dear God, don't let me be like that poor soul in Skibbereen who went to town for meal and couldn't get any to buy, and the government store groaning under the weight of it, God rest him.

Despite having been reassured by Denis the day before that it was usually open on Sundays, as he crossed the bridge towards Castle Street the terrible fear grew large in Pádraig's mind that he was going to find it closed. But that Edward Ashe Corn Merchants were clearly happy to be the exception to the rule when desperate souls were travelling in from the outer realms of the district, he soon found to be true. Denis had been right when he'd said, 'The merchant never sleeps when there is money to be made.'

The rain that had dogged the early part of the walk was now holding off and the worry of the meal getting wet on the way home was certainly diminished, though a glance at the sky told Pádraig not to be too sure.

'How much?' the vendor asked of him.

'*An mór 'tá air sin?*' Pádraig asked back, and lifted his chin gesturing at the casks of flour in the background.

Pádraig followed the man's eyes to the numbers chalked on the slate board but had no understanding of the lettering and looked back to the guide saying nothing.

'Two-and-six a stone.' The man said, then gestured the price with the digits of his hands.

'*Dhá chloich.*' Pádraig held up two digits of his own, making an impulsive decision to only take two stone instead of three. The price was a bit higher than he had expected. *But 'tis going nowhere but up*, he thought to himself. It was really the weather that kept him undecided. If it got bad and he was carrying the lot, the meal might be destroyed altogether. At least this way there was something to fall back on, and yet he didn't fancy the thought of another trip there and back just for the one stone another Sunday.

Pádraig watched silently as the aproned stranger poured, then ladled the coarse yellow dust that hissed into the bowl of the scales until the stack of brass weights began to shift on the other side.

A trí! Pádraig heard himself say in his mind. '*Trí!*' he said out loud, surprised by the urgency of his own voice.

'Three?' the man asked, making sure.

Pádraig nodded. The clerk lifted the bowl of flour out of the scales and poured the two stone of meal, already weighed, onto a prepared paper sheet. But he refrained from completing the wrap and began the process over, removing half the weights.

Before pouring anew, he stopped, as if in thought. 'Where are you headed out to?' he asked.

'Huh?'

'Ballyvourney? Donaghmore? Kiln–'

'Clondrohid,' Pádraig cut in.

'Clondrohid,' the vendor repeated. '*Clondrohid?*'

He paused to scratch the back of his head, scanned the floor behind him, then looked to the cloth sack Pádraig was holding and scanned the floor again.

Watching the man at work and moved at the sight of his kind consideration of the customer's predicament, Pádraig felt the hair tingle on the back of his neck. Spying an empty flour sack, the clerk shook it off and slapped it against his leg to get the dust out. Then, putting it to one side, he wrapped the first measure up in numerous sheets of paper, tying it off with string.

'Now.' He gestured to Pádraig to hand him the sack, laid the parcel at its centre, weighed off the extra stone, wrapped it, tied it and lowered it into the sack on top of the other. He then transferred the whole lot into the second sack from up off the floor, tied the whole lot off with a rope and patted both sides lightly, leaving his hands there as he lifted his eyes to look Pádraig straight in the face. 'Clondrohid?'

Pádraig grunted a yes.

'You're a better man than me,' the vendor said quietly.

'Right so. Seven …' he held up one fully open hand, and the thumb and index of the other '... and six,' as, lowering the index, he kept the thumb standing alone.

Aware of how grubby his hands were, Pádraig took out his money and pinged out the seven silver shillings, one on top of the other, added the sixpence, then put the four copper pennies back into his pocket and pulled the sack up onto his back, thanking the clerk with a nod.

Pádraig left the shop contemplating that he would need to sell twopence worth of meal to a neighbour or someone on the works to make up the sixpence he owed the gangsman. But by the time he had crossed the bridge out of Macroom, he was already preoccupied with the dead weight on his back and was regretting having taken the extra stone.

Out past Masseytown he rifled through the options in his mind. It was too late to go back.

A little further on when he'd be passing near the works, he could take the one stone out and hide it somewhere until the next day when he could carry it home – if it wasn't plundered by rats. Finding somewhere dry where no one would see him at it was the thing. If he struggled on with the weight he would be worse off than coming home after a day's labouring at this stage. He had no idea what Diarmuidín weighed. He had counted on the meal being around the same, but hadn't factored in the awkwardness of its bulk, nor that constant work and hunger had weakened his constitution over the weeks since he'd ceased daily carrying his child to the union and back. If he found a good stick somewhere he could tie the smaller cloth with the one stone onto it and pitch it over his shoulder, carry the other in his left hand, and swap them over along the way ... *There must be somewhere dry I can stuff the sack with the one stone in it.*

Pádraig pictured himself hiding the meal somewhere near the road he'd be working on in the morning. But no sooner than he'd thought it, he could imagine the guard on the tool hut spying him and rubbing his hands together at the opportunity to relieve him of his plunder.

Before long, still calculating his options as he struggled on, Pádraig had passed the turn-off for the works and knew it would be even more conspicuous to be seen turning back towards them. He marched on, troubled by the thoughts of what might happen if he could not get the entire three stone home. Whether he was to get it there in sections or all at once, it had to be intact. Without all of it, there was no clear way they could see themselves through the weeks ahead until he'd be paid again. He had made a decision. The soundest his circumstances had afforded at the time: to take as much as he could carry, with the knowledge that the price was only going to continue rising, and hazarding a bet that two trips would cost him more energy than one in the long run. But now, beginning to feel the effects of the dead weight, he was not so sure it had been the right one.

In desperation, he began to scan the road ahead in his mind for anywhere he knew well enough to hide something. Somewhere he wouldn't be seen or noticed. But how long would it take to get in off the road somewhere and unpack it, bury it or cover it up with something, and be sure someone would not see him coming back out? Nowhere that was safe from the elements came to mind either. Could he risk an unknown location?

He was frequently unnerved at the passing of strangers, who looked at him as though seeing something foreign in their landscape … a struggling being, perhaps not at the peak of his physical health. One man carrying an abundance of food, obvious as a flour sack, and families starving all around the place. He knew he was a vulnerable target.

Pádraig was sweating profusely and struggling with his burden and deadening muscles when a few light drops began to fall from the sky, pattering on his hair and dotting the outside of the old linen sack.

*

Two-and-a-half hours later the door of the cabin swung open, and, with a large gash over his right eyebrow, Pádraig wobbled through the door, flopping the sack down with a grunt.

'Jesus, Mary and Joseph, what happened to you?' Cáit worried over him.

Pádraig just lay on the floor looking dazed, trying to catch his breath.

'I couldn't leave it,' he muttered. 'Too much.'

'What do you mean?' Cáit was confused. Pádraig wasn't making any sense. She tried to turn his head toward the dim light of the fire to see how bad the cut was, but it was a mess, and he was resisting.

'Fell … I fell,' he said, still labouring heavily. 'A root, in the road. Couldn't stop myself … Couldn't stop myself going.'

Cáit tore a rag from the end of her shawl and agonised over whether to touch a wound she couldn't see. Dragging up a few strands of old straw into the embers she waited for a small flicker of the light to show the damage and winced at the sight of the gory crimson mess above his eyebrow. The wound appeared to have stopped bleeding, at least, and was already crusting over, but it would need cleaning.

'I saw her …' he said.

'Saw who?'

'Onóra … your sister, at the union.'

'Onóra? At the union? When? What were you doing there?'

But before she could get any sense out of him, Pádraig was out cold, asleep. Despite how desperate she was to find out about her sister, she knew he needed rest. In the meantime, she went about boiling water and making a tiny bit of caked meal into a hot poultice. He screamed when she pressed it over the cut and held it there, her other hand covering his eye to save from burning it. 'Christ above in heaven, woman!' he cursed, as she kept her weight on him.

'Go back to sleep,' Cáit told him and left him to rest, slumped back to the floor, until she could prepare a plate of meal for him to eat.

*

'Come on, husband, sit up,' Cáit said, slapping and shaking Pádraig until he came to. 'You have to eat something. Sit up and eat this now, or you'll be going nowhere tomorrow.'

She spooned some of the gruel into his mouth until he took the spoon himself.

'Are you hurt anywhere else?'

'It … no.' The way he was turning his neck and stretching to check himself reassured Cáit that nothing else was badly damaged. He was probably aching all over, sore and stiff.

'Where did you see her?'

'What?'

'What were you doing at the union?'

'Who?' He looked bewildered.

'Onóra! *Tigh na mbocht.* You said you saw her there!' She pleaded for an answer, hoping it wasn't just a dream he'd had.

'Oh …' Pádraig rubbed his forehead and winced at the pain. 'It was … 'twas when I was going for the relief.'

'What?' she said, disappointed. 'Not today? How long ago was that?'

'It was not today. It was the last day …'

'What? What are you talking about? Was she in good health? Did you talk to her?'

It was too much to answer all at once. Pádraig felt his face contort and shook his head, but his brain hurt. He didn't know where to start or how to do the least damage with his answers, and his wits were not in the best shape for this conversation after what he had just been through. 'I did not … I mean she was in good health, she was fine … she looked fine, but I couldn't talk to her … it was the Master …' Exasperated, he struggled to tie a sentence together. 'She was being led through the yard by the head woman and I would have … She would have got into trouble if I …' He fumbled over the words but managed to get the drift out, without making matters worse. 'I thought I might see her another day, but leaving the yard that day, they told me it was up. There was no more. I didn't know how to tell you …'

Cáit spent a long time staring into the fire, with tears in her eyes, not knowing whether to be angry at Pádraig, or relieved, or what anything meant any more. She lay with her back to him in the darkness, he drifting away again and she unable to sleep, trying to piece together what he'd said, wondering where her sister was now and what might become of her. The news was a shock. Being so far away, Cáit had not been in contact with any of her people for months. In the absence of any news from them, she had somehow presumed they were untouched by the same conditions they were enduring here, but it was all too clear now – no one was safe and the fears she had buried were being realised. How naïve she'd been. If Onóra was still alive, and healthy a month or so ago, that was something. Maybe she was being looked after. But did her being in the poorhouse mean their parents were dead? Or perhaps they were in the union too?

Cáit gripped her mouth with fear. What about the rest of them? She should have never let Pádraig bring her out here into the wilds, she thought bitterly. The memory and the weight of the decision to leave her family upon his suggestion grew back up and filled her mind again. But it felt much heavier now, like being trapped, to be stuck so far away as she was from her people, helpless to do anything for them.

Pádraig's wound, gory as it was, would heal. *A wound of the heart is much deeper.* The grief for a glimpse, the longing to embrace your own dear loved ones, but not knowing if they were well, if they were alive or dead, the feelings of loss – no poultice or medicine could hope to heal those wounds. Nothing but knowing they were alive and seeing as much with her own two eyes … a cure she might never have again. She felt she might die of sorrow and, laying her head on the straw, she wept until she fell asleep.

*

By the light of dawn, when the children stirred, Pádraig was long gone again. In the blurred reflection of a stream along the way, he tried to wash his eye, wincing, and assess the damage. When the men set to work not long after, there was no hiding it. The various looks and comments told him it was certainly noticeable, but that he'd live.

'Holy Mother of God. What did you run into?' one of his new comrades wanted to know.

'Talking when he should have been listening, I'd say,' another answered for him.

35

DESTINED FOR RUIN

Having been single-handedly running the shop for over a week, Thomas French jumped with alarm when, as soon as the bell had rung signalling the exit of the last customer, his employer, Cornelius Creed, suddenly appeared behind him.

'Mr Creed!'

'Apologies, Mr French.'

Removing his coat, Creed, who had taken leave over a week before without explanation, acknowledged the sudden end of his indefinite absence, then locked the door and drew the blinds. French, unsure of how to react in the face of this mysterious behaviour, sought to busy himself by closing up the books, placing them in the safe and locking it, before turning back to gather up the rags on the counter in need of processing.

'I, eh … I didn't hear you come in, sir.'

'You did not, Mr French. I drew up the cart outside, off the square and let myself in through the back.'

'Oh. Of course, sir.'

The explanation was unusual, to say the least. But French knew when to keep his head low. 'Shall I?' With an armful of rags he feinted at moving towards the back rooms, seeking permission to continue with his duties now that the shop was officially closed for the day.

'Go ahead, Mr French.' Creed answered with the absent-minded consent of a distracted individual. 'And when you're done closing up I would like to have a word with you.'

'Yes, sir.' French was resigned already to whatever unwelcome news was in store for him, but feeling puzzled he lingered a moment, looking rapidly left and right as he searched his memory for a clue to anything he might have done wrong.

'Thank you; you may continue as you were.'

'Thank you, sir.'

Out in the store French tried to keep his mind together as he sorted and logged the items, pondering whatever revelation might await him at the other end of his task. He dared not dawdle and went about the process as efficiently as he could manage, but it was impossible to concentrate. The unlikely combination of pressure and trepidation led to his checking, then having to recheck a number of the items, the resulting delay only increasing his sense of agitation as he realised he was merely staving off the inevitable.

Weighing things up as he worked, he reasoned that though cantankerous at times, Creed was a good employer who paid consistently and had kept him in steady, respectable employment for almost two years. French had repaid his employer's faith in him with complete respect and deference, obeying Creed's every whim with unquestioning loyalty.

Listening and spying nervously for any sense of what was coming, he tiptoed half way back into the shop and out again a number of times, alive and attentive to every nuance of Creed's presence now that he'd returned, all the while fearful of disimproving his lot by delaying further, thereby testing the patience of the temperamental being he sensed – in that moment more than ever – was the orchestrator of his fate.

Creed was labouring over something, but as to what, no definitive clue carried from the room wherein he sat quiet at his writing station behind the counter.

Peering sidelong through the frame of the doorway French could glean nothing from the scrunching of paper that passed back and forth from the menacing jaws of one hand to the other; the rick of the rejected drafts being periodically dropped and catapulted into the waste paper basket; little, but perhaps an attempt to deceive the reality of the moment, from the smothering of his writing implements beneath a newspaper; and nothing still from the opening and closing of the heavy drawer of the desk that repeatedly offered up its fresh blank pages to hide the clandestine works of a tortured writer.

As the gears of many clocks around the shop ticked down the minutes ever so slowly, while somehow sounding faster, the little premises of Cornelius Creed, Pawnbroker's on the south side of the square became a hot room, muting whatever new pandemonium might be unfolding beyond in the world outside.

But French, too, was tortured. At home of late, his elderly mother had been pressing him, unaware that she was adding to his worries, questioning how long 'that lovely Mr Creed' could manage to keep on another employee the way things were going. 'Are you showing him enough loyalty, Thomas? I'm sure there's ten more would take your place just as quick,' she would say, and crying, 'Who'll look after us when you're broke, and we're turfed out of here for not payin' the rent?'

And maybe his mother had been right, French suddenly realised. Only weeks ago he'd overheard Creed relating committee business, talking of replacing 'doleful workers' who had been given 'ceremonial positions' on the public works. 'The committee should be employing some of the emaciated poor labourers instead – those who are starving to support their families,' he had said.

Could he now be thinking of leading by example and replacing me? 'God!' French gasped into the dark. Unable to recall a single task he had ever refused, or one he had failed to perform adequately, French could find no good reason that Creed might now doubt his abilities or question his reliability. Unless he felt French had simply slipped into the mark of an employee so at ease in the task as to be taking his position for granted. *He must know how much I depend on this situation!*

But what if it was nothing to do with him at all? There were those rumours that fever was in the workhouse now. With the condition of the poor spiralling downwards and nothing but the depths of winter ahead, it could be only a matter of time before the tinderbox caught fire. No one seemed to know how the sickness passed from one person to the other. But it was certain that anyone in frequent contact with the wretched and starving poor was at risk. And a pawnbroker and his clerk at the centre of a busy town, labouring under the strains of a sick and miserable population of paupers, were as treacherously positioned as it was possible to be.

Cornelius Creed, Pawnbroker's was the principal conduit, if such a thing existed, through which the whole unblessed lot of the poor passed as they came and went to that hellhole of a place. Maybe Creed was afraid of the disease and planned on having him man the shop alone indefinitely? French scrunched his eyelids tightly, as his imagination sewed together the patches of a wayward kite.

Whichever scenario, it didn't matter: without the steady income of his tenure, French and his mother would be on the same road to disaster as every other family in the barony, thrown on the mercy of charity, the poorhouse and the grace of the Almighty. Out in the air, fumbling to close the heavy iron lock on the goods store, he pressed his forehead into the ice-cold condensation of the door frame and sighed, before turning to go inside and meet his fate.

He found his employer composed now, with hat, coat, umbrella and gloves already retrieved from their hooks and ready by his side. Creed was sitting still, lips resting on his thumbs, hands clasped together over his elbows, supported by the counter of the thick wooden desk. Before him lay three white envelopes.

French stopped in the doorway and swallowed as quietly as he could, sensing a change in the state of things – the unavoidable approach of a disaster he could still not predict.

'Mr French, I have come to a decision.' Creed looked straight ahead to whatever beheld his vision and could only have sensed French was there by sound alone.

'Yes, sir.' He heard himself reply, as meek as a lamb.

'These times are unprecedented. No man can be sure of the best course to take in lessening the blows of fate when madness is looming from every direction. One would hope that at a certain point it would become obvious ... and a reasonable man might cease to ignore what he hoped the signs were not telling him.' The oration was slow and deliberate, with long pauses between the parts of his sentences.

'It becomes difficult to know if the service you are providing is of benefit. Or, if you are simply placing yourself in the path of a reckless wind, eager to gather up everyone before it.' He lowered his head and appeared to have finished for a moment.

'Sir, if I may speak. I believe the community ...'

'Please, Mr French ...' Creed raised a hand, which cut French off in mid-sentence and nearly stopped his heart. His employer, regaining his thoughts, joined his fingertips back to their almost prayerful poise. 'I have decided to close the shop. Mm ... mm ... Not immediately of course. I intend putting the premises up for sale, and I'll wind the business down in the meantime.'

French was frozen inside and out with the shock.

'Of course, you're wondering how all this affects you in the here and now. I will not cast you out so carelessly at such a perilous time, rest assured ... In the short term, you will continue as you have done of late. The two of us being here will be of no utility. And in the meantime, I intend directing my efforts where they might be of more value.

'If someone happens to buy the premises intact I will recommend that you stay on in your position. But I would not hold out any great hope for that, Mr French. In fact, the writing is on the wall in that regard for the foreseeable time to come, I believe. The business of a pawnbroker is destined for ruin. A pawnbroker ... hmmm ...'

Creed seemed amused at the sound of the word leaving his own mouth. *This is Massy Warren's doing!* French suddenly thought.

'A pawnbroker ... a pawnbroker, as you know, derives the vast bulk of dividends from redeemed pledges, and not from the sale of forfeited articles. But – were the calamity ahead somehow, even now, to be prevented from deteriorating further, at the very least – most of the poor creatures who avail of this service will never again have the wherewithal to redeem their sorry tickets ... their pledges. Not, at least, in this lifetime. And a proprietor is to be cast adrift along with a boatload of these ... relics of their blighted existence.'

Flicking his wrist as though expressing an earnest wish to rid himself of their capture, Creed looked around the shop and spoke to the accumulation of objects. 'A worthless collection of depressing, pestilent souvenirs, of ... of what the government would have us believe, a Malthusian catastrophe. Hah!

'Mr French, I know you have your mother to look after. You have been a dependable employee to me since we began here. I will not leave you wanting. Even *if*, as I say, the premises is bought or closed in the short term,' Creed cleared his throat repeatedly, and abruptly, as though he were battling his emotions, 'I should require someone to manage the store, I dare say. But you *must* think of the future.'

Creed stood, stepped out from behind the desk and began to dress for the rain. French was too disoriented at first to be able to interpret the peculiar actions of his employer, though he sensed there was meaning behind the buttoning of the coat and the careful tightening of gloves along each finger. Mr Creed picked up the three envelopes and put them into the hand that French found he had outstretched to receive them.

'On your way in tomorrow, Mr French, if you find the post office master to have opened up for a change, I would like you to send these on the next despatch.'

'Of course, sir.'

'Do you have any questions, Mr French?'

'It's ... It's a lot to take in, sir.'

French puzzled at the sensation of the envelopes now within his grip and, taking his own overcoat from the stand behind the door, slid them into the inside pocket, whereupon he caught a glimpse of the destination written across the face of the uppermost packet: 'Cork Examiner, Patrick Street, Cork'. *Not 'to the editor'*, French thought.

'I'll be going out the front, Mr French. Which way for you?'

'The same, sir.'

'You have locked the safe?'

'I have, sir. The safe is locked.'

It now dawned on the clerk that Creed had not returned to stay. The bell rang overhead as they began to exit into the street amid the fog of their own breaths. French felt as though he needed to lie down and think through the import of his employer's words.

'Are you all right, Mr French?'

'I think so, sir. I am. You're... going ...?'

'Paulellen and I will stay out there another while. Oh... one other thing, Mr French. Walk with me a moment.'

'Of course, sir.'

'It's very important that from tomorrow on ...' Their voices disappeared temporarily amidst the rattle of a coach as it trundled across the square, finally coming to a halt outside the hotel near to where the two had stopped. '... more. Do you understand?'

'I have it clear, sir.'

'Good evening, Mr French.'

'Good evening, Mr Creed, sir.'

French nodded in deference to his employer, and left in the opposite direction.

36

OUT OF LITTLE

Regarding his own expressionless stare in a mirror, Charles Edward Parke Gordon sat on the edge of the soft mattress, his mind as blank as his face. The thick, slow throb of the blood pulsating behind his left eardrum was the only thing close to drawing his focus, but he was neither soothed nor bothered by its constancy.

He did not feel like a husband. And though it had been over two months since his young wife had made him one, at only thirty years of age he did not feel like a widower either.

Though this puzzle had burdened his mind of late, lost now in the woven pattern of the curtain before him, he was not frozen, trapped in a moment remembering Louisa's white flowing dress at the chapel of St Mary de Lode in Gloucester; did not picture her bathed within the leaf-kissed light of the wavering churchyard trees as she smiled on the face of her father, Edward Day, weeping as he gave away the hand of his youngest daughter that sunlit June morning the year before; nor did he, the absent father, conjure in his thoughts the anxious cries of the helpless child, their infant son whom she had left behind, and whose face he was still yet to behold; and, for a change, Gordon was not even preoccupied with impressing, or living up to the expectations of, his own father, 'The Colonel', whose name – being the eldest son and the proud heir of – he had been entrusted to carry and to bring honour to, just as his father had before him.

In that moment, numb, and stoic, Captain Charles Edward Parke Gordon did not feel much of anything. He was simply there.

Tat tat tat. Someone tapped on the door.

'Captain Gordon, sir?'

'Yes?'

'Your car, sir.'

'I'll be down presently.'

'Sir.'

Gordon listened to the footsteps fading down the hallway, then rose and began to dress, wearily and without haste.

When, some ten minutes later, Gordon stepped into the car, his assistant, Mr Limerick, shouted out the window of his own side. 'Thank you. You may proceed.'

'Hup!' With a flick of his wrists, the driver gave the horses their whip to depart, and Gordon felt the whole arrangement of animals, straps, buckles and furnishings shudder beneath him, setting all in forward motion into the busy street.

'Driver! Stop! Oy!'

'Hike!' The driver pulled hard on the reins, troubling the animals who voiced their displeasure at the aborted start; Gordon watched Mr Limerick peering out the window with confusion at the servant running after the coach. Having caught up, the young man unlocked the door of the carriage and held up a brown leather satchel.

'You left this in the hallway, sir,' he shouted.

Gordon blew out his lips at the inconvenience, then took receipt of the bag with reluctance. But despite the servant continuing to linger outside, perhaps awaiting further instruction or a tip, Gordon sat looking straight ahead with the satchel now atop his knees, displaying a sure unwillingness to engage in conversation.

'Everything all right, sir?'

'Perfectly fine, Mr Limerick.'

'Thank you.' The assistant wore a look of concern as, with a nod, he released the servant and shouted aloft, 'Once more, driver.'

The seat above creaked and Gordon, exhaling impatiently through his nose, imagined its occupant turning to check they were actually clear this time.

'Ya!' Out the window, Gordon watched the empty-handed servant retreat back into the warmth of the lodging house. To the sounds of the reins slapping the horses' flanks, the jumblement of hooves, the clanging metal bits and the violent chatter of imperfect wheels over uneven stone, the car made a burst for the street once more, supported by its unyielding axles and groaning iron springs.

*

From his knee-deep trench on the public works line of road 151, Pádraig threw a momentary glance to the man making conversation with him, but continued working. The most striking thing about him, Pádraig noticed – as his new neighbour on the line as of that morning removed his hat momentarily and reaffixed it – was a prominent baldness to the crown of his head. *Sál trí stoca*, Pádraig thought to himself. *The heel through shoe.*

'There is a lot of controversy surrounding this stretch of road, you know?' the man continued. 'Some fella – Splain, I think they said his name was – went and had a conflab with that Captain Gordon yesterday. Or lodged a grievance, more to the point. This stretch we're working here is part of Daniel Conors's land. Now, I don't know if the fella Splain was acting on Conors's behalf or what, but the way I hear it, he complained to Gordon that the road has all been laid down in the wrong place. Would you fathom it?

'And apparently Conors raised this with Gordon as far back as October, but the captain was too occupied with other matters and only sent his second down yesterday. So this fella Limerick arrives and says, "Yep! It's all wrong." All two hundred and eight perches of it! That's why we're all moved over here now this morning. He had to strike a new line parallel to the other one, only ten or eleven perches away. Two months after the start of it! Can you credit all that?'

The speaker had a look around to make sure neither the gangsman nor any of the stewards were looking, then rubbed the inside and outside of his hand on his patchy old soldier's jacket and stuck it out to greet his new ditch-mate.

Pádraig, blissfully unaware of what the man was saying to him, only turned his head again because he noticed he was no longer talking.

'Ned. Ned Brien Swiney, Slevean Road.'

'Ua Buaćalla.' Pádraig shook the man's hand.

'O'Buachalla. Nice to meet ye. Don't mind me. I talk a bit, but I'm no harm. I've seen ye in the queues and that. I know you haven't the English and I haven't much of the Irish meself, but sure what of it? We're all one and the same.'

Ned went on discussing and sharing his thoughts on what a piece of work Captain Gordon was. Pádraig, Ned's audience of one, liked the easy, friendly tone of his companion's voice, regardless of the language barrier.

It had been over a week now since the gangs – and the trio of Pádraig, Denis and Jeremiah – had been split up. The whole operation was running to a new system of 'task work', whereby the men were to be paid by the amount of individual work they did, instead of by a daily rate. The maximum they could earn was still eightpence a day but the work was substantially harder, and was to be measured. It was when they'd arrived at work on the Monday following that first payout that each man had been allotted a section of road to work himself. But the stones they were breaking now were field stones.

They were tougher somehow and needed a particular kind of stroke to split them. As of yet, no one seemed to have mastered it. It was exhausting. With men no longer sharing tasks there was no let up, and the result was badly blistered hands all around. But worst of all had been the shock around the second paying out of the wages: on 11 December, one week after the start of the task work, not one out of the whole complement of four hundred men had earned more than sixpence for any one day: and that sixpence had, at the higher end of the scale, been a rarity. Some men had received as little as one penny for a whole day's work!

A meagre one shilling and eightpence Pádraig had had put into his hand for the five days that week, including the Saturday before the task work when they were still on the day rate but were rained off early. The first day on the new system Pádraig had gone at it hard, with no distractions except for trying to see how other men were splitting the stones. He'd felt he'd got a lot done, compared with some others at least, but the next day, Tuesday, his hands were out in blisters. By Wednesday they'd been so sore it was hard to swing the hammer at all, and his work rate was slowed severely. On Thursday the broken blisters, scabbing up, had reopened painfully throughout the day and he'd had the added new discomfort of severe cramping in his calves and the soles of his feet.

Pádraig was annoyed at himself, and surprised that his hands were so soft. In all his working life, doing bits here and there and tending to his own, his hands had never been as sore, or as torn up. The only consolation was that the work had seemed to be affecting everyone the same way. The men had all been idle for so long before the works started up that most were simply unused to the intensity.

'That was some shock all the same wasn't it, O'Buachalla? The wages … the *airgead*?'

Pádraig knew what 'the wages' were by now and, though resistant to it, was already gaining a sense of the other odd word here and there, just as he had thought he would.

'How they expect a man to feed a family under these conditions is just baffling.' Ned was talking. 'Starvation wages, some of the men are calling them now. And I don't mind telling ye, I tend to agree. It doesn't take much arithmetic to figure it out … I mean, if you take that a man has to buy his meal now at what … two, and six or seven a stone? The average number in a labourer's family is at least six, and his wages on the works, at very best, but one might say near impossible under the present circumstances, is eightpence a day. At that price, it any case, a day's wages will only purchase around three-and-a-half pounds or so of flour. Earning a full eightpence a day, would give, at most, half a pound of the coarse aul' bread to each family member for the entire day.

'Of course, that's presuming they don't need to part with any of the other unavoidable pence for heat, light or the rent, nor any other indispensable necessities, to say nothing of clothes which, well, if things be suffered to continue the way they're goin', will soon be as rare a commodity as a bed or as food itself.'

Even though Pádraig had no idea of what Ned was saying to him, he sensed that the contents of his diatribe was none too distant from the inner talk he was having with himself. The same issues were, unsurprisingly, heavy on the minds of almost every man there.

On the basis of the first wages they'd received, which seemed luxurious by comparison now, and taking the weather and the stoppages for the lack of daylight into account, Pádraig had calculated that for his small family he was bringing home just over fivepence a day on average, which would afford him and the family just under twenty pounds of meal a week, or two-and-three-quarter pounds total a day – *if* he didn't have to spend on anything else.

He could afford to give himself almost, but not quite, a pound of bread a day on that, surviving on which he would – weekly – have to put in four to six days' manual labour and walk anywhere between forty-eight and seventy-two miles to get there and back depending on how many days' work the weather allowed. Cáit would get about three-quarters of a pound or just under, which was feeding Diarmuidín too, still nursing.

'Síle, who is four now, can have half a pound a day.' Pádraig recalled planning it out with Cáit.

'And Diarmuidín needs a mouthful or two,' she had argued. 'At two years old he needs to be eating something solid every day.'

But all that was on the old wages! he thought, clattering away at the stubborn rock before him. Now he faced a whole different level of problems.

Something coinciding with Ned's tone of complaint pulled Pádraig back out of his thoughts and into the present.

'We're being worked to death, basically, on wages that wouldn't support an idle man and his family …'

'Shssh …' Pádraig said with his head down, so that Ned instantly quieted, as aware now as he was of the approach of two overseers strolling along the line – a ditch full of bodies for as far as could be seen, of rolling shoulders and backs breaching the trenches, heaving up and earthing down beneath a skin of coats glazed with polished dirt and sending off a malodorous air that mixed old and new sweat with noxious fumes, as with each clink of the hundreds of hammers that pierced and then rained down into its depths, the rocks spat out their ancient secrets on fragments of pummelled powder and sulphuric dust.

'It should not seem such a hard thing to accomplish, to pay a man the wages he has earned at the end of a week. But when you find that, across the country, there are approximately three hundred thousand men now on the books, and all at the mercy of a completely new system of wages that must be tailored to each. It is ghastly, on either end.'

'Three hundred thousand and growing, Mr Ronayne.'

'Indeed, Mr Barry. And sadly, I think it will inevitably be found that in the resulting confusion, the wages will become less frequent, then fall further and further behind.'

'I sincerely hope you're wrong, sir.'

37

OUT OF NOTHING

Thunderous rain had begun to fall on top of thunderous rain from the night before. But the ground wasn't thirsty and said, *Enough.*

Ned Brien Swiney leaned on his shovel and looked to the sky. 'More in the night and more in the morning. I wonder how long they'll let it go on like this?'

He uncoupled his hands, gripped the shaft, and began to dig. 'They've called off the works in Dublin ... because of the snow, I believe ... I mean, the order was given in Dublin ... For counties in the west ... There'll be some numbers of them ... left to go hungry now, I suppose... If it's not bad enough to be cold, God help them.'

Krzhhziwhou!

The spade punctuated Ned's sentences intermittently, chopping into the sodden earth, letting rainwater in and drawing ground water up. 'But we don't stop down here. Not all of us at least ... The man unable to continue ... or who drops out ... is simply replaced by the next poor soul on the list ... Always someone more desperate than himself ... lined up waiting.'

Kurrfff!

'But on the whole ... he can no longer afford ... to stop on the mere whim of bad weather ... him who wants to survive ... 'Tis too frequent now ... and once you're wet, you're wet ... There's no shelter ... and nowhere to go but home ... That's a matter of miles for some ... and by the time a man's got there ... he could be dry ... and wet again ... Or just still wet!'

Kraaaawf!

'And at that ... sure he might as well ... stay here working ... earning money ... however little it does be ... as be wet and cold at home ... sleeping in the same clothes.'

Kriiift!

'And besides ... whenever the rain does stop ... he'll be dry quicker ... working than sitting still.' Ned stopped and joined his hands over the butt of the spade handle again a moment. 'And the Quarter Sessions started up yesterday at the courthouse.'

Krzhhuck!

'Every Pat, Jack ... and Michael is to be tried for something, I suppose ... Distraints ... evictions ... and God knows what else ... 'Twill be all the poor ... pursued by the law for being poor ... And turfed out on their ears.'

Kreeeeuw!

'They'll know all about the rain then ... God Almighty, when the rain comes down does it come down ... All across the country these December weeks ... are to be seen ranks of men like us here ... Peasant battalions ... nay, legions.'

Krzhziwhou!

'Men on their knees and haunches ... Sloshing about in the mud ... for pennies that wouldn't keep the family pig ... let alone keep the body and soul of a family together.'

Krzhziffrf!

'The strongest men ... the heads of families ... of almost an entire class of our people ... A grey, peasant army of labourers.'

Kijhhrfff!

'Blending the blood of fallen chieftains ... dispossessed tenants ... wandering poets and rootless slaves ... into ...'

Kaaaaarwf!

'... the poorest of the poor ... Us who work the land ... but never own the land ... Here are we ... being paid to ...'

Krzhhziwhou!

'... trifle with ... and tease the appetite of hunger ... so these foreign masters ...'

Kiouw!

'... whose ancestors took the land from ours ... and subjected them to ...'

Kiioouuuuw!

'... one barbaric law after another ... can ease their consciences ...'

Krhoowft!

'... while we stay quiet ... and die off ... as our wives and children grow weaker at home.'

Kiiioouuffih!

All of a sudden, Pádraig noticed that Ned was no longer talking. He checked and searched the horizon for any cause of disturbance that might have caused his neighbour to go to ground. But Ned was fine. Pádraig relaxed again. Not a steward or a ganger in sight. They'd be sheltering from the rain, like any smart man who had a choice would be.

Somehow, despite the hush of the downfall, the clinking hammers, the spades, the rude splashing and splodging of the mud and the sporadic coughing of the unwell, all was quiet. The tranquil haze that now came over him was almost too comfortable. Was he cold? Was he not cold? Pádraig couldn't tell. Were his lacerated toes red or blue? He wasn't sure. Crouching there in his trench, he felt as if he might be sleeping on the edge of the abyss. But the latest clink of the hammer made a glance off the rock and with a dull thud it pounded his thumb. Boom! The pain shot through Pádraig's whole body and up and down the length of him calling all his senses back to waking. He winced as discreetly as he could, but Ned's head whipped around to see what he'd done to himself. At the same time a cry was heard further along the line, followed by a commotion, and one by one the hammers stopped ringing. But as the silence caught the attention of the men along the line, it carried abroad and alerted the stewards too. The overseer on duty came running out of the shelter with a coat over his head, too hurried to grab an umbrella, as, in the ditches, necks strained to spy the source of the moaning and discern what had happened. Like a wind through the reeds, words and hushed whispers passed along from one trench to another. 'Murphy ... the weaver.' Pádraig heard. They were two words he understood well enough and before he knew it, he had hobbled out of his own hole in the ground and was trying to run through the stiffness of his joints in the direction of the gathering flock of labourers that shielded his approach from the view of the gangsmen and stewards approaching on horseback from the opposite direction.

Forcing his way between the spectators Pádraig found Denis lying on his side in the mud, and crying like a child.

'Up! Come on! Get up!' Pádraig urged his friend to get to his feet. But Denis seemed unable to move and howled in pain when Pádraig tried to lift him.

Over the weeks, daily hunkered down in one position for hours at a time through the cold and the wet, Pádraig had watched as the comrade he'd grown to have an affection for had become increasingly hunched over. Denis, who'd spent his working days as a weaver, was at the stage of his life when he should have been doing less and being looked after by his children instead of facing the prospect of a gruelling routine of outdoor manual labour. He had already been in a debilitated state when he'd begun a place on the works; the conditions had taken their toll and fast accelerated the decline of his health, until now, when it looked as though Denis had simply seized up and seemed to have all but resigned himself to the mud.

'Me shoe ...' Denis cried out through the tears and the spittle that webbed his gasping lips. 'Me fucking shoe!'

Pádraig turned to see the upper of a shoe on one of Denis's feet and the other half of it still stuck in the mud. The shoe. The one shoe that had been mended and stitched back together nearly as many times as he'd put it on and taken it off. It had given up. And so, it seemed, had

Denis. One of the men standing nearby pulled the sole of the shoe out of the mud and handed it to Pádraig. Denis grabbed it and smothered it into his chest.

'Back to work! Get back!' Roberts, the overseer, climbed off his horse and began pushing men aside and pulling them away from the scene. 'Get back!'

'Back to work or you'll be docked!' another of the stewards bellowed.

Pádraig was the last to be pulled away and, resigned that there was nothing more he could do for his friend, reluctantly took a few steps backwards as instructed.

'Can you walk?' Roberts snapped at the fallen man, who didn't answer but just sobbed pitifully. 'Can you walk, man?'

'Return to your spot', the under-steward shouted at Pádraig, who was still standing by, watching helplessly, feeling as though he too were stuck to the ground, and that when the overseer pushed him back another step, and then another, that he too was being pulled apart.

'Stretcher!' the gangsman shouted.

'Stretcher!' the steward relayed, louder.

Pádraig wandered half backwards to his own section, not knowing why, or how, to go back to his task.

'O'Buachalla! O'Buachalla, he'll be all right. Don't get yourself into trouble. You've mouths to feed yerself, man.' Ned steered him back towards his own trench, and although Pádraig heard only the sound of the words, he was guided by his neighbour's caring tone.

Two men came running through the hissing rain with a stretcher from the sheds, as some of the hammers slowly began to clink again, more for the sake of blocking out the reality and providing the semblance of effort than to accomplish their task in earnest.

'Right, take him away. Johnson, get one of the horses, and a car to take him home.'

'Yes, Mr Roberts.'

Denis was lifted, grimacing, onto the stretcher and carried away still weeping with shame and anguish, a broken man. Some gawked as he passed and some turned away. At length, when he was gone, Pádraig looked down and, his jaw locked in anger, remembered the pain. With the hammer in his grip but frozen between actions, he watched the blood as, running down his thumb in rivulets, it mixed with the rain and blended to a purple-brown mud, the lot coated – as a rock shattered beneath his hammer – with the ancient white and grey powders that, blown asunder, were fused with the rest and swallowed just as quick. *As quick and as violent as this life,* he thought, *wrought of the earth, and pulled back to it, just as ruthlessly.*

'E ... lth ... u ... pt.'

Pádraig spat out of the side of his mouth, then left his pit again and walked to the spring some fifty feet away to dunk his cup for a mouthful of water. Between breaks, it was an act of open defiance and frustration. 'O'Buachalla!' Pádraig heard Ned call to him in a voice of hushed shock that said he feared this was going to end horribly. But somehow the stewards either did not notice or chose to ignore the action. Having taken his drink Pádraig wandered back to his spot and began working again without a word to any man.

Though naturally affected by the whole incident, the men could scarce afford to spend too long thinking about what had happened. Already listless, jaded and emotionally drained, if they could allow themselves to think at all, they had themselves to think about. But there was pity and feelings of *thank God it's not me,* even of envy, for the release. Pádraig could sense it in the mood of the men. In the hammers. They sounded different now.

When the fire of anger in him had begun to die down, Pádraig began to wonder what would become of Denis. It was possible he'd recover from his injury but how would he earn now? How would his family fare against the odds? *They'll be blessed if they make it through to the end of the year on the wages he's owed ... if they're clever with it. But then what'll he get for the recent days he worked? With his back as bad as it was, he'll be lucky if it equals two days' wages. No wonder he lost his hope. Then there'll be debts.*

'He probably owes more out than he can count on, the poor soul.' Ned was talking again. 'Everyone inevitably owes something to somebody. The wages go ... and you're struggling to hang on for the next lot, so you borrow again, and you keep trying to somehow stay up with your debts. But that's the way of it, isn't it? One year after the next ... Until the day comes that you're called on to pay the last debt ... to the last inexorable creditor.' Ned looked to the sky as he spoke, rocking his shovel from side to side to free it from the sucking mud.

'How strange ...' the words continued to flow, comforting Pádraig though he had lost the sense of them, '... that out of little, much is paid; that out of nothing, all is paid.'

Did you lose a shoe? Pádraig remembered himself asking.

No, I found one, Denis had answered.

And the shoe. That blighted ... God-accursed shoe. Pádraig shook his lowered head, with the rain rolling down his cheeks. *Denis had clung to it as if its fate were tied to his own,* he thought.

The weather had intensified. Afternoon's light, waning, was masked behind ominous cloud and would not return. Pádraig felt the sting of the cold in his blue-white skin and the tail of a shiver that pulled through him.

Miserable shoes. What good are shoes ... to stand in mud, I ask you. What good is one leaky shoe? Why was it so important to him, a one damned, leaky shoe?

Laying down the hammer and gathering up a pick out of the wooden barrow, Pádraig fought to get his head around it, deferring to his older friend's cracked wisdom. His reasoning mind searched and questioned, but found nothing. Pádraig disliked shoes. Begrudgingly, he could say he understood their value, but he had always found them to be so restrictive, and heard himself argue with his father years before: *If God wanted you to have shoes you'd be born wearing them,* Pádraig had said. *Vain comforts is all they are. The only shoe I need is the skin on my feet.*

Oh, a necessary evil perhaps, but it's an awful poor man has no shoes at all, his father had maintained.

Raising the pickaxe high above his head, those words still ringing in his mind, Pádraig's mind struck back to the memory of another cold day, early in '45, when not a month in Doire Liath, he'd wandered into town, the words of the talk with Cáit still drying in his mouth. *We get our sciolláns into the ground, Cáit. We dig our heels in. And with the help of God, we'll be all right.*

*

They had been through the worst of it. Despite the fact that they'd been living from hand to mouth and barely surviving. Even though their station had been perilous. They had come back from the roads. The eviction was behind them. They had survived a desperate winter. Homeless. At the mercy of strangers. Had got resettled in a little bothán of their own. Even up in the wilds, exposed to the elements on a godforsaken wind-battered hill, exposed and overlooking half of Cork. At least they had a cabin to themselves. And a chance …

That bitter February, Pádraig had made the journey into town with a bundle under his arm. Looking like a giant hive full of bustle and bother, the big town sprawling out in front of him was an attack on the senses for someone coming in out of the spacious countryside. He'd been to Macroom before. But poor country people like him avoided the town. A gaping eyesore of clamour and haste. Any number of people banging into each other. He couldn't understand the attraction.

That same morning he had gently pulled the new blanket off Cáit and the children, leaving them with the old one and the coat. He rolled the precious cargo into the new blanket and bundled it up under his arm. If he was to get anything into the ground that spring he was going to need money. But pausing before he left, he leaned down and teased a strand of yellow straw out of Síle's hair, stroked her head and climbed out through the doorway. It was still too early in the year to be pawning the blanket, really. The weather would be cold until April or May if they were unlucky, but they'd almost worked their way through the sack of meal Ua Laoghaire had given them. It was a risk Pádraig just had to take.

He walked in amongst the confusion, doing his best to conceal the large lump under his waistcoat. His ears were assaulted by a forest of strange sounds. Not having a word of English, Pádraig was nervous and worried about having to deal with someone who only spoke the Béarla.

If it was not that the situation at Doire Liath was so precarious he might have been more worried still. He did not know a sinner here and had no idea how many desperate souls were on the prowl – empty mouths and empty bellies who might be driven by want to attempt God only knows what to quell their hunger.

The wealth was startling and ever-present.

Everywhere, betwixt and between the aimlessly wandering, begging poor of Macroom, Pádraig saw windows full of bread; hook-hung butcher's meat dripping with fresh blood and laden with fat; baskets of muck-caked vegetables; milk; beer; barrels of butter; corn, wheat, flour and oats by the sackful; leather boots and buckled shoes; tobacco by the pound; and every tool and trinket a man needed to be self-sufficient. His mouth watered as he went along, his gut aching with the hunger. So far as he could see you could get practically anything ... if you had the *airgead*. The poor hordes that pickled the streets all around him clearly had none, or virtually none. They appeared just to skulk around and drool, ogle, dream ... waiting for a morsel, or a falling crumb.

Pádraig wandered about the town, amazed at the concoction of humanity on display and the environment that contained it.

He didn't know where the pawnbroker's was. Nor what it looked like. But half-mesmerised and glad of any distraction from his own hunger, he carried the treasure on in search of its redemptive destination. Walking awkwardly on the strange surface of the cobbled streets, he felt himself out of place, as obvious a foreign body as a speck of grit in the mouth of a clam. But all at once, with a sense of alarm, Pádraig felt as though he was being stalked.

'You look lost, my friend.'

Pádraig spun around to stare squarely into the face of an apparition that had broken through the skin of this other world.

'*An goite amú atánn tú, a fhir óig?*' A pair of earnest old eyes, under an overgrowth of wiry charcoal and white brows, peered into his and awaited an answer.

The shock of the sudden confrontation put Pádraig on instant alert and he was ready for battle. The foe before him, at least twice his age and resting on a stick, looked too feeble to be trouble, but with the hackles up on his back and the hair of his neck tingling, Pádraig looked all around him to see what else might be coming, expecting to be set upon from behind as part of a strategy.

'*Clondrohid?*' the old man proffered matter-of-factly, keeping steady eye contact.

Still unable to respond, searching for danger, Pádraig perceived the man to express a lack of hope for the outcome when, removing his crooked old hat with one hand, he leaned his balding head forward and scratched the back of his neck with the unused fingers, the other hand leaning on the knobbly stick for balance all the while.

'How did you know where I was from?' Pádraig finally spoke, still unsettled.

'Because you came that way.' The old man, crowding his eyebrows, wore the puzzled look of one who felt they both should have known what was obvious, but he appeared to Pádraig to be displaying supernatural powers. He could have been coming from any one of a dozen other parishes in off that road.

'I'm after the pawnbroker's.'

'Of course you are.' With one hand the old man motioned towards the lump under Pádraig's waistcoat, then, switching hands on the stick while nodding his head, he opened the other arm towards the square inviting Pádraig to stroll with him.

Though still wary of the stranger's motives, Pádraig began to walk slowly alongside him.

'Shannie.' The old man offered his hand.

'Shannie?' Pádraig reluctantly allowed the stranger his grip.

'Shanahan. O'Seanacháin.'

'Ua Buaćalla,' Pádraig responded, feeling less concerned for his safety – if only by degrees – as they walked.

'Ua Buaćalla! A noble Cork name. Creed or Wiseman?'

Pádraig didn't speak, but looked to his new guide to elaborate.

'No preference? Creed it is then … Cornelius Creed is a better class of a man. Has a heart for the poor. Wiseman is all right in a pinch, but only if you're desperate. Creed is one of our own. More our colour, if you get me,' Shannie said with a wink. 'Have you the English?'

'I do not.' Pádraig's answer was resolute and full-voiced.

'Then you'll need someone to talk for you.'

Pádraig felt suddenly sceptical again.

Plying his craft with years of expertise, Shannie knew his man, expected suspicion, and was prepared when he saw it. He had the ways of the world and knew that honesty was the best way to make any transaction run smoothly and to the benefit of all.

Considering himself an opportunist, but not a rogue, Shannie knew he was too old to have someone coming after him, but young enough to appreciate the value of a satisfied customer who might have cause to avail of his services again. 'What have you to trade, clothes? A blanket?'

Pádraig, more backward, looked guarded.

'*Clondrohid* …' Shannie said again, and pouted in thought, leaving a pause. 'What's your first name?'

'Pádraig.'

'Pádraig …' Shannie stopped, and turned to face Pádraig square on.

'Look.' Pointing a finger toward his own face, the old man continued, 'I've a mouth to feed too, and *this* is how I put food in it. I can help you to sell your items for the best price that can be got for them. In return, you give me enough to bring home a morsel or two for mine.

'If you get a small price, there's less for me, so it's in *my* interest to help *you* do better. If I get you more than you would have got yourself, and you pay me some of that, then we're both better off.'

With the visitor clearly still considering the proposition, and anxious, the arrangement was in the balance.

'I'm not a swindler. I can send you off home with a few bob in your pocket but you have to trust me. You show me what you've got, and together we decide on a plan of action. Fair?'

Shannie, donning his most genuine and sincere face, gave Pádraig long enough time to answer so that he knew he wasn't being pressured. 'Stand in here with me.' With a comforting air, he shepherded his prospective business partner into a doorway, where he was sure to feel less exposed.

Pádraig knew he had no option but to take the offer at face value. He had no English himself. 'Listen, Ua Seanacháin. I am a young man but I'm a father, with young children and a wife depending on me. We've just … by the skin of our necks … got through a rough time. An eviction and a bad winter on the roads.'

'I know, son. We're all weathering the same storm.'

'What's in here …' Pádraig said, tapping at the bulge under his coat, 'is all I've got … to give us a chance of getting back up off our knees and making it through the next bit.'

'I hear.'

'I've walked near seven miles this day to do my business. And in the name of God …' The old man nodded along, encouraging the words out, as Pádraig stopped short and shook his head. 'God have mercy on me for questioning your honesty, old man, but I've no room left to take chances.'

'Listen, *Clondrohid* …'

'Pádraig!'

'Pádraig. We are the same, you and I,' the old man said, leaning and gripping one of Pádraig's arms with one hand and, with the stick in the other, poking his finger into his breastbone. 'You and me are the honest poor.' He turned his finger to his own chest then but stayed leaning on Pádraig for balance as he put his weight on the stick again. 'All we can do is our best in these hard times. But I am a man of my word. I'm not out to fool anyone. You need to pawn something and I can help you do it. I'm not doing it for *nothing*. But I can be of use to you, if you let me be. I'm fair ... and I'm honest.

'You have my word on it. If you wish.'

Baring his head for a second time, Shannie took off the battered old hat, placed it over his heart and, with the stick between his ribs and the elbow of his arm for support again, extended the other hand to Pádraig. Feeling won over by the man's sincerity, Pádraig grabbed the hand and shook it solemnly before turning away from the street to take the bundle out from under his arm. Some minutes later the old man led his customer into the crowded square and began to navigate the mass of beggars and stalls towards a row of establishments on the south side.

The one service that drew the poor in and took their trade above all others was the pawnbroker's. Macroom had two. Two proprietors of an institution that worked in reverse to all others the town had to offer. Every other trader was supplied through the back and purveyed its wares through the front, working that way consistently, year-round, administering goods in return for money.

The pawnbroker's, viewed from above, would appear to breathe in during the summer months, inhaling goods when the poor were most stretched and breathing out from autumn to spring, expelling goods when the poor were cash-rich enough on the back of the harvest to redeem their pledges. Though loathed, and traditionally seen as parasitic, the pawnbroker provided a narrow bridge between the cashless class and the world of commerce and trade. A pauper who was broke but had an item of value could exchange it for cash and then enter the market, transformed from mendicant to merchant as it were, if only temporarily.

'No ... For what you've got, Creed is definitely the right man. Trust me. There's only two of them and they're chalk and cheese. If you'd something of a different class to sell, it might be Wiseman you'd call to. He deals in more exclusive paraphernalia. Can be a bit of a snoot. Might turn his nose up at ye. No ... and Creed is not long at it either. He's still a bit soft.' Shannie winked again, enjoying his own roguishness, and feeling excited by the prospect of the sport that lay ahead.

As they refined their path towards a particular establishment, Shannie caught sight of a small brigade of souls who, idle outside, began to stir as he came into view with his mark. 'Blast ... they've found me again.' Shannie let on this was unexpected, worried his latest client might still be unsettled at the last moment. They knew Shannie by his trade, and as always – like a pack of stray dogs – came out to scavenge on the green carcass he'd have straggling along.

A decrepit old man was the first to break from the pack and come out to greet them.

'Oh, I hope ye have favourable dealings, sir. Mr Shanahan'll look after ye, God save him. And maybe if ye do well you could spare the price of a half a loaf so a man could feed his family.'

The plea fell on deaf ears seeing as Pádraig couldn't understand him. Shannie felt no obligation to clarify the misunderstanding and he and his man were absorbed by the crowd before its leader had finished his long sentence.

Shannie parted them deftly with an arm extended. But knew to stay on their good side. 'Excuse us, gentlemen,' he said as he pushed through.

Inside, a brass bell above the door was triggered and heralded their custom. But the proprietor was already behind the counter and the sound seemed merely to confirm what his eyes had probably told him, as, wearing a cynical gaze, he peered back over his lenses, first looking to Shannie and then to the visitor. His greeting said neither 'Welcome' nor 'Woe-come' and Creed, clearly not surprised that he had visitors, turned back to licking and thumbing a page of his paper.

In turn, Shannie knew Creed well and understood that this indifference was the beginning of their negotiation. The pawnbroker was a man of healthy appearance, nearing middle age, with pale blue eyes and long grey hair, balding on top, and dressed without ceremony.

At length he looked up. 'Good morning, Mr Shanahan. You're off to an early start today.'

The sarcastic tone of the greeting did not dismay Shannie, who was happy he'd landed the first blow by inducing Creed to speak first on this occasion; he was about to respond when another man, plainer still, but podgy, appeared from the back, apparently responding to the bell.

'Would you like me to …'

'Handle this, Mr French? I would not. But thank you,' Creed answered, closing the paper with two hands to thumb to the next page, all the while keeping an eye on them. The clerk turned tail and disappeared as quickly as he'd come.

'Good morning, Mr Creed, sir.' Shannie spoke with jollity and bowed as he removed his hat, then gave a cough that encouraged Pádraig to do the same. ''Tis a fine morning and even finer to be bringing someone into your fine establishment, sir … to do business.' He smiled at Pádraig as he finished the sentence, looking pleased.

'I wish I could share your enthusiasm, Mr Shanahan. Every time that bell rings, I'm one step closer to bankruptcy, whether it be psychological or financial.'

'Well, sir, I hope that day will never come. God bless you, sir. You're a great friend to the poor.'

'That's exactly the problem, Mr Shanahan. You think I'm a soft touch, so you keep bringing me this constant stream of hapless wonders, thinking I can save them all.'

'Ah, every day the world turns, sir. We just do our best one at a time. But God be good to you, Mr Creed – many is the man has had an easier path because of your kindness.'

With the head of the knobbly stick in the pit of his arm, Shannie, enjoying the repartee, was practically bouncing on the tips of his toes.

Holding his beaten-up old hat in both hands just above his knees, he pinched the brim and grinned a wide smile, emitting the slew of treacle-toned pleasantries and compliments. It was a daily ritual and Shannie knew they were both well able for each other.

Their audience of one, whom Shannie sensed was sweating beside him, must have had no idea what was happening. But at least he was staying still, if staring around with curiosity while he waited.

'Who is this poor soul you've brought in to me?'

'This poor man, Mr Creed, has walked all the way from Mullach an Ois this very day, with not a rag on his feet the whole journey.'

Creed, who was now unveiling counter displays, turned from his task to look at the subjects and raise an eyebrow that as good as said, *Now you're turning it on*. Mullach an Ois was a mountain peak almost three times as far as Clondrohid and even Pádraig had turned to stare at Shannie with curiosity.

Absurd as the claim was, Creed said nothing to challenge it. Listening daily to the stories, and pleas, however much they were embellished, was all part of the dance. And the cat-and-mouse game he and Shannie played as they tried to outsmart each other was the gratification he got for his generosity. Despite the difficulties of the time, there was no danger of financial ruin. Creed knew he was a bad businessman, but he could afford to be. With seventy-five acres to his name and being the owner of his premises by the grace of inheritance, the shop was really just a means of keeping himself occupied.

He could entertain himself here and stay on top of his living costs without having to touch his land. 'Go on ...'

'This man has five young children. His poor wife is dead and he's taken in three of her sister's boys. They're all living in a skelp in a hole in the ground above in the wilds beyond Clondrohid ... and not one of them has eaten a scrap for seven days straight.'

Creed turned fast to lock eyes with the chanter, who had suddenly stopped talking.

'… Or maybe it was seven children and three or four days without food. The old noggin. I might be getting confused.' Shannie scratched his chin, squinting one eye.

'But really, Mr Creed …' he added after a pause, pleading in a more earnest, quietened tone. 'They're on the road since Christmas time, at the mercy of charity, and only recently found a place to settle where they wouldn't be disturbed, but left in peace to try and get on surviving like the rest of us …' Creed looked Pádraig up and down and sighed pitifully. '… And now he's here, making an effort to try and get his family back off their knees, to some semblance of a dignified existence …'

Pádraig had been unable to understand even the least part of what was being said, and having finally stopped moving for some time, was feeling utterly exhausted and weak with hunger. Suddenly overcome, he stumbled and tried to steady himself on the counter.

'Oh, bedad, I think he's going to go …' Shannie made a rush for Pádraig as if to catch a falling tree, noticing that Creed seemed panicked for a moment too, stuck behind the counter as he was.

Shannie steadied his charge, half pulling him off his axis at the same time for theatrical effect, then, whipping a rag out of his pocket, mopped the brow of the bemused Pádraig, who was suitably disoriented looking now.

Be Jays … you are not as green as ye look, Shannie thought to himself, impressed. The glassy eyes and collapsing knees of his companion were perfect.

'Are ye all right? Stay with me!' Shannie shook Pádraig, gave his face a little slap, and stared into his eyes, delighted with himself, and feeling like a performing magician with the perfect accomplice. This was the best one yet.

'Right. What has he brought?' Creed asked, sold for a penny. As Pádraig returned to his senses, Creed's and Shanahan's eyes both fell to the bundle in the crook of his arm. Aware that he was up, he moved suddenly, then hesitated.

'Pádraig Ua Buaćalla,' Shanahan said, evidently to introduce him, but also letting Pádraig know that now *was* in fact the time to come forward.

His eyes flicked between the two men before, lowering his head, Pádraig gently placed the blanket on the glass counter in front of him.

The pawnbroker was perched on a stool behind the counter, but already leaning on one elbow and in position to view the contents directly below his gaze. Shanahan, too, closed in on Pádraig's left, to complete the intimate gathering.

'This treasure is all the good man has in the w–'

'Mr Shanahan. Please!'

Having checked his companion, the pawnbroker then signalled for Pádraig to continue – he unravelled the blanket slowly, feeling the weight of the world and of all his young family's hopes on his shoulders.

For a moment the noise and bustle of the square outside fell away as, with forlorn acceptance, Pádraig unveiled the pair of brown shoes within, staring at them with a mixture of sadness and pride. '*Bróga m'athar.*'

After a long moment, Shannie clicked his tongue, and rocking his head, followed. '*Is beag rud nách buaine ná an duine.*'

'What's that?' Creed asked.

'The smallest thing outlives us ...'

Pádraig continued to stare at the shoes. *It's a poor man hasn't a pair of shoes to his name, to take him to Mass of a Sunday.* He heard his father's voice, still talking from long before.

And he remembered how as a youth he had responded cheekily to his father, pointing and saying, 'You'll never catch me wearing them leather hooves. I have the shoes God gave me, and they never wore out yet.' But he had worn them once. The very shoes before them now. He wore them in that chapel that day when they were married in '38. The chapel in Macroom, somewhere near here. 'Just while we're inside,' he had told Cáit and, having relented, put the shoes on for the few minutes to keep her happy. But he had despised the sensation – just walking as far as the altar and back in them was enough and they had come off again as soon as he was outside.

'His father's shoes.' Shannie spoke to Creed with his eyes closed, his voice as rich with sympathy as he could manage. 'His poor, dead, father's …'

'Christ, Mr Shanahan …'

'God rest him, he was a dacent man.' Shanahan pulled out his kerchief once more, and blew his nose dramatically.

Pádraig looked shocked at this behaviour and then less than pleased at the state of the rag in Shanny's hand, remembering that it had mopped his brow only moments ago.

The pawnbroker rolled his eyes across the ceiling and rested his jaw in his upturned hands. 'I can't give him very much for these.'

'Good God,' Shannie retorted abrasively. 'After putting the man through all that! Look at them, they're hardly worn, if ever at all.'

'I can see with my own eyes, Mr Shanahan, but that they're not new.'

'Good as new to someone who needs a pair.'

'I could give him two-and-six maybe.'

'Goh! Two and …? Ah, Mr Creed.' Shannie wrung the brim of the bent old hat and paced to nowhere and back in dramatics. 'They're worth a pound if they're worth anything! Is that two-and-six per *shoe*?'

'It is not per shoe, Mr Shanahan.'

'This honest man is hoping to put seed into the ground to sustain his family through the season …'

'I understand all that, but I can only work with what I'm given.'

'He has to buy the seed – it's not going to fall out of the sky.'

'Yes, Mr Shanahan, that's all well and good.'

'And he's come into you here in good faith, with these family heirlooms. A pair of them!'

'Now, Mr Shanahan …'

'And you're trying to put him into an early grave. Where's the respect?'

'Mr Shanahan, this is a business. I can do my best, but I don't give money away.'

'And you a dacent Christian man, Mr Creed.'

They were on the verge of success now. Shannie was sure of it. So long as Pádraig could hold his nerve. But checking for a moment as he continued his rant, he caught a glimpse of Ua Buaćalla, who was beside himself and looking with frantic eyes from one to the other as if wondering where it had all gone wrong. Shannie knew he'd have to wrap it up quickly.

'There's always George Wiseman's shop over the way,' Creed said. 'Or he could seek a loan from one of the lenders. Edward Ashe. Philip Cross. William Garde Browne. They're all getting rich as Croesus off the principal. Two-and-six. That's thirty pence.'

'Judas got that and he done away with himself …'

'MISTER–'

'Would ye have him take his family straight to the poorhouse in Masseytown and be done with it?'

'MISTER SHANAHAN! PLEASE!'

Shannie fell silent, knowing he had pushed Creed as far as he could take him, but that it was this point he had needed to get him to. He permitted his rival the illusion of having regained control and now stood back to allow the magic to work.

'Now – this is a short-term loan, or when does he intend to redeem his ticket?'

And as calmly as if he'd walked in the door only moments before with no care in the world, Shannie moved in to complete the trap, relieved to sense he had not laboured in vain. 'I believe Mr Ua Buaćalla is hoping to reacquire the valuable items as soon as his station is improved.' In effortless voice he loosened the shirt on his neck and kicked at Pádraig below the sightline of the counter.

'And when would this be? One month? Two months?'

'Mr Ua Buaćalla has great plans, and intends to–'

'Long term it is. Very well …'

As Creed wrote *Long term* into his ledger, Shannie stayed quiet, lest he undo anything, but struggled not to look as smug as a cat with a mouthful of bird. It was in the book now.

'I believe this woollen garment is up for bidding too, Mr Creed.' Shannie thumbed the blanket to indicate its fine quality.

'Yes, I presumed that,' Creed said but kept his nose in the book, clearly refusing to indulge his tormentor.

'Fine ram's wool.'

Creed shook his head and, still writing, read aloud. 'One … pair … of … shoes … and one … blanket.'

'And one pair of laces.'

'The laces are part of the shoes, Mr Shanahan. They don't work without them!'

'Ah, we'll throw in the laces.' Shannie winked at Pádraig, who had visibly calmed down now that the transaction was underway.

'Very well. Reluctantly, I'm prepared to loan Mr O'Buachalla six and threepence, on the basis–'

'Six? Six and threepence? Did I hear you right? Mr Creed, this is robbery!' Shannie slapped the tweed hat against his thigh and spun away from the counter in protest.

'Mr Shanahan, the entry is only in pencil. I can erase it if you wish and you can take this man elsewhere.'

'His father'll turn in his grave!'

'I assure you I'm the only one being robbed here. Now do you accept, Mr Shanahan?'

'God in heaven. Right so, only on account of I've other urgent business to attend to myself. And this man has to get back to his wife, and seven starving orphan childer. I'll accept six and eight on his beha–'

'Six and three. Not a penny more.'

'I don't know how ye sleep at night, robbing good Christian men, Mr Creed. Six and seven.'

'Six and three.'

'God forgive me, you're a hard man. Very well. Six and sixpence.'

'Three. Six and three.'

'Six and fivepence.'

'NO! Seventy-five pence! Six and three.'

'All right. Seventy-six! Seventy-six! Done.'

'Why do I torture myself? Six and fourpence. I won't be sorry if I don't see you for the rest of the week, Mr Shanahan.' Creed said, correcting the sum with the pencil.

'He's got nine months to redeem the pledge, by which time the interest will have accrued at seventeen pence per annum, which rounds up to a florin and ten pence. Total with principal and interest will be eighty-five pence; seven and a penny.'

'Cold as stone,' Shannie said under his breath, but spoke loud enough to still be audible.

'I'm sorry, Mr Shanahan?'

'God bless ye, sir.'

Creed shuffled into a back room, returned with the money and, after handing it to Pádraig, thanked him for his business.

As Pádraig stared at the coins in his hand and the two prepared to leave, the pawnbroker nodded respectfully to Shannie. Pleased that there was something of a knowing gleam in his glance, the old hawker returned the approval with a dignified bow of his own, then led his man out through the door under the bell.

'Mr Creed.'

'Good day, Mr Shanahan.'

Creed, needing to bring himself under control before engaging another customer, retained the task of processing the items for himself and, having given Mr French the counter, tied the laces together. Carrying them out, he stacked the shoes in the store with a tag that read 'Pádraig O'Buachalla, Clondrohid' along with the date, and the number '96' corresponding to the entry in his ledger.

He sighed deeply as he put the shoes away, knowing he'd given significantly more than they were worth – and that in all likelihood, judging by the condition of the 'claimant', they would not be retrieved. He would process the blanket next.

Leaving the shop, Pádraig gripped the money tightly and held it out of sight as he followed the old man quickly through the square, until, sure that the last of the beggars had dropped off and given up following them, they found a quieter spot and stopped in a doorway a couple of streets away.

'Are you happy?' asked Shannie.

'I think so.'

'We got a good bit over the odds.'

'I'm in your debt, Ua Seanacháin.'

'It's my pleasure, Pádraig Ua Buaćalla.'

'How much is your share?'

'Ah. My children are fed and grown young men and women. It's just my wife and myself mostly. If you can give me enough to put a morsel on the table for today I'll be happy, and I'll thank you for it.'

'That's more than fair.' Pádraig was really feeling the cramps of hunger now. He'd been so fervent in his emotions, he'd almost forgotten. 'Where can we get some food?'

'Follow me.'

Coming out onto the north side of the square again, Shannie led Pádraig to Thomas Cotter's, a bakery, and waited outside as Pádraig bought them each a penny loaf.

The old guide then walked his customer down Castle Street, to the edge of the bridge that split the town.

'Clondrohid. Here we part.'

Pádraig took out the coins, and gave the old man another penny. 'I hope our paths cross again some time, Ua Seanacháin.'

'I hope you never have need of me, Pádraig Ua Buaćalla. But if you do, my services will be open to you as required.'

The two shook hands solemnly and parted company.

Walking off the west side of the bridge, Pádraig, impatient with hunger, tried to eat a lump of the bread but was spotted passing Barrack Lane and set upon by beggars who tried him with every kind of heart-rending plea until he was forced to run away with the bread under his coat, at which point their pleas turned to such a variety of curses that were they arrows, he thought, they would have lodged by the dozen in his back. He knew if he'd given them so much as a crumb they wouldn't have left him alone until it was gone.

The hunger was much more pronounced now and Pádraig knew he'd have to eat something soon. Finding the measure of what a walk into town meant from their new homeplace in Doire Liath had taken a significant effort. But tired as he was, completing six-and-a-half miles to get there was only the halfway mark. Getting home would make it a thirteen-mile round trip and Pádraig knew that a fire that burns no sticks goes cold. That kind of exertion, even at a gentle pace, would deplete the healthiest man were he to try it on nothing and yet he walked faster, trying to shake the cramps.

After the union, he told himself, acutely aware – from the numerous poor souls idle and hanging around on the far side of the road – that he was coming up to the turn-off for the workhouse at Masseytown. Pádraig kept his head down and marched on to avoid their attention, but they were too busy begging at the gate to notice him on the other side. They wouldn't have bothered another pauper anyway, with no obvious food on him, but they might have smelled the warm bread, and his feet couldn't carry him away fast enough.

The feelings of sickness and pain in his guts intensified to the point of a cold sweat until finally, when he'd found a quiet spot by the river, Pádraig sat down and broke a fist-sized chunk off the still-warm loaf. The smell was so good and the dough so soft that he wanted to just take his time eating it, but he hurried it into him for fear that someone might notice.

It was dry, though, and to get a lump of it down that stuck in his gullet he had to gulp water from the stream. The water was like liquid light. He drank and ate more until he was full very quickly. Then, but for the remainder of what he was eating in one hand, Pádraig put the rest back under his waistcoat in case he might have struggled to stop himself. In a moment of panic he suddenly remembered the money and grabbed at his pocket, but the coins were still there. He hadn't noticed their jangling for a while and they could have easily fallen into the stream … or perhaps into one of the beggars' pockets.

'Clondrohid,' Pádraig muttered to himself with an amused grunt. Feeling less anxious, his hunger sated, he could finally relax for a moment. And gazing down at his bare, dirty, shoeless feet there as he'd chewed the last bite left in his hand, his eyes had drifted from the river before him to imagining how excited the children were going to be when he walked through the door with bread.

*

Cling! The bell of the raining pickaxe struck the rock and rang through the air as Pádraig noticed that Ned was talking again.

'There was an ad appeared in the Cork paper yesterday. I do sometimes find a paper around the square and the like.'

Krzhziurrf!

'The pawnbroker Creed is selling up.'

38

THE TERROR OF TYRANTS

F *riday, 18 December*
Though the suffering and privations of the appalled and afflicted residents of this town and locality have hitherto been recorded in your columns, yet I deem it no intrusion on the feelings and sympathies of your readers to recur again to a subject, which, did it evoke in the outset, a kindly and natural commiseration, must, now that it has arrived at the full growth and maturity of its horrors, startle and appal the most inconsiderate and unreflecting.

Justin McCarthy scribbled the words hastily into his notebook in anticipation of the article he'd been assigned to compile over the forty-eight hours to come and deliver back to his editor at the *Cork Examiner* for Monday's publication of the editorial. Having just now stepped off the evening car to Macroom he sought advice as to what sights might best represent the needs of the town to the reading public, and where he ought to devote most of his efforts and limited time.

It was a hard thing for him to fathom, that he, but a sixteen-year-old boy, could be entrusted with the huge responsibility of being – albeit not exclusively – the eyes and ears of such an important institution as John Francis Maguire's own *Examiner,* during the greatest crisis the country had ever known. But more than that: trusted to be the voice and the emissary of the poor he was encountering, presenting them to the world at large and recording their fate for posterity. And yet, it was so. Although he felt immensely conscious of the tremendous weight thrust upon his shoulders, Justin believed he was carrying it well, and, indeed, Mr Maguire had recently reinforced that belief, commending his performance as 'showing great promise'.

Maguire cited often the value of nurturing younger talent and had stood behind this conviction when he'd assigned both Justin and his friend Tom Crosbie the role of travelling reporters. So it was a shame, but a matter Justin fully appreciated, that he and Tom could not be credited with their articles under their own names. Maguire was astute enough to know that were his readership aware that the correspondents were but sixteen and seventeen years old their writings might not be taken as seriously as they deserved to be – not to mention by those who, given any opportunity, would have the 'partisan publication' undermined and ridiculed. So Justin and his friend's articles were attributed to 'Our Special Reporter', 'Another Special Reporter' and other such anonymous designations. The uniqueness of the position the two shared only increased the strength of their friendship and Justin felt that he and Tom were comrades in fire. Most frequently – as on this occasion – they were sent out alone across the region, each to assess, then report on the true state of affairs. But so ably mentored as they were by their faithful employer, Justin had every confidence that he and his friend could do and were doing just that.

Given all that he had encountered during his travels, Justin scarcely needed extra incentive to be diligent in his role. But if ever he became disheartened, Maguire's inspiring words were all the fuel he needed. And now, looking up, as he scanned the evening skyline of Macroom, Justin again heard the words in his mind: *The liberal press, my boys, is the terror of tyrants! And with a little guidance from me, and not a small amount of ink, that is exactly what you two will become.*

Arriving in a new town, Justin had always found the clergy to be a useful source of advice on what to take in and, guided by the horizon, he decided to begin with the established church. Upon reaching the rectory, near the river, he stepped inside and asked to see the pastor.

'This way,' the sacristan told him. 'Mr Swanzy is a very busy man. But you're lucky. It so happens I just saw him come in from his errands. He's been out all day. Now what is it your name is? Is the minister expecting you?'

'He is not, sir. I'm from the *Examiner*.'

'Of course. Here we are. Just a moment.'

Justin didn't have to wait long before he was shown into the vestry.

'The vicar will see you now.'

Henry Swanzy was a tall man of middle age, though sturdily framed. As he offered his greeting the vicar looked surprised, even astonished, but Justin was accustomed to the spectacle of his elders balking at his appearance. Even so, he was keen to proceed and had found he achieved more respect when he took the initiative and cut straight to the matters at hand.

'Thank you for seeing me, Mr Swanzy,' Justin said, taking a notebook and pencil from his shoulder bag. 'I'm here for the *Examiner* ...'

'Yes?'

'... to write a piece on the condition of the town, and its inhabitants.'

'Yes.' The minister was not giving much back so far.

'I confess myself to be unfamiliar with the layout of the town and its ramifications for the variety of persons I might hope to meet.'

'I see.'

'And I have often found it to be of great benefit to consult the clergy of a locality to discover where I might best focus my attention. I take no denominational sides in such serious matters as the stark times we are witness to, sir. It was simply the case that stepping off the mail car I noticed the steeple was closer than the cross.'

Justin found the vicar to be aptly poised with elbows and hands in a suitably prayerful clasp. He had so far held both index fingertips to his upper lip, removing them but slightly for each new affirmative. By his expression, he seemed still to be assessing the rudiments of Justin's introduction, but so far he had shown no inclination that he might indulge his guest any more than he might need to. Having dispensed with his full remit, Justin decided now to stop talking and see what would come.

'Yes of course ...' the minister, finally, answered. 'You may have noticed the frequency of beggars and undernourished specimens about the town already.'

'I have, sir.'

'I'm afraid you needn't go much further to get a sense of the desperation that prevails here and throughout the barony. As much as anywhere else, I expect.'

Justin nodded in agreement.

'I would suggest that you undertake a tour ... of some of the domestic abodes in the vicinity of the square. In the immediacy of its laneways and alleys, situated in the wretched hovels of the poor, you will find an amount of misery adequate to fill several columns of your journal, I should imagine. Beyond that, I am afraid I have my own family to attend to among other matters now and cannot be of much more assistance to you.'

'Of course. You've been most helpful, sir.'

'But a word of warning, young man ... '

'Yes?'

'Be prepared to meet much ...

'I am, sir.'

'For I fear to say it, but a boy of your tender years – you are likely to witness things that will live long in the trouble of your memory.'

McCarthy nodded to show he understood, but had a response. 'I am afraid I have already encountered such things in my travels, Mr Swanzy. But I thank you for your kindness nonetheless.'

The minister returned a single, respectful nod. 'There is a pawnbroker, Creed. He hasn't been seen much lately as it happens, but he corresponds regularly enough with your journal. If you can track him down, perhaps he may be of use to you.'

'Thank you, sir. I will ask of him. One other question if it's not too much trouble, Mr Swanzy?' Both men were on their feet now. 'I am instructed to enquire about the Quarter Sessions while I'm here, but was made aware they may be spoken for?'

'They began on Wednesday and are still running, I believe. There may be some business yet, but it couldn't be much even under the present circumstances. They're normally disposed of in a day.'

'Oh. Good. And – the courthouse, sir?'

'It's on Barrack Lane. If you cross the bridge and take the second right.'

'You've been very helpful, Mr Swanzy, sir. Thank you kindly.'

'You're most welcome. You can find your way out?'

'Of course, sir.'

'Good, good.'

It was dark already and with a cold fog in the air Justin made straight for the square again, intent on finding Bartholomew Donovan's Lodging House, where Tom told him he'd stayed before at a very reasonable expense. Justin's last thoughts before sleep were of the inadequate habiliments of any of the poor out in the cold that night.

*

On Saturday morning, Justin navigated the town and made his way to the courthouse, eager to catch what might be the last of the Petty Sessions.

Indeed, a trial was just about to get under way in the crowded building and Justin made his way through the densely packed public gallery to find one of the last seats near the front.

Upon the bench were seated a number of justices in customary wigs and gowns and, in time for their introductions, Justin conscientiously took down the names of Mr James Little, Special Magistrate; Mr John Borlaise Warren, Justice of the Peace; Mr Massy H. Warren, JP; Mr Splain, JP; Mr Nettles, JP; Mr Warren Crooke, Magistrate and the Assistant Barrister Moody, presiding.

Writing swiftly in his notebook as he did so, Justin concentrated on getting to grips with the basics of a case brought by the crown prosecution, with a certain Mr Sheahan, the appellant.

According to a Mr Gallwey, solicitor for the crown, it appeared that a conviction had been obtained against a Mr John Grace for supposedly stealing a flail used for threshing corn. The object was valued at sixpence.

Mr Gallwey proceeded to examine Mr Sheahan, a man who, with his back to Justin, wore a seemingly borrowed velvet coat that did not fit, and had his unkempt hair plaited with a ribbon. It was upon Mr Sheahan's application that the conviction had been obtained and Mr Gallway attempted to prove that he, Sheahan, had detected Mr Grace stealing the flail from inside the door of his employer's yard, 'Sheahan himself being at the time in such a position as to amply observe the appellant picking up the flail and leaving the yard with it some time later under his coat.'

It appeared a simple case, thought Justin, and as presented, perhaps an easily plausible one.

Next, Mr Downing, for the defence, questioning Mr Sheahan, asked, 'Did you actually see Mr Grace put the flail under his coat?'

'I did not, but …'

'Did any time elapse between the appellant's picking up of the flail and his leaving the yard?'

'A little.'

'How long would you say?'

'Perhaps a half hour.'

'I see. And was there anyone else on the premises around the time that Mr Grace left the yard?'

'There were numerous persons.'

'And could you be a wholly certain that none of those people left carrying a flail under their coat?'

'I could not, sir.'

'Thank you. And when Mr Grace eventually did leave the yard, did you see him carrying the item?'

'I did not, sir.'

'Could you see it under his coat?'

'I could not, sir.'

'So how do you know he had taken it?'

'Because I saw him pick it up earlier.'

'How much earlier? Approximately half an hour – correct?'

'Yes, sir.'

'And do you suppose it's possible that he may have put it down at any time between?'

'I didn't see him put it down.'

'Were you watching him the entire time?'

'Not the entire time.'

Mr Downing then asked of the bench if they saw any point in his continuing the questioning. The larceny went unproved and the prisoner was acquitted and released. Mr Sheahan looked somewhat relieved if not a little embarrassed stepping down and Justin could not help but suppose it had been at the behest of someone unseen that Sheahan, who clearly looked out of place dressed as he was, had taken a case against something of an equal, yet showed no real ambition to enforce the accusation.

Amid the bustle, the next case called was against John McCarthy, a man from the neighbourhood of Skibbereen, who was led into position in iron handcuffs, where he stood upright but looked miserable and uncomfortable, much like Mr Grace before him. Though it looked more like it had been for two years to Justin, Mr McCarthy had been the last two days in the gaol of that town following a dispute with the landlord, Mr O'Driscoll, and his agent, Mr Bird, regarding the rent and the distraint of the contents of his cabin for moneys owed. The said contents included furniture, the man's horse and forty sheaves of corn that were all he and his family had to live on. While the men in the employ of the agent had been removing the table, the accused's daughter had put her hand on the item and begged them to stop, after which the police were called, who the next day had taken Mr McCarthy and his two sons away to the jail where they'd been since.

Mr Gallwey, Mr Fitzmaurice and Mr Michael O'Connell would conduct the prosecution and Mr Philip O'Connell the defence.

John Hurley, the agent's driver, was called for examination by Mr Gallwey and, once standing in the dock, tugged briskly at the bottom of his short coat to get himself comfortable.

'Are you the driver for the agent for Mr O'Driscoll?' Mr Gallwey began.

'I am.'

'Did you conduct a distraint on his behalf, on Wednesday last, on the lands of Shreelane, for rent?'

'I did.'

'And what happened?'

'Hmm. Ahem.' John Hurley cleared his throat and straightened his coat once more. 'I attempted to impound the furniture, but the prisoners would not allow me to conduct my business.'

Cross-examined by Mr Philip O'Connell, Mr Hurley accepted that he had not been assaulted, nor injured, and was not abused, except by McCarthy's saying, 'The devil a one of you shall take this table.'

At this, laughter and amusement abounded, coming mostly from the gallery behind Justin.

Through a series of questions that followed, the agent's driver admitted that he knew Mr O'Driscoll's tenants were in the habit of signing bills to the bank in lieu of the rent; did not *think* they were asked to do so before the rent was due; had heard that the prisoner and his sons *had* signed a bill for rent; and believed that the landlord, Mr O'Driscoll, had put the bill in the bank and got money upon it.

'But there was rent due besides,' he argued.

'How much rent?'

'There were three-and-a-half years' rent due.'

'And had the time for paying the note on the bank arrived when you carried out this distraint?'

'It had not.'

Hurley's response was greeted by some sensation in the gallery.

'What did you distrain, sir?'

'The man's horse, his corn, and the furniture.'

'Did you leave the unfortunate man anything to sustain his family?'

'Mr McCarthy stole some of the confiscated corn back. I only managed to take away forty-six loads.'

Disruption rained in from the gallery once more, though this time it was marked by a graver, angrier tone.

'Quiet!' With one word, Mr Moody quelled the noise.

'And where did you put them?' Mr Philip O'Connell continued his questioning when the furore had abated.

'I impounded the horse and put the corn in a garden near Mr O'Driscoll's house.'

'Did you count them?'

'I did.'

'Who else was in attendance?'

'Two or three others.'

'Who was the auctioneer?'

'I was.'

'Did you bid yourself?'

'I was not the buyer, but got the corn afterwards myself.' Gasps were heard throughout the court.

'How much did the corn sell for?'

'I sold every six weights for eightpence.'

It seemed to Justin that the entire gallery erupted in disgust at the swindle, during which time some members of the court actually left the bench, including Mr Michael O'Connell for the prosecution, a sense of decency and shame apparent in their actions. But whatever the emotion, from where he was sitting it looked as though they wanted nothing more to do with the proceedings and, in Michael O'Connell's case, his client.

'And gracious God! Did you not also take the straw upon which the poor family slept?'

'I did not take the straw on which they slept, but I did take a stack of straw that was outside.'

'The Devil's henchman!' A voice shouted amid more chaos.

'Quiet!' Mr Moody shouted again.

'You say you distrained all of these items before the bill was even due. Why did you do so, Mr Hurley?' The wigged figure of Mr Gallwey took over once again. With his back now to his client, the prosecutor eyeballed the court with the question, and Justin fully anticipated some attempt at retrieving a semblance of propriety for Hurley's behaviour.

'Because we heard that the prisoners were top-dressing their corn.'

'Exactly so.' Mr Gallwey satisfied himself, and sat again.

'Was it not by the produce of the corn they were to meet that bill?' Mr O'Connell, still standing, asked.

'I suppose so.'

'Exactly so. I have no more questions for Mr Hurley.'

Feeling exhilarated, Justin strove desperately to keep up with the proceedings and scribble down all he could as the court took its breath and jostled the change.

'Mr George Bird.' Wearing a long grey coat and a black top hat that, once removed, revealed a head of dead straight shiny black hair, the next person to be examined and called to the stand was the agent himself, a young, robust man, Mr Fitzmaurice having called him to obtain the agent's support for the prosecution's case.

'Mr Bird. How much is the yearly rent on the prisoner's holdings?'

'Twenty-two pounds,' the man answered calmly, sweeping the fringe of his locks to one side.

'Did you direct Mr Hurley to conduct the distraint?'

'I did.'

'On what grounds?'

'On the grounds that I heard they were top-dressing the corn, and because he owed a gale of rent not included on the bill.'

'One gale? How much in total did the prisoner owe?'

'Including the bill and all, twelve months' rent.'

'Twelve months total. Are you sure of that?'

'I am sure.'

Mr O'Connell rose to cross-examine the agent for the defendant. 'Mr Bird. Define a gale.'

'Half a year's rent.'

'Half a year, thank you. Mr Bird ... John Hurley, your driver, swore that the prisoner owed three-and-a-half years' rent.'

'That is untrue.'

'How is that so?'

'Mr O'Driscoll is in the habit of raising money from the bank on the strength of his tenants' bills, because he pays large head rents. In the bill passed by these prisoners, several other tenants had joined, and as a result the amount was much larger in the bill than the amount McCarthy alone owed.'

Some of the gallery appeared to be confused by this revelation.

'That's very interesting, Mr Bird. And was this bill passed into the bank?'

'It was.'

'Can you say which?'

'I can – the Provincial Bank.'

'And had Mr O'Driscoll the money of this bill in his pocket when the distress was made?'

'Yes, sir.' Murmurs began again in the background.

'Yet the bill was not then due?'

'No, sir.'

Justin could scarcely believe the implications. The defendant, John McCarthy, had joined with other tenants of Mr O'Driscoll to submit a bill for the bank in advance of their payment of rent. Mr O'Driscoll had raised cash on the strength of the bill, and the bank therefore held the bill against the tenants.

But in the misguided belief that Mr McCarthy was responsible for the entirety of the bill, and on account of what at least was being portrayed as a gulf of misunderstanding between his agent and his driver, Mr O'Driscoll had set them both against John McCarthy for the distraint of goods worth more than three full gales, even though McCarthy's own share was for but one gale and that not yet due. In doing so the landlord had robbed him of what was his rightful property in place of rent that McCarthy himself did not owe, and at the same time stole from him that property which not only afforded him his ability to survive but, ironically, would enable him to raise what was owed to the bank for his part in the bill that he had, with honesty, already submitted. And none of this even considered the injury inflicted upon the health of the man and his family in the process.

Once again, the court was filled with the turbulent noise of unrest.

'And these poor wretches, including this man here, liable at the bank for the whole amount, but minus the worldly goods and chattels that enable them to raise their part in it?' The defence solicitor's bitter words were more of a summation than a question and were directed at the bench, regardless of the witness.

'Certainly.' Mr Moody, in a grave tone, affirmed the observation.

'You may go down,' Mr O'Connell told Mr Bird. 'It should also be understood by the court that Mr McCarthy's horse, unfed and uncared for, was released from the pound but died this morning and the family have been fasting for two days, with no means of nourishment.'

A shout of 'Outrage!' rose out of the general disquiet.

Justin looked across at the silver-haired O'Driscoll, who he knew to be a Justice of the Peace himself in Skibbereen. Sitting with his agents now, he displayed a remarkable air of calm despite the storm that had grown up around him. Judging by the fact that he had taken off neither his hat nor his gloves but rested with his hands atop the silver head of a cane, Justin guessed O'Driscoll had not planned on staying long. At that moment O'Driscoll leaned down and whispered something to Mr Gallwey, who then stood and asked the first witness, John Hurley, to rise again.

'Mr Hurley, was it by Mr O'Driscoll's directions you distrained McCarthy?'

'Certainly not. Mr O'Driscoll allows me to act as I please.'

This brought the gallery to all out uproar and fearing an outburst of violence Justin almost readied himself to leave.

'Silence! We'll have silence now! Thank you!' Mr Moody near cleaved the bench in two as he wielded the gavel with such force in his attempts to restore authority, but he eventually succeeded as Mr Hurley was excused again as quickly as he'd been called, hurriedly leaving the table. After a brief pause during which Justin caught up with wording the scene, Mr O'Connell moved to address the complement of eight jurors.

'Gentleman of the jury, the last question put by the Crown Prosecutor shows you the nature of this case. It is so disgraceful that the odium is sought to be placed on the agent to shelter the principal. I could understand and could credit the excuse if, in this court, Mr O'Driscoll had, upon hearing the facts sworn today, said, "I was ignorant of the real facts until now, and I give up the prosecution."

'He has not done so. And between principal, agent and driver, let the disgrace and the odium be shared. Gentlemen, you have often heard the noble descriptions respecting that mutual and reciprocal kind feeling which should exist between landlord and tenant, but here today, during this crisis, and the season of cold and miserable weather, not one week before Christmas – that time which is sacred to all Christian families – you have had demonstrated before you the means by which that desirable object is to be inculcated on the part of the landlords, by first procuring the note of the tenant, then taking him from his wretched family and having him incarcerated, not to mention the distraint itself, and at last taking him a distance of thirty-five miles to be prosecuted by landlord, agent and driver. Good God, is there no sympathy for the wretched! Or where is this system to end?'

A long silence followed, which no one dared to break, held aloft as a triumph by the righteous among the room and respected as something to be broken at their own peril by those perpetrators of the injustice, Justin sensed.

'Gentlemen, I am afraid to trust myself in going over a recital of the prosecution of this wretched man. I am unwilling to say anything disrespectful of Mr O'Driscoll, but do what is in your power. Let John McCarthy home to his wife and children, destitute and miserable as they are.'

The jury, without deliberation, acquitted the prisoner Mr McCarthy, who at being unshackled cried bitter tears of woe and relief at the announcement.

Justin mopped up his account, satisfied it was good enough to be tidied later, as the courtroom around him became a transience of gesturing limbs, of tongues talking, and of the bustle of coming and going, as all owners of its moving parts sought to take advantage of what would be a brief adjournment.

Had he wanted to observe more, Justin was sure he could have filled his notebook there alone, but he had so much ground to cover. Instead, he fought his way out through the crush, stopping only to gather some details from a court official as he left, and made back for the centre of town, where he might find directions for the union, along with whatever else chance might place in his path.

Crossing the bridge again, he couldn't help but admire the beautiful river that ran north to south below it, splitting the west edge of the town from the east. The water looked cold and constant, but bubbled merrily down the weir, travelled underneath the arches and came out flat and still on the other side. The wise old Sullane on its way to the Lee, Justin guessed, but a long way yet for a fish to the Cork city he knew well.

As the bridge passed beneath his footsteps, the town appeared to open between two towers before him: on the left, the steeple of the rectory he'd visited the night previous; and the turret of Macroom Castle to the right, with battlements that harked back to the town's medieval past. But while they were deceptively similar in size and shape, perhaps by design, he mused, the purpose of one was to keep people out and of the other to draw them in. He walked on the right side of the street, and the wall of the castle grounds led him back to the edge of the square, the heart of the town, where a number of soldiers were coming and going beneath its gate.

'Can I help you, young man? You look lost.'

Justin spun around to meet the pleasant face of an elderly pauper who rested on a stick and smiled at him through teeth as crooked as a row of falling houses.

'Are you familiar with the town? This is the fine residence of the Honourable William White Hedges, our resident gentleman, the owner of the town and lord of the soil. But you won't find him here today if you were hoping to have an audience with *him*.'

'I, eh ...' McCarthy instinctively checked if his notebook, or some obvious item, was sticking out, advertising his profession.

'Eight months and more he hasn't been seen around here.' The old man didn't wait for an answer. 'No! Our resident landlord, the honourable proprietor of the castle and its princely estate, deems an English atmosphere and English society more congenial to his inclinations than the peat-impregnated mists that envelop the emerald mountains of Macroom. And sure, the resident gentry taking their cue from him are similarly neglectful and indifferent. They seldom interfere save when they wish to thwart or impede measures that otherwise might give increased employment.'

On the one hand McCarthy found himself wondering if the man before him stood around the square, a permanent fixture and living signpost to visitors, magically foreseeing what they wished to know when they landed in its midst, while on the other his mind, so taken by the extravagant language pouring out of the man's mouth, was too excited at the prospect of catching the falling pearls he was hearing to risk stalling such a gift as this horse with trivial questions. It was as if the article McCarthy hoped to write was simply rolling off the man's tongue, but he dared not be so brazen as to produce his tools yet.

'Landlords, taken *en masse*,' the pauper barely stopped for breath, 'cannot be regarded as the promoters or protectors of the people's prosperity. Of course, some of the gentry here would have you believe it is otherwise, but if the condition of the people be a criterion wherefrom to form a judgement …'

The old man, using his stick as a central balance, swapped hands frequently, pivoting on the support, unveiling various sights to his right and left extending one arm or the other as he described them.

'As you can see, all around here, but even more so out in the country, the most universal destitution exists. Squalor, misery and famine are the prevalent bedfellows of all our poor. Food and raiment are utter strangers to the unhappy people. At night they are forced to litter themselves together in the tattered, often rain-soaked garments, which they have laboured in for a miserable penny … *if* they've been lucky enough to gain employment on the works, that is.

'And you'd want to be lucky indeed. At least, some people consider it luck. But that's debatable. About seven hundred are employed on the road to connect Bantry and Ballyvourney about ten miles west of here … but 'tis very stony ground out there and be's hard to make much gain on the task. There's about four hundred more employed a couple of miles to the east, cutting a line through Daniel Conor's land, but that's about it for the whole district. The poor men are often paid late and might have already spent most of their wages on credit, getting meal "on time" from the gangers and the like … Dacent men some of them, if the truth be known, but on the whole 'tis a paltry and trifling enterprise. If it were to be effective at all, 'twould need to be proliferated fourfold! The demand for employment is hourly increasing. Indian meal is selling at eightpence a stone and the price of every other article of human consumption is rising in God-awful proportions alongside.

'A fearful crisis is upon the people, to be plain, and the whole blasted lot helped along by the exploded fallacies and absurd obstructions of that terrible science Russell and his government are sworn to uphold – political economy – and that weighed in the balance against the health, the hopes and the very existence of millions of our people.

'But a few revolving weeks must sink the beam, when the result of the next government meeting, I should think, must be a liberal and bounteous extension of relief, else the absolute decimation of the labouring population of Ireland.'

The speaker came to a dead stop with an expression that defaulted to a riddlesome grin inviting neither criticism nor praise, and within a moment's passing McCarthy had to question if the man had spoken at all, or if he'd imagined the whole lot.

But alas! if only during the last moments of the gentle condemnation Justin had finally taken the courage to open his notebook. 'I'm sorry, could you repeat that please, sir?'

'When parliament meet on the nineteenth, or ... which part?'

'Sorry, sir. I mean could you repeat all of what you've said?'

'Well. Eh ... heh.' The old man seemed confused and flustered for the first time. Leaning on the stick with one hand, he took his cap off with the other and agitated the band of white hair between his neck and ears with the free fingers. 'How am I supposed to remember all that? I don't know what I said, sure.'

'It's just I found it really informative and I'd like to cite some of it, with your permission of course, sir. I write for the newspaper.'

'Ah ... and the two of us standing out here with scarce enough blood in our veins to withstand the freezing cold. Buy me a bowl of hot soup and sure it might pierce my memory.'

'Actually, I haven't yet eaten myself,' Justin remarked, reminded of his hunger. 'I accept your offer, sir. In fact, I saw an attractive inn here earlier, Meskell's I think it was ...'

'Ah, you couldn't drink the piss outta there, you'd be sick as a sewer – the Arms is the only place.'

'The Arms?'

'The Queen's Arms hotel. If it's good enough for O'Connell, says you.' The old man winked.

'A hotel? Will it be expensive?'

'Not if you don't eat too much.'

Justin smiled. Through his jacket he felt the old man gently gripping his arm as he began to lead the way. The warmth of the grasp only increased what affection Justin already felt for his guide – to buy him a bowl of soup was the least he could do in return for a second helping of such inspired eloquence.

'Good morning! Ye hoors,' his companion muttered through smiling teeth as he tipped his hat at two soldiers passing nearby.

'Those soldiers?' Justin queried.

'Forty-seventh regiment. Five weeks they've been here. We have no barracks, but Mr Hedges sent word that it'd be all right. They were welcome to use Macroom Castle demesne for their temporary lodgings, if they wouldn't mind. They've been billeted here since. Another affliction and an additional incubus, which the people regard as at least as paramount an evil as all the others they have to contend with. Here we are now ...'

Entering the hotel, Justin was instantly aware of the disparaging reactions of the staff and the gentrified clientele. His companion continued, oblivious, pulling Justin along as he went.

'*Cork Examiner!*' In voice for all to hear, the bedraggled chaperone pointed at Justin. 'They all know me,' he added, much to the amusement of Justin, who doubted that the staff would have let him in on his own.

'Will you be dining?' a waiter asked when they'd seated themselves.

'Indeed we will. I'll have black pudding, bread, a bowl of soup and a cup of tea, thank you. What'll ye have yourself, young man?'

At the peril of embarrassing himself, as he sensed he was about to squander a whole week's wages, Justin decided that, though the prices were sure to be extravagant, the expense would be worth the story and, ravenous, took the plunge on sating his own hunger too.

'Just soup for me, please.'

'What's your own name, young man?' the old man asked when the waiter had gone.

'Justin. Justin McCarthy.'

'Ooh, that's a good name. A good Cork name.'

'Thank you. And yours, sir?' McCarthy asked, and unsheathed the tools of his trade once more.

'A. Nonymous.' With his hands gripping the edge of the table and the stick against the side of his chair, the old man grinned, playfully coy, then collected the stick in one hand and leaned in to confide in Justin, now unfolding the notebook. 'There are some people around here… might be a small bit envious of my being a feature in your newspaper, young McCarthy. Proud people. Mr Creed, the pawnbroker for one; he's our usual local correspondent with the *Examiner*. I wouldn't like to be putting anyone's nose out of joint, if you get my drift? You can call me William yourself, though, if you like. That's what me mother called me.'

'I understand, Mr William, sir.'

'Just William. No need for the mister.'

'As you wish – William. But yes, Mr Swanzy, the minister, mentioned the pawnbroker too.

'Now come to think of it I should have maybe said ex-pawnbroker. Sure 'tis your own newspaper has been advertising the sale of his premises in its most recent numbers. Ah, he's a dacent skin of a man, if a bit uptight. Suffers with the nerves betimes. Anyway, selling up now. A fine premises too. Some of the more unsavoury types haven't made it easy for him. He'll be a great loss to the poor of this vicinity.'

'And where would I find him?'

'He hasn't been seen around the place. Mr Creed can be his own worst enemy. Says too much. But that comes with the territory of the writer, I suppose, doesn't it?' The old pauper winked. 'Has the clerk running the shop now, Mr French, but sure there's no craic out of him at all.

You're very young, if you don't mind me saying, to have such worldly ways about you. How old are you, young McCarthy?'

'Sixteen.'

'Sixteen? Oh, that's a good age to be getting into the thick of it, rolling up your sleeves. Tough times, though, lad. Do you enjoy the work?'

'I love writing and I enjoy seeing the country and getting the word out about what is happening.'

'Well, them is all the right tools, you'd have to wager. I believe you'll do well, young man.'

William trailed off, distracted as the food arrived, and Justin took advantage of the opportunity to question his subject, who ate as ravenously now as he had talked. Justin was fascinated by him. Despite his many years and a body ravaged by time, William had a mind as free and nimble as the movements of a wild hare on the run. He could be artful and poetic one moment; humorous and trite the next; philosophical; a mine of information; or a shameless gossip. Regardless of his downtrodden appearance, he had a wit and an intelligence that any person would aspire to. It crossed Justin's mind that he could sit there with the old man to get it all, being entertained all the while into the bargain. But he had a job to do, and really wanting to see the hard reality of the country for himself, Justin did his best to keep William on the subject of the condition of the people of Macroom and gather what information he needed. He had yet to visit the workhouse and to see some of those houses in the lanes and streets around the square. It was a huge amount to take on in one day but he was driven and had a sense of moral responsibility that kept him from shying away from the task.

'Well, if you want to see the wilds of it, Ballyvourney has plenty to offer. You can catch the mail car for Tralee at one. That'll take ye. The poorhouse is back the way you came over the bridge, not half a mile from here. That's a terrible sad place.' The old man shook his head and stared into nowhere. 'You mind yourself going in there. God bless the poor souls that have to suffer it.'

Justin downed the last of his tea, thanked his newfound comrade, and slipped him a coin as he departed.

'Oh, 'tis very kind you are.' The hand took it and put it away just as rapidly, presumably lest anyone else see it. It seemed to be swallowed by William's pocket so fast that even he hadn't looked at it.

'I think I'll just hang on here and finish the last of the pot if you don't mind, young McCarthy. You're very generous and thank you for the soup and the bread. I enjoyed your company. I like a good listener.'

'Thank you, Mr … William.'

'God bless, and good luck to ye – oh, eh, when will the article …?' he shouted as Justin hurried across the lobby towards the door.

'Monday! If not, Wednesday. But Monday. I'm promised Monday.'

'Monday so. Right. Very good.'

The old man talked away to himself but as soon as the boy was out of sight he gathered up every scrap of what was left and moveable on the table, wrapped it in a napkin and stuffed it under his coat, then polished off the last of his absent companion's soup, slurping out the bottom of the bowl with his fingers.

Seconds later the principal waiter appeared around the corner and poked his head in over the snug.

'Everything to your liking?'

'Oh, the finest as always, Mr Greene. The boy didn't leave a morsel, look it. Hah?'

'I see that. He doesn't seem to have left his spoon either, or might it be he knocked it off the table in his haste?'

'Be God, I'll have a look for it now. Oh, would ye look at that?'

'Oh, it's great eyes ye have, Mr Shanahan. Is there anything else we can do for ye, now that your young friend has left without paying his bill?'

'What? He did not. The little …'

'I'm in jest, Mr Shanahan. He paid for it all.'

'The … Oh, ye had me, ye had me,' he laughed deferentially. 'What a nice young man. Well, that's me all set up for the day so.' The old man slapped the flanks of his frayed old coat. 'Thank you, Mr Greene. I'll see myself out.'

*

That evening, by the light of a candle in his room at the inn, Justin McCarthy did his best to detail as much of what he'd seen as his jarred mind would deliver, and distil the notes into something that would do the poor people of the district justice.

The destitution is advanced and widespread, nor is it confined to the lower classes alone. Though, as must ever be the case, it is they who feel it most poignantly. And while referring to that class, I think it will be quite in place to lay before you a few scenes, which came under my observation, the recollection of which even at this moment, harrow me with indescribable horror and amazement. Scenes such as I hope it shall never again be my lot to witness.

I might premise that I was prepared to meet much, and determined to endorse a great deal. But I must confess that my expectation was far surpassed, and I might say, magnified significantly. This evening, upon the recommendation of the Rev. Pastor of Macroom, I set about exploring the town to get a sense of the misery and poverty for myself.

The first wretched door I was emboldened to knock upon attracted my attention from the circumstance of hearing the voices of several children crying aloud …

Justin fell asleep writing in the small hours of Sunday morning, but arose early and made his way back to Cork, there to hurriedly finish preparations on his article in time for a final once over by Maguire himself ahead of the Sunday night printing.

39

THE PARADOX OF SECRECY

For the sixth day running, Thomas French slid the bolts into place above the back door of Cornelius Creed, Pawnbroker's without having had any sign that the proprietor had returned to the premises. Nothing had been moved at his writing desk. There was no fresh dung in the car house. No change to the safe. Only a week had passed since the previous Monday when Creed had surprised him with the astonishing revelation of his decision to sell the shop. And it was only last Wednesday that the news had been related to the rest of the public via the advertisement that French had posted on his employer's behalf. It had been a mere seven days, all told. But it felt like a lifetime.

After locking the safe and tidying up, French took his hat and coat and, standing for a moment at the bottom of the back stairs, listened for any signs of life from above but confirmed, with disappointment, that it was just as he'd suspected. Still. He left through the front.

At the end of a long day, it was all weighing heavily upon his mind. Though he was quite equal to the individual tasks involved, he was feeling increasingly worn out at not knowing what the future held: when *would* Creed be back? 'Another while' was such an undefined length of time. And what had Creed meant when he'd told French that he would look after him? And that he wouldn't throw him into the street ... Was it this? The gift of operating the shop alone in the middle of a crisis? And in the weeks running up to Christmas, no less. Was it the stress of trying to explain away his employer's absence? And with the added burden of having to deal with enquiries about the sale on top of everything else ...

How could he be sure he was carrying out Creed's instructions correctly? Should he be using discretion, or just continue to carry them out to the letter? 'It's the not knowing!'

'How long did he say he'd be away for, Thomas?'

'Oh, Mother,' French threw his head back, weary at the thought of answering the same question again. *Paulellen and I will stay away a few days more*, was all he told me.'

'He must have said something else?' she asked.

'Nothing of any consequence. That was the essence of it, Mother.'

'Well, that's not very much to go on, is it? And there's been no sightings of him at all?' She paused to take the bowl he was handing her. 'Surely *someone* has seen him, Thomas. Doesn't he report on all those meetings to the paper?'

Sitting by the fire with a blanket over her lap in the old reeling chair he had bought from the shop, French's mother kept on with the questions as she stirred the heat out of the soup he had made for her. Through the calmness of her nightly interrogations she seemed oblivious that her constant reminding him of his woes was only intensifying the ordeal and increasing his desperation.

'Usually, he does,' French went on trying to humour her, 'but not a word of his writing has been printed this month.'

He watched with pity as, from out of an old bowl with a thousand cracks in it that owed them nothing, his mother sipped at the watery broth. She held the vessel so close to her chin that the spoon never had to go far from her mouth, and gripped a rag within the palm of the same hand in case anything went astray.

What was going to become of them? His mother was mostly in good health, and still lucid a lot of the time. But her becoming frequently forgetful … that was only going to get worse. The pattern of her coherence was so random now. He worried about leaving her on her own for long periods. And he missed having an equal to converse with.

'What's everyone else saying?' she asked.

'Oh! What they haven't proposed would be easier to rattle off. Anyway

– don't you fret about it, Mother.' He took the napkin and wiped her chin. 'Drink your soup while it's still hot.'

'But isn't that the paradox of secrecy?' She took the cloth and finished the job herself, dabbing repeatedly at her lips, then at the shirt above her breast. 'You can't blame the poor souls, Thomas. People talk when they've nothing to talk about. You know what they say – what's nobody's business is everyone's business.'

There was some wisdom in her yet, French consoled himself.

'But God help him. Isn't he a good man, promising to look after you?'

'He is, Mother. But in the meantime, it's me that has to face the firing squad every day.'

Thomas closed his eyes in frustration. *Oh, to be hiding away out there, like Mr Creed with his racing horses,* he thought.

The following morning French awoke with the same underlying panic and stress in the pit of his stomach, as though a storm were swirling up inside his head. Rising from the straw mattress and pulling on his trousers he searched for the root of his growing anxiety, determined to address it with reason and logic.

Mr Creed asked me to look after the shop on my own for a while. So why am I so surprised? It has only been a week. The pressure he's under must be catastrophic, to have brought him to the point of selling the shop. If I'm feeling so overwhelmed, how must he be feeling? A few days more. I can manage for a few days more. Creed has been good to us. And he's a kind man. This is his hour of need. He's depending on me. I mustn't let him down.

In the dim of their room on Slevean Lane, French filled the bucket in the corner and pulled up his braces. Combing his hair in the light of the dirty window he sighed, staying motionless for a moment. As quietly as he could, he raised the fire, then sat on the edge of the reeling chair to put on his shoes and watched it smoulder as he drained a bowl of the cold soup still left in the pot from the night before, swinging the remainder out away from the heat of the rekindled embers. The bowl rinsed clean, he slid his arms through the sleeves of his military overcoat and hoisted it up over his back; then he pulled on his mittens and leaned across the low bed to check her breathing. *All is well,* he thought as he heard the short, quiet pulling and blowing of air that came and went through her nostrils. But how long more would he have with her? He feared a future alone without his mother's company. French placed a kiss upon his fingers and laid it onto the shoulder of the sleeping old woman, whose long white hair lay loose around her head, then pulled the lip of the blanket up a little higher. 'I'll see you tonight, Mother,' he whispered. 'Agnes will be by soon.' His sister would surely not forget again.

As French stepped out the door, the hat met his head with a boxy thump.

Surely Creed's presence is being missed elsewhere too? Today is Tuesday; the Relief Committee meeting will be starting shortly. They'll be feeling his absence there. And Creed must be missing the weekly meetings too. He lives for them, and his writing!

French suddenly put the pieces together in his head and wondered if Creed might in fact be attending the meetings and just not reporting on the matter. It was true that no articles had shown up in the papers, but maybe that other rumour held some water: that the paper had censored Creed and had dissociated itself from his writing after the sensation of his 'Exalted Fly' article. *It is possible,* he thought. *And Creed has already come into town at least once. Why not again? No ...* That was highly unlikely. If Creed had come back into town, French would have heard about it. But even if he was not attending the meetings, perhaps the Relief Committee would know something of his plans. Or of when indeed he intended to return. And surely he had cause to communicate with *them* in his absence. They depended on him!

French turned onto the square and looked ahead to the crowd already assembling.

He was not looking forward to another day of handling custom. It was not his strong point, working the counter – even under normal conditions, before the shop had experienced an increase in visitors.

But regular customers were one thing. These time-wasters – curious types, clearly uninterested in buying or selling anything – asking nosy, infuriating questions.

French had been taking a small pleasure in dashing the hopes of those who'd feigned interest and said they were enquiring about the shop itself. He simply asked them all to leave their details, then watched the disgruntled expressions that, every time so far, confirmed for him who was and wasn't actually interested. His mother had been right when she'd made the observation about nobody's business becoming everybody's business. And Creed had been right too, during the *soirée* affair. 'It does not take much to get the wheel of the rumour mill creaking and turning around here, Mr French,' he'd said, 'greased by the gossip-hungry lickspittle of wagging tongues. The gall of some of these people, bandying theories around like snuff at a wake!' *That was really the beginning of this whole run of ill,* French thought.

It was as if Creed had seen the future, he mused, but this latest wave of scandalmongering made the *soirée* look like a picnic. 'Has Mr Creed left the country?' 'Have his writings been banned from the paper?' 'How much is he selling the shop for?' 'Has your employer contracted fever?' It was exasperating.

Reaching the door of the shop, French parted the new crowd of paupers outside, some of them less willing to be patient than others and hardly allowing him space to get to the door.

'Where is Mr Creed?'

'Is he back yet?'

'You'll just have to wait until I get set up, I'm afraid,' French told them collectively, fumbling with the keys and hunching his back towards the gathering as he pressed his face to the door frame and tried to get the low lock open. 'But if it will save any of you the time, I am redeeming pledges only. I will not be taking any new pledges.' French tried his best to retain a polite demeanour but found his patience near shattered as he finally managed to get the door open.

'What does he mean?' one of the paupers asked as French wedged himself in through the narrowly opened door, then locked it again from the inside.

He took his hat and coat off and hung both on the rack, then stood in the middle of the shop and stopped a moment to stare out through the warped glass at the distorted figures, refracted and tear-stained by the rained-upon windows. He worried in that moment whether he was becoming more like Creed, and wondered what he would do if his employer never came back. *It's as well to just get on with it,* he thought. *Now …*

French unlocked the door which, needing no help, was forced inwards by numerous figures at the front.

'Please! Now, as I've said, I cannot accept any new pledges. Please take your time,' he implored them as they pushed past each other.

A clatter of footsteps accompanied one desperate person pressing against another to get to the unmanned counter as French stayed pinned to the wall, holding the door open as the miserable scene unfolded before him.

'Is there anyone here wishing to redeem a pledge?' He sidled around them and got behind the counter at last.

'How much will you give me for this spinning wheel?' French followed the sound to a weary, thin woman with turned-down corners to her mouth, bearing what clearly was an item that no longer functioned.

'I am not taking any new pledges, I'm afraid, ma'am.'

'Where is Mr Creed?' she said with desperation in her eyes. 'He'll take it. I know he will.'

'Mr Creed is not here.'

'But I've come three miles with it,' she said, wearing every step of the journey in her face.

'I sympathise with you, ma'am. But for now, it's just me here, and I cannot take–'

'Will you please take this jug off my hands, sir? The blessings of God upon ye, an honest man.'

'Please spare a few shillings for this blanket, sir.'

More and more of the paupers tried to foist their items on him, holding them aloft and pushing them through the bars, causing him to lean away.

'You are not hearing what I say,' French pleaded.

'Has he lost his will?' A better-dressed woman beside a hooded figure shouted from behind them.

'He's gone to live on his seventy-five acres, I heard!'

'The spinning wheel, sir, please ... I have starving children.'

'When is he coming back?'

'I have a bowl, sir, if you'll take a look?'

'Redeeming pledges only. Do you all understand what that means?' French fought to make himself heard above the noise.

'Where is Mr Creed?' a man repeated.

'Ahh!' An elderly woman at the centre of the pack let out a sound of anguish and appeared to be struggling to breathe as the crush threatened to swallow her at its midst. French realised he was the only person in the room who could see her and, catching a glimpse, as if of a woman drowning in a sea of people, gasping, French saw the face of his mother.

'STOP!' He shot his two hands aloft.

The room came to a standstill as he rushed out from behind the counter and pushed his way through to help the woman up. 'You there, bring me that chair, please.' He sent a man in behind the counter.

'Thank you. Now, dear. You sit here, look.' French eased the broken old woman onto the chair and talked to her with his hand on her back, as, gasping for her breath, her shoulders and chin went up and down and she fanned air at herself, staring at him with panic in her eyes.

'Now please ...' he said, addressing the crowd in an effort to pre-empt any more madness. 'No matter how many times you ask: *Mr Creed will not be here today*. Or any other day in the foreseeable future, I'm afraid. I am the only person running the premises in the meantime and as I have told you all, I will not be accepting any new pledges. That means I will not be taking in *any new items*. Those are my instructions. I can redeem existing pledges only and those upon full payment of the loan that was granted in trust of the items, along with interest accrued. I realise that some of you are in severe distress, and you have my sympathies. But as it is not within my power to help you if you are not here to redeem an item, I must ask you to kindly vacate the premises and return at such time as Mr Creed *has* returned, if you so wish.'

French watched and allowed himself a measure of shame as, dejected, another light of hope having been extinguished before their eyes, in flittered raiment and in various stages of physical neglect, almost all of the hapless souls lowered their heads and began to depart, taking with them whatever items they had hoped would change their fortune for a day or two.

'Does anybody know this woman, or where she lives?' he asked the disappearing crowd.

40

On the Eve of Starvation

D espite the extra hardship evident on the faces of the poor, which was but an increase by degree when compared with any other winter of the 1840s, 23 December 1846 in the town of Macroom had the same appearance as that of any earlier year. With two days until Christmas, the market square was a busyness of preparations. Servants of the well-to-do were sent to gather last-minute cooking supplies, extravagant gifts and orders from the suppliers of specialist wines and exotic goods to decorate the dinner table. Passengers arrived and left, in bians, mail cars, hired cars and private horse and traps, carrying books, wooden toys and all manner of luxuries, as the beggars and paupers of the town walked amongst it all, hoping to catch a crumb, or to unlock someone's kindness at the time of year when it was likely to be felt most.

One of those returning, not to his permanent home, but back to base after a long week criss-crossing the various districts of the county, administering to the duties of an Officer of the Public Works, was Captain Gordon. His cart trundled into Main Street out of the direction of the Bantry Road, ready to deliver its exhausted cargo like something it had shovelled up after running him under its wheels.

Throughout his time away, Gordon had generated hostile press and ire everywhere he went, as though he couldn't get enough of it: narrowly avoiding a lynching in Castletown; accused of corruption in Kilnameaky; and blamed for bringing the country to rebellion in Ballinaboy. Skibbereen, the *Examiner* had announced, was 'too hot' for Gordon, and the source of more threats. He was sought all over the western half of the county, in Bantry, Bandon and the four divisions of the Carberies.

Even as far away as Mayo, where last he had been stationed before being posted to Macroom, the people were still baying for the blood of 'The Scotchman'.

On that day, Gordon felt he was quite possibly the most disliked man in the entire county of Cork, representing, as he did, the elusive face of the Board of Works, and therefore becoming the focus of all the complaints and contempt associated with its name. But he needn't have gone any further than the Muskerries to have achieved that status.

Gordon didn't care a snuff about the public reaction and cared even less now that he was unshackling the burden of his duties and could put it all to the back of his mind. Far behind now, the road stretched out of all those godforsaken towns whose whining functionaries he'd had to endure over the previous ten days.

Rocking back and forth as his cart careered across the cobbled plain of the square, Gordon issued an instruction to his driver. The young man acknowledged his request, and, before he was to discharge Gordon to his lodgings at the east end of Main Street, he brought the vehicle to a temporary stop facing Peter Williams's post office. From there Gordon watched him disembark to fetch what mail might have accumulated in his absence, and kept himself concealed within.

Its wheels spinning as it set off again, the soldier's cart vacated the same be-rutted spot on the cobbles of south square, where later that evening, rather less conspicuously, Creed and Paulellen's arrival was timed not only to engage the discretion of darkness, but to avoid unnecessarily encountering the ever-increasing flow of paupers hoping to raise a few pence on whatever they had left and buy something from the meal store to get them through the desolate days ahead. The Creeds had timed it correctly and – save for a single mendicant, seeming too stiffened by cold and hunger-induced lethargy to shift from his hard-won turf – Creed fancied not a soul had noticed them.

The first to step down from the car, Creed tied off the reins, then helped Paulellen to alight.

'You go ahead, dear. If Mr French is still within, ask him to come out and take the horses round the back.'

Collecting the bags, he followed her into the seclusion of the closed shop, while the horses' breath fogged and condensed in the frigid air of the dimly lit street.

*

The next morning, Christmas Eve, to the sound of the eight o'clock bells, Paulellen donned her winter coat and prepared to face the task of gathering supplies for what was sure to be a less-than-joyous Christmas dinner. But having heard no signs of life from her husband by the time she was ready to leave, Paulellen returned to the dark bedroom and sat on the edge of the bed, in two minds about whether or not to disturb him.

'Don't worry, I'm awake.' Creed pre-empted her decision with muffled words that told her he was lying on his front with his face half buried in the pillow.

'How are you feeling? Did we come back too soon?'

'No.' The answer was whispered, and weak.

To Paulellen, the affirmative one-word answer didn't carry half as much enthusiasm as it had the potential to, and a feeling of pity – accompanied by the wish that she could embrace him and absorb all his troubles – welled up within her. But knowing he would need to fix himself, for pride's sake, she resisted and instead gently patted the prone outline of his leg through the blankets.

'Take your time now. Just because we're home doesn't mean you have to jump straight back into work. For the sake of one day you might as well wait and pick up again after the break.'

'I know. I know. But …'

'But what?'

'I don't want Alicia to see me like this.'

'Cornelius. She's your sister! She'll understand, whatever it is—'

'I just don't want to ruin Christmas for everyone, indulging melancholy and worrying her with my petty woes. Promise me …' The sound of his voice indicated that his posture was changing, as, rising up onto his elbows, he beseeched her. 'Just promise me we won't make this the focus of the visit.'

'Of course not. Don't be worrying.' She paused. 'I'm going to go and start gathering the bits and pieces for dinner. Is there anything in particular you'd like?'

'God, no. Please, whatever you do, don't go wasting money on silly fripperies and frivolities at a time like this.'

'Ah, come now, it's Christmas. And you're such a fussy eater. I want to make sure you're …'

'Those are my wishes now and the best gift you can give me is just that. Your understanding is all precious to me, Paull. Let's just try to have as normal a day as we can. Agreed?'

'Of course. Of course. What time did she say they'll be here?'

'Oh, I can't say. You know Alicia. She won't be here too early, anyway.'

'Sure, it doesn't matter. Whatever time. We'll see her when she arrives.' Paulellen patted his leg once more, and stood. 'Right, I'm going.'

Once she'd left the room Creed lay his head back on the pillow and sighed heartily. He'd meant everything he said, but secretly he hoped Alicia would spot that he wasn't feeling well, and that, as only his sister could, she would unravel all the strands of his problems and somehow make him feel better about everything.

Paulellen was as sweet and as caring as Creed could hope his wife would be, but he knew a married couple had to keep some things sacred at the risk of losing respect for each other. Alicia was his little sister and only sibling, and he had always idolised, even worshipped, her. Nothing she said failed to please him. And she was all that was left of his family now.

Suddenly, distracted from his own apathy, Creed found himself climbing out from under the blankets and sitting on the side of the bed. From beneath the plastered laths and joists that separated the floors, he heard the mumbled strains of a conversation between Paulellen and Mr French, who had arrived to open up. It was impossible to make out much of it.

'You're ever so kind, Mr French. God bless you.'

'Yes, ma'am.'

The bell over the door rang as the clerk's words were followed by the stillness of the empty shop.

*

Half a mile away, on the works between Chapel Cross and Macroom Cross, the weary, exhausted creatures who that morning had begun their last day of works before 'the stop' had just been whistled off and were carrying themselves towards the ditch for the nine o'clock suck.

All were anxious to find out how many days the works would be shut down for. On the one hand, they felt worry and trepidation at how long they'd be without a means of affording themselves some sustenance. On the other, they quietly longed for a chance to rest.

But this morning, and on this day of all days, the great concern was whether or not they were to be paid. No one had received anything since 11 December and everyone was down to the last of their reserves, having stretched their credit and the generosity of their neighbours to their limits. Hopes were desperate that they would not be let down on such an occasion as Christmas.

Being positioned so conveniently close to the centre of town that he found discarded newspapers regularly and being one of the few among the men to 'have the letters', Ned Brien Swiney's reading had become a highlight for those with the interest or the strength to listen and stay awake during the breaks. Even when Ned couldn't find a paper himself, several other labourers had developed the habit of bringing scraps along for him to read. Ned wasn't the only literate person among them, but since he'd introduced the men to the distraction, it had become accepted that the honour of reading to them was his.

He nearly always read during the late break and knew it gave the other men, as well as himself, something to look forward to. Smoking aside, the early suck was reserved for the small enjoyment of eating fragments of griddle bread and whatever scraps could be pulled from greasy cloths and pockets – fragments that for just a few moments promised the unkeepable promise: to cure the primeval and unreasoning hunger that consumed them for the rest of their waking hours. The reality over the last few days, however, was that some of the men, Ned included, had little or nothing to entertain their hunger. And with the hope of today's wages as the entertainment come the longer break, Ned suspected they would welcome a change to the usual pattern.

'Well … Since I'm having a pauper's breakfast this morning, I might as well read now,' he volunteered.

'What's a pauper's breakfast?'

'Did you never hear of that one?' Two men discussed Ned's phrase. 'A clay-pipe smoke and a gobful of cack, I'd say.'

'Ha!' The inquisitor, who was smoking already, was not amused.

'Anyone see anything? How's it looking?' asked Ned as he began to open his coat.

'All clear. C'mon, Ned,' a bearded man said, hugging his own shoulders, and looking cold now that he'd stopped moving.

Careful not to tear the treasure, damp as it was from sweat and the morning's rain that had seeped through his clothes, Ned proudly pulled out a couple of sheets and unfolded them. At the same time, squatting low in a motley circle, the ground being wet, his audience arranged themselves to provide cover for the 'Bard of Slevean'.

Some of the stewards were disapproving of the activity, ready to come down on the men at any opportunity. But Ned had noticed that Mr Roberts, the head overseer, who'd been profiting handsomely buying meal for some labourers, albeit at a levied rate in lieu of their wages, turned a blind eye. Even so, the mark drawn between the men and their masters remained a very clear one and consequently Ned's listeners were always on the alert when he read to them.

Though deep within the complement of four hundred beings, Ned and his cluster were in no real danger of being discovered in their enjoyment by the stewards, dishevelled sentinels took turns standing watch at the edge of the ditch, resting stubbled chins over spade handles and sucking on *dúidíní* if they had them. It made Ned proud to think that the ceremony he had enabled provided a badly needed source of stimulation for his companions, right down to the almost enjoyable thrill of 'keeping yellow' for the gangsmen.

That morning, from an assortment of mouth-watering advertisements on the front page of the *Examiner* giving details of Christmas delicacies that he imagined were being prepared that very moment to grace the tables of the rich and powerful of the Muskerries, and the whole of the county of Cork, for the sake of the unusual occasion, Ned began by giving his audience the choice of what they wished him to read.

'Christmas fruit?' he offered.

'Oh, yes please!'

'No!' came several voices.

'Right. What about this? A circular, as of the fifteenth, by Joseph Walker, secretary to the Board of Works?'

'Yes!'

'Never mind the fruits! What's going to happen to us on the works?' someone shouted.

The circular was the clear winner. Ned cleared his throat and began to read. '*Due to the sufferings labourers have lately been exposed to when the works have been stopped by severe snow or rain, it has been decided to issue a directive to the effect that on such occasions …*'

'Read up, please.'

'Shhhhssh!'

'Ahem.' Ned scanned the horizon before attempting to speak louder. '*It has been decided to issue a directive to the effect that on such occasions, the labourers are to attend roll call on the given morning. And all who attend will, if it is impossible to set them to work, be entered on the pay list for a day's daily rate.'*

'Oh! That's a welcome development,' someone said.

'Shhhsh. Keep going, Ned.'

'In the case that the weather is fine at or by the nine o'clock break, permitting them to begin, they will still get the full day; while if at, or after twelve, they will be paid for as many hours left between that and the end of the day.'

'Aw ...'

'Sure, a man can't feed himself and his family even on a full day's rate.'

'But wait ...' Ned said. If there was any doubting the placatory nature of that supposed generosity, the language of the last bit would put the nail in the coffin.

'Go on.'

'In order to guard against abuse, it says, *the inspecting officers or engineers will be careful that this system of relief is never resorted to when there is work to be performed, in breaking stone, or scraping snow off the roads,* etcetera.'

The multitude groaned in unison, with some apparently not surprised by the miserly gesture.

'They give it with one hand and take it away with the other,' a grey-bearded man grumbled.

'Go back to Christmas fruit.'

'Yes. Christmas fruit, please!'

'Christmas fruit. Right. Where was it? Oh, here. *From the Foreign and Home Fruit Establishment.* Eh ... *et* – something in French – *at 83 Patrick Street, prime turkey figs in drums, preserved oranges and lemons, carved, whole ...'*

'God in heaven!' One of the men threw his head back and closed his eyes.

'Bonbons, pastilles, brandy fruits, potted meats, American and French apples, Royal Dessert and Vanilla Biscuits.'

'What in the divil is a bonbon?'

'Oh Lord …' Another man lay on his back holding his stomach.

'Ah, enough of that imperial cack! C'mon get to the news that'll mean something to our own class of people!'

'Tut. There goes my only Christmas dinner,' another said.

'Let me see,' Ned relented, wishing to keep them happy, and scanned along the columns. 'Christmas presents?'

'Anything about Macroom?'

'Eh, no … no … oh, the advertisement for the pawnbroker's is still in. That's the only thing on this page.'

'Oh, yes. What does it say again?'

As he was about to read, a rough-shorn man sitting on his haunches nearby grunted at Ned and, chewing with his mouth full, broke off a piece of his griddle bread and extended his arm to offer it, nodding at Ned to take it. It was Pádraig O'Buachalla who, despite his not understanding Ned's English, had obviously noticed he had nothing to eat. Ned, who had talked to Pádraig, his ditch companion, most days throughout the weeks previous, was taken aback by the kindness. He had heard barely two words out of his neighbour in all that time, but this gesture, and the sobriety of the day Pádraig had chosen to make it, said more to Ned than any words could ever have done. The sense of decency seemed to carry and all within view fell quiet for a moment until a few among their ranks followed the example and gave something to a neighbour who had even less than they.

Ned, in awe, shook his head in disbelief and watched as Pádraig ate the rest of his own. Then, holding the small cake in his closed hand, he continued, and read the advertisement aloud: '*To be let or the interest sold. Superior house of business, with extensive back concerns, on the Square of Macroom. Nine-hundred-year lease can be given. Apply to Mr C. Creed, Macroom.*'

'Any steam packets?'

'Amen to that. Get me the devil out of here. Any going to New York or America?'

'Erm … Bristol; Liverpool; London; London again. No. All to England.'

'Ah, bad cess to that.'

'Go on, Ned, turn over the page.'

'Nothing from the Union?' a young man asked dolefully, resting his chin on folded arms.

'Cork Union?'

'Just Macroom.'

'No. Sorry,' Ned said.

The man's head sank.

Having exhausted the first page, Ned carefully turned over to the next.

'Anything more about the works? What've we to look forward to next year?'

'I did see something … *Future legislation for Ireland. A cluster of new measures. We at the* Examiner *quote – from the* London Daily News – *the following programme of measures, to be introduced at the opening of the next sessions by Her Majesty's Ministers. The measures are indeed extensive and embrace a wide space of legislation for Ireland.*'

'We heard that before.'

'Indeed we have,' Ned muttered in agreement, then began to read, '*Poor Law – Wastelands – Peasant Proprietors – Emigration – Drainage. Parliament will meet on January nineteenth.*'

'Good God – that's near a month away.'

'But that's good. It means the works will continue until then at least.'

'Oh. This is true.'

The interruptions came frequently and Ned waited patiently each time before picking up.

'How many of us will still be alive by then?' another of the older men interjected. By the look of him, Ned considered he had good reason to ask the question.

'*Poor Law,*' he resumed. '*With respect to the Poor Laws now in operation for the relief of the poor in Ireland, the only one worth speaking of is the Labour Rate Act under which three hundred thousand able-bodied men,*' *or nearly half a million individuals, are at this moment living upon Government wages.*

'*A proposal to render permanent that law, no matter how amended, would require, we fancy, even more than the constitutional courage and coolness of Lord John Russell. His great thought, we should imagine, must be in what way he can most speedily and solely get rid of that terrible measure.*'

'Well, that's all very well for the *Examiner* to say, but what have we got to keep us from starving without it?'

'No. It's not the *Examiner* speaking there. They're quoting from the *London Daily News*. Maguire and his *Examiner* are in favour of the Works,' Ned explained. 'Obviously *they* want to dismantle them, though,' he added dispiritedly.

'What?' One exclaimed aghast as heavy heads shook all around at the all-but-foretold confirmation of a disappointment they had come to expect. For a moment Ned felt conflicted about the benefit of his reading aloud, fearing how accustomed to let-downs and bad news the men had become. The way their luck was running, almost all of whatever news filled the papers was bound to be bad. But it was better to be equipped with knowledge, he reasoned, and the men themselves chose to hear it, if even for the sake of the distraction alone. The tale came to Ned's mind of O'Connell and of his meeting a man on a country road breaking rocks to build a wall. He asked the Liberator, 'Who do you think is going to win the parliamentary election?' To this it was rumoured O'Connell had replied, 'Well, it matters little to you who wins, my good man, because either way you'll still be breaking rocks.'

And yet, each man must have hope – Ned reasoned upon remembering the yarn – and has to believe that his fate was not preordained.

'John Russell the hole of me arse! Bring back Peel any day.'

'Russell *and* Peel mine!' another argued. 'Bring back an Irish parliament, and self-government.'

'*Drainage ...*' Ned moved on. '*The act for promoting employment by advances to landlords for drainage can hardly be said to be in operation in Ireland, because it is so framed that few have chosen to use it.'*

'That's true. All the parasite, cockatrice landlords are absent, that's why.'

'*But*,' Ned read on, '*the Poor Law, which gives workhouse relief to some seventy to eighty thousand aged and infirm persons will probably receive some modifications. There is only one question connected with the Poor Law, which is of any primary importance, and that is whether a right to relief in any shape whatever is to be granted to the able-bodied.'*

'Good God in heaven,' exclaimed one of the men.

'*Indoor relief to such a multitude is plainly impossible. The present workhouses, which it cost about a million and a half to build, should be multiplied tenfold to contain them!'*

'More death houses for the poor,' the same voice offered up, sounding defeated.

'*Outdoor relief, with some kind of labour test, is that for which advocates of the Poor Law contend. It is the only practical way for easing the burden on the souls …'*

'So, some of them have a heart for the poor!' someone shouted.

'Perhaps.' Over the corner of his page Ned saw a boy, scarcely sixteen years old, the owner of the voice, throwing his fist up, in hope. 'But wait, listen … *Upon this point we do not hesitate to express our firm belief that ministers will not, either by rendering the Labour Rate Act, or by any other measure, establish a practice so fraught with mischief.'*

It was the sting in the tail. All were dejected and those who had contained their joy at the prospect of an easier way through the months ahead now joined in a kind of dissatisfied chorus.

'There you go.' Ned folded the paper back up to bring it home for the fire.

'Lord h' mercy,' another said, as a torn scrap of a different paper was passed along a few hands until it reached Ned. Though only a rip, it still showed the date, the twenty-first, which they'd missed. Ned, aware that time was ebbing away, silently scanned the only complete article it beheld.

Indian corn sellers are making a whacking profit at the expense of the poor. Indian corn is lately selling at sixteen pounds and seventeen pounds a ton, although we have it reliably that cargo is being received ex-ship at ten pounds fifteen shillings a ton. To the fortunate buyer, this market price would leave seven pounds a ton, or seventy-five per cent in profit! This is the legitimate course of trade so lauded and protected by the Whig premier.

Believing that they'd had enough bad news and that the price per ton was so far from the sphere of the men's thoughts, Ned decided to spare them the extra woe. 'No news of food depots.' Curses filled the squad as the whistle blew, bringing the poor man's parliament to a close for the time being.

'They'd better bring the wages to cheer us all up.' One man offered the men a last hope as Ned sent the same scrap back along the hands.

*

While Ned and the men on road number 151 were returning to the line after the morning suck, the boardroom at M.U. was an opus of clattering chairs, as around its table the first participants of an especially convened meeting of the Guardians were taking their seats. The meeting had been brought forward from 26 December. To the concern of all, and especially Warren Crooke, the medical officer, the capacity of the workhouse had now been exceeded by almost one half of its designated volume.

'State of the house?' Edward Ashe enquired to open the proceedings, proceedings that, Warren hoped, would for once spur the Guardians to more urgent measures than was their wont.

'Eight hundred and forty-four this morning, December the twenty-fourth.'

'Thank you, Mr Burdon. Eight hundred and forty-four.' Ashe re-

recorded the number in his own logbook. 'And for the record, as this is our last meeting of the year, could you speak to how this number relates to those preceding figures over the year?'

'Of course, Mr Chairman. It goes without saying that numbers of admissions have increased rapidly in recent months, but if it pleases the board, to offer a summation of the year as it stands. March twenty-first saw the house record its lowest number at two hundred and six, thereafter keeping a steady average of around two hundred and fifty to three hundred inmates monthly throughout the summer, until the period between October and November, during which there was the most significant increase of three hundred and eight-seven new paupers, recorded as of November twenty-first, when the house was counted at six hundred and ninety-two. And, of course, that number has consistently risen until the present juncture.'

'Thank you, Mr Burdon,' said Ashe.

'How many admissions can we realistically continue to accept, with numbers already two hundred and forty-four over capacity?' Cornelius Murphy directed the question to the chair. Not all of the Guardians, unfortunately, thought Warren, were as diligent as Murphy.

'It is not recommended that we go over capacity at all, Mr Murphy. And yet here we are. But perhaps the question is best put to Dr Crooke.'

Surprised at how quickly the attention of the Guardians had turned to him, Warren took a moment to compose himself and, especially, to hide his irritation at Ashe's rather convenient passing of the burning mantle – the same Ashe whose habit was one of keeping his top hat on the table in front of him when all others hung theirs upon the rack, and whose current activity of picking away some imaginary specks of dust from his waistcoat confirmed to Warren Crooke that he was a man more concerned with ceremony and status than with achieving meaningful action.

Warren might have remained seated. The committee members would hear him clearly enough. But to emphasise what he had to say, he stood to answer.

413

'The problem is that disease and contagion, at a certain point, follow overcrowding as a matter of inevitability. Due to the lack of workhouse uniforms to dress them in, some paupers are being admitted in their own filthy clothes, which, of course, does not and will not help the situation. The privies are overwhelmed and jamming up. But, more importantly, any person bringing sickness into the overcrowded conditions is akin to presenting a lit match to a bed of straw. And of course, it is no surprise that the greater the instance of admission, the higher the chance of introducing such contagions.

'You are all aware that we have already had dysentery to contend with …'

'Dr Crooke,' Father Lee jumped ahead.

'Yes, Father Lee?'

'Is there any evidence so far of a correlation between the recent upsurge in admissions and increased cases of illness, or even of mortality within the house? How does it compare with other periods, for example?'

'This month? To date, the twenty-fourth of December' – Crooke, knowing that his answer was going to bring sensation, banged his finger on the table to indicate with exactitude – 'there have been more than thirty deaths. And I anticipate that there will be two more before the sun has set.'

'More than?' the priest repeated, shocked. 'More than thirty deaths! What is the exact number?' He blinked repeatedly, stunned.

Having felt so many cold bodies under his hand of late that his dreams were frequently troubled, Warren buried his tongue in his cheek before answering, almost reticent to admit such realities even to himself. Then suddenly, angrily wishing to summon productive action from the Guardians, he answered, 'As of this morning … thirty-five.'

Father Lee tried to get something out, but only the last sound seemed to carry. '… five? And the number for the corresponding period last year?'

'Five.'

'Five?'

Warren nodded in the affirmative while Lee lowered his head.

Sweeping the room, the doctor could see that several of the board were almost as ashamed as he was at finding themselves insufficient in the face of the catastrophe.

'Thirty-five?' The priest asked again, his long face becoming even more equine in disbelief. 'So, the mortality rate is seven times what it was last year – and we're not even through with December yet!'

Nobody spoke. Warren feared there were no words to lessen Lee's horror. What more could be said? If anything, the priest's response was beneficial to the moment and to his hope of eliciting a worthy response from the otherwise conservative body.

'Have their spiritual needs been taken care of? Who has been administering to the dying?' Lee, in that moment, a hand held to the side of his face, seemed to have unknowingly placed his ecclesiastical duties ahead of those of his being a Guardian.

'Of course, Father Lee. The chaplain has been on hand at all times,' Mr Ashe interrupted.

'Good heavens. And this in a house where only weeks ago a resolution was passed to the effect that a second physician was not necessary?' put forward Patrick O'Riordan.

Warren sighed. He knew that despite his efforts at restraint, the fact that he had half-heartedly thrown his hands up articulated his frustration with the majority of men around him. 'That was not by my vote.'

Ashe gave a grunt of awkwardness and, unjoining his hands, sat up. 'Gentlemen, I believe that is past business and was decided upon.'

Warren looked directly at Ashe. 'It was, Mr Chairman, but–'

'The real problem as I see it, and I'm sure you'll agree,' Reverend Mr Swanzy butted in, 'is how to keep people from requiring the accommodation of the workhouse.'

'I apologise, Mr Swanzy.' Father Lee shot to his feet and swept the roof and the walls of the room with an earnest gaze before speaking. 'Dr Crooke, I feel I have to ask – is there fever in the house?'

The tension was palpable. The critical moment had come.

'Dr Crooke?'

'There are currently seven patients in the fever ward.'

'Good Lord. The rumours are true?'

'Dr Crooke believes he has the situation under control, Father Lee,' said Ashe.

'Under control? But there have been thirty-five deaths, Mr Ashe!'

'I have *never* used those words, Mr Chairman. I simply said I am doing all that is within my power,' Warren interrupted, angry at the misrepresentation.

'Of course, Dr Crooke. That is correct, Father Lee. Now with respect, I suggest we must get on with the business of what changes we *can* effect to improve the situation from the ground up. Or what else are we for?'

'Hear, hear!' The table only half-heartedly agreed with Ashe, with some members still adrift on the fright of the revelation.

'Now, Mr Swanzy, you had a ques—'

'But where to from here?' Lee interrupted again. 'With fever in the house, I mean – please spell it out for us, Dr Crooke. What are the wider repercussions of having reached this point?'

Warren Crooke drew a breath, finally forced to examine the subject he wished he could avoid.

'The real problem is that, inevitably, gathering paupers together this way puts very many people in the way of deadly contagion. By allowing unwell inmates to leave the house, as we must do, we run the possibility of sending a large quantity of newly infected hosts back out into the community, completely ignorant, as they wander back to their cabins and dens, that they might be carrying a deadly disease capable of infecting their entire family. It becomes a vicious circle. In a word, wildfire.'

'Good God,' Lee said.

'I propose that we focus on solutions that address the requirements of the poor to prevent their reaching the point of needing the accommodation of the workhouse.' Swanzy sought to bring the discussion to practicality.

'If I may offer an insight?'

'Yes, Mr Burdon.'

While the clerk spoke, Warren resumed his seat.

'In the short term, this week of the year usually sees a temporary fall in the number of inmates, due to some less desperate cases signing out for Christmas.'

'While that's very interesting indeed, I dare say it does not solve anything for those within, Mr Burdon. And, dare I add further, one can hardly call this a usual year.' Con Murphy interjected, with an observation that echoed Dr Crooke's thoughts. The clerk seemed taken aback, and buried his head in the books.

'Yes, of course, Mr Murphy,' Burdon responded.

'But back to solutions.' The chairman was attempting to keep the meeting on track and despite his anger towards him, Warren appreciated that Ashe was at least making an effort to get the most out of the board in the interests of its meeting the demands of the crisis.

'Yes, Mr Lucy?'

'As it stands it appears that we will have to wait until Parliament reconvenes on the nineteenth of January to know the fate of the Poor Law. But I fear we *must see* an amendment that affords some kind of outdoor relief again.' Daniel Lucy was without doubt the leading exponent of such measures among those present and appeared now to seize the opportunity to re-popularise the idea.

'Hear, hear!' Father Lee called out, if rather too loudly.

But the approval was not unanimous and, emanating from those previous opponents of the outdoor relief system, already withdrawn by the board the previous October, Warren could observe the frowns and mutters of dissension.

'With respect, Mr Lucy, I do not think it appropriate to raise matters of the Relief Committee here,' said Swanzy, looking around the table for support.

Crooke watched on anxiously as Lucy tried another approach and hoped that he was being listened to. 'The Relief Committee are all but impotent in this matter, their finances having been practically exhausted for some weeks now.'

'That is beside the point,' Swanzy argued.

'I have heard of soup kitchens opening in various other neighbouring districts, Mr Swanzy,' Lucy went on. 'Inishannon, and Skibbereen for example. Why not Macroom? The need is clear.'

'Is that not also Relief Committee business, Mr Lucy?' asked Ashe. 'Michael O'Connell has called a public meeting at the courthouse on the fifth of January for the purpose of establishing a soup kitchen in the town. Surely all are aware. In the meantime, this is our last meeting before the year's end ...'

'That's all well and good, Mr Chairman.' Lucy's persistence was admirable. 'But this is only the twenty-fourth of December and with the fullest of admiration for Michael O'Connell, it should be the duty *not only* of the Relief Committee, but of the Board of Guardians too, to bring such matters to bear.' Lucy's reasoning was sound, Dr Crooke felt, but he knew that unless some of the committee had experienced a change of heart – which was certainly possible in light of the myriad developments – Daniel Lucy was not going to witness the urgent call to response he might have hoped for.

'Please, Mr Lucy,' the chair begged to curtail the speaker's distraction.

'Now, when the Assistant General Commissariat visited the boardroom here on the eighth of December, those of us Guardians who are also members of the Relief Committee announced that on the strength of a charitable assistance by the Sackville Street Society we were about to open a soup shop.'

'Mr Lucy, please. As chairman of that same Relief Committee, I am well aware of these matters. But if it helps bring this diversion to an end, I might remind you that we also stated at that committee meeting, in the presence of Mr Bishop, that our funds were very close to exhaustion from having sold extensive amounts of meal to almost eight hundred families at reduced rates. Now, we sadly can't have it every way and with respect I say again, this is a meeting exclusively held for matters directly relating to the Poor Law. As Guardians we must keep our business so directed.'

'Mr Chairman?'

'Yes, Mr Murphy.'

'The other solution, or part thereof of course, would be to increase employment.'

Ashe nodded. The chairman welcomed the change of subject, although his expression was somewhat ambiguous. 'That is certainly worth discussing, Mr Murphy. Gentlemen – under the present conditions, some would debate whether the system is ultimately of benefit to the labourers currently engaged on it. Considering the problems that have followed in its wake it is also conceivable that before too long the works might be dismantled altogether as a form of government relief. But, until we know more, I propose we pass a resolution to consult Captain Gordon on the matter.'

'Hear, hear.'

'Thank you, Mr Chairman.' Murphy sat down.

'In the meantime, may I suggest that we dedicate what time we have left to what might be done to improve the conditions of the inmates given the state of the house at the present moment, and the significance of the season?'

*

Outside Peter Williams's post office in the square, with Paulellen beside him, Creed had been waiting nervously for Alicia and Denis to arrive on the five o'clock mail coach.

With arms held up like a blind man, finding his way between the other parties reuniting before them, Creed gripped Alicia tightly, leaving Paulellen to embrace his sister's husband, Denis, who greeted her with a polite kiss on the cheek. Creed found himself calmed by Alicia's affection until, seeing Paulellen over his shoulder, she broke away to greet his wife with a fond and warm smile.

'Paulellen! How are you? It's so nice to be home. Thank you for having us.'

'You're most welcome, Alicia. You both look so healthy. Hasn't Alicia blossomed, Cornelius?'

'Oh, stop away,' Alicia replied, embarrassed.

'No, really, you're flourishing,' Paulellen insisted, as Creed extended his hand to his brother-in-law.

'Denis. Welcome.'

'Con,' Denis said, masculine and aloof.

'Let me help you with that.' Creed offered to take one of the bags.

'How's Macroom?' the younger man asked.

'Well …' Beneath a sweeping arm, Creed unveiled the microcosm of the square behind him as an example of the world.

'Silly question, I suppose,' Denis admitted.

'Sadly! But there'll be time for that. It's great to see you both. Come now. Let's all get in out of this gloomy, damp evening.'

With Alicia and Paulellen arm in arm ahead of him, Creed walked the short distance to the door of the shop in the company of Denis.

'Excuse me, please. Excuse me.' With the bag in one hand, Creed broke ahead suddenly, clearing a path through the paupers queuing up at the door of the shop.

'Oh.' Alicia recoiled, suddenly uncomfortable, and stepped back until the entrance was clear enough.

'Please make space … Mr French will see to you all shortly.'

'Mr Creed, sir!' French was caught up behind the crowded counter, seemingly surprised to behold Creed again, and was eager for his attention.

'Hello, Mr Creed,' another voice called behind him.

Creed turned to see Edward Ashe, who, to judge by the bags, had also met someone in the square. It was inevitable that he'd run into someone eventually, Creed reasoned silently. The question had simply been who and when.

'Hello, Mr Ashe.'

'We haven't seen you for a while, Mr Creed; is everything well?'

'All is well, thank you, Mr Ashe. But I'm indisposed right now, I'm afraid. As you can see ...'

'Of course, Mr Creed.'

'... we are receiving guests.'

'Well, the best of the season to you and your guests, Mr Creed. Everything is relative of course.'

'Thank you, Mr Ashe,' Creed bowed. 'And to you too.'

Creed was trying desperately to normalise his responses in front of Alicia in the hope of forestalling the conversation that would inevitably follow if she became aware of his situation. He gave an awkward glance to Paulellen, who only half acknowledged him.

At least Ashe, noticing the awkwardness, had withdrawn fairly quickly.

'You remember Mr French, Alicia?'

'Yes, I think so. Hello, Mr French.'

The clerk, in that heavy maroon jacket, was doing his utmost to politely juggle the mob while greeting Creed, Paulellen and their guests, but the pressure showed in his perspiration.

'Hello, Alicia. I am very pleased to see you.'

'Everything in order, Mr French?'

'Eh. When you have a moment, Mr Creed.' The awkward darting of French's eyes told Creed he was desperate to enquire or confide something, but Creed had enough on his mind at the moment. He was relieved that all parties on the home side, French included, were doing their best to assume the appearance of normality. The visitors did not appear to have noticed anything out of place, or if they had, they were too considerate to show it, and for once Creed was thankful for the terrible specimens of poverty and distress on hand, hoping, with desperation, that they were providing his guests with a convenient distraction from any visible oddity in his own behaviour.

French again lowered the half door of the counter as the guests passed through. 'How long shall I stay open, sir?'

'At your discretion, Mr French.' Creed nodded but avoided eye contact with the clerk and led the party of arrivals hurriedly up the stairs.

'Oh, dear God,' Alicia said, blessing herself when they reached the upper rooms.

'I know, the smell is dreadful ...' Creed shook his head.

'No – I mean, yes ... but the poor creatures.' Alicia held her hand to her heart.

'Oh. Naturally.'

'So pitiful. It's ... even worse than we've seen in Cork.'

'Certainly. And that's only scraping the skin of it.' Creed was aware he had opened the door to expanding more on the subject, but he was in no real mood to elaborate.

'But look ...' Paulellen interrupted, her clasped hands under one side of her neck. 'Let's get you settled in.'

'Yes!' Creed agreed, nodding, the bag put down at last.

'There'll be plenty of time for all of that. It's Christmas Eve. Cornelius, can you show them?'

'Of course. The usual room, dear?'

'Yes. Alicia's old room. It's all ready.'

Denis came forward, a package in his hand. 'This is the, eh ...'

'Oh ... Thank you, Denis.' Paulellen took the packet.

'Ah, the music sheet, and the books for Ellen and Charlotte,' Creed remembered.

'Yes, I *think* they're the ones you asked for in the letter,' Alicia said.

'Thank you so much for remembering.' Paulellen was thrilled. 'Charlotte will be so excited. That's kind of you both. Thank you.'

'Well, Alicia went and got it.'

Despite being only partly present in his distracted state, Creed was amused to see that Denis was eager to untangle himself from any responsibility.

'Ah, but it was a joint effort.' Alicia laughed.

Creed held on to the buoy of pleasantry and, picking up the bag again, led Denis to the guest bedroom, while the sounds of the women's conversation filled the hall as they moved into the kitchen.

'Now, let's get a cup of tea. Are you hungry?'

Creed heard Paulellen behind him as he struggled with the weight of the bag, walking ahead of a silent Denis.

'How long were you on that mail coach?'

'Oh, it was so uncomfortable, Paulellen. Sure, we couldn't see a thing for the last hour …'

*

Early that afternoon, as a slow rain had set in, the men had abruptly been let off and sent home with one arm longer than the other, no sign of the two weeks owed to them and on *Bigil Lae Nollag*.

As soon as it had become clear to Mr Barrett that the men would not be paid, a disagreement broke out between himself and the visiting paymaster, Mr Gibbs Ross. Arguing within the shelter of Barrett's hut, to the hush of rain outside, Ross had refused to issue the men their pay on the grounds that the clerk – present between them – had no paperwork ready for him, having mistakenly sent the relevant materials on to the paymaster in Bantry.

'He believed he was following the protocol of the previous system,' Barrett said, attempting to cut off Mr Ross's opportunity for excuses.

'Mr Barrett, I understand your frustration. In your pay clerk's defence, he evidently received no prior notification of the change. But while there are bound to be many cases of oversight and neglect held inseparable from so extensive a system called into sudden operation, I hope to your satisfaction it is neither owing to a case of negligence nor malice on my part, or of any other person present in this instance that we find ourselves so compromised. I myself have not traversed a distance of thirty-five miles for the sake of my good health.' The paymaster, who seemed to keep his eyebrows high, in expression of constant surprise, was the face of innocence.

'Compromised? *We* are compromised, Mr Ross?'

'There's–'

Mr Ross clearly wanted to elaborate but Barrett cut him off. 'The position of those men out there: *that* is the definition of compromised. Doubtless your claims regarding the overall system are well grounded, but it changes nothing of the fact that there are four hundred men on these works who have not been paid for two weeks, labouring under the most extreme conditions, who will now be returning to their families without reward, and on the twenty-fourth of December!

'Good God, man, you have the money with you. It surely can't be that hard to issue payment for the men today!' Barrett's temper was directed at Ross, but he also took in the pay clerk, who was sitting quietly between the warring parties with his head kept low.

Ross, as Barrett was discovering, was the kind of man who found it hard to admit any possibility of fault on his part, even though there had been ample time in advance of his visit for him to ensure that the paperwork under the task system should have been directed to him, or reserved for his use.

'Whose job was it to inform the clerks of these changes? Or, more to the point, were you aware of the change yourself, Mr Ross? In which case might you have simply sent word on in advance?'

'I do appreciate the difficulty of the situation, Mr Barrett. I do. But you might appreciate that it is not such a simple thing as it may seem when one considers the nature and the extent of my work, carrying out these payments.

'Now that they are working by task, every man's work has to be measured and calculated by cubic yards, and that converted to a monetary value, before the necessary sums can be readied in silver and copper coins for each man to get what is his due placed in his hand. Then recollect, there are in excess of three hundred thousand persons at more than ten thousand separate locations across the country at present.'

'And you are looking after each one of those, are you? Figures, Mr Ross, convenient statistical figures.'

'I'm merely demonstrating the difficulties, Mr Barrett. If there were ten thousand paymasters, the payments could be carried out weekly.'

'Tst …' Barrett found that his hands were clenched and squeezed them tighter before releasing them.

Ross continued making his excuses. 'If there were five hundred, each would have twenty separate parties to pay, at so many miles asunder. Furthermore, even when things go as planned, when the day comes to issue payment, many of these men do not answer when their name is called out and when, by reason of their absence, the lists cannot be closed, the pay clerk is obliged to table these lists again the next day of payment, and go over them again …'

'Now, Mr Ross!'

'… calling those absent on the previous day again. This gives much trouble and occupies much time.'

'Mr Ross!'

'I'm simply trying to help you understand the complexities of even my own list of tasks, Mr Barrett. I cannot be expected to also look after the duties of the administrative head of the Relief Commission, informing each associate everywhere I might go. This should all happen from the top down.'

'Mr Ross! Can we please concentrate on this one aspect and, instead of swiping at shadows, speak to the substance! Can you pay the men?'

'When the paperwork can be retrieved, showing me who is entitled to …'

'Can you pay the men TODAY?'

'I cannot.'

'Very well. Please do whatever is required to have this rectified at your earliest convenience. Now, if you'll excuse me, I have other matters I need to attend to. That'll be all, thank you.'

Barrett left a perplexed-looking Gibbs Ross inside his cabin and proceeded straight to the gangsman.

'Mr Roberts.'

'Mr Ross, sir?'

'It seems the men will *not* be paid today.'

'I beg your pardon, sir?'

'I know. It's beyond my control and frustrating in the extreme. I have tried to remedy the situation in every way, but to no avail. As soon as the weather breaks again, let the men off, that for God's sake they may be home before dark in time to see their families.'

*

'Right. Away off home with you. That's it,' Roberts shouted, walking along the line, addressing the group as an entity, as it broke and disintegrated a yard at a time in line with his footsteps, the men climbing out of their pits and ditches, confused and realising the worst.

'What about the wages?' one asked in disbelief.

'There'll be no pay today. That's it. Up out of it. Off with you now.'

Heartlessly callous in delivering the blow, Roberts clapped his hands as he went, knowing there was no way to dress it up, angry at the providence of the situation, and angry too that he would not be reconciling those outstanding balances with the men he had bought meal for 'on time'.

'We have families to feed …' He heard the shout of a man very near to him and in his side vision saw the figure falling to his knees as if breaking down. But Roberts walked on, a short trail of his inferiors trying to catch up behind him to help do his bidding.

At this moment, he had not the stomach to deal with individual cases or nurture each labourer through his troubles. Roberts had his own woes to deal with. He wasn't even sure if *he* was going to be paid.

'Send them home. Go on.' Re-shouldering his falling braces and turning to get out of the rain, Roberts spoke to one of the stewards who'd caught up, and, delegating the task to the younger man, set his muck-laden, unlaced boots against the flow, looking anywhere but into the faces of the labourers who fell away on each side of his large strides.

It was with utter devastation and bitterness that Pádraig turned for home facing the unbearable prospect of arriving empty-handed. The grimace-inducing hunger; exhaustion; the pain of swollen joints; of cracked, waterlogged, blistered skin were almost nothing when compared with imagining Cáit and his two children looking up at him, hungry still despite all his efforts.

How could it be that tomorrow – Christmas Day of all days – his children, whose father was working himself into an early grave, would be just as cold, hungry, miserable, wronged and dismissed by the world as the children of those families whose fathers couldn't get work? After all he'd come through, and after all he'd surmounted, Pádraig had never felt as low or as hopeless and lost in his whole life. It was as if he walked more slowly with each step, unable to face the vision that waited at his journey's end.

And yet, behind the devastation, he longed more than anything to embrace them. It was the only reward left for him. When everything else was being removed, one joy at a time. In spite of every life-sapping effort that brought no reward, in spite of each false hope that toyed with his fate, something within him was still stronger than all the desolation, decay and hunger. Stronger even than the will to survive.

No force, no level of pain, weariness or deprivation save death itself, could equal the unwritten instinct that now fuelled every step he took upon this earth – even when every speck and pore of his physical being cried for him to lie down, whether for a moment or an eternity. The depthless need for his children and for Cáit, the woman he loved, to be safe, to endure and not to suffer – that was what kept him moving. *He* did not matter. But he had to stay alive for them. And so his feet moved.

He knew that if he had to, one drop at a time he would use himself up, to shield them from the anguish, from the hunger, the cold and the pain. He would battle all these until the last one was beaten, or until there was nothing left of him and he'd vanished from existence.

The route home was marked with nothing but more signs of want. Pádraig, supposing he and the men had been sent home to their families early as a gesture of mercy, now realised the irony of such a decision; had the men completed a full shift, many would have only reached home under the cover of darkness, when their children were sleeping, and would therefore have been spared what the daylight could not save them from. Even now, only halfway home, the light only emphasised the cruelty of winter, in the leafless trees and the exposed desperation – the struggle of all living things to cling to life when everything around was dying.

Every so often along the way he saw a young girl, a boy, or a woman out gathering firewood; at least nature supplied that, and in abundance. But no one was outdoors who did not need to be – who could not waste their energy on any activity not essential to survival. No bough of holly, garland of ivy or twig laden with berries decorated the desolate cabins and skelps of the poor, the usual custom that Pádraig remembered from his own childhood. The people had not whitewashed their cabins and outhouses with buckets of lime as they had done in years long past. Everything was spent, and at the deepest ebb of the flow of life.

And it was cold. Pádraig hugged his fingers beneath the pits of his arms and buried his chin into his neck, constantly shifting his coat to hide as much of himself as he could from the wind. He walked and trudged on for a long time, until at last, bone tired, the next step was the one to deliver him to the top of the hill.

Pádraig stumbled over the doorway to find Cáit distraught with a sick Diarmuidín in her arms. She looked at his hands and with the frightened whites of her eyes looked up and stared into his. He shook his head and attempted to speak, but couldn't.

Síle, sitting up on a pile of rocks behind the door, looked up with teary eyes at the tall, skeletal man who lately she had seen only when the weather was hardest. As she reached out her arms to him, the hope-worn figure sank to one knee and gripped her desperately, crying as he fell. She felt his wet face, as choking the stifled cries and sobbing, he buried his head in the crook of her neck, and she cried too, squeezing him back.

All his hopes for this little girl were dying inside him. All the faith a little girl should have in a father was dying like a waning candle in her eyes. The hopes his own mother and father had had for him, like their parents and grandparents before them – that their descendants, their children, their grandchildren, would have a better life than they had – were disappearing.

No one is coming to save us.

The answer for this foe, this hunger, was hidden somewhere far from view, gone after hope.

All the generations that carried us here, for what? I have no answer, the voice inside him screamed. *I am useless! I am worthless in the face of this evil.*

He felt her small frame and his own shaking together.

How can I save you? I cannot save you.

The urge to wail out across the clench of his teeth welled up. He supressed it, but was taken over by a struggle to breathe; he heard his mouth make a sucking gasp at air, then filled. He held his breath and listened with barely a wince.

The little cries.

Stop, stop, stop, he told himself, realising he was scaring the life out of her, his dear little girl. Feelings of guilt, a sinking within himself – it dived, deeper than any despair he'd ever felt. It was as if the floor of his soul were being dragged, smashed, broken on a reef. An awareness of panic wrenched at his guts and twisted his thoughts. Heat akin to the molten metal of a forge, but changing love to fear. Self-loathing … hatred … seething rage. The turmoil of a living hell churned in his mind.

Help! he screamed within himself. *Help! Help! Help! God!*

But there was nothing. Nothing but a death. He felt the anchor of his sorrow plunge and crash, having at last reached the bottom, settling heavily as it came to rest in the sands of an ocean floor.

Then stillness … and sound, echoing within unfocused senses and lost equilibrium. But moisture, the burning fatigue of his scalp. A comfort in the warmth of her skin. Her weight as a living object … the helplessness … divinity … the sadness of her tears. The love, hope and brokenness of her arms gripping his neck, as she tried to fix him, even in the depth of her own fears. Defenceless in her trust, he let go. It was a feeling that would cripple evil. Love, crippled.

A familiar strength called back from the source of everything. A sense of resistance. And Diarmuidín's crying – something summoned beyond feeling within him. A duty. Instinct. A necessity to shelter. *I cannot let go. I cannot break.*

He heard the thought within himself as, descending once more, plummeting, with gravity removed, the sound of hammers surrounded and encircled his emotions.

Walking … steps … hunger.

Clink. Clink.

Pain. Weariness. Descent.

41

The Innkeeper's Regret

A gunshot rang out in the early morning and echoed like a ricochet around the quiet, empty town of Macroom. In the long-standing absence of its latest resident – the honourable William White Hedges – the officers of the 47th Regiment, enjoying the luxury of the castle at his invitation, were hunting on the grounds. The lower-ranked soldiers of the regiment, generally confined to the less stately surroundings of the stables and servants' quarters lately converted to a makeshift barracks and mess hall had, as usual, been up and drilling since 6 a.m., under their drill sergeant.

Afterwards, eating breakfast, they were given an extra half ration of oatmeal for the occasion of Christmas Day. Their second and only other meal for the day would consist of the conventional three-quarter pound of dry bread and a portion of salted beef. Still awaiting news of a new posting, they would spend much of the day at their leisure, washing clothes and drinking their daily ration of beer and rum, given to alleviate the boredom and to relieve the twenty-hour fast between dinner and their next meal.

From old sweats down to underage boys who'd lied about their age, more than half of them had joined up to escape destitution and poverty not so dissimilar to that which surrounded them.

*

At Doire Liath, Pádraig awoke to the sound of falling rain and of rivulets of water filtering through the sodden roof above, dripping intermittently and splitting the close, dank air that smelled of malodorous humanity.

Lying awake with his eyes open, he listened to the breathing of the children: Diarmuidín snuffling through the trapped phlegm that had plagued his chest for months and Síle wheezing, still asleep. Foreseeing the emptiness of the day that lay ahead, he wished for them and for Cáit that they could sleep through it, and not feel the hollow of the hunger he had now within him. For himself, he wished that he was walking towards Macroom again, to arrive wet, and if even he was the only man there, to hunker down in the sodden ditch and beat and burst the rocks asunder, stung by the cold, and wincing with the agonies of being stuck in that position until the darkness came again and he would wander home once more to hide himself in the deadness of exhausted sleep, instead of lying there feeling helpless, useless and poor to his young family.

*

Just over the way in Liscarrigane, with the grass of seven cows and plenty of strong hands to tend the small farm, Diarmuid Ua Laoghaire and his family, as tenant farmers, were that bit better off than the labouring poor all around them.

It being Christmas morning, the youngest, Peadar, a late surprise to his parents, was proud to have been given the task of looking in on the animals. At this one time of year in the country, for their part in the Holy Nativity, a little extra attention was paid to them, and the ass, the cow and a few sheep, for a day and a night, were kept inside out of the weather. It was a great novelty for the seven-year-old boy, who had wild aspirations, beyond his father's means, to one day be a priest.

It was also a great treat that he was to be allowed a hen's egg for breakfast, an annual tradition, and one he'd been looking forward to in the weeks leading up to this day.

'Well, how's all beyond in the stable?' old grey Diarmuid asked Peadar as he joined the family at the table.

'All is well, Father,' he answered, feeling very grown up.

'Good, Peadar.

'Will you say grace for us?'

'I will.' Peadar jumped at the chance, surprised. Excitedly – having taken in the table with his eyes – he joined his hands and solemnly bowed his head, squeezing his eyelids tight. It was a day of privileges.

'Lord, bless this food. Bless the hungry and the poor. And those less fortunate than ourselves. *In ainm an Athar, agus an Mhic, agus an Spioraid Naoimh*, amen.'

It was a little too soon, but before he'd finished, Peadar opened his eyes again to survey the table as all joined with him in the closing prayer and simultaneously blessed themselves touching forehead, then navel, then left shoulder and right shoulder, to make the sign of the cross.

Peadar looked to his father, who nodded his approval, and before anything else could distract him he cracked into the chalk-white shell and split it open to dig out the golden runny yolk as he felt the hand of his sister Margaret rubbing his head but ignored it and continued to savour his prize.

'Peadar?' Diarmuid, at the head of the table, spoke hesitantly.

'Yes, Father?'

'Do you remember one Christmas here not so long ago, it was people in the stable and not the animals?'

'I do, Father.' Peadar prepared himself for some erudite lesson.

Diarmuid tapped a finger on the table's edge, seemingly deciding. 'When the breakfast is over, I want you to …'

But Peadar, reading the faces up and down the table, perceived his mother, Siobhán, at the other end, locking with his father's gaze as she slowly shook her head.

Peadar was not entirely sure what his father had in mind, but guessed it involved him taking something to Muintir Buaċalla; some eggs perhaps. His mother, with a look, seemed to say he was too delicate in years yet to handle what sights might meet him there and was making her feelings clear on it.

His father stopped mid-sentence, chewed his jaw a while, then drew back his head, seeming quietly to agree with her wishes.

'No matter,' he said. 'Always remember there are people worse off than ourselves, Peadar.'

'I will try to, Father.'

Old Diarmuid, watery-eyed, with a work-worn hand, leaned over the table and tossed the mop of his hair.

Peadar returned the sad smile, looking up at his noble father.

*

At Macroom Union, fever had arrived and had catapulted the burden of dysentery and the recent outbreak of measles to a new level. The situation was pushing the facility itself, and the abilities of the staff, far beyond anything manageable or humane, leading Dr Crooke to have recorded in his log on Christmas Eve:

> I may never again behold a sight more pathetic than that of the two hundred perished beings sitting collected around the small turf fire in the boys' ward today, and it being the source of most of the apartment's sparse light. Even with three windows open and ventilation in the cold walls and floors, the fetid and oppressive smell exposes a want of the proper attention to cleanliness. Almost a hundred girls inhabit the adjacent dormitory, under the same offensive conditions.

> The charm of infancy has all but disappeared and a miserable collection of prematurely haggard faces is in its place – the effects of cold, unhealthy living conditions and long-felt hunger. With a lack of workhouse uniforms to go around and most in their year-long tattered clothes, all are very ragged.

> It would be hard for any visitor to believe or accept the consolation that those children here but a matter of weeks or more look markedly better and healthier than those more recently admitted and are easily distinguishable. But it is true, however uncannily, that physically, they are faring better under these conditions than those outside at the present moment.

> Currently, of the 755 inmates within, 112 are in the hospital, in various stages of illness and recovery, with patients dying almost daily. It is by now impossible to maintain separation between the sick and those not

yet sick. Housed between the fever hospital and the infirmary, patients are having to share the confined spaces two to three occupying one bed at a time, which mostly consists merely of straw. But throughout the house at large there is nothing but straw mattresses as a usual circumstance.

On Christmas morning, gathered at the main door and sending up their heart-rending pleas, a family of paupers in the last stages of hunger were begging to be admitted. Inside, hidden from their view, the porter, fearing he could do nothing to help, pretended not to hear but consoled himself that if they were aware of the conditions within, they might change their minds. But the truth was that the extent of their suffering and deprivation had reached such a critical point that they were willing to risk the by now widely rumoured fatal conditions and contagions within.

Arriving behind them, a mother whose husband was owed wages on the works, wages that even when issued had been proving far short of adequate to support her large family, banged on the door incessantly, imploring someone to take in even two or three of her children.

Fearing the noise would attract the attention of the Matron – or even worse, the Master – the porter eventually opened the door, but only to discourage the solicitations that threatened his position.

'I'm sorry, ma'am. The Guardians will not sit again until Saturday the first, I am told. Please come back then.'

'We'll be dead by then,' she shouted.

'We've come all the way from Inchigeelagh,' the father of the family pleaded.

'I'm sorry but I can let no one in without the approval of the board, and we are well past full.'

The porter answered longingly, wishing he could do anything to help them but fully aware that even when the board was in session, capacity was so far exceeded that they were having to exercise the greatest discrimination and impartiality, selecting only the most destitute of objects for admission.

He struggled to close the door again and begged them not to trouble themselves by waiting longer.

The porter watched the families wandering away again through the window, the image of the man's feet and hands stuck in his mind, mottled as they were with patches of red and blue from bad circulation. The whole group looked so cold. The way the children had dangled their frozen hands out in front of their bodies, almost as if they didn't belong to them. To reach Inchigeelagh, he reasoned, the family would have to retrace their steps some eight or nine miles, little ones and all. It was doubtful whether they would all see home.

*

In Massytown, Denis Murphy had for some time been lying prostrate in a stupor of self-pity and bitterness.

Living from day to day, an hour at a time, surviving on what little his wife and children could beg, he and his family had fallen to their lowest.

Even before Denis had come off the works injured, whatever wages he'd had coming to him were already owed in debts to neighbours and relatives, and he and Anne had borrowed even more since. Over the past week and a half lying listless on their straw bed, his loom and weaving tools long since pawned, Denis had searched his mind. But with half the winter still ahead, in the middle of a universal food shortage with no one coming to their aid, and knowing that the works was no longer an option for him, he could see no way to get back to a point of equilibrium. More than once his thoughts had turned to Pádraig and he'd wondered how his comrade was faring. But realising the inevitability of his own fate, Denis himself had all but given up.

As he had done yesterday and would do again tomorrow, he would spend the day confined to the cheerless tenement room his family inhabited without even the comfort of heat or light. Mostly oblivious of his wife's comings and goings, Denis had a sense that it might be Christmas Day, but he no longer cared whether it was or not.

'Sure, even if I had something to give ye, there'd be nowhere open to spend it today.' Ned answered his wife, who, determined to find something to feed their family at any cost, was wrapping a scarf around her head by the door.

'Oh, there'd be something to be had somewhere if you had the gumption to go and find it, don't you worry about that.' Ned knew Mary was trying to lay the gauntlet of shame at her husband's feet, as the two youngest children – who'd been crying since they woke up – held onto her legs. 'God forgive me,' she said, 'but I can't listen to any more of this.'

'Where are ye going? Come back here, Mary Silke,' Ned shouted as she stormed out. But she gave no answer.

*

Wakened by the moans of sickness from the tenants in the loft above, Jeremiah O'Leary hardly believed it was Christmas Day.

'Thank God we borrowed early,' he told his wife beside him. Supporting himself, his wife and six children on the wages of the works, they had run out of food by the twenty-second, even before the break up. While most of the labourers working alongside him – who'd managed to stretch out what they had for longer, sure that they'd be paid up before the stop – now found themselves without a plan to fall back on, he and his wife had been forced to address their needs early and, through the sheer luck of poorer timing, had something to eat for Christmas Day.

'Thank God,' she said in turn.

'It's coarse yellow meal,' he reasoned, 'but it's the difference between something and nothing.'

*

Bookending the south edge of the town, off opposite ends of the square, the O'Learys and the Swineys occupied accommodations in Holland's Lane and Slevean Road. Between them and Denis Murphy's family to the north-west, the three loosely triangulated the town and drew an accurate representation of the plummeting health and fortunes of the thousands of poor inhabiting the fifteen lanes throughout the vicinity of Macroom itself. The picture of all that lay between was no more than a condensed jumble-shop version of what was to be seen out in the hills and cabins of the countryside, albeit with less space, and all the more piteous for their proximity to comparative wealth and resources that some others were lucky enough to enjoy.

By ten o'clock on the morning of Christmas Day, the O'Riordan household at the east end of Main Street was lively with the noise of three girls and a boy with their new toys. The younger girls were arguing over who got the best gift and which girl would inherit what from the girl above her in age.

In the midst of the happy chaos, Ellen, the eldest, was perched studiously atop her piano stool. With the aid of a book in her hand, a special gift from the Creeds, she was familiarising herself with the apparent genius of a composer named Franz Liszt.

Her mother appeared at the door. 'Now, children, I want you all ready for Mass in one hour. You can play with your toys all day after we get back, but remember what you promised your father – we're all going to the schoolhouse straight after Mass to help out.'

While his family enjoyed their Christmas morning at home, Patrick O'Riordan was one of the Relief Committee volunteers out visiting the crowded slums in the lanes, giving emergency food and water to those unlikely to make the journey to the schoolhouse and informing all others of the plan to distribute soup and bread there later that morning.

'The whole town is pauperised,' Pat said to Daniel Lucy as they left a particularly miserable abode in Duggan's Lane where a man, woman and four children were huddled around a fire against a backdrop of soot-stained bricks and blackened walls.

'We haven't eaten for twenty-four hours,' the father told them. They seemed glad to learn of the event at the schoolhouse, but Pat couldn't see how they might endure such conditions much longer.

Induced to enter another house where groaning was heard from within, Dan Lucy found a man stretched out on dirty straw in violent pain. By the swelling in the man's lower legs, Pat guessed the condition to be dropsy.

'Where are your family?' Lucy inquired.

'*Ag bualadh ag dóirse*,' he replied. 'Knocking the doors.'

The sick man begged them for water, which Pat administered. He drained almost the entire bottle. 'I've been battling an unsupportable thirst for two days,' the man sobbed.

*

Though the morning was frigid – its bite as fresh as the trickling waters of the Sullane gently flowing under the nine arches of the bridge nearby – and though the sky above the houses and slate roofs of the rain-wet town was grey and ominous, between showers the light that pierced the apse of St Coleman's was transformed by the stained-glass windows. Vital and dense as a spectral flood, beams of sunlight backlit the altar of the dead Christ and washed the faces of the congregants in cobalt, crimson, ochre and greens – rich as fresh resinous paint pushed under a palette knife and smeared through the plastered arches and pillars of the simple church.

Down the far away back of the building, the squeak of a turning shoe and the slow cry of a door-hinge announced the last of the incoming parishioners, as against a backdrop of the melancholy scenes playing out across the vast and tragic stage of Macroom and its surroundings that morning, Father Lee took to the pulpit and all within held their breath in anticipation of his Holy Sermon.

> The weary, dreary, dripping rain,
> From morn till night, from night till morn,
> Along the hills and o'er the plain,
> Strikes down the green and yellow corn;
> The flood lies deep upon the ground,

No ripening heat the cold sun yields,
And rank and rotting lies around

The glory of the summer fields!
How full of fears, how racked with pain,
How torn with care the heart must be,
Of him who sees his golden grain
Laid prostrate thus o'er lawn and lea;
For all that nature doth desire,
All that the shivering mortal shields,
The Christmas fare, the winter's fire,
All comes from out the summer fields.

'So wrote a poet, in recent years, who it seems well understood the link between the cycle of the seasons and the life of the Irish peasant, who like the bee in nature works all summer long, and in winter must survive on what he has gathered, when the land no longer provides. But what happens when summer does not provide?

'Though the poet speaks of corn, the principle holds for any crop. And while the labourer is not a bee, mankind is a community. Much like a hive, one depends on the many, and the many on the one.

'And God created it so. The word "religion" itself stems from the Latin *re* – meaning again – and *ligo* – to bind, to connect. And so the answer must be that we protect and support each other. That in times of need, we must spread the wealth, for the good of all.

'Today, we offer our Mass to those around us, and in our midst, who need our protection, and are shut out by the wealthy. And we ask that God will hear them.

'Brethren, let us acknowledge our sins, and prepare ourselves to celebrate the sacred mysteries.'

At the rectory in Castle Street, the Reverend Henry Swanzy, having completed his opening prayers, now turned towards pew after pew of parishioners, each face as open as a chalice before a church wine, ready to receive his spiritual blessings on the feast of Christ's birth.

Climbing to the pulpit, he saw, looking down from on high, spread throughout the gathering, separated by their families, the many faces familiar to him from his work at the Relief Committee, the Loan fund, and beyond. The Warren families, the Crooke family, Robert Nettles, Richard Ashe, Edward Ashe, Henry Coppinger, Benjamin Swete, Herbert Baldwin, William Woodley, John Orpen, Philip Cross, Peter Williams, Francis Woodley, John Hawkes, John Pearson and many prominent others.

'Friends, it has come that time once again when we bid adieu to one year and stand on the threshold of another. A new year – another revolution of time.

'Will it bring new hopes, increased freedom, the amelioration of the institutions and the elevation of the millions that form the population of the Empire? How many a departed year has left us the legacy of a past and fruitless experience? How many a welcomed one spanned, as it were, the cerulean arch of the future, promising all bright things, but evanescent in its brightness as it was, fleeting in its realities?

'As Christians, it is incumbent upon each of us, to "love thy neighbour", to "do unto others" – phrases we hear so often that the weight they bear upon our conscience burdens us little. Some of you will have read of the deputation who lately travelled from Skibbereen to London, to solicit an appeal to English sympathies ...'

At that exact moment, Father Lee addressed the same article. 'Much has been said of that envoy, which lately travelled to London. The Rev. Mr Townsend and Rev. Mr Caulfield account for their failure in that their success bears no proportion to their expectation, or to the wants they represent.

'The avenues usually open to appeals from all quarters of the earth were industriously closed up before them. They encountered prejudices inflamed by misrepresentation, selfishness malevolently awakened, and doubts shamefully insinuated. The savings banks were quoted in reply to them, as if deposits could disprove hunger.

'England, who competes with the nations of the earth in riches – with many of them in the arts – with them all in learning. Is it rich, proud, enlightened, civilised, liberty-loving or benevolent to boast of superiority over other nations, when to this one, with whom she has united herself, is miserly of her wealth and paltry in her responses?'

'What will the historian say,' Swanzy posited, 'of a nation which boasts of a grandeur without parallel and offers its institutions – constitutional and social – as models to the world? How will he reconcile the denial of private aid to perishing humanity in a sister kingdom, by the citizens of that which has created a partnership of weal or woe? What will other nations now say of the contrast between the two?

'In one, the luxury of the Sybarite: its palaces elegant; its mansions grand and opulent; its equipages splendorous; its shows magnificent; its streets and dwellings resonating with the sounds of happiness. In the other, where is the trace of general comfort? Or the sound of mirth? The record of happiness? The traces of *national* comfort are not visible. The prevailing sound is the voice of men, even noblemen, lamenting misery.'

Massy Warren, crossing his legs, didn't feel so at odds with the happiness to which Swanzy alluded. His own two boys were full of mirth and doing fine.

'It should not be necessary,' Father Lee allowed, 'to make it clear that we accept willingly and gladly that large sections of the English people and the press who have shown the most liberal sympathy to the poor of Ireland. But, assuredly, years must elapse before the hateful prejudices engendered by a portion of the press – the ungenerous repudiation by wealthy Englishmen, and the invidious responses given to Deputations – will be blotted from the memory of Ireland.'

Swanzy, now finding himself uncharacteristically impassioned, even embarrassed, agreed with the description in the English newspaper. He saw daily in Macroom those same things that the deputation to London had seen.

'It is a hard lot enough to be in such a state of destitution as to be starving, but to have the sufferers misrepresented and caricatured, raises a question: who is more to be pitied, the sufferer or his defamer? In the judgement of Heaven, the question is decided, for *he that despiseth the poor, reproacheth his Maker.*'

Aware of the ruffled feathers that began to show themselves in the form of sidewards looks and raised eyebrows, Swanzy simply raised his voice.

'That same deputation,' Father Lee shouted above the intermittent winter coughs, 'while abroad, obtained an audience with Sir George Grey at the Home Office and requested that a Queen's letter be issued to encourage a collection throughout England for the relief of distress in Ireland.

'The response, we are told, received by mail after Mr Grey had consulted with his peers, was that *Her Majesty's government feel that a Queen's letter is not, at the present moment, the most appropriate mode of raising funds for the relief of these cases of distress.*'

A hum of discontent rippled throughout the chapel.

'They added, *Much must remain to be done by individuals, owners of property, and by private charity.* To be sure there must. But who better – from fortune, mercifulness and generous sympathy – to head this charity than the benevolent mistress of a mighty empire, having for her subjects the wealthiest aristocracy and princely merchants the world has ever produced. Let the Queen of Great Britain appeal to private and voluntary aid for the widespread misery of this portion of her dominions; then England, Scotland, Wales *and* Ireland would surely respond cheerfully and practically to so well-timed an act of their gracious mistress.

'If we *form one empire*, as we are told a hundred times, then treat it as so – if we are *not* then, in God's name, leave us to ourselves and our resources.'

James O'Riordan watched his father's face. He'd never seen him look quite so serious or upset with his large fists clenched and bound trembling to his thighs, stricken jaw muscles twitching beneath the skin of his face and moisture at the corners of his eyes.

'But do not mystify reason and pervert the meaning of words by assuming a tone to command respect in one season and another in the season of a fearful emergency requiring all the *kindliness* and all the *justice* of a responsible government.

'I wish to read from a letter by that lion of the west, Archbishop John McHale, addressed to the current Premier of England, Lord John Russell.'

Lee knew that naming both a hero of the people and the obvious culprit of the woes of the nation in the same breath – not to mention pitting them against one another – was enough to raise the passions of the dead; at this point in the sermon, the emotions of his congregation were already running high. Nevertheless …

'*My Lord*, he begins.' Lee leaned one elbow on the lectern, letting all understand that he would not be going anywhere any time soon.

'*By one of those awful calamities with which Providence sometimes visits states and nations, five millions of people, forming an integral portion of a flourishing and mighty Empire, are entirely deprived of food and consigned to all the horrors of famine. The Prime Minister is naturally and rightfully appealed to, to relieve the suffering part with an equitable application of the wealth of the entire body, and he replies to them, to look to themselves, and to rely on their own resources. Self-reliance is a fine theme when sufficient for any crisis but to tell a people to supply themselves with food when both food and the means of procuring it are gone, appears like the requisition of the Hebrews, to make bricks without materials. And does your lordship, too, advocate, by this singular letter, the nullity of the Imperial Union?'*

Lee paused and gripped the lectern in both hands, while the

assemblage expressed their agreement with murmurs and even a distinct 'hear, hear'.

'*For forty-six years the people of Ireland have been feeding those of England with the choicest produce of their agriculture and pasture – and while they thus exported their wheat and beef in profusions, their own food became gradually deteriorated in each successive year, until the mass of the peasantry was exclusively thrown on the potato.*

'*New improvements in agriculture were projected, scientific reforms in the rearing and feeding of cattle were discussed and adopted; but to the mass of the people the practical fruit of those improvements was a fresh interdict of the use of flesh meat and flour, and a further extension of the dominion of a less nutritive kind of that same vegetable, to the exclusive use of which they were inexorably doomed.*

'*No matter; a cry of Irish prosperity was raised by those who subject the growers of corn to the uniform consumption of an inferior quality of food; the same cry was re-echoed from the shores of England, gladdened with that abundance by which its inhabitants were supplied, careless of the misery by which that abundance was productive in Ireland; losing sight altogether of the dietary destitution which, during the spring and summer months, her people were uniformly fated to endure.'*

'Much as we ourselves here in Macroom bear witness daily, careless of the cries of the poor that go aloft, the sufferers of that destitution. But at length their cries, and all the cries, have reached to Heaven! And He who has created the poor as well as the rich has answered, "Now will I hear – the time of retribution is come," sayeth the Lord. "By reason of the misery of the needy, and the groans of the poor, now will I arise."'

From the palate of the rector the sentiment was carried, as though relayed: 'In a great national chastisement, all must in some degree be involved; and though many of the poor are made victims, perhaps from their want of due resignation, and to teach them that there can be still deeper misery than that which they have endured, the entire destruction of the potato crop reads as an awful lesson of the cruelty, by which that aliment has been made an instrument.'

And Father Lee answered as though in tune: 'An instrument of rapacious wealth – of dire oppression, and of national degradation. The simple tuber, intended by the Almighty as a valuable adjunct of human sustenance to his creatures, has here been abused by man. And by its destruction will it show what some have been ignorant of – that the interests of all are identified.'

Swanzy: 'That one class cannot permanently flourish and another be abandoned to decay.'

Lee: 'That the people cannot be pushed to the verge of starvation without landlords and rulers sharing in all the perils of their position. The perishing potato is the most formidable agitator the oppressors of the people have ever had yet to wrestle with.'

Swanzy: 'Unity is a force of creation, but if abused a force of destruction. For it warns that if we obey its countenance, all shall profit. But should we deny it, shall we fall together.

Lee: 'Let them believe, however, and tremble, that they shall one day hear the judge of *all* things pronounce their tremendous doom. "For I was in hunger and ye fed me not. Thirsty, and you gave me no drink. Naked, wretched, and cold, and you clothed me none."' Slowing to catch his breath and finish the line, the priest was audibly overcome.

The minister paused a moment within the silence, before collecting with a prayer.

'O God, heavenly Father, whose gift it is that the rain doth fall, the earth is fruitful, beasts do increase, and fishes do multiply; behold, we beseech Thee, the afflictions of Thy people; and grant that the scarcity and dearth, which we do now most justly suffer for our iniquity, may, through thy goodness be mercifully turned into cheapness and plenty; for the love of Jesus Christ our Lord, to whom, with thee and the Holy Ghost, be all honour and glory, now and for ever, amen.'

At the chapel, the first collection was announced and the woven plates sent out to gather the gentle chink of donations from the pockets of the merchants and the servants of the parish. Out along one row and back along another they travelled, crossing laps of woollen trousers, shawl-covered knees, passing winter coats and tweed hats.

Father Barry, as curate, informed the givers: 'With many children among us today, I think it preferable not to go into too much detail. With our own eyes, we have all seen the many examples of extreme want and desperation around us. At our doors, in the lanes, in the fields, upon the streets, coming and going from the Union house, even outside the door of this church on your way in today. We have witnessed their degradation and their manifold descent throughout the year.

'After Mass this morning, along with members of the Relief Committee, myself, Father Lee, Father Foley, our staff and some of the leading gentlemen and ladies of the town, many of yourselves among them, will meet at the National School House next door, where soup is to be distributed in an attempt to alleviate the distress of those in the most stricken of circumstances. I needn't remind you, the limited resources of the Relief Committee are in constant need of replenishing and they cannot hope to keep pace with the deficit among those it aims to serve.

'It might help you to know, as you pass the plates around today, that your contribution to this collection will go towards the purchase of bread, which is to be provided to the committee at a reduced cost thanks to the benevolence of the ever-generous proprietors of numerous bakeries in the town, which in essence will bolster our very limited resources. I am informed that a similar collection is being offered at the rectory by Reverend Henry Swanzy, and his congregation.'

By now the last plates had reached the top of the church and were being consolidated into one basket by the church volunteers.

'If, by some miracle, anything is left over, it will necessarily sustain those same poor in the challenging days to come, which naturally promise to be even more difficult, without the added incentive of Christmas to motivate the generosity of others.

'God save the hearers.'

As the collection plate was passed at the rectory, Swanzy was making a similar appeal:

'But if the prospects of our unhappy land and its stricken people look gloomy, both for the past and in the future, let us address ourselves to the kindness of individual sympathies and the human beauties of the gentlest of all virtues. It knits us all together – the members of the mighty family of the Earth. Wherever sorrow is, there is sympathy – for tyranny there is tears – for orphans, asylums, there are pity and commiseration. All these are bright, redeeming traits in the hardness of our callous nature, superinduced in the stony world in which we are compelled to live and have our being. We can't all be legislators, but we can all love our neighbour – we can't all give grants from a princely exchequer, but we can do the next best thing: give all we can. It is the season of Christmas – alas, not old and merry Christmas. It is the season of the new year – alas, not a *happy* new year for millions. It is the season of festivity now turned to fasting – of firesides once sparkling with the beauty of home affection and innocence, now quenched and desolate. "Their lights are fled. Their garlands dead."

'In your own mirthful mercy and sober enjoyments of God Almighty's gifts, when gentle beings climb round your knees like young tendrils, and soft voices fall upon your ear, and lids are lifted looking into your eyes for love, then think of a Christmas and New Year for others, the sorrowful and sore afflicted.

'Therefore, I implore any and all of those among you who have it in your power – as means permit – as Christians and true representatives of this church within the community, to think of what you can spare, on behalf of the impoverished, starving poor of the district. To, if you can, make a subscription to the Relief Committee, whether it be the one in the town here, or to that of any other parish in the barony. Perhaps you have old clothes, or blankets surplus to your needs. You can bring them here and we will distribute them for you, or if you wish to do so yourself, I assure you, you will not need to walk far to find a grateful recipient.

'If it be in your power to offer employment, any such generosity cannot be without its good. Whatever you can offer, as little or as much is sure to be greatly appreciated by somebody, some family … someone's hungry children. We shall now have a poem, read to us by one of the younger members of our congregation, to reflect on the moment.'

A young girl, the daughter of Henry Minhear, approached the altar with paper in hand.

'From "Winter" by Mary Howitt,' she announced, head down.

There's stillness in the harvest-field
And blackness in the mountain glen;
And cloud that will not pass away
From the hill tops for many a day
And stillness round the homes of men.

In rich men's halls the fire is piled
And furry robes keep out the weather;
In poor men's huts the fire is low
Through broken panes the keen winds blow
And old and young are cold together.

Oh, poverty's disconsolate!
Its pains are many, its foes are strong
The rich man in his joyful cheer
Wishes 'twas winter through the year

The poor man 'mid his wants profound
With all his little children round
Prays God that winter won't be long.

'Many thanks, young lady – very well considered.' Swanzy thanked the shy girl as she walked briskly from the altar.

'God, whose nature and property is ever to have mercy and to forgive, receive our humble petitions; and though we be tied and bound with the chain of our sins, yet let the pitifulness of thy great mercy loose us; for the honour of Jesus Christ, our mediator and advocate. Amen.'

Nearing the end of the Mass at St Coleman's, from the raised lectern, Father Lee looked down on his congregation once more and, as he had anticipated, found many prominent families of the town under the sweep of his gaze – the Lucys, Scannells, Donovans, Welplys, O'Riordans, McNamaras, Creeds, Murphys, Ryans, Lehys, Duggans, McSwineys, Horgans and Fitzgeralds.

Noticeable to Lee by their absence were the poorer families of the town. Having by now pawned whatever decent clothes and shoes they'd had and fearing their dishevelled condition would be offensive to God, the clergy and the senses of the Holy, they no longer attended Mass for the most part. But as Lee gripped the stand he noticed the quiet entrance of a crooked old figure at the other end of the church. Leaning on a stick, the man removed his hat and, finding a quiet place among those who – kneeling on the back of the last pew and standing in the dark corners – hid themselves from view at the rear, bowed his head. Sensing his attentive presence out of all his flock, Lee began to speak, quietly and full of care.

'Today, is a day we use to remind ourselves that we are all poor. Some are poor in wealth, some in spirit, health, morals. We are poor in that we owe to each other, and to God, more than we could ever accumulate in life. Poor until we reach Heaven.

'Today we remind ourselves that we are all poor. Christmas Day, the day of the birth of our Lord, the son of God, Jesus Christ, born into this world as poor as any among us.

'His parents homeless and without shelter on the eve of His birth, turned away and shunned, at their most desperate, so that they had to fend for themselves, and so that the soul of all souls, a helpless infant baby, was born in a stable, much like any we might see in the countryside, open to the weather, soiled by animals, in the company of the beasts. The light of the world, laid down in a manger, we are told. A manger – a feeding trough for the animals. As the hymn says, "No crib for a bed." A scene that many of our own poor would not find unfamiliar.

'On the significance of this day, our kindness is important even more so – a day we feel most for our fellow beings, and those suffering around us. Today, we remind ourselves that we are all poor ...'

Mid-sentence, Lee turned to something that always captivated the imagination of the children and stoked the pride of those present who, some years before, had organised and raised the funds for 'something so worthy of grandeur and sacredness' to be executed by a master carver for the benefit of the parish. For just a moment, with an open hand, he displayed the life-sized marble figure, which lay beneath the table of the altar: the Dead Christ, in white polished stone.

'... we remind ourselves that the greatest among us was born poor in a stable. Christmas Day. A day we celebrate, a day we get together on as families. Little children rejoice in the opening of gifts. Adults give each other presents. We give gifts to ourselves. We eat well, dress well and of course we give ourselves a respite from our labours.

'But every day is Christmas Day for the family that is in need, in the way that it was the day before the first Christmas Day. We have had almost two thousand years to anoint it, to retell the tale, and to hear it again and again throughout our lives. For those who were there, it was a normal day. There was no such thing as Christmas yet. Every day is Christmas Eve for those who need shelter, and for the mother, the father, and the infant who need our kindness, and our gentleness.

'The account of the innkeeper and the baby Christ – the infant Jesus.

'"Pity me," he said. "Pity me my destiny."

'The innkeeper. Who one year after another prepared food and served it to his guests. Each day, unaware of what was coming, he busied himself with his chores. Year in, year out.

'"Set the tables; fetch the wine; down to the cellar, don't bang your head." Day upon day. And when our Lord came, he didn't see him.

'"How could I have known?' he said. "He was just a baby … an unborn baby. Pity me. Pity me my destiny," he said.

'"All my life I waited for my joy, my king, my treasure. But when he came, what can I say? I turned him away. There at the door, I didn't know. They bowed their heads, I didn't know. They walked away. I didn't know. I let them walk away. I know! I let them go. Even though …

'"All my life I'd waited, for my joy, my king, my treasure. In a forest full of leaves, spinning leaves… How was I supposed to know the one? In a forest full of mirrors, full of me! How was I supposed to see the sun? Pity me. Pity me my destiny.

'"I would have given him my bed. Heaven knows. And as a pillow for his head, heaven knows. I'd have laid my life down there and then, heaven knows. I don't know how I missed him. I should have bowed and kissed him …

'"For, all my life I lived for him. My joy. My king. My treasure. And when he came …

'"What can I say? I turned him away … I turned him away … Don't turn him away."'

Father Lee's voice trembled, and had faded almost to the point of weakness, so that remarkably, though it carried, he could scarcely hear himself.

Just beyond her peripheral vision, but attuned to his every inflection even through the grip of their gloved hands, Paulellen felt the wave of a supressed sigh that spread its way through her husband's body.

*

At midday, after Mass, a mêlée of haggard faces breached a sea of black shawls that covered the bodies of mothers, daughters, sisters and wives from head to foot as the desperate vied for position at the schoolhouse, where the crowd had been growing ere the word spread that morning. There were men among them, but either shame or a sense of chivalry bade them stay back until the first wave were seen to.

'The bakers of the town have once again stepped up and kindly bolstered the inadequate supply of soup that our relief committee has managed to put on.' Standing on a chair, Father Lee attempted to address the hungry. But within the minds of most, the louder, nearer voice of self-preservation overrode any function for patience, or outward gratitude, and his words fell on deaf ears.

'When will we get a soup depot?' a male voice shouted.

'We're working on that and hope to have some news of it soon. In fact, a meeting is to be held for that very purpose on the fifth of January. Please try to have patience; we are doing all we can.'

'I think it's too much for them, Pat. I'm going to take them home,' Mary O'Riordan told her husband, concerned at the sight of her younger children cowering behind the servers, already much affected by the scene. He nodded his agreement and she removed them at once.

'I know it's very hard to see, children,' she consoled them as she whisked them away. 'Those poor souls have no one else to turn to, and it's up to people like us to help them as much as we can. Your father and I are very proud of you all for helping today, and your uncles James and Samuel will be too.'

'Will Daddy be safe?'

'Of course he will, James. They're just hungry; he's going to help them.'

*

Mary Silke, holding her shawl tight at the neck, pushing her way to the front, had kept her face well hidden until Mary O'Riordan had left. Holding out the empty can, she was forced to partly reveal her face, but hoped Pat wouldn't notice her. A lifetime ago, in '25, before he had a family, Pat had been a sponsor at her and Ned's wedding. He had courted her sister Sarah back then, and he and Ned were thick as blood. Now, pursing her lips, she struggled to hide the missing teeth and the void of having no words for him. How far apart their lives had grown.

Pat, pouring soup from a jug into the tins held aloft to him, was sure he'd recognised Mary Silke among the crowd before him. If it was her, he thought, life had not been kind, and for the sake of her dignity, fearing that the shock of her diminished appearance might be mirrored in his face, he dared not acknowledge her directly. Instead he gripped her hand around the can as he filled the vessel to the brim and with guilt and sadness watched her scurrying away. There was a rush for the front as the bread appeared.

'Patience please! Patience!' Father Lee shouted, passing a bag to each of the volunteers.

*

Later in the afternoon, at the cottage in Gurteenroe, the Welply family and all and sundry were celebrating the day as normally as they could at James and Marie's, where dinner conversation other than about the crisis included the ongoing feud between O'Connell's Repeal Association and its mutinous seceders, being led by William Smith O'Brien.

Having finished their meal, James and Samuel shut out the noise of the children and were enjoying the peace and privacy of James's study.

'Perhaps he'll see sense and change his mind,' observed James, loosening the breast of his shirt and sitting back with a lit pipe in his hand.

Samuel shrugged. 'I don't know, James. Selling up might be the wisest move for him. And if he *is* thinking of sailing … Well, you couldn't blame him for entertaining the idea. It must have crossed everyone's mind by now. Wouldn't you say?' Sam didn't sit so much as recline his rump against the edge of the thick desk, dressed in knee-length stockings and patent leather shoes, with one leg propped up upon a box.

'I don't know. It hasn't mine.' James wasn't convinced.

'Oh?' Sam grinned.

'Have you ever thought about it?' James answered with a question.

'Well, I've not made any decisions that I'm keeping from you, if that's what you mean. But if things keep going the way they are, I think Dorcas and I would consider trying to give the children a better chance elsewhere.'

'Hmm.' James said nothing for a moment but simply drew on his pipe as he considered the splintering of his wider family. 'I suppose it would be no different from our own people leaving Wales a hundred years ago.'

'Exactly,' Sam said, staring out the window.

'If you do ever decide to, at least you might have a friend there ahead of you now.' James laughed a mild laugh and lit his pipe again. 'All speculation, of course …'

'The Creeds and the Welplys in America …' Sam turned back, smiling. 'Now that would be something.'

*

Nearing three o'clock at Codrum House, over an extravagant Christmas luncheon put on for the extended Hutchinson Warren family, Massy was launching into a speech in response to a comment his wife had just made.

'Bridget Hawkes Penrose Warren! The people of this barony are *poor*?'

'They're so poor.'

Massy dusted off his mouth with a linen napkin and propped himself up at the head of the long table. 'Well, you're right, dear, at least in the sense that there are varying degrees of poverty. Is their degradation more pronounced than in other years? Admittedly, yes. But what do they ever do to change their situation? Not much, I say. How poor *are* the poor generally? Or more to the point – how poor do they have to be before they decide to do something about it? Don't try to answer, dear. It's a futile conundrum.

'But in the meantime, I have to look after my family and my livelihood. Am I right, John?' Massy chewed on the remnants of his meat as he spoke, stopping to pick something from his teeth.

John Borlaise Warren murmured in assent, his mouth full.

Massy, picking up his knife again, hadn't finished his rhapsodical waxing. Slicing into another hunk of the succulent pork languishing in gravy on his plate, he took in his relatives one at a time with his gaze. 'Is it my fault that they are poor? Did I personally make them poor? No.

'Each man can but do the best he can for his own. But I am doing my share to improve the lot of the average Macrompian peasant, I'll have you all know.' Massy pointed his knife at numerous family members around the table, looking along it as if sighting a rifle, pre-empting their judgements and winning a knowing laugh for his efforts. 'I actively involve myself in the dealings of the Relief Committee on a weekly basis. But much more besides: if I and the other proprietors of the town, Ashe, Nettles and such, can successfully negotiate to have the new Macroom Railway run through our lands, it will bring industry to the barony and improve the lot of one and all.'

'Perhaps you a little more than the poor, Massy, no?' John joked.

'Well, naturally, yes ...'

Everyone laughed.

'But doesn't the philosopher say that the most meritorious charity is to give a man a trade? Which is a much better idea than my making *myself* broke feeding the parasites,' he scoffed.

'Massy!'

'Sorry, dear. Figure of speech.'

*

Over a roast dinner above the shop in South Square, Alicia decided she could contain her concerns no longer. 'Are you tired, Cornelius? You look like you've been working very hard.'

Paulellen winced, seeming to anticipate an awkward conversation.

'In truth, I, eh, haven't been very …' Creed stuttered, fussing over his food.

'I've been telling him for months he needs to take a break, Alicia,' Paulellen cut in. 'He spreads himself far too thin. I mean, the Relief Committee, the shop, writing for the paper, the race meetings – it's too much for anyone.'

'That's a multitude of vocations.' Hearing the strain in Paulellen's voice, Alicia responded in support. 'I don't know how you manage your time, Con.'

'There, you see?' Paulellen looked to her husband as she dressed the meat on her plate between sentences. 'Even Alicia agrees with me. I know you want to help people, Con, but there's a point when you have start looking after yourself – isn't that right, Alicia?'

'She's absolutely right, Con.' Alicia caught a fleeting look of disapproval from Denis.

Quickly looking back to her food lest Paulellen or Cornelius spot the transaction, Alicia kicked her husband's leg under the table. But, keen to keep everyone happy, as soon as she was sure they weren't looking, she playfully admonished the scowl and shook her head at Denis.

A fervent supporter of O'Brien's in the recent split in the association, Denis saw his brother-in-law as a devout Repealer – one of the conservative enemies of change and someone with a vested interest in hanging on to his middle-class opulence, even at the risk of a long, slow waltz with the Whigs in London. A dance that Denis felt had been going nowhere ever since O'Connell had lost his nerve in '43.

In reaction Young Ireland had lost *its* patience: with the Union, the government and, ultimately, the great old leader of the movement too. The battle for Repeal was over forty years old, but the Liberator's movement had failed. Agitation had failed.

Not having seen Creed since before the split had begun, essentially making enemies of the two, Denis was desperate to lock horns and get his teeth into an argument with his brother-in-law.

'This is just gorgeous, Paulellen. What a treat. Thank you. We've been so looking forward to it.'

Alicia tried desperately to create a harmonious table. Hers was a delicate position: she was newly married, and her brother and her husband – who between them meant everything to her – were still getting to know each other. And then this. A fracture right down the middle of the one thing they had in common and them on either side of it. What timing! She just wanted everyone to get on. And Denis was being a grump.

But something was off on the other end. She'd been noticing it ever since they'd arrived: signs of deep unhappiness in her brother's behaviour. Cornelius was prone to bouts of melancholy, but she hadn't seen him to be so within himself for a long time. The Cornelius she knew would never be so undecided about what time the shop was to close. Then there was that man, Mr Ashe, outside the shop after they'd arrived. He had said he hadn't seen Creed for weeks!

'So, Con – your last letter to Alicia said you'd been thinking about selling up. It looks like you've gone ahead with that plan?' Denis seemed almost to echo Alicia's thoughts, if a little more bluntly than she might have enunciated them herself.

'Oh. We saw the advertisement in the paper,' she explained, trying to even out the tone.

'Why *are* you selling up, Cornelius?' Denis asked again, clearly pointed in his choice of words.

But convinced that he was unlikely to escalate the inquisition any further, Alicia felt she could temper the conversation. And as her brother seemed in no hurry to bring the subject up himself, she waited now to see how he might respond.

'Indeed. Quite. Indeed …' Creed, finishing something in his mouth, began an answer. 'I apologise; I've been meaning to write since. And it must have seemed obvious. It was too late to begin a conversation about it last night. And then today … Well, I didn't want to clutter the occasion with … But, well, it seems it's upon us now.'

It pained Alicia to see Cornelius, usually so articulate, struggling to speak. He finished chewing, then wiped his mouth, but held on to his napkin like a conch.

'It's simple …' He had mustered the courage to elaborate. 'There is no future in the trade of the pawnbroker. Not for the next year at least. Perhaps even for a number of years to come. It's a sad state of affairs, no doubt, but the people who depend upon my service the most are lately in such a predicament that it's all but certain a great deal of them – through no fault of their own, of course – will not be able to redeem their pledges. We class this as a forfeiture. Now, it's standard practice to legislate for a certain percentage of forfeitures every year, but given the scale of the unfolding calamity, the business is simply unsustainable.'

While Alicia saw the coherence of his short speech as a healthy sign that Cornelius was returning back to himself, the Cornelius who would always take the opportunity to provide nuance and to impress everybody with his intellect, she worried – knowing his politics – that Denis, specifically, would be horrified at the seemingly callous and impersonal approach in her brother's breakdown of the facts. As Cornelius continued on, she sought an appropriate opportunity to change the subject, but consoled herself that somehow the atmosphere was retaining a peaceable quality in the meantime.

'In the aftermath, on the back of these forfeitures, which will amount to many hundreds of pounds in unredeemed pledges – and I mean even by stopping now, as opposed to next year, or the year after, when the full scale of the horrors will have unfolded, because there are so many in such severe straits already that it's highly doubtful they will ever afford to settle their debts – it is almost certain that what I'll be left with in place of those redemptions is a terrible collection of morbid souvenirs.

'That's it strictly in commercial terms of course, just to answer your question – why I'm selling. I'm sure I'm not the only one. The whole cart is beginning to roll. But what could anyone expect after forty-two years of the Union.'

'I can't disagree with you there,' Denis said, sitting back, as Creed continued, 'This used to be a prosperous town ...'

Oh good – some agreement. Alicia settled. The potential for bad weather around the table was dissipating.

'Oh, yes. Forty years ago Macroom was, comparatively, a thriving municipality. There were four tan yards; the spinning of worsted was a staple trade and gave a means of procuring bread in the town and villages to three hundred families at least; there were two principal factories for coarse broadcloths, and from twenty-five to thirty houses manufacturing narrow cloths and friezes, all now utterly extinct. Gone entirely.

'There were two to three hundred shoemakers and brogue-makers – fifty of each class is now the utmost. But they are not by any means fully employed nowadays, and on so essential an article of comfort. The population has doubled ...'

'Tea, anyone?' Paulellen offered. She had been the first to finish her dinner and, fanning herself as she got up, seemed keen to get some relief from the oppressive heat in the room.

'Yes, please.' Denis absentmindedly accepted the offer.

'I'd love some tea, Paull!' Alicia exclaimed. 'But let me make it, please. You've done enough.'

'No, Alicia. Stay where you are,' Paulellen insisted, raising a hand. 'You're a guest now.'

Creed continued, 'There were six or seven master smiths, making farming implements, tools for housework and such, and keeping thirty men constantly. Good smiths could easily earn from a pound to thirty shillings a week. They can now be had for two and sixpence a week, plus diet. There are not more than ten of them about the town now, jobbing.

'There were five or six master hatters – keeping four to six men each, on wages of ten shillings a week – with diet, according to the custom of the town – there are now *two* shops with one man each, on wages of two to three shillings a week. Besides all these lost advantages, at that time there were around forty or fifty families living here on private fortunes, fully resident and diffusing employment and comfort. There is now only one!' Creed held up one finger to illustrate his point.

'The disappearance of private fortunes? Surely that's a good thing?' Denis interrupted his flow. 'Bad cess to the lot of them.'

'Well – within the Ascendancy? Yes, that could well be so *if*, that is, they were to be replaced by domestic industry; *someone* has to invest in local enterprise. But that's another conversation. Employment was plentiful and wages remunerative. In England, one in fifty of the population is engaged in manufactures; in Ireland, not one in five hundred. Parliamentary papers would have you believe that the number of manufacturing workmen has increased in percentage in Ireland since, by a factor of eighteen to one. Not so. Beware the union of the shark and its prey, I say.'

'Huh.' Denis wrinkled his brow, only mildly amused at the image. With elbows now up on the table, his hands under his nose, one over the other like a fist in a glove covering his pregnant mouth, he continued to endure the cascading list, but he was too preoccupied with anger to absorb the value and the weight of the exposition.

It was all very well to list the evils of the Act of Union with the efficiency of a librarian and to proselytise on what it had done to Irish society; Denis knew plenty about the ill consequences of the Act and was in full agreement with the Repeal Association on every nuance of it. Where he and Creed differed was in how they each behaved under that Act. And what he could not understand was how a man who spoke as Creed did on the subject could simultaneously take up and operate the business of a pawnbroker under the auspices of providing a service to his already downtrodden fellow countrymen and women. It had always got under Denis's skin, and now he had cause to display his feelings on it. But, remarkably, his brother-in-law was still talking.

'At the turn of the century, no one with the name of a tradesman would think of receiving less than a pound a week. The best that can be got now is about two and six a day – *when employed* – but any tradesmen now is happy if he can average seven or eight shillings a week, the year round. In fact, I know of a tradesman who recently offered himself for as little as *two shillings a week* and couldn't get employment even at that miserable rate.'

Creed paused a moment, while Paulellen poured a cup in front of him.

'Thank you, dear. The condition of agricultural labourers, of course, is "utterly deplorable" even at the best of times. During spring and harvest – under normal circumstances, whatever that means – they get employment at sixpence a day with diet, and eight without. Many of them have large families, of course. They couldn't survive on that but for what their wives obtain going about begging potatoes.

'I needn't attempt to depict the squalid conditions familiar to those of whom I'm speaking – you've seen it for yourself I'm sure … three or four families often living in one miserable hut on straw wads, scarcely any covering but their day rags. And no such thing as a change of linen.'

'Oh … God help them.' Alicia, shuddering, interrupted his speech.

'Is that not shocking to humanity? Endeavouring to live and support a family on sixpence a day? But how can it be otherwise when there is no employment for the people? All are thrown upon the land, a source which has long since been inadequate to the needs of the vast majority of the claimants.'

'What about pawn offices, Cornelius? Were there any of those back in the day?' Finally, Denis threw in his lure, and waited.

'Pawn offices? Ha! A pawn office was practically unheard of. Even ten or twelve years ago such a thing was not known. And that holds for Macroom, as well as many, many other rural towns. But now they're commonplace everywhere. And what are the deposits in these places? The blankets, the coats, the clothing of the industrious people. Everything and anything whereon a few pence can be raised to buy a few potatoes. They have thrived on the wreck of the Union.'

'On that point there … If you don't mind me asking, Cornelius … With all your knowledge and intellect, but most of all, with all your concern for the poor: what in God's name possessed you to become a pawnbroker, of all things?'

As Denis had hoped, Creed halted, stunned.

'Well …'

'You have to be aware that it's one of the most reviled vocations in the history of vocations!'

'Denis. Please!' said his wife.

'I'm sorry, but it just … Well, it seems like an absolute double standard to me. Doing good for the poor on one hand and charging interest with the other.'

'Denis,' Alicia pleaded, almost lovingly. 'We're guests here.'

'And what has that got to do with anything?' Denis was finding it very hard to draw the horses back now.

'Right – eh, well …' Creed hesitated, surprised by the attack within the presumed safety of the family circle. 'I would like to think I …'

'He's not like other pawnbrokers,' Paulellen broke in, speaking up for her husband. Creed, though grateful, still felt disoriented.

'Oh. No?' Denis feigned surprise, evidently unable to hold back the sarcastic taunt.

'Well. That's honest.' Creed was still reeling.

'What did you expect?'

'Denis!' Paulellen barked, uncharacteristically losing her composure, and bringing the ambush to a halt. 'Cornelius?' She spoke as she might have to someone who'd nodded off, but Creed did not yet feel lucid enough to respond. 'I'm afraid Alicia is right, Denis. You are our guests. And perhaps opinions like that are best addressed to the company you keep elsewhere.' Looking from one to the other, she surveyed the visitors for a reaction.

What bothered her even more than Denis's outburst was that Alicia didn't seem to disagree. Or if she did, she had not the decency to stand up for her own brother. 'And if no one else will stand up for him, Alicia, then I will.'

'Paull, please, that's not nec–' Creed, though clearly wounded, spoke at last, and attempted to exonerate his sister. But Paulellen had not yet cleared what was stuck in her gullet, and her cheeks were flushed with the heat of her temper.

'Cornelius is tireless in his efforts on behalf of the poor of this entire district. He has himself run ragged, in fact, if you can't see it.'

'It's not necessary to say so, Paull.'

Again, she ignored her husband's interruption. 'And I should think he would be much better served with some support, in place of an attack like that, at such a difficult time. Especially considering how good he's been to–'

'Paull!' Creed gently but firmly planted the flat of his right hand on the table, making the cutlery ring.

'No. I'm afraid it does not sit right with me, Cornelius.' She drew a breath. 'I'm sorry.'

Getting up, she began to clear the dishes. 'My passion has got the better of me. But …' She struggled not to curse. 'Politics should *never* cross the dinner table.'

The cool swipe she made was designed to underscore the reality that Denis's criticism was motivated by his own idealistic agenda, and his aggressive stance as a Young Irelander. *Just when he was starting to come back to himself.* She commiserated with herself silently, as much as with Cornelius, but realised she was angry at him too, for not standing up for himself.

Despite attempts made at pleasantries throughout a tense dessert, a cordial atmosphere was impossible to recover. Creed didn't speak much at all for the remainder of the short evening. All were pensive, and hurt, and in the end, guests and hosts retired early.

*

At mid-evening, holed up in his digs on Main Street and finished with the wine, Gordon pushed himself out of the rocking chair. He knelt before a large chest on the floor, and from it produced a long bottle of amber-brown liquid. *From the 75th Regiment of Foot. Long live the Queen.* The tag about its neck bore the handwritten words.

The last he'd heard, the men were stationed in Athlone. The regiment. It was the only home he'd known since he was seventeen, when he'd been commissioned as an ensign. South Africa. They were the best years.

Blindly Gordon leaned back, resting one elbow on the edge of the seat and, uncorking the bottle, clumsily poured himself an approximate measure. He took the first swig and placed both glass and bottle on the low table beside him to fumble through the contents of the chest. As he did so he scattered a packet of letters around the floor. Holding the glass again, closer to his ear than his mouth, he picked one up and thumbed it open with the same hand.

Jan '46
It is with great sadness that I write to inform you
of the passing of your beloved Aunt Margaret.

Sincerely, Charles Edward Gordon (Lt–Col.)

Blinking heavily, his head hanging low, Gordon held the letter by his thigh for a moment, then dropped it and selected another.

25 Sept.1846
Clifton Place
Exeter

Dear Charles,

It is I, your young expectant bride …

Any day now! Of course, I understand that duty comes first, but I hope with the good news that they'll grant you leave, and we will be together as a family for the first time.

Your loving Louisa

On the hall table behind the door was an untouched plate of dinner, dropped off by the maid that afternoon, and an unanswered note from the officers of the 47th, requesting the pleasure of his company at Macroom Castle that evening.

By then Gordon had dispensed with the glass and was drinking straight from the bottle. Rocking gently, he stared at the wall. Tears ran down his cheeks as he poured in more of the liquid that released them, a lock of soft hair clasped in the grip of one hand. But before much longer, the chair had stilled. In full uniform, with medals on, its passenger was adrift, listening to the charge of the Xhosa on the plains below the Winterberg mountains.

*

In Doire Liath, the wind was howling and sucking again outside, beating the bluff and the little stone cabins around it. Lying in the dark by the smouldering fire, Pádraig was still going over the night before, when he and Cáit had argued.

'How could it all be gone?' He had belted the words out. 'We were barely scraping the top off it. Starving ourselves to stretch it out!'

'I know, Pádraig! I know! But I'd the women coming to me every day at the well. Crying that their children are fading away in front of them. You don't know what that's like! None of the other husbands here *got* on the works.' Cáit had flung the words back in a broken voice.

'They were takin' ye in, Cáit!'

'I wasn't taken in! I'm no fool!'

'Well, how come we've nothing left then?'

'Because!' Cáit broke down, hiding her face in the side of her shawl. 'I know what it's like to lose a child. I had to give them something. It was the Christian thing to do.'

Pádraig had found himself with nothing to say. He knew she was right, but the consequences were grave.

'How was I to know you wouldn't be paid?'

'Don't sit against the damp wall,' she said softly, when the tempers had died down a while later. She rested her head on his shoulder, he with his arm over his knee.

'I thought we were doing all right,' she said.

Pádraig's stomach was a mess. *We're not!* he wanted to shout, but he couldn't let it out on her. That made him all the more angry. *I near burst my head carrying the stuff home*, he could almost hear himself say. *And all for you to go dishing it up to the neighbours. Into the mouths of strangers!*

He was crying inside, but he was unable to cry any more. Everything was in reserves now. Even tears. It was better to say nothing. And less tiring.

In truth, she hadn't even given that much away. It was more that with hunger constantly banging at the door it had been very hard to keep the measures small. Over the weeks, a spoon more here, another spoonful there. Into the pot. They were small amounts. Not enough to notice the difference in one meal shared out between four. An extra bite each maybe. But when you got to the end of the sack, it all added up.

'Who was it?' he asked eventually. His voice was calmer, but still clipped.

'Caitilín, once or twice.'

'Kitty Uí Laeire? That …' Pádraig halted the utterance, breathing out through his nose and turning his face to heaven. 'God forgive me.'

'Máire Rua,' she said.

'O Jaysus. I don't want to know any more.'

'What if it was the other way round, I kept thinking?'

But now, a full day later, he just lay there. There was no more to be said about it. He was still angry, but with the benefit of a little perspective he could see it better. It wasn't her fault the works hadn't paid him. And she was a kind person. He loved her for that. What if it *had* been the other way round. He would have wanted someone to be kind to them. *Not like those who took advantage of her. They don't care what happens to us. So long as there's something in their children's bellies.* Pádraig hated himself for thinking that. *Our being generous and kind isn't going to keep the children alive, though.* His thoughts went around and around. *How long can we keep going like this? How long can any of us keep going like this?*

But it's better to be the kinder person, he reasoned. *Better on the soul at least. And God knows we've been the recipients of some of the greatest kindness of all ourselves, when Diarmuid Ua Laoghaire took us in at Liscarrigane.*

He could still see it clearly: huddled there in the ditch, trying to keep the blankets over them. The savage wind that fought to suck the breath back out of his mouth; sharp snows cutting at his eyelids; the burning heat in his chest and throat contrasted with the cold everywhere else in his body and the noise of nothingness so severe that it had him deafened to the world. Then the face of Ua Laoghaire appearing above them.

But even when someone had left a small cake of bread at their door earlier that day, that had made the difference between the pain of hunger and just feeling hungry. That kindness. With his nose buried in Diarmuidín's hair and the fire dying, Pádraig struggled to keep his eyes open.

*

Later that night, unable to sleep, disturbed by the ghost of the conversation and memories of childhood in the house, Alicia climbed out of bed and left Denis sleeping, only to find a forlorn figure sitting in the darkness at the kitchen table.

'You're awake?' Creed said gently.

'Couldn't sleep. You either?' she answered softly.

'There's tea in the pot,' he whispered.

'Thank you. Maybe I'll get some.' Alicia turned to the glow of the stove.

'Cups are—'

'I know.' Quietly she laughed back over her shoulder. As if she could have forgotten.

The ping of the spout on the porcelain rim were comforting in their familiarity. With the tea in her hand, Alicia pulled out a chair for herself and sat, but neither spoke for what seemed a long time.

'Listen,' he began. Paulellen ...'

'No. It's fine, Con.' She stopped him, 'Paulellen was right.'

'She can be over-protective of me, sometimes,' he insisted, 'She doesn't mean any harm.'

'Don't worry. I know,' Alicia said, wrapping her hands around the warm cup. An open pause was filled by nothing but blackness and the warmth of the stove.

'It's always funny staying here.' She tried to lighten the subject. 'So many memories ... Can you believe Father had a weekday school here?' Alicia's eyes swept the emptiness, picturing the past.

'Reading, writing, arithmetic, grammar and the Roman Catholic Catechism,' Creed began the motto, but they finished it together, ending with an obligatory laugh whose cadence was short-lived.

'Hardly ever now. But I remember that.' In their rippled wake, his words, barely spoken, carried affection, laughter and sorrow for the unforgiving speed of time. 'He'd hardly know the place now, Old Dan,' he followed.

'Mmm.' They both spoke softly, as if afraid to disturb the night.

'He was right, you know,' Creed said after an interval.

'About what?' she wondered.

'About me.'

'Father?'

'No. Denis. Earlier.'

'Oh, Cornelius! You're a good man. Denis is just ... he's just very idealistic.'

'I've been very conflicted,' he pushed, leading Alicia to sense he was finally going to reveal what was preoccupying him deep down.

'You don't have to,' she offered.

'No – I ... For quite a while there I had myself convinced that I could do some good.'

'But you do!'

'I know, but Denis was right. Any good I do outside of this place is undone by what I do here, in the shop.'

'But you do provide … it is a service to some degree, isn't it? I mean. Where else can they go?'

'That's what I told myself too. But …'

'But what?' she asked.

A heavy sigh filled the inky lung of the empty room.

'I've been trying very hard. You know? But I feel like I'm up against thick old walls, sandwiched somewhere uselessly in the middle, between the rich and the poor. Like a cog in the teeth of a wheel.'

'What do you mean?' Alicia said. 'A cog can drive a wheel, can't it?'

'No! You don't understand,' he asserted. 'This is old money. The Yeomanry. Power. The weight of the establishment behind them. Denis understood that. He could see what I had managed to keep hidden from myself for all that time, until quite recently … That so long as I remained in this line of business, I could never argue the moral high ground. It made me too easy a target for anyone who'd wish to discredit me, or my intentions, whenever it suited them. He proved that today, and so easily.'

'But he's just young. And frustrated,' Alicia argued, trying to rescue her brother from himself, but sensing that he was already gone beyond wherever she could reach.

'I know, but he demonstrated how easy it is to undermine me. I'm a hypocrite! In their eyes at least. Doing this makes me one. And it gave them licence to carry on however they would wish to. It's a stain upon my character. It counteracts anything I have ever done, and perhaps ever will do.'

'Do you say so?' she asked, full of worry.

'I say so.

'This business – I saw an opportunity when John Wiseman closed up. But the idea was so stupid, impulsive and short-sighted. I can see that now.

'I told myself it would be a leisure interest. A trickle of income on the side. Small amounts. That wouldn't do much harm to anyone. That it was a *useful* service even. But no matter how you dress it … It is the business of making money from those who are already so low in their station that they have no choice but to avail of it.'

'Cornelius, if you're that unhappy then perhaps you're right. You should follow your instincts.'

He didn't speak, but in the almost pitch darkness, lit only by the dim blush of the stove, Alicia could perceive him by his faint silhouette, nodding in affirmation as he drew a fast breath up through his nose and slowly let it out again.

'So how bad is it?' she asked, 'Will you lose the …'

'No.' His response was assured. 'I'm not going broke. I have my land. The equity of the shop here, and its assets. The horses. Ha!' He laughed as though at the ridiculousness of his own vanity. 'No. It was just pointless to carry on. On paper. And a much worse year is still to come.'

'Maybe you got out just in time then?'

'But that's not the worst of it. I rationalised to myself as soon as I decided to sell that I would just redeem the old pledges. And I stopped giving out tickets. Because it would make no sense to take in new pledges on articles that cannot be redeemed from a shop that has closed up.'

'I understand,' she said, but she did not yet.

'But *really* … behind that,' he leaned forward, 'if I admit it, I was really *saving myself*. Over the last two weeks I've been turning them all away.' He sat back, sounding like he was on the edge of his emotions.

Alicia didn't speak.

'Don't you understand?' he said. 'In the hour of their greatest need. At what might be the most critical juncture in the lives of some of these terrified creatures, I left them at the mercy of their poverty … to save my own skin. Me … the righteous hypocrite!'

'How many?' Alicia asked, aghast.

'Over the last couple of weeks? Hundreds.' Despite an obvious reluctance to let them go, the words escaped on his breath, barely over the level of a whisper. 'And just as you said, where else can they go? Don't you see … I'm the innkeeper!'

He gasped and began to shake violently as Alicia grabbed his fist through the darkness and squeezed it for courage. His other hand jumped to cover his mouth.

Even in darkness he closed his eyes to shut out the world he'd created. 'How did I … How did I become this person?'

They could not see each other's tears.

42

TWO GORDONS

'Don't worry, he'll come round soon enough,' Paulellen said, standing in the doorway of the shop.

'I hope so,' Alicia replied.

'He's just been through a hard time lately. It's mostly exhaustion, I think.'

'I'm really sorry, Paull,' Alicia said, and as if apologising for him too, looked to the quiet Denis, who stood to the side with his head down.

'Come on. Let Paulellen in out of the cold,' was all Denis said as he picked up the bags and made for the coach that was pulling up outside the hotel.

Paulellen shook her head, then turned her attention to Alicia, who had lingered and held out her arms to embrace her.

'Will you ask Con to write to me?' Alicia pleaded.

'Of course. And you know he will.'

'I'm sorry Denis was so …'

'Stop. You don't need to apologise for him. They're old enough to look after themselves, Alicia. Go on. You don't want to miss the coach.' Paulellen strove to keep her voice soft but even to her own ears it was full of disappointment, and anger. She felt genuinely forgiving of Alicia, who was clearly suffering. Excusing Denis was another matter.

'I'll write soon, tell him,' Alicia said, walking backwards.

'Make sure and keep covered up on the car. You'll catch an awful cold in that weather.'

*

Nec Aspera Terrent announced the Latin engraving on the mount of his signet ring: 'No fear on earth' – the regiment's motto. It wobbled and danced above the knuckle of his little finger, as beneath a rocking hand the nib scribbled and ripped furiously across the page of a letter to the Board of Works.

Gordon was working through a stack of correspondence built up upon his desk and next addressed the petition of one Father James O'Driscoll, parish priest of Inchigeelagh, who had written the letter now opened to his left.

'I cannot describe to you the extent of the suffering of the poor in the three weeks that have elapsed since the stoppage on the Inchigeelagh and South Carrigboy lines,' O'Driscoll had pleaded. 'I beg you will have the goodness to drop me a note stating how soon these people are to be set to work, that I may hold out some assurance to them.'

In passing O'Driscoll also informed Gordon that 'under a mistaken impression that I myself have been too tardy in urging you to employ them, the people in question are, as I understand it, determined to proceed in a body to Macroom, to represent their condition to you, in the hope of awakening your sympathy and being re-employed.'

With teeth clenched as he wrote, Gordon replied to the priest:

26th December 1846

I had intended doing everything in my power to go on the southern part of the Inchigeelagh line next week, but since a threat is made use of, I take such as an intimidation, and will now longer delay the work, until I find that subsequent good conduct renders them deserving of consideration. I make no promises but this, should the people come into town at any time in a body, it will cause a further suspension, and very likely lead to the works in other parts of Kilmichael also being suspended.

Henry William Gordon (Captain)

Inspector for the Board of Works

Macroom.

Near his feet, against the leg of the table, stood his brown leather satchel, its casing stamped with the lettering BOARD OF WORKS. Gordon lifted the flap and placed the letter inside.

*

It was a regret of Creed's that he had a certain amount of unfinished business weighing heavily upon his mind. But not so deep a regret as to detain him from deciding upon his final journey. One of the outstanding items listed in his thoughts was the missive he had drafted for the *Cork Examiner* in consideration of the two Captain Gordons. Lying next to Paulellen in the darkness of their bedroom above the shop, he went over the piece in his mind:

Although two men could not be imagined who were more dissimilar in temperament – one upright and sober, the other to be often found vomiting into a bucket by his bed, sleeping off the damage of the night before – it has been the misfortune not only of the poor labourers below them on the works, but also of those local officials working on behalf of the poor of Macroom, to have been required to deal with two British officers of the same name and rank: Captain Henry William Gordon, 59th Regiment, Inspector for the Board of Works and Captain Charles Parke Edward Gordon, 75th Regiment, Engineer to the Board of Works, who between them, have ensured that lately, 'Gordon' has become the most hated name in Macroom since Malachy Duggan.

This correspondent once discovered the satchel belonging to the inspector and had it hurriedly delivered it to him via coach, and at some personal expense; an act of common courtesy that in the light of subsequent events now feels as misplaced as being polite enough to hold a book being offered by the outstretched arm of the Devil, so that he may search his pockets for a key to the particular gate of hell behind which one is about to be locked.

If Macroom and the Muskerries had not enough to worry about in 1846, it would seem that the Board of Works had thought it fine and fair to add the confusion of sending two foreign military officers of identical name and equal rank into one district, each to engage with local government officials here, and do the bidding of its offices, heedless of the problems such a peculiarity might cause.

Since the spring of this year, a slew of other captains, lieutenants, and majors of the British army have been drafted into the Board of Works. Seemingly idle, while their regiments, garrisoned in Ireland, lie dormant, awaiting a sortie to some distant battlefield, or mutinous outpost of the far-flung empire, the government has decided it fit to utilise and repurpose the skills of these officers: already on the payroll; highly trained in dealing with large groups of men; and accustomed to dishing out the discipline needed to control such, where necessary without qualm.

Independent of one another it seems, the same two Gordons have blazed a trail of terror across this country in that short time. From Louth to Letterkenny, Cork to Culdaff, and at numerous points between, the name 'Captain Gordon' is by now greeted with infamy. But to further confuse matters, 'The Scotchman', a cognomen given one of them in ire by someone along the way, having failed to stick fully to its intended Gordon, now floats randomly between the two, often misdirecting praise, or ignominy in the wake of a particular event, to the wrong one.

Although one Gordon certainly appears to be less vindictive than the other, the reports they have effected, and the bridges they have burnt in a matter of just nine months, read as a litany of havoc and mayhem. The indecipherable crossing of their paths along the way has not helped to defuse the chaos.

That the two would end up in the same district – this one – where they might not only cause twice the trouble but hinder the already compromised efforts of those here to deal with the unfolding crisis, is uncanny. And yet here they are to be found, inflicted upon the hapless population of Macroom and the surrounding parishes.

Two Captain Gordons!

43

ALL HUMAN AID IS VAIN

'Robert! I thought I heard a carriage.'

At Codrum House, Robert Warren stepped through the door, answered to him by a servant boy who, although dressed to look more sophisticated than he was, could not have been more than fifteen. Massy had appeared in the hallway just in time to greet Robert, who was calling unannounced.

'Good day and belated Christmas wishes, brother.' Robert removed his hat, gloves and winter frock coat, handing them to the servant. 'Thank you, young man.'

'Maurice, close the door – you'll have the house frozen,' Massy instructed the boy.

'Maurice, is it? Be a good fellow and fetch the basket from my carriage for the lady of the house, won't you?'

'Do as he says, Maurice. Run along.'

'Yes, sir.' The boy bowed and kept his eyes to the floor.

'Hello, Robert. What brings you to Codrum?' Sliding a hand along the rail of the stair while pinching up the knee of her red gown to avoid tripping, Bridget, Massy's wife, appeared along the grand staircase.

'Bridget, dear. Greetings of the season. And to the Penrose and the Hawkes families.' Robert bowed in kind, calling to mind the incident between Massy and Bridget's father, John Hawkes, wondering if it had caused tension within the household. 'In answer to your question, I am here to consult your dear husband on a matter of great importance.'

'Of course, Robert. I shall leave you both to it. But all is well in Killinardrish, we trust?'

'As much as can be expected anywhere under the circumstances.' He smiled, feeling awkward about addressing that which burdened his mind to a lady, but not wanting to answer in pretence.

'Indeed.' Bridget replied. She understood, he felt, but evidently reluctant to engage the subject further, she turned to retreat up the stairs as the servant boy returned with the basket of covered foods. At this, Robert, knowing he would not be staying long, sought to complete the formalities. 'Mary and the children send their regards. For the time of year …' He gestured to the home-cooked gifts and looked to both Massy and Bridget.

'So kind, Robert.' Bridget answered for both. 'You'll return our best to all, naturally?'

'Of course, dear.'

'Gentlemen,' Bridget said, ascending the last section of the staircase.

'Come through, Robert.' Massy led the way. 'Cook is preparing some trout for lunch as I speak. You'll stay and join us?' Dressed in a jacket with two rows of brass buttons running parallel from waist to chin, Massy seemed always to be wearing the latest preposterous fashions, but looked chivalrous on this occasion, Robert had to admit.

'Oh, that splendid cook of yours. I do have an evening service; otherwise I would certainly consider extending my stay. Trout, you say. Did you catch it yourself?'

'In this cold? Heavens no!' Massy laughed. 'Now, to what do I owe the pleasure, dear brother?' Robert detected the playful hint of a patronising tone in his younger brother's words, but ignored it as typical of Massy's barbed personality, as, now in the study, the two took to armchairs facing each other. 'I did not expect I'd see you again until Relief Committee business had resumed in January.'

Robert took a breath and got straight to the point. 'In light of the dire circumstances that abound, Massy, I plan to convene a meeting of the principal clergy of the barony – of the Established Church – with the aim of petitioning for external assistance on behalf of the poor of our barony.'

An irksome shift in posture as Massy crossed his legs gave Robert a sense of his brother's discomfort with the subject. It was no less than he'd anticipated, but focusing his eyes on one of Massy's buckled shoes dangling above the other, he carried on. 'I am in need of a suitable venue, at a central location, in which to conduct it. Some of the ministers will be coming from as far as–'

As he spoke, Massy interrupted, turning his head slightly away and lifting high his chin, clearly displaying a wish not to involve himself in such an undertaking. 'Robert, I'm not sure I am the–'

'As sometime chairman of the Relief Committee, I hoped you would secure me the use of the boardroom at the workhouse for the purpose. You have some sway there, have you not?'

'Yes.' Massy seemed to draw his head even further away, if it were possible. 'I'd rather not, Robert.'

'May I ask why?'

'It's simply not a matter I would find a valuable use of my time. I have much–'

'Use of your time?' Robert pinched up the knee of one trouser leg to lean further forward out of the chair. 'Massy. Don't you think it's time you began to–'

'No.' Condescendingly calm, Massy cut him off. 'I shan't be preached to on matters that do not concern me, Robert. I do enough for my part, serving the interests of the poor.'

'Come now, brother.' Robert lowered his head and, feeling that it was time for his brother to be acquainted with some harsh facts, stared at him from beneath a frown so deep that he could perceive his own bushy old eyebrows. 'These events concern us all. But in this instance, *you* perhaps more than anyone, Massy.'

'*Me*? How so?' Massy scoffed.

'I did not come to you by mere chance, but to give you … This has gone too far.'

'What specifically has gone too far, Robert?'

'Your … It is all well and good to pose as …' Robert said raising his voice, then, realising that a heated discussion would achieve no good results, he stopped himself and began again. 'I am aware that you give generously of your time to attend the meetings, and I commend you for that. But …'

'But?'

'But outside of that, in public life …' Robert lowered his voice to the level of an earnest confidant. 'You have done nothing but make a mockery of the poor and impede every measure–'

'Oh, give over, Robert!'

'… that seeks to relieve them.' Robert pushed his point as the two crossed each other.

'That is not true!' Clearly discomfited, Massy shifted again, laughing nervously to conceal the embarrassment.

'Massy.' Holding out his hands, Robert squeezed his eyes closed, regretting the points he was about to raise, but had inevitably known he would have to. 'The incident with the race winnings, and refusing to accept them for the committee.'

'That …' Massy attempted to protest, but Robert had much on his mind. 'The lashing of your father-in-law, John Hawkes, for his kindly gesture …' He lowered his voice further still and motioned to the ceiling, sensitive to Bridget's potential feelings on the subject.

'Now hold on! That's a family matter.'

'At every turn, Massy: scoffing at the Repealers; attacking Mr Barrett. I was there, at that meeting, you might recall. Your attack was vociferous!' Counting the incidents off with his fingers, Robert calmly but determinedly cut through Massy's numerous attempts to interrupt, feeling that it was necessary to take him to task where no one else had tried. 'At the presentment sessions, you argued for a three-month term of relief, when it was clear to all that six, at the least, would make any meaningful difference.'

'That is a matter of opinion! But what is so amusing is that the presentments were as good as quashed by your own hand, Robert!'

'My intentions were honourable.'

'Well, at least my three months might have been passed!'

But Robert was only nearing the crux of his argument: 'And then that *ridiculous* letter to the paper …'

'What letter?'

'… which served no purpose but to maliciously injure the reputation of an honest man. You have that poor pawnbroker half demented, who, incidentally, does try very hard to achieve some good on behalf of the wretched.'

'The *soirée*?' Massy laughed. 'I thought you were serious, Robert. But wait – did you mean Creed? And for a moment there I thought you said he was *honest*? The man is a *pawnbroker*, for heaven's sake!' Gleeful with sarcasm, Massy rose out of his chair to parade before the glowing fire. 'Anyway, what makes you even think that was me?' His anger, replaced by excitement, Massy's eyes sparkled at the chance for some sport.

'Was it not you?' Robert knew the look and was determined not to indulge it, but heard himself respond. It was as if they'd reverted to their boyhood arguments again, he realised, all vows and vocations thrown from the window. Resolving then to regain his composure, Robert wished he could even shame a truthful answer out of his brother, but knew now he could not.

'No one came forward with so much as a horsehair's proof of my being the author of that satire,' Massy pressed again. 'They couldn't have. There was none!'

Instead of arguing, Robert lifted his own head and listened calmly with arms folded, intent on letting Massy blow himself out.

'Oh, don't do that. I hate it when you give me that – godly face, Robert. You're so damned pious. Just when I was beginning to enjoy myself too.

'Very well! Very well! It *was* me. But for God's sake, the whole matter died away months ago. This is the first time I've even heard mention of it since the blasted summer. And that must *never* leave this room, Robert!' Massy wagged his finger as if to seal his order, then, having relented at last, leaned his elbows on the mantlepiece above the fire with his back turned – sulking, Robert supposed.

Aware of the superior smile he now wore, Robert adjusted his face to achieve a more serious expression and lowered his head, struggling with the mixture of feelings Massy's admission had inspired in him: relief at the confession on the one hand, and a sense of disturbance at the malice it revealed.

'The issues I speak of are trivial,' Robert began, 'when compared with the odium you harbour for the poor, Massy. Your heart is hardened towards them. And it can do you *no good*, in the short run or the long. Is it not time to realise that – along with many others – you will have to stand before God … with all of this on your conscience?'

'Oh, please, Robert!' Massy rolled his eyes, feigning boredom, so that Robert felt himself infuriated at last.

'I am concerned for your soul, Massy!' He raised his voice forcefully and stood, resisting with great difficulty the urge to shake his brother, instinctively knowing it would come to the wrong result. 'Don't you realise? I'm giving you a chance to atone. I could have gone to Henry Swanzy, Ashe or any of the others. But I want *you* to do this! *You* must do something of virtue … something that demonstrates contrition, lest you be damned, Massy, now, and forever after.'

Robert, after a silence, opened his eyes to find himself with his own fist cupped before his face, awaiting Massy's response, who seemed to be lost in thought, considering the weight of the words.

'If only something so simple could lighten the burden of sin upon it,' Massy said at last, looking out the window. Turning back, he gave Robert a reluctant grin and rolled his eyes. 'Oh, look … If you promise not to go spreading it about that I had anything to do with it, I will arrange for your use of the boardroom. Just don't go saving the *whole* heathen race from their demise!' he added dryly.

'MASSY!' Fearing his brother would undo what little good he had managed to wring out of him, Robert sought to bury the utterance.

'How soon do you require it?'

'As soon as it is possible to arrange. Before the year is out, in fact.'

'Well, that doesn't leave much time, does it?'

'It does not, I'll permit you that.'

'Today is the twenty-ninth, Robert!'

'Could it be got for tomorrow?' Robert was pleased. Even if Massy was not fully committed to the gesture, it was a huge leap for him, and so very encouraging of more, he hoped.

'Well, apart from the inmates of the workhouse, I doubt there'll be anyone else spending much time there before next week. I shall speak to Edward Ashe, who I think is at home. I'm sure I saw his coach this morning.'

'You have no idea how happy I am to hear that, Massy,' Robert said, joining his hands. 'Right. I have a lot of messages to organise, if I am to achieve the results I aim to. So I must be going.'

'I can't convince you to stay for lunch then?' Massy asked, with an air of longing and even sadness, Robert noticed.

'Thank you, Massy, I'll make a point of it next time, I promise. But I really must get back.'

Donning his outer garments once again, handed to him by the boy who now stood with hands behind his back, Robert alighted from the first step and turned to Massy, in the doorway. 'Brother. I know it is not something you might usually be inclined to, but for your own sake … it would please me greatly if you would find your way somehow to contrive a peace with the pawnbroker.'

'I'm sorry, what was that, Robert? I'm finding it hard to hear. I think Cook is calling me. It must be lunch.' Massy laughed dismissively, retreating.

'Just think about it, please, Massy,' Robert said as he climbed into his waiting car, hoping the good will he'd inspired in his brother might propagate more, however doubtful it was that it might stretch quite that far.

'I will do that much, Robert. Good day to you now! I hope the road is not *too* rocky on your way back. Regards to all in Killinardrish.' Bowing, Massy gestured to the boy to close the door, then vanished within.

'Oh. He's gone?' Bridget appeared in the hallway behind Massy. 'Cook is just about to serve.'

'He couldn't stay,' Massy said staring at the back of the door. 'Has urgent business to attend to.'

'And what was the matter of great import? He seemed in earnest …' Bridget's voice began to fade as she headed for the dining room.

'He wants me to make peace with Cornelius Creed,' Massy shouted just loud enough for her to hear, then turned and followed. 'Hmm!' he mused quietly.

'Cornelius Creed? The pawnbroker?' his wife asked, as Massy unfurled the napkin across his knee at one end of the table. 'The same man who's been upsetting you all year in the papers?'

'The very fellow.'

*

Killinardrish, Cannaway, Macroom, 30 Dec. '46.

My dear Henry,

It is many years since you took your position as Vicar of Trinity Chapel, Westminster, and I hesitate to presume on our former friendship, but l have been requested by our clerical body here to forward to you the accompany-ing document and to beg that you will have the kindness to get it inserted in some of the London newspapers and make any other use of it you think likely to promote the object we have in view.

It is truly deplorable, at such a time, to be obliged to persuade the people at the other side of the water that our poor are starving and need all the help that can be given. None, however, but those who witness it can form an adequate idea of the state of destitution and misery in which I may say the whole population of our parishes are sunk. Statements of deaths by starvation are bad enough, but they give but a faint idea of the real state of the case. We see our poor people wasting away by hundreds and we can truly say that the number who have a fourth subsistence do not amount to one in five. I assure you most solemnly that in my own parish, which is by no means the worst off, I know not how the vital spark is kept alive in the great mass of the people.

We have a meal-store here and I am obliged to turn regular meal merchant. It is open on two days in the week, when I take my stand behind the counter from morning till night. I sell on these two days more than one hundred pounds' worth of food, at a small reduction in price, and cannot imagine where the poor creatures procure the money they pay for it. The sales, however, are diminishing as the want of food increases, for, in fact, they have sold every article they could dispose of and now many families of six, eight or ten persons eke out a miserable existence on 14 lbs of meal from one day to another. Many are the instances when they have been without a morsel of food for twenty-four hours and still they are patient to a degree I could not have imagined, and express themselves satisfied at every exertion that is made for them.

Disconnected efforts to collect subscriptions for separate localities will never meet the case. One parish will receive large aid, while many others will receive little or nothing, and often these are the most in need, not having persons of influence to represent their state. We hope, and indeed are sure, that you will use all your influence to promote the contents of the accompanying petition.

Yours, dear Henry, very sincerely,
Robert Warren.

At a meeting of the clergymen of the Established Church from nine extensive parishes, held in Macroom, on Wednesday, 30 December 1846, it was unanimously resolved that the following document should be forwarded to some of the most influential clergymen in England, with a request that they would give it publicity:

Having for some time past observed the grossest misrepresentations published in a portion of the English press respecting the state of Ireland, and fearing that these may prevent many of the benevolent in England from coming forward to assist in relieving our grievously afflicted poor, we, the undersigned ministers of the Established Church in the district of Macroom, county of

Cork, feel ourselves called on to bear our testimony to the prevailing fearful distress, and to contradict, in the most direct terms, those mis-statements.

It is an admitted fact that of the crop, on which from four to five millions of the inhabitants of Ireland depended for subsistence, five-sixths were totally destroyed by the visitation of God, so that on the first of November, scarcely a vestige of their ordinary food remained to a population which, according to the 5th Annual Report of the Poor Law Commissioners, represents the most wretched and pauperised population in Europe.

With this fact before them, the editors of these publications should have hesitated before they made the charge of exaggeration. Is it not evident to every honest and reflecting mind, that nothing but the most grievous destitution must prevail? We lament to say that such is the case, and we pledge ourselves as Christian men and ministers of the Gospel, that so far from any statement we have seen having been too highly coloured, we have not seen one which adequately represents the destitution and misery with which we are in daily contact, and which, great as it is, we fear is only the commencement of what we are to anticipate.

On our English friends, and particularly on our brethren in the ministry, we would earnestly call to come forward zealously and liberally to our aid. We solemnly assert, as in the sight of God, that if large pecuniary means are not put into the hands of the relief committees so as to enable them to reduce the price of provisions for the poor, and to assist those families who have no person able to labour for them in the public works, famine in its most awful form must be felt in every part of the land, and that to an extent never before witnessed in this country.

The poor have parted literally with every saleable article they possessed: their strength is daily wasting away, so that when put to task-work, in many instances they are unable to earn even 8d. per day. If the Christian public of England do not, as they have nobly done on former occasions, when the exigency was by no means so great, contribute liberally for their support, thousands and tens of thousands must perish.

We should beg to recommend the formation of a central committee in

London, to collect subscriptions and disburse the funds as in 1822, and of district committees in this country, through whom the funds may be distributed to the parochial relief committees.

Regarding, as we do, this visitation to be a judgement from God for our transgressions, national and individual, while we call upon all to use their best exertions to alleviate the distress, we desire unfeignedly to acknowledge our manifold sins, by which we have most justly provoked God's wrath and indignation, and to humble ourselves under the mighty hand of Him without whose blessing all human aid is vain.

Richard B. Kirchhoffer, Rector of Ballyvourney.

Henry E. Sadlier, Rector of Inchigeelagh.

John W. Baldwin, Curate of Kilnamartery.

Hume Babington, Rector of Mohevidy.

John Torrens Kyle, Rector of Clondrohid.

Robert Warren, Rector of Camaway.

Samuel G. Fairtclough, Rector Ahinagh.

Henry McGlintock, Rector of Kilmichael.

Henry Swanzy, Rector of Macroom.

44

THE SMALLEST THING
OUTLIVES US

I n the early still of the morning, Creed found himself wandering the shop, struggling with whether or not to follow through with his decision.

Fearing that the footsteps he now heard overhead – which told him that Paulellen was up and about – might cross to the stairway and descend to find him, Creed sought the sanctuary of the store behind the shop, where she would never suspect him to be. There he hung the iron padlock on the outside of the door – as close to locked as it could be made to look – and pulled the door in behind him.

His eyes watered from the stinging cold, as, inside the small, cloistered space, behind him, in front, and to each side, he found himself surrounded by row upon row of the belongings of the poor: the countless precious items he had relieved them of, one pauper at a time, stacked to the inch upon shelves over the height of his head. And there Creed suddenly realised that with every pledge and with each shilling and penny he had given out, he had unwittingly bought from those poor of the district the many bricks of his own tomb.

In that moment, behind the shelves, on the middle of the back wall, in the reflection of the store's one window, he caught a glimpse of a greyed, haggard, frightened man staring squarely at him. It had been a long time since he had seen himself without glasses on his face and he fretted at the ghostly reduction of his former self and at one who looked and felt even poorer than so many of those he had sent away bereft of their belongings. A cackle of laughter rose up and he watched it burst forth from the man before him, who seemed to find the seriousness of it all highly amusing. The Creed in the window laughed until slow, silent tears choked and replaced the strains of confused merriment and until, blinking through the blur of his sorrows as he lowered his head, the real Creed's eyes fell upon a pair of shoes, tied together, stacked among the countless others. A tag dangled from a string inside the left one. He drew it out and read the pencil markings of the log entry in his own hand: '*96*' – the ninety-sixth entry that month – *Feb 11th '45. Pádraig O'Buachalla. Clondrohid.* The whole description had a diagonal strike through it and Creed flipped it over, to find a single word on the reverse, showing that French had marked the item as *unclaimed.*

What must have happened to Pádraig O'Buachalla? 'He may well be dead,' Creed said aloud, and closing his eyes, bowed his head in reverence.

From out of nowhere, the image of Shannie, the old sharp, blossomed in his mind and Creed stood catatonic, remembering those earliest days of having opened the shop, when there had been less at stake and when he had enjoyed the casual trading of insults and strategic manoeuvrings, through what then had appeared the harmless daily exchanges with that swift-footed, silver-tongued old rival, Mr Shanahan. Creed had not seen him since before December. Even that seemed like an age ago. *That canny old rogue. If ever there was a survivor … He of all people will see this through. My hat upon it.*

Creed became aware that the shoes in his hand felt heavy. *My father's shoes,* he remembered the young man saying. O'Buachalla had the face and hands of someone aged twenty-six or twenty-seven, but was probably younger. A tall, strong-looking young man, who but for the tragedy of the circumstances, Creed was sure, would be still alive out there, raising a healthy family; no care for where his family's next meal was to come from; not struggling and perishing slowly, one day at a time for however long it was that he had lasted; and never in need of the services of a parasitic wretch like Cornelius Creed the pawnbroker.

Creed stopped and closed his eyes, absorbing another wave of the self-loathing heat that for weeks had sapped his energy and frayed his nerves. How he wished now he could smash and burn that sign over the door, or erase it from the past. But he could not. There was but one way to do that. Creed opened his eyes, and gazed into nothing.

But he had helped the poor. A part of him still knew that and felt it, somewhere behind the confusion. A softness was there, though he struggled to hold on to it. His intentions had been good, he reasoned. In many cases he'd given his customers well over the odds for their items, to his own detriment. If he were to consult the book under the counter in the shop now, he was sure that the corresponding entry would show that he had given Pádraig O'Buachalla more than what was fair. Because of him, that man would have been in a position to feed his family for at least a few weeks more and would have, perhaps, during that time, found another way to keep himself alive because of it. Beyond that, what could he have done? What could anyone, other than Lord John Russell, or God himself, have done?

But all that was so long ago, Creed thought, and he rubbed his eyes, trying to escape the veil of exhaustion. Pádraig O'Buachalla had already been in need of a pawnbroker before this great wandering catastrophe had even begun. If O'Buachalla's survival had been so perilous even before it, how could he have survived the two years since? *The smallest thing outlives us.*

Creed stared at the shoes with sadness. He couldn't remember the Irish for it now, but that was along the lines of what the old hawker had translated it as. And how true it was. With all its awareness and ability to affect its own fate, a single life was so delicate. Yet the shoes – the dead, lifeless objects in his hand – had survived, and had walked through numerous lives, seeing each of its owners under: Pádraig O'Buachalla; Pádraig's father, and maybe other owners before them. The poor dealt in second-, third- and fourth-hand clothes all the time. But now the shoes had found their way to Creed. At that moment, he felt suddenly as if they had been meant for him. Reduced as he now was to the humble, wretched shadow of himself that felt just as poor as the man whose name the tag of the unclaimed shoes bore – Pádraig O'Buachalla – who was so poor that he had not even worn them into the shop himself but had carried them in under a blanket and passed them across the counter, the last valuable item he had in this world … *to me … to Cornelius Creed, their latest owner.*

We are all poor in the sight of Heaven. Creed heard the words of Father Thomas in his mind as, holding them in his hand, he looked down and realised that he too had no shoes on, as if to complete the transformation. It was poetic justice. He began to smile, suddenly as unburdened as ever he had felt. He had nothing left to lose. For the first time since he could remember, Creed's mind slowed down and the world around him seemed peaceful and still. Feeling the wondrous calm of his shoulders softening, he breathed a huge sigh, knowing he was free.

It was still early. Creed shivered with the cold. Through the window the last fledgling sun of the year was glowing, pouring liquid gold through the naked skeleton of the winter tree outside. Molten blotches spilled and dripped from its limbs, singeing and drowning its shadow below. In a sweeter season the same wild cherry tree had played host to an embarrassment of birds and had mothered a peerless fanfare of lush green leaves, flowers and seeds. Now arid and abandoned, it held upon the frosted skin of a bare branch but a single lonely sparrow attempting to warm itself in the light.

'The little birds in silence dream,' he whispered. And watching the tiny creature, Creed heard the song from a long-ago page in the book of his memory, and the sweet voice of Mary Welply singing:

'Tis night – all's still save yon bright stream
Which now as 'neath the sun's light flows
The little birds in silence dream
And flowerlets on their stems repose;
The moon smiles on that gentle tide –

That tide's the calm and crystal Lee,
List, o'er its waters gently glide
Sounds of the sweetest melody.

By the time Creed registered that the sparrow had flown away, he had rolled the shoes up in a blanket and tucked them under his arm. Passing through the shop, he heard the footsteps again above.

'Is that you, dear?' Paulellen shouted down to him.

'I'm just going for a walk by the river, dear.'

'Oh, good. I'm so pleased. The air will do you wonders,' she called back, her voice fading behind him.

The bell jangled overhead as Creed pulled open the door and stepped outside.

THE RIVER BELOW

'Just pull in there a moment.'

'What's the matter, dear?' Bridget Penrose Hawkes wondered at the strangeness of her husband having the driver stop in the middle of the bridge. But now that the coach was stationary he appeared to be looking at something over the side.

Bridget could faintly hear a dog's barks echoing off the pillars beneath, but she was blind to the scene otherwise. 'What can you see?' she insisted. Massy, leaning his head out the window of the vehicle, didn't answer.

'Oh, come on, Massy. It's freezing.'

'Carry on, driver,' she said eventually. Massy sat back as the coach began to move.

'I think that was Welply's dog.' Clearly lost in thought, he spoke to himself.

'What do you mean? What's so unusual about someone walking their dog?'

'It's nothing, Bridget.' He shook his head dismissively.

'More of your strange behaviour, Massy. I really don't know why you insisted we come into town anyway. I hope it wasn't inspired by Robert's notion of your reconciling with that man?'

'Of course not.'

Massy looked straight ahead and rocked to and fro as the cart kept over the cobbles.

My Name Is Pádraig
Ua Buaćalla

O utside the cabin on Doire Liath the evening wind was howling as Pádraig, awake, lay still, Cáit and the children sleeping before him.

Back at the works on the twenty-eighth the men had finally been paid. That day, Pádraig had left the line early and carried home just over a stone and a quarter of meal, exhausting the wages, having only earned three shillings and sixpence on the task for the eleven days, excluding Sundays, that had come and gone since he'd been last paid on the eleventh. By his reckoning there had been two days when the weather was so bad that it had prevented him going at all, and one half-day, when, on the fourteenth, they'd been sent home in light snow. Other than that, it was estimated by the men that each of them had been cut an hour's earnings out of every day for the shortening light. The rest of the deductions, Pádraig imagined, were a consequence of the difficulties of breaking rocks in such harsh conditions, with numb fingers, and slowed physical ability. He himself had managed to earn almost sixpence for each full day it had been possible to work. But some men had received much less. It was a paltry return for such a long period and the only consolation was that if he had been paid before Christmas, they would probably have gone through it all by now and would have had nothing left to keep them going for the next week or two.

Pádraig's intestines rumbled in the darkness, and he worried that the new meal he'd managed to buy was already dwindling fast. But what was far more worrying was that having necessarily fasted on the two days between Christmas Day and the works starting up again, his strength had been so depleted that it had almost killed him to get back to Macroom. By the time he was paid at the end of that first delirious day and had gone to buy some bread, almost three full days had passed from the time he'd last eaten. Since then, as he'd tried to build his strength back up, it was proving more difficult than ever to rise up in the morning and make the journey in and out to the line. So much so that he now questioned whether the little labour he was managing would merit the effort it was taking to get there and back, when next the wages would be paid.

Since the return, a quietness had hung over the men. There was a noticeable absence of those who, it was assumed, had lacked the strength to start again, or worse. It struck Pádraig that not returning to collect what they were owed said a lot about the condition of those missing. Even Clench, the big man from Holland's Lane, had not been heard of.

But Pádraig was keeping mostly to himself. Reserving all his energy for the monumental efforts that were sapping every ounce of it, he could not afford to spend much time thinking about anything else.

This day marked the end of the toughest year he had ever known. By far. That anyone alive could remember, it seemed. But the fact that it was ending brought Pádraig no comfort. Tomorrow was to be the start of another year. One that promised to be much harder and even longer yet. He could not bring his mind to imagine how it was possible for their circumstances to get worse. But deep inside himself, he knew that they would.

Turning to roll from his back onto his side, Pádraig winced. He was so sore and bone-tired that he felt as he imagined he might if he'd been run over by a pack of horses. How he was to do it all again in the morning? And the day after that? He did not know how yet. Squeezing his eyes tight in the darkness, for now, listening to the screaming winds that howled over the ridge behind, he would try to forget about all of that. And rest.

My name is Pádraig Ua Buaćalla, son of Pádraig Óg Ua Buaćalla and Maighréad Ní Ghóilin, of Carraig Na Madraidhe.

An image filled Pádraig's mind: rough, flaxen short trousers and calloused bare feet. His father's legs, viewed from the floor. It was from when he had been a baby. And cloths … His mother, hanging cloths out to dry, after the children. Yellow gorse. And shale rocks. His earliest memories. They brought a sense of comfort and almost carried him off to sleep. But with the passing of time still in his mind, it struck him that for as long as it could be remembered, his people had been living this way, hand to mouth, going against the grain … Existing. It wasn't the only realisation. It had dawned on him lately that he'd always quietly assumed that life would get easier, not just for him, but for the poor in general. That their lot would improve. In his lifetime they had seen Emancipation. There had been attempts to dissolve the union. For a while it had seemed that things *were* getting better. There had been hope. But this past year had told him beyond doubt that the lives of the poor would not improve. Or that if they did, he would not see it; that he had been foolish even to think it. It was a huge blow to his understanding of the world, on top of everything else. It would not stop him trying, but it was harder to see the good in things.

Beside him, Cáit's breathing sounded laboured as she slept. He could remember when once it had been peaceful and even. Looking at her in the dim light, for a moment he thought he saw his mother. But realising his mistake, he noticed for the first time that Cáit looked old. He felt an overwhelming sorrow at seeing what life had done to her. *The shadow of herself and only a woman of twenty-five. Going grey. Losing her teeth.* She could not even feed Diarmuidín. *Trying to feed her children, and abandoned in her plight by even the last vestige of her own body.* Pádraig could not think of a more cruel trick in all of nature than for a mother – whose instinct, above all else, was to feed her children – to have seen the last of her milk dry up, with her children starving in front of her. He loved her so much for the strength of the woman she was. They were still here. Together. Trying. And still, the helpless snuffling little creatures clung to their mother ever tighter on the floor. His poor little children. What chance had they in a world like this? One of them too small and the other smaller. He searched his mind, and as he sometimes did when he was in trouble, asked himself what his parents would have done in the same situation. But there was no answer. They had never faced anything like this. *What could anyone do differently if these were their children. Work harder? Walk further? Eat less, so the children could have more?* Full of desperation and grief, Pádraig listened for an answer. But there was none.

What a curse. The curse of all curses. In spite of everything you have tried, to watch helplessly as your children grow weaker, thinner… and quieter, until they're too small for their own bones. Too small for their own heads. Oh, God, give us anything but this. We would gladly suffer anything, but not this!

Pádraig wondered what his mother would say if she saw his children right then. She would cry, he thought. But he was already doing that.

How many others were in the same situation? He knew that he and Cáit were not alone and he pitied, and prayed and felt sorry for all those people around him who could not feed their children either. He saw Muintir Laeire in the cabin behind the ridge, Muintir Éalaighthe on the other side, all their neighbours, Máire Rua and Labhrás Ua Duinnín beyond … Peig na Croise … Muintir Buaćalla in Barrantawnaknock … His mind travelled further and further away out from the cabin on Doire Liath, over the thousands of poor in the cabins and skelps scattered across the wild hills and bogs, to his own people in the homeplace at Carrigaphooka, in Kilaclug, and Inchinlinane; further and further towards Macroom, to Cáit's sister, Onóra, at the union, all the outdoor paupers he'd seen in the yard getting relief there; the men and their families on the works, Denis Murphy's family, if Denis was still alive, Jeremiah O'Leary, Ned's family, Clench … The poor of the whole barony … Cáit's people, Muintir Oiscín in Carrigadrohid. Shannie, the old man who'd guided him to the pawnbroker's, and who had said that all the poor of the world are as precariously placed as an egg in the mouth of a pig.

Pádraig looked to his children in the darkness and pictured all those people, hanging on by the skin of their teeth, existing as they had done for generations from one end of the year to the other on their tiny parcels of land. Each one of them pressed and stretched so far that their very existences were, as his and Cáit's were now, as precarious as the old pauper had said. The whole lot of them stripped of every last hope of self-reliance, until their very lives had come to depend upon one simple gift of nature that grew for only six months of the year. He could see it all.

Every one of them, struggling each day with ever more difficulty, after a lifetime of existing, trying to grow enough to eat, enough to pay rent, to clothe themselves, and to put a light in the darkness, all the while hoping and praying with every bit of faith they had that the one simple crop they now leaned upon, like a straw balancing the weight of the world, would not give a bad harvest.

But it had. It *had* failed. And its failing would reap untold destruction. Never before so fully as this, and never ever, when there had been so many, so entirely at the mercy of its success. From every side, the world seemed to want them to go. Winter was trying to freeze them out. Fever and sickness, it was said, had come to prey on them too. The ground would not sustain them. Hunger was devouring them from within. The sky sought to wash them away. And to judge by the efforts of their keepers – the landlords, the gentry, and the government of the foreign invaders, who had ever seemed uncaring and were now practically working them to death to keep them alive – he supposed they might be just as happy to see every man, woman and child of them scattered to the wind. The wind that howled ever louder outside. With his face in the straw, Pádraig did not need to listen hard to hear it. It was howling and screaming over the teeth of the ridge with everything caught up in its grasp: the pig, the egg and them at the middle of it all. Pádraig Ua Buaćalla and his little family around him, holding on against the cold wind blasting them from every direction.

In the darkness of the tiny cabin, up there on Doire Liath, at the edge of the world, Pádraig lay staring at the faint outlines of his wife and children. Through the darkness it appeared that they were almost gone already, fading slowly before his eyes. He reached out his arm, to make sure they were still really there. As though, if he could touch them, it would stop them from disappearing.

The wind whistled and screeched up the stubborn stone walls that held up the clattering roof, like an offering.

How will we ever hang on?

My name is Pádraig Ua Buaćalla.

ACKNOWLEDGEMENTS

Sincere thanks to:

Nicki Howard at Gill, without whose instinct and initiative this story would never have found its way to the page.

Marianne Gunn O'Connor for adding grist to the mill, with blind faith and enthusiasm.

For being a joy to work with and always insightful: Conor Kostick, my editor, whose great instincts and ideas are an integral part of this book.

My neighbour, Sheila Nicholas, who let slip that she was a copyist just as I was transferring the longhand first draft onto the computer, and then dug in with me from over the wall.

Suzanne Doyle, my music manager, who bravely held the reins of the other horse at times over the last year while I went wandering in a different century.

Warmest gratitude to the Macroom and Skibbereen brigade for their kindness and friendship, and for punting the ferry across the wide waters that lie between this land and the one of the past: Fr Michael Kelleher, Maura O'Flynn, John Kelleher, Tadhg Creedon, the late Máire MacSuíbhne, Margaret Murphy, Dr Con Kelleher, Jack Buckley, Jim Cooney and Catherine Lynch.

Thanks, with admiration, to my fellow enthusiasts in this realm, whose welcome embrace at the National Famine Summer School I was so grateful to receive after the release of my Chronicles album: Prof Christine Kinealy, Dr Jason King, Caroilin Callery, Kieron Tuohy, Cathal Póirtéir and John O'Driscoll, to name a few.

For inspiration in the other tongue: Colm Mac Con Iomaire, John and Sheila Conneely, and Louis de Paor.

My greatest thanks to those around me – wholeheartedly supportive, as ever: my family, who are the mountain from which I see the world. Not least of all, love to Eimear, for accepting when I so frequently locked myself into a room with 'the other woman' over the last three years. And to little Londubh, who sat on my shoulders for many long walks during lockdown and who, on so many levels, helped me to feel the weight, and to understand.

Thanks also to: Prof Joseph O'Connor. The team at Gill, all so pleasant to work with. Brendan Graham. The late Shay Healy. Edwin Garland. Joe Lancaster. Pauline Scanlon. John Sheahan. John Dolan, features editor and assistant editor at *The Echo*. Jane Davies, curator, Lancashire Infantry Museum. Charles Reid, Gordon Highlanders Museum. Dr Jonny Geber, University of Edinburgh. Marion Acreman, Kilkenny Famine Experience. Will de Búrca of De Búrca Rare Books, for the invaluable original copy of Peadar Ua Laoghaire's *Mo Sgéal Féin*. Joe and Deirdre Hayes, for the use of another quaint cottage. Dominique Ellickson. Daragh Bohan. Patrick Maher. Caitríona Frost. Liadain O'Donovan. Hugh Comerford. Amy Saunders.

A debt of gratitude is owed to John O'Connor, the opening page of whose illuminating history *The Workhouses of Ireland* introduced me many years ago to Peadar Ua Laoghaire's account of the Ua Buacalla family.

POSTAGE ONE PENNY

Sir Randolph Rothe
Castle
Dublin

M A C
N O
18